LEGEND
of the
COCO PALMS RESORT

RITA D'ORAZIO

Wasteland Press

www.wastelandpress.net
Shelbyville, KY USA

Legend of the Coco Palms Resort
by Rita D'Orazio

First Printing – April 2020
ISBN: 978-1-68111-140-7

Printed in the U.S.A.

0   1   2   3   4   5

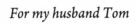

For my husband Tom

PROLOGUE

Kaua'i, Hawai'i is home to the famous Coco Palms Resort.

This waterfront property along the Wailua River coast was once home to Kaua'i's royal family. The last reigning monarch, Queen Deborah, owned a twenty-four-room hotel here. When Deborah passed away in 1853, the land was put up for sale. The property changed hands many times over the years, but no one was ever able to turn a profit.

In the 1950s, then-owner Gerry Gartner turned the quaint hotel into a 320-room luxury resort; but still, it didn't gain worldwide attention until 1961, when new manager Genie Evans joined his team. She brought to the island one of Hollywood's elite: the King of Rock and Roll, Elvis Presley.

The movie *Blue Hawaii*, which was filmed at the Coco Palms, has remained synonymous with Elvis's name to this day. After his death, who'd have predicted the Coco Palms would become even more popular? Swarms of fans visited the resort for years and years.

Unfortunately, all that ended on September 11, 1992, when Hurricane Iniki left the Coco Palms nothing more than an empty shell.

Iniki destroyed fourteen hundred homes that day, as it battered the island of Kaua'i for over forty minutes. To this day, Iniki is still one of the largest hurricanes in history to have hit the Hawaiian Islands. It took months to restore electricity in the more rural areas, but no sooner had the storm passed than the locals rallied together to start cleanup.

In the years that followed most of Kaua'i was rebuilt, along with numerous new land developments throughout the island. The only building that has never been touched—for over a quarter of a century now—has been the Coco Palms Resort. It sits dormant, holding onto its memories of years passed.

To this day, two things remain a mystery on the island of Kaua'i. First, what is the location of Queen Deborah's remains? And second, why has the Coco Palms remained stuck in 1992?

CHAPTER ONE:

Genie Evans
(1960)

I'm sitting at my desk in downtown Dallas, going over briefing notes before my next meeting, when my private line lights up. Only a handful of people have my number, which gives me the advantage of knowing whom I'm greeting on the other end of the receiver. But today, here I am, listening to a strange male voice—so much for the best-laid plans.

"Good morning, Miss Evans. I hope I haven't gotten you at a bad time?"

"First of all, you have, and secondly, it's slightly after the noon hour."

"I apologize. Please, let me start over. My name is Gerry Gartner. We have a mutual friend, Dean Davis—he suggested I give you a call."

"Funny. I've never heard of you, Mr. Gartner. Quite frankly, I'm surprised at Dean for giving out my private number. This better be a matter of life and death."

"Don't be mad at Dean; he was reluctant at first. Please, let me explain."

"Start explaining. I'm a very busy woman and about to head into a meeting."

"Miss Evans, I desperately need your help. Dean has sung your praises over the years. He tells me that you're one of the finest businesswomen around. I'm hoping you could shed some light on my dilemma."

"You have about two minutes to keep my attention."

"I'll do my best, but—"

"No buts, Mr. Gartner, time is ticking. Maybe you can start by telling me where you're calling from, because either you're a late sleeper, or we're in two different time zones."

I hear him laugh. I hadn't realized I was being witty. He replies, "Sorry, I've lost my manners today. I have to admit I'm a little nervous speaking with you."

"You're going to be a lot more nervous when I tell you time is up. Push forward, Mr. Gartner."

He coughs loudly. Nervousness has obviously made his throat dry. He squeaks, "I'm calling from the island of Kaua'i."

"Can't say I'm familiar with it."

"It's one of the Hawaiian Islands, northernmost."

"Mr. Gartner, unless you've struck oil, I can't imagine what we're talking about here. Sorry, but time's up."

"Just a few more moments! Can we schedule a time that's more convenient for you? And before you say no, let me give you a quick scope of what it is I need."

"One more minute."

"About eight years ago, I bought a 250-acre coconut grove. I've taken a pre-existing twenty-four-room hotel and turned it into a 320-room luxury resort," Gerry says, sounding like an anxious auctioneer. "What I need is someone to run and manage the place. I was—"

I interrupt before he can say another word. "You do realize I'm in the oil business, right? Or did Dean forget to mention it, which I highly doubt. That's why I mentioned striking oil earlier."

I hear his nervous cough yet again, along with what sounds like a throat lozenge being unwrapped. I feel myself getting even more impatient. I hear the candy clicking inside his mouth as he finally replies, "I'm aware of what you do for a living, Miss Evans. But what captured my attention were your prior accomplishments. I know that you've taken two other failing businesses before your current job and turned them into thriving conglomerates."

"Impressive. You've done your homework."

"What do you say? Can we set up a time to talk again?"

"Give me your number," I say. "I can't promise anything right now. I really need to run to my next meeting." I hang up without saying goodbye. I wasn't kidding when I said I needed to run.

Later that afternoon, the meeting is dragging. I can't wait for it to wrap up. For the first time in years, I'm having difficulty focusing. My mind keeps drifting back to that odd phone conversation, and I wish I'd had more time to spare. I'd like to know how Mr. Gartner envisions my help with his resort. I guess I could satisfy my curiosity by asking Dean. After giving out my number like that, I think buying me a proper supper and giving me some insight into Mr. Gartner is the least that he could do.

The next evening, I arrive on time to find Dean waiting for me at the bar. He gets up to kiss my cheek, holding a bourbon on the rocks in his left hand.

"You sly dog, you," I say as he hands me my bourbon. "Y'always know how to get the best of me."

Dean gives me his usual boyish smile. There isn't anything that could put us at odds, nothing, not even a private number. What Dean and I have is like a brother–sister relationship, maybe even better than what most blood siblings have. But I still berate him as we are shown to our usual table.

"How dare you give my number to a total stranger? You know how busy I am. Who is this crackpot you've sicced on me?"

"For the love of God, you have such a flare for the dramatic. You make it sound as if Gerry's a dog who's got hold of your leg."

I raise my hand into the air as if swatting away a fly. I dismiss his comment with a blink of my false eyelashes. I've been trying to look more glamorous these days. Maybe Dean's right; I can be quite dramatic in all areas of life. Maybe this is what happens when you reach middle age and find yourself still unattached in an era where that's not well accepted. Maybe my drama is a substitute for becoming a cat woman, or even worse, a sad old spinster. Urrgh ... why must we have such horrid labels? I know exactly why I never married. What society won't acknowledge is that I've been too busy working and building a good life for myself, which I will never apologize for. I've never imagined myself in a kitchen waiting on any man or child. I refuse to be like my mother, God rest her soul. I mean no disrespect, but poor Ma. All she ever did was wait on my father. She was too smart for that. He could have done his own chores.

"Hey!" Dean says. "Where'd you go?"

"Sorry. My dramatic mind, as you put it, drifted."

"Okay, listen, I'm sorry I gave your number out. You have to believe me when I say I only had your best interest at heart."

I look at him with skepticism. "Please, do explain," I reply.

"You do realize that Gerry is one of the richest real estate moguls in the world?"

"No," I say, "I didn't get that information from him. He mentioned buying a coconut grove, but lots of people invest in foreign land."

"Don't let his humble ways fool you. The guy is loaded and worldly. Gerry loves Hawai'i, but he has no clue when it comes to managing a resort. He saw the place as an opportunity for his future retirement, but underestimated the skill it takes to run the place well."

"Why me? Why would you suggest me when you know I've been in the oil business? Are you trying to run your friend into the ground?" I laugh. "I don't think it's for me. Plus, do I look like the exotic type? I know nothing about hotel management, let alone Hawaiian traditions. It sounds menial, in all honesty."

"You haven't seen the place, so don't make hasty judgments. You've been miserable for quite some time, and it's not like you. As your dearest friend, I can see that you're ready for a change. I know deep in my soul that this is perfect for you. Please trust me on this. At least give it some consideration."

I gulp my bourbon. It's not easy to hear your best friend insinuate that you're a sad sack—it's really quite disturbing. Am I really that miserable? I always thought of myself as having a vibrant personality.

"I know what you're thinking," says Dean.

"Well. Please do enlighten me. It seems that you know me better than I know myself these days."

"Not true and you know it. You can't sit there and deny that you've lost your spark. Where has it gone?" asks Dean with deep concern. So much so that his face is reminiscent of a melted wax figure from Madame Tussauds.

"If I knew where my spark was, do you not think I'd have ignited it?"

We both laugh at my exposed flaw. Aging and being alone are getting the better of me, something I never saw coming.

"In six months, you know I'll be fifty?" As I say the words out loud, I know Dean is right. I finish my bourbon and order another. Why am I feeling pitiful? It isn't in my nature, nor is wearing false eyelashes. I quickly try to regroup. I really don't have anything to be miserable about. Here I am, sitting with a dear old friend whom I've known since high school. We are both successful and financially independent—what is my problem? I'm lucky to be sitting here with Dean, about to dig into our favorite grilled prime rib, done just the way we like it, rare. What the hell is there to fear?

Back at home that night, I find myself tossing and turning. I had one too many shots, which never makes for a great night's sleep. I get up to warm up a mug of milk. I need to put my restless mind at ease, since I have a big day ahead of me. It's not just the bourbon affecting me, it's the unfinished conversation with Mr. Gartner. Something in his voice left me wanting to hear more. I decide I'll give him a call first thing in the morning. Well … maybe not *first* thing, seeing as he's on Hawaiian Standard Time. Once I've made my mind up to call him, I feel relaxed and fall into a deep, peaceful sleep. Making positive decisions has always been my equivalent of never going to bed mad.

Four weeks later, descending the stairs of the airplane in Kaua'i, I'm enraptured by the sweet floral scent lingering in the air. I was expecting scorching heat, but instead, I am welcomed by balmy trade winds. The scene as I look out over the tarmac is even more dreamlike than I'd imagined. I can see tall palms swaying for miles. The mountain views are straight out of a storybook. How can such a tiny airport and island feel larger than life? Unexplainable—that's all I can say about it—plus I'm having one of those once-in-a-lifetime experiences that I know I'll never get to feel again. At moments like this, I wish I had a built-in tape reel that could replay what I'm seeing and smelling, over and over whenever I want to—but that's not how we're wired, unfortunately. So I take another deep breath of fresh scented air, then step onto the tarmac.

From where I'm standing, I can see three female hula dancers. They are swaying gently to the sounds of an elderly gentleman strumming his ukulele. What a way to be welcomed to the island. A beautiful Polynesian girl greets me with "Aloha" and places a fresh floral *lei* around my neck. The scent I smelled earlier is now filling my senses to the limit.

"Aloha," I reply. I don't want to come across as crazy, but I can't take my eyes off her. Never have I seen anyone so exotically beautiful. I walk over to take a peek at the hula dancers, all of whom are just as attractive and way out of my league.

Mr. Gartner may change his mind about this arrangement when he sees little old me. I'm as plain as Texas toast—okay, bad analogy; it's actually thicker than regular toast. I'm more like a cozy cup of warm milk. Let's just say I'm pretty plain. There isn't a set of false eyelashes that could hide the fact. The girls here, they're blessed. I can't change my God-given features, but what I could do is try and sway my hips as they do. Depending on how long I stay, maybe some hula lessons will be on my list of to-do's. I want to know what their hand gestures represent. Something tells me I'm missing out on a lovely story with every one of those arm extensions which they perform so effortlessly. It's as if they're one with the swaying palm trees in the background. I want to drink and eat whatever it is that makes them this way. I haven't even made it off the tarmac and I'm in love with everything I see.

I come out of my trance when I hear my name being called. After a few moments I spot the lips that are mouthing my name aloud. In the crowd is a middle-aged man, no taller than five foot ten, maybe more like five-nine. He's definitely easy to pick out in his bright, tropical print shirt and baggy white pants. I might be wrong, but I don't believe he's of Hawaiian descent. Dean and I never discussed that. He approaches me and gets in so close that I'm lucky if there's six inches between our faces. Obviously, he doesn't respect personal space. I can see by his wide-eyed expression that something about me has taken him by surprise. I'm sure he didn't expect me to look the way I do, but he's a far cry from the tall, dark playboy mogul I was expecting.

"You must be Mr. Gartner," I say, extending my hand to shake his.

"Please, call me Gerry. This mister business is too formal for the island. Aloha, and welcome to paradise," says Gerry in a friendly tone. He appears much more relaxed than he came across the few times we've spoken on the phone. "You must have some bags to retrieve?"

"Yes, most definitely. I wasn't sure how long I'd be here, so I didn't exactly travel light."

Gerry directs me to the luggage turnstile, which is outdoors—something I've never seen before. He carries my bags to the car, a convertible no less. Not that I have the best hair in the world, but by the time that convertible gets through with me, I'll look like I've put a finger in an electrical socket. What can I do? I don't even have a kerchief to tie around my head. I don't complain because I want to come across as confident, without the slightest of concerns. I roll up my side window to form a wind barrier. As we continue driving, I catch a glimpse of my reflection in the window. Good lord! Looking back at me is the arse end of a squirrel.

CHAPTER TWO:

Abigail "Abby" Parker (2013)

It's a cold, snowy New York night, which apparently is only going to get worse. I am dying to get home before the big dump of snow starts coming down, but Stan has other plans for me.

"Hey doll," Stan says when I pick up the phone on my desk. "Can you come to my office?"

There are a few things about my boss that I detest but can't bring myself to tell him. One in particular is him calling me "doll." I want to tell him off every time he utters the word. My girlfriend suggested I sue on count of harassment. As if! I'm a junior in the law firm. The only thing suing would get me is fired. Not to mention homeless from not being able to pay my bills.

I knock before entering Stan's office. He yells for me to come in.

"Listen," he says as I approach his desk, "I need you to take my place tonight. Something's come up that I need to take care of. You'll have to network for me at this party."

"What party?"

"Real estate developers and investors," says Stan as he hands me the address on a piece of paper. The party is being held way the hell out in downtown Jersey. There is no way I'm taking a ferry in this blizzard.

"You are aware that there's a storm advisory?"

"What's the big deal? You've never lived through a winter storm before? You'll be indoors."

"I'm worried about getting home."

"Come on doll, I thought you'd be thrilled. Maybe you can pick up a new client. Being a junior and all, you can use the help."

I don't say another word. I don't want to come across as ungrateful. Any other time, I'd have been thrilled. I put the paper in my pocket and turn to walk out.

"Hey, hey, where you going? I haven't told you why I was going. Sit, I need to fill you in. What's wrong with you, doll?"

I am half listening. I'm thinking about my previous plan, of picking up a container of matzo soup at my favorite deli. The plan was to relax and watch the snowfall, not to be in it. I've been dreaming of my warm, white-and-grey Zen apartment all day long. I like to alternate subtle pops of color throughout my apartment according to my mood. Currently I'm into red accent pieces and white vases with fresh green foliage.

Stan says, "There's these two brothers I want you to meet. They're land developers that I'm trying to bring on as new clients, so charm the pants off them, doll."

I've never hit anyone, but Stan gives me the urge to smack him upside the head. I feel as if I should be standing in a smoke-filled gin-joint every time he says the word doll.

"I'll do my best, Stan," I say with clenched teeth.

I make a quick stop at home to change for the party. At least I've convinced Stan to pay for my transportation due to the weather. As a junior, my expenses are limited. I quickly shower and throw on my go-to black designer pantsuit. I have just the perfect white blouse, which shows the right amount of cleavage. I cover my exposed flesh with multiple strands of pearls—sexy, but still very professional. I brush out my long dark hair and give it a quick once-over with the flat iron. My makeup is still pretty decent after a full day of work. I apply dark eyeshadow for a smoky-eye effect and some individual lashes, which I load with extra glue seeing as it's windy outside. I choose a bright red lip color followed with a spritz of perfume and high-heeled black booties.

By the time I get back downstairs, the snow has started falling furiously. I can't believe how much has accumulated. My booties are not going to keep my feet dry by the return trip. Stupid move, but it's too late to run back upstairs and change. I spot a cab approaching with its light on. I decide to make a mad dash before someone else sees it and tries to flag it down. I'm waving my arm like an accelerated windshield wiper to get his attention. The cab stops in front of me. I open the door and get in, but the cab driver tells me to get out.

"Hey lady, someone called in for a ride and it ain't you. You need to get out."

"Well, why'd you have your light on?"

"Because I'm picking up a passenger. Now get out," screams the driver.

I try negotiating with him to drop me off after he takes his passenger to wherever the person needs to go. I don't care what it costs, because I can't put a price on getting out of these blizzard-like conditions. Avoiding icicles building on my hair, not to mention frostbitten feet in my short boots, is worth any price.

The driver won't hear of it. "Get out!" he tells me again, when suddenly the door opens opposite me. Our screaming match comes to an abrupt halt.

The stranger says, "Hey, hey … what's going on?" The driver keeps rambling on, while my jaw drops. I've never seen anyone more handsome in my entire life.

"I'm sorry, man," the driver says, "This chick won't get out of the cab."

The gorgeous stranger looks at me and smiles. "Where you going?"

I try to get the words out, but my mouth feels like I've taken an oversized bite of a peanut-butter-and-banana sandwich. I dig into my pocket and pull out the piece of paper with the address, which I end up showing him, thanks to my lack of words.

The stranger laughs. "You won't believe this, but I'm heading to the exact same place. At least I'll have company for the long ride."

I can't believe my luck. He extends his hand to introduce himself. I'm slightly reluctant to touch his flesh. I feel as though I'll explode on impact. "Noah King," he says, "and you are?"

"Abby. Abby Parker," I reply with a trembling voice.

"Pleased to meet you, Abby," says Noah as he holds my hand, my stomach doing backflips.

CHAPTER THREE:

Genie Evans

(1960)

Gerry mentioned that we'd reach a point on the highway when the water would appear and become one with the sky. I can't take my eyes off the white-capped waves. They are rolling in one after the other in a seductively hypnotizing manner. From a distance the waves don't appear to be very large, but as we drive closer, it becomes clear that they're enormous, a surfer's dream.

I know we've reached our destination upon seeing the Coco Palms sign on my left. The white lettering is in a font I've never seen before. Each letter has a tropical curvy look, if that's even a thing—definitely custom-made. What makes it stand out even more is the dark distressed wood the letters are painted on.

We come to a complete stop and Gerry parks the car. I don't dare look at my reflection in the window again, as I'm positive that my bushy squirrel head has gotten much fluffier. It feels as if I'm wearing earmuffs. While I try to tame my fluffy mane I hear Gerry say, "Come, I can't wait to show you the place. I'll unload the luggage later."

As I turn to look at the resort, it's definitely hard to miss the hanging shell. This is no ordinary shell. It has to be at least ten feet in height. There it is at the main entrance, suspended by God knows what, dangling in the center of a pyramid-shaped roof. Can't say I've ever seen anything of the sort. I find myself saying with nervous laughter, "I sure hope that thing is on nice and sturdy." I envision it falling on my head and killing me before I can get a hula lesson in.

"She's a beauty!" Gerry exclaims as he stares up at the shell proudly. He takes hold of my elbow and escorts me into the resort, but I'm still fixated on the shell. How can one not be? It's the size of a baby elephant suspended in midair.

"Is it real?" I ask, thinking he'll say it's a manufactured piece, but his laughter answers my question otherwise.

"Heavens, yes, it's real. There are plenty of these monsters out there," Gerry says, pointing to the roaring blue ocean. In all honesty, I'm not sure I want to know what monsters surround me. I'd much rather take a look around the grounds and the resort itself, because what I've seen in a few short steps from the parking lot is breathtaking. Note to self: make sure you get to know the names of all the gorgeous tropical flowers surrounding the front entrance.

Gerry walks ahead of me into the hotel. Since he can't see what I'm doing, I decide to run past the gargantuan seashell. Another note to self: if you decide to take the job, check the safety of the shell's installation, ASAP. Concentrating on the shell, I find myself slamming into Gerry's back. He quickly turns to see what's hit him. I nervously laugh it off. "Oops. I guess I missed a step."

Gerry looks at me suspiciously. I deflect by gushing over the high cathedral ceiling. It has to be twenty feet high. I'm quickly realizing that Gerry doesn't do small. I bet his motto is "Go big, or go home." Or "The bigger the better." Anyhow, you get the gist.

The sun is beaming through stained-glass inserts. Through the sun's rays I can see transparent reflections of color. It's reminiscent of an indoor rainbow, if such a thing existed. In the reception area my eyes settle on the front counter, which is made of the same wood as the building outdoors. It's reminiscent of driftwood but with a more polished finish.

Standing behind the counter is a gaggle of gorgeous girls. Some are scurrying around with papers in their hands and others are stationary, checking people in and out. I'm quite certain that the hiring process was not a difficult task for Gerry. It's as if they've all just walked off the set of an exotic fashion shoot wearing the same bold and bright tropical-print dresses. Each girl has her dark hair pulled back in a perfect chignon with an unblemished fresh flower placed strategically above her ear, each with a different color. These girls are stunning natural beauties wearing minimal makeup.

The longer I stare at them, the worse my self-doubt is becoming. I have to remind myself of why I am here. It's a job opportunity, not a beauty pageant. But I have to give it to Mr. Gartner—he definitely has an eye for detail. By the looks of the well-fitted dresses, it is evident that Gerry isn't partial to muumuus. I'll kill him if I find he's laid a muumuu out for me to wear. I unexpectedly give out a small chuckle. Gerry looks at me as if I'm semi-insane. He ignores my outburst and introduces me to each of the girls. They are warm and inviting—just the friendly faces needed to make guests feel welcome. I need to keep my self-doubt in check; it just started appearing, like a bad blemish, around my forty-ninth birthday.

"Come," says Gerry. "I have a few vacant rooms on the second floor I'd like you to see. If you have any suggestions about the décor, or anything for that matter, please let me know. I welcome your opinion; that's why I asked you here. Wait until you to see the ocean view from upstairs," he continues as we keep climbing the stairs.

"Can't wait," I respond a little too quickly—probably because my brain is still focused on the exotic girls on the lower level. I catch myself saying, "You've hired some very lovely girls. I also noticed that your wait staff appear to be all male."

"Very observant, Miss Evans. I have two female hostesses that rotate shifts for the supper hour and another set for the daytime, but, yes, I like an all-male serving staff. Is that a problem?" asks Gerry.

"Not if I'm looking for eye candy," I laugh.

He looks confused at my response. The joke seems to have flown over his head. Before anyone says another word, his pager goes off. I watch as he unclips the pager from his belt to look at it. "I hope you don't mind," he says, "I have to make a call. It's quite urgent."

"No problem. I'll be fine. There's a lot for me to take in."

"Why don't you get yourself a drink downstairs? I'll come look for you as soon as I'm done."

"Okay. You go ahead. I'll make my own way down."

He walks briskly down the long hallway, disappearing down the staircase. I don't feel like going back down just yet. I want to look around. The first thing to catch my eye up here is the colorful carpeting. The array of colors causes my eyes to blink rapidly—the way they do when I look through a kaleidoscope. The longer I stare, the more the shapes bounce in and out at me. This carpet could be the inception to the psychedelic era. Gerry is a man ahead of his time without knowing it. We may have to have a chat about his choice—another mental note taken.

I decide to descend via the other set of stairs. As I stroll down the hallway, I find the walls to be stark. Did he do this intentionally, to offset the flood of color coming from the carpet? I still think the walls need something to make them less institutional. They need more of a tropical feel. By this point I'm on mental note overload. I need to start jotting my ideas down. The one thing I truly love is the massive window at the end of the hallway. It not only brings in the sunlight, but it's wide open to let in the balmy breeze and aromas of the tropics.

This is what the walls need, the feel of the outdoors coming in to seduce the guests. Minus the carpet, which is better suited for a funky Manhattan hotel.

Approaching the staircase, I notice the door is wide open to one of the suites. I expect someone to be there, but not a soul appears. I stand and stare as if willing some movement. I walk a bit closer—I have to anyway, in order to get to the stairs—and peer in, my eyes adjusting to the darkness. It's eerily quiet, when suddenly a cool breeze starts circling my lower extremities. It feels as if my feet are turning into immoveable blocks of ice. I swear I'm going *lōlō*. How is this even possible? As I make another attempt to free my feet, I'm relieved to hear Gerry's pounding footsteps approaching from below. I don't want him to see me this way, so I try to leap with more force. Whatever had me in its grip suddenly lets go, and I find myself face down on the kaleidoscope carpeting. I can hear panic in Gerry's voice as he runs up the last few steps. I get myself up before I have to endure any further embarrassment. I'm sure by this point he's wondering how a bumbling fool has become one of the world's most successful businesswomen. I know I'm not making a great first impression, but nothing like this has ever happened to me before. For the most part, I'm always composed. I have a quirky side, I'll admit, but clumsy I'm not.

"What in God's name happened?" exclaims Gerry. "Are you all right?"

"I'm—" I don't get to finish thanks to the slamming of the open door, which startles both of us. Gerry's face drains of color.

"What's going on?" I ask. "Why the shocked look on your face?"

It takes him a few moments to answer me. He glares at the door. "Are you sure you're okay?"

"Yes, yes, I'm fine. To be honest, I'm really not sure what just transpired."

"It's that damn room."

"What seems to be the problem?"

Gerry keeps shaking his head in disgust. "No one is to ever go in that room. It's off limits to everyone. When I say no one goes in there, I mean no one. Understood?"

What am I to say? I just got here. He is smart enough to pick up on my blank expression.

"I didn't mean to yell," he says. "That room has made me so mad over the years. I swear it's possessed. I will never go in there again as long as I live. It's given me nothing but grief."

I'm shocked to hear the words coming out of his mouth. Does this man actually believe in black magic? Maybe he's the one that's *lōlō*.

I don't know why, but somehow crazy is one of the first Hawaiian words I learned from the book I purchased a couple of weeks prior to leaving Texas. In all honesty, I liked how the word sounded. *Lōlō*. But maybe, just maybe, it was a premonition on my part. Somehow my inner being was telling me that crazy things were about to happen. Nah, couldn't be. This manner of thinking is totally *lōlō*.

To lighten the mood, I say, "How about we take a walk outdoors? I'd much rather look at those swaying palm trees."

Gerry smiles and takes my arm gently as we start down to the main level. "Come. I'll take you for a stroll along the lagoon. If you'd like, we can take one of the canoes out."

"That sounds lovely," I say. I turn back like a curious cat—only to have the door open and slam shut again, which leaves my spine tingling.

CHAPTER FOUR:

Abby Parker

(2013)

Five minutes have elapsed since I hopped into the back of a cab with a complete stranger named Noah. I try to look inconspicuous, but my eyes can't stop shifting side to side. I'm positive he can sense I'm looking at him. There really isn't much space between us, which leads me to cock my head each time I glance over. I'm sure I look like I have tics from his point of view. If it weren't for the extra lashes I glued on at the last minute, I'd have a much better chance to see him with my peripheral vision. There's no way I can get a good look at him unless I do a 180-degree turn in my seat, but that's a bit much. I'm not sure what's happened to my usual composed demeanor. It's as if an alien twin has taken over. I know I need to stop, because if someone were doing this to me, I'd be so annoyed. This isn't my first experience sharing a cab with a stranger, but there is something different, a pulsating energy surrounding us. Either that, or I'm about to have a coronary. The blood rushing through my veins is making my heart pump uncontrollably. I'm starting to feel short of breath. All I know is that I'm not myself. Ninety-nine percent of the time I'm in control. This might be my first time admitting I'm a control freak.

The longer I sit, the more I can feel a tiny rumble of gas floating through my intestine. Oh no, this can't be happening. The last thing I need is for my irritable bowel to take over. This condition started when I tried my first case. Stan told me to get help. He said it sounded like a volcano about to erupt. I believed him, considering he was sitting in the back of the room. After that I tried to get Zen … to the point of doing hot yoga. I started to see a change within a few weeks. It really helped with my anxiety and noisy bowels. I have managed to keep it in check up until now. I really don't want this handsome stranger to remember me by my gurgling sounds. To keep him from hearing, I need to break the silence. But Noah beat me to it.

"So, Abby, what do you do for a living?"

I tell myself to calm down, breathe and talk slowly.

"I'm a lawyer. I work in our corporate division."

"Interesting. Who do you work for?"

"Brickman and Brickman," I say.

"Hmm … sounds familiar, but can't say I've ever dealt with them. May have heard the name through my colleagues. The name definitely stands out."

I want him to keep talking, and not just because it camouflages my stomach noises. I love his deep, non-anxious voice. It's extremely sexy and soothing.

Working for Stan, with his obnoxious ways, has made me forget that real cultured gentlemen do exist. I respect Stan, but most days I feel as if I'm working with a mobster-type lawyer—the kind you find in the old black-and-white flicks. Even though I know my tall, dark, handsome stranger's name, he's still a stranger—but awkwardly enough, I sense a familiarity. It's as if I've known him all my life. I wonder what he's thinking, sitting beside me? If he could hear my thoughts, he'd be jumping out of a speeding cab. Of course, we aren't moving at all.

The cab driver interrupts my thoughts. He turns his head slightly towards the back, at all times keeping his eyes on the road ahead. "Sorry folks, but there seems to be a pile-up. Looks like we may be here for a while."

"What's your best guesstimate?" Noah asks.

"Oh man … I hate to break it to you, but we could be here all night."

Somehow, I don't care—I'm elated.

Noah pulls out his cellphone. As he frantically taps away at the keys, a thought comes to me. Does he have a date for the party? Yes, why else would he be typing at record-breaking speed? These parties are usually nothing but schmoozing and trying to snag new clients, so a date isn't always a good idea, but who knows. He finally stops tapping his phone but hasn't put it away. I bet he's waiting for a response. Within twenty seconds a beep goes off. He looks over at me.

"Sorry about that. I'll turn it off."

As much as I want to say *no worries*, I don't. Part of me wishes he'd put it away and focus on me. That is being a bit presumptuous, not to mention entirely neurotic. I give my head a little imaginary shake, hoping the sane and in-control Abby will return. How can this stranger be melting my heart like a snowman on a sunny day? None of my old boyfriends had this much of an effect on me. It's as if he's read my mind. He puts the device in his pocket and pulls out an unopened miniature bottle of water. He turns to me and asks, "Would you like the first sip?"

"I'd love some, but only if you're sure. I don't want to —"

He unscrews the bottle and hands it to me. "Ladies first."

I wouldn't have minded if he took the first sip. Somehow, knowing his lips would have touched the bottle's mouth, then mine, makes my heart pump out of control. I'm sure he'd have made the water taste that much better. I can't control the crazy thoughts swirling in my head, but I do get my stomach gurgles to settle down. This man is making me batty. I believe I'm experiencing love at first sight, or lust, maybe both. I pass the bottle back to him and his hand has a grip over mine. We look into each other's eyes simultaneously. Crazy-me slowly leans into him. My eyes close as I gently kiss his full lips. He takes the bottle and places it on the seat, and we both lean back into the smelly leather of the yellow cab. His hand has taken hold of my face as he kisses me. His flesh touching mine makes it feel as if the driver has cranked the heat up to a hundred degrees. Again, we are on the same wavelength. Noah asks the cab driver, "Would you mind opening the back window about an inch, please?"

I can hear the driver mumbling and the tone of his voice clearly relays displeasure. He's going on about how the snow is going to get in, along with a litany of other complaints, but finally I feel fresh air. I peek out one eye and see that he is looking at us in his mirror. For the first time in my life, I wish I was in a limo—the type that has a tinted panel between the driver and us.

I know I'm treading dangerous water with this complete stranger, but I've already jumped in headfirst and I don't feel myself slowing down. I want to drown in the scent of his skin. I had no idea I could feel so attracted to someone I just met. I want to get to know every inch of him. Apparently, so does he. I can feel his warm hands outlining my body.

He whispers in my ear, "I think we need to put on the brakes. Our driver will throw us out into the deep freeze soon."

I know we should stop, but I need another minute of him. I wriggle my way back up to a proper sitting position as I say, "I'm sorry, I don't know what's gotten into me. I don't want you to—" He stops me from saying another word by planting his warm lips on mine. They feel like plush pillows.

"No need to explain," he says.

That gets me wondering. Is he used to this? Do women always end up making out with him wherever he goes? I'm being stupid. Why wouldn't they? After all, I just did.

"Hey, what's going on in there?" he asks as he gently touches my temple.

"Nothing important."

"Just so you know, I don't do this either," he chuckles. "Sorry for laughing, but this is really out of character for me."

Not another word is needed. I truly believe him. He has a genuine air about him. I feel as if I'm looking at my soul mate. He comes across as very confident and comfortable with himself. I love a confident man, especially one without conceit. This man truly appears to not know how beautiful he is.

"So, Noah. How do you think the party is going?"

We both laugh. Noah looks at his watch. "Looks like we may not make the party. You realize we've been in this cab almost three hours?"

"I'd be lying if I said I'm disappointed about missing it. Although I *am* concerned about when we'll actually get back."

Noah leans over to talk to the driver. "How much longer?"

"Another twenty minutes, give or take. The heavy traffic cleared about a half hour ago. You were otherwise occupied," says the driver with a smirk, as he peers into his mirror.

"The only people that'll be left at the party will be the diehard drinkers," Noah says to me. "It was a two-hour cocktail party."

"Oh, I wasn't aware. My boss never mentioned it, and in all honesty I didn't ask. I was filling in for him last minute."

"Well, I for one am sure glad he didn't make it," says Noah as he holds my hand. "I won't be going back tonight. I have a room booked."

Suddenly I feel my stomach drop, like it does in those fast elevators. So, is he meeting a girl? He probably has a hookup in Jersey. Why wouldn't he? Look at him. Shit!

"Uh-oh," he says. "Someone has drifted again. Did you hear what I said?"

"About staying over?"

"Yes."

"Would you like to share my room?"

"You're not meeting anyone?" No sooner have I said the words out loud than I wish I could retract them. They sounded desperate. Damn!

"What? Why would you think that?"

"Jersey's really not that far, and if you were only going to a cocktail—"

"Whoa there, counselor. I was going to meet up with an old university friend, but once I got stuck in traffic with you, I was hoping things would take a different route. Even before you kissed me," he laughs.

I'm mortified for thinking the worst. I guess his frantic tapping earlier was to cancel out on his friend.

"Well?" he says. "What do you say? Would you like to join me? I have a beautiful suite, compliments of my firm. I'm staying right where the party was taking place. Waterfront room! Breakfast in bed overlooking the Hudson River."

"You can stop. I was going to say yes before the amenities."

The next morning I text Stan and tell him I'll be late. He responds by apologizing that his clients had canceled due to the weather conditions. Talk about irony. He tells me to take the day off after hearing how I sat in a cab for hours and had to spend the night. Well, maybe the latter part wasn't entirely true, but he didn't need to know. My guilt almost has me turning down his generous offer, but his acts of generosity are few, so I take it.

I'm standing in front of the floor-to-ceiling window. The Hudson River is waking up to the warmth of the bright sunrise.

As I watch the glistening water, I feel Noah's arms wrap around my body from behind. I can't think of a better way to start my day.

CHAPTER FIVE:

Genie

"What do you think?" I ask Gerry. The last of the shell basins are being installed in the bathrooms.

"I love them. Don't know why I didn't think of it."

"I believe it's what you hired me for, Mr. Gartner."

Gerry turns to me with furrowed brows. "Don't you think it's about time you call me Gerry? Seriously! It's been six months. I can't take another minute of it."

"I wasn't aware you felt so strongly about it."

"Jesus, Genie. I've asked you over and over to call me Gerry. Our relationship passed the business stage a while back. And, don't start giving me excuses about what the staff might think, because frankly, I don't care. It's time you ..."

Gerry is pacing. He keeps pushing his hair back, which I've noticed is one of his many nervous habits. I just want him to be calm and focused on the bathroom right now.

"Okay, okay," I say, whispering. "We don't need everyone to hear us. Back to the basins."

Gerry smiles, which has me promising to do my best to be less formal in public. "I don't know what to say, Genie," he says. "The shell basins are spectacular. They make a world of difference. Everything you've done these past months has been stupendous. You truly have an eye for detail."

I can tell Gerry sincerely appreciates my efforts. It isn't so much the words he uses as the lightness that gleams in his face. He gives me a kiss on the cheek. "I must be off, but I'll be back first thing in the morning."

"You best get going," I tell him. "You wouldn't want to miss your flight. I've got things covered." He hugs me tight and leaves for his monthly day trip to Honolulu. Gerry still has business to attend to on the island of Oʻahu. I just wish he weren't staying over in his old apartment. I try hard not to think this way, but the overnights make me paranoid about which of his ladies he may be spending the night with. Even though Gerry has been taking less and less frequent trips to Honolulu and conducting more of his business dealings remotely, I can't help myself from going to negative thoughts.

When Gerry tells me that I'm special, I truly believe he means it. It's tough for any person to go from being a notorious flirt to monogamous overnight. I respect Gerry for who he is. He's never promised me anything he hasn't delivered on. He's been nothing but kind and attentive since my arrival. As long as I keep my expectations of him in check, I should remain sane. It makes the indiscretions less painful. Well, not really—but for the time being, as long as he treats me well, that's all that matters. Plus, I know what I signed up for.

What I truly adore about Gerry is that he accepts me for me. For the first time in my life, I've met a non-judgmental man. He trusts me as a businesswoman, which is more than I can say for the men in my past. He's trusting of my ability—to the point that he's given me free rein to do as I please with the resort. Much more freedom than I'd anticipated. Which led me to installing the shell basins, which I imported from the island of O'ahu. I figure if he can hang a gigantic shell in the front entrance, why not follow that through in each room? I want the Coco Palms to be exclusive, to have something that no other resort in the world has. And we have shells right outside our doorstep. We need to utilize everything Mother Nature has to offer.

The first installations were in the single bungalows, which Gerry calls cottages. The two-suite cottage, number 25, was the main living quarters of the last reigning Queen. I figured I'd experiment with the cottages before disturbing the bathrooms in the main building.

While basins were being installed, the bright carpets were torn out of all the cottages. In their place I put in a combination of wood and ceramic flooring. I thought it more appropriate to have ceramic in the bathrooms and natural wood throughout the remainder of the rooms—much more suitable for the tropics. I also had stonemasons install a mosaic of seashells and stones on the bottom portion of the walls in the cottages only. I hired some local children—accompanied by adults, of course—to collect the shells and unique stones. The shells and stones are an extension of the outdoors, complementing the custom-built shutters for the wraparound windows. They bring lightness to the dark wood ceilings, which felt oppressive but would have been too costly to redo. My team staggered their shifts around the clock to reduce impact on the guests.

After the first cottage was fully refurbished, I hired a professional photographer to come and take photos. I wanted to revamp the brochure as soon as possible. I needed to get my marketing plan in place. It's the only way I could start to bring worldwide attention to the Coco Palms.

Today, the last of the rooms in the main building are getting their finishing touches. It feels good to know we'll be done. As much as I want to make over Room #256, I've been warned never to enter. I'm like a cat—everything piques my curiosity—but I don't want to betray Gerry. After my initial incident with the room's door opening and closing, it never happened again. I still feel the chill every time I walk by, but I keep that to myself. I'd be lying if I said it doesn't give me the heebie-jeebies, but as the months have passed, I've come to terms with it. I tend to believe that supernatural entities exist, but I've learned not to discuss them any longer with Gerry. He thinks it's all hogwash.

I've also convinced Gerry to change the color scheme of the chapel, which is hidden away near the lagoon. Here stood this beautiful architectural masterpiece, but it was almost impossible to find. As much as I didn't want to cut down natural habitat, it was badly needed, particularly for safety. I couldn't have guests tripping over the large roots that were protruding from the ground. I had the soil around the chapel excavated, and cleared a good six feet of trees around its perimeter. Cobblestones have been laid to match the walkways alongside the lagoon. I found a local nursery that planted my favorite tropical flowers all around the chapel. Hiring local experts has been a great way of meeting people. They've offered me an abundance of insight into the Hawaiian culture, which in turn has provided me with ideas for the resort.

As I'm outside instructing the painters on the exterior color for the chapel, I hear Gerry yelling for me.

"Gerry! What are you doing here? I thought you'd left for a meeting?"

"I did, and now I'm back."

"That was a fast meeting." I don't know what else to say. He's looking at me strangely—to the point of making me a bit uncomfortable. He's carrying a box with a red ribbon tied around it, which he hands to me.

"Here," he says. "I thought you might like this."

Caught totally off guard, I say nothing and take the box. I untie the ribbon and lift the lid to find a floral garment. I put the box down on the ground so I can get the dress out. As I raise it up and it unfolds, I find myself staring at one of the most beautiful dresses I've ever seen. It's reminiscent of what the girls at reception wear, but Gerry has chosen a subtler floral design.

"Do you like it?" he asks enthusiastically.

"Like it? I love it." I hold the dress up to my body. "This is stunning. Thank you so much. I don't know what else to say."

"Say you'll wear it tonight. I'd like to take you to a *lūʻau*."

"Really? Me?"

Gerry laughs. "Yes you, unless there's someone standing behind you by the name of Genie."

I can feel my cheeks burning up. I can't believe he bought me a dress. He obviously thinks I have a curvaceous body, or he'd have bought me a *muʻumuʻu*. The gesture speaks volumes to me. I can't wait to try it on.

"Well? Is that a yes?"

"Yes," I say. "Sorry, you caught me off guard. I wasn't expecting to see you, number one, and then you give me a dress?"

By this point I know my cheeks are flaming red. It's hard for me to accept a compliment, let alone a gift. Neither has happened very often in my life. I was always a friend or an older-sister type. I can count the lovers I've had on one hand—and may I add, the experiences were nothing to write home about.

Gerry starts away. "Meet you in the lobby at five PM, and don't be late," he says with such confidence.

"I won't. And thank you again," I reply as he keeps walking.

I stand by the lagoon, staring down at the beautiful dress resting in the box. I needed to try it on, so I turn to start back to my room, only I can't move. I feel an odd tightness around my ankles. I look down, but there's nothing there. Again I try to lift my foot. My crazy mind starts racing. Is the walkway built on some sort of quicksand? But my logical side knows it can't be, or it would have sunk long ago. Plus, everything is leveled, and I'm not knee-deep in anything. I do, however, start to feel the same chill I've felt when I'm near Room #256. Suddenly, I'm blinded by something shining in my eyes. The sun seems to be reflecting off something. I close my eyes for fear that my pupils will combust. With one last attempt to move, I land flat on my face with my floral-print dress crushed beneath me.

I hear a woman's voice say, "You really should be more careful, dear."

I look around but can't see anyone. Quickly I jump to my feet. There by the lagoon's edge is a double-hulled canoe, but no one is on it. I can still hear a booming female voice. Maybe I've hit my head, which would explain my hallucination. The strange thing is I can no longer feel the coldness. If anything, I'm sweating. I pick my dress up off the ground, thankful that it hasn't been soiled. I'm not entirely sure I want to look over at the canoe. I could swear that's where the voice is coming from. Except I now hear a low murmur sweep past me, saying, "You could have at least given an old lady a hand."

I'm convinced I'm going mad due to the tropical heat. What did I eat earlier? All I see is the bright sun shining into my eyes. And with every second that goes by, the voice becomes fainter and fainter. How could any of this be possible? Who was talking to me? Veering around the corner of the cottages, I hear, "Aren't you the least bit curious?"

I see a faint shadow of an elderly woman. I rub my eyes frantically with my floral dress as I hear her say, "You wouldn't want to wrinkle your outfit. Come now. Gerry will be disappointed."

"Who are you?"

"I'm your fairy godmother," she says, roaring with laughter.

"How do you know Gerry gave me this dress? Are you spying on me? What's your name?"

"Now, now, dear. Which of the questions would you like me to answer first?"

"How about starting with your name?"

"Deborah, Queen Deborah."

"As in …"

"Ah … so you have heard of me."

"But you died. Like hundreds of years ago."

"Let's not exaggerate. It's more like over one hundred, but under two."

I can feel my head spinning and my breath becoming shallow. The daylight is turning into night. I must be dying. That's it. I have crossed over into the other life. But strangely enough, I find myself with my eyes wide open. Here I am in a strange, yet familiar room. Who is this old woman looking down at me? Please don't let me be dead!

"You're not dead," she says.

"Oh great, you're also a mind reader? Where am I?"

"My room. You fainted, so I thought it best to get you out of the sun and heat. Mind you, I'm a ghost, so guiding you here was a bit wobbly for both of us," laughed Deborah.

"So, I'm not dead?"

"No. Come, you must get up. You don't want to be late getting to that *lū'au*."

"How do you know so much about me?"

"I've been watching you since you got here. I knew right away that you were one person I could be friends with."

"Friends? You scared me half to death. Plus, shouldn't friends be able to see one another? Why couldn't I see you down at the lagoon? How is it possible that I can see you now?"

"There you go again with the multiple questions. How about I start with this: I need to feel that I can trust a person, and then I have the capability to allow you to see me. Believe me, I haven't trusted anyone in a ver-r-r-ry long time. I'd have to say a good hundred years."

I start to feel woozy again. It's insane to think that I'm talking to some sort of apparition.

"Try to keep in mind that I'm capable of reading one's mind," says Deborah jokingly. "So, try not to have too many bad thoughts about me."

I catch myself laughing out loud. I didn't realize ghosts could be so spunky.

CHAPTER SIX:

Abby

After making mad, passionate love with Noah all night, I lie on my side watching him sleep. Who watches someone sleep? I thought this was irrational behavior, the type of nonsense I'd read about in *Cosmo*, until it happened to me. I can't get enough of his face. I take in every breath, his chest heaving up and down, causing my body to burn with desire. His peaceful sleep has my nerve endings twitching. I want nothing more than for him to wake and make love to me again, but I also fear he'll wake and want to leave. Maybe he's had his fun and won't even wait to have breakfast with me? My paranoia is in full swing. We are strangers after all, and he is sleeping, not looking at my face wanting to take it in. Oh my God … I've lost my mind. Never have I slept with a total stranger. I am a well-educated woman and was brought up quite conservatively.

I scramble in my purse to grab my phone. It's five AM. Should I try and nudge him awake? If I'm never going to see him again, maybe he should just leave as soon as possible. I can't take the agony of the unknown any longer. I gently slide in nice and tight against his body. He can sense I'm next to him. He slowly begins to run his hands over my body, his eyes still shut. I can't control my urges. I need him, and just like that, it's as if we have one mind.

He whispers in my ear. "I've never wanted anyone as much as I want you. Is it insane to say I love you?"

As much as my crazy side wants to believe he loves me, it sounds too much like the classic *Cosmo* article. I need to think that it is pure physical attraction. Somehow, thinking about it that way will lessen the blow when he never calls me.

We lie in bed until the sun rises over the Hudson. He is partially sitting up, playing with my hair as my head rests on his chest. Every follicle is aroused by his touch. I need to stop being so foolish. I put my bra and panties on and walk over to the floor-to-ceiling window. It isn't long before I feel his warm arms wrapped around me, and he says, "I don't want us to end here. Let's take the day off. What do you say?" He kisses my neck. "And before you ask or start to think that I do this all the time, I don't. I've been with the firm for almost three years and never taken a sick day."

"Neither have I," I reply.

"There you go. We have something in common. How about some breakfast? Maybe we can plan our day over coffee. But for now ..."

And just like that, our bodies are pressed against the steamed-up windowpane, my arms pinned against the glass as he makes love to me. His touch leaves me lifeless as a ragdoll. There isn't an inch of my body that his tongue hasn't tasted. We are like two starving wolverines trying to get as much food as we can while we have our prey, except without violence, of course. Noah is a gentle and considerate lover.

It is noon when we finally get our wits about us. As much as I don't want to go, we need to get back to Manhattan. Never would I have thought we'd be in the back of a cab together again, except this time it's a limo, the kind with a partition.

"What are your plans for the rest of the day?" he asks.

"I haven't given it much thought."

"Would it be presumptuous of me to ask if you'd like to have dinner? If you want to be alone, I understand."

"Sure," I reply, a bit too eagerly. "I mean sure, I'd love to have dinner with you." I wish I hadn't sounded like a giddy schoolgirl, but too late. "What'd you have in mind?"

"I haven't gotten that far into the plan."

"Do you need to go home first? Or—"

"No, I don't need to be anywhere, except with you. But if you need some space, just say the word."

"Are you insane? I don't even want there to be space between us in this cab," I say as I close in on him. "How about you come to my place and we order in?" I think this last suggestion may have made me sound truly desperate. I feel myself beginning to perspire. Last thing I want is for him to feel my wet palm.

"Decision made," says Noah, still holding my hand. "I'd have suggested my place, but there may be a few food containers laying around."

Whew, I dodged that bullet. "No worries on my part. I have to tell you up front, I'm a wee bit of a clean freak."

"There's no such thing as a wee bit. I'd venture to guess you're full-blown neurotic."

"You haven't even known me for twenty-four hours and you call me neurotic?"

"Well?"

We both laugh. I can't keep a straight face. "I confess, yes, I tend to like things in a certain order. Hate seeing clothes on the floor. Huge pet peeve."

"Think I may have opened a can of worms."

Noah stayed over, and only went back to his apartment to collect his things. From that day on, we were a couple. We were in love and crazy about one another. After two years of living together, never in a million years would I have predicted he'd leave me the way he did. It left me broken and distraught. I could barely work for about a month. I thank my parents for being there, and Stan for not firing me. My work right now is what keeps me going. I love what I do, but it has also been nine months since Noah left. I'm not saying I'm over him. I've just learned to cope.

Looking back at the situation, I fully understand why my parents check up on me. Had I been a betting woman,

I'd never have put money on the possibility that I, of all people, would fall apart the way I did. My therapist believes I'll be stronger than ever, though, and I have to agree. I've become fierce in my job. Stan tells me so every chance he gets.

CHAPTER SEVEN:

Genie

There we go. I take one more glance at myself in the mirror, add another touch of red lipstick, and I'm ready for the *lūʻau*. I still can't believe how good I look. I feel like a new woman. Who'd have known that such a form-fitting dress could look so spectacular on me? Somehow Gerry did. I can't wait for him to see me in it. For the first time since I arrived, I feel as if I truly fit in and have gotten out of plain Genie mode, which I'm sure is mostly in my own head anyway. Lately I've been feeling younger and full of energy. Maybe Dean was right. I won't let him know just yet, though. I give out a small chuckle.

As I'm walking from my cottage, I hear Gerry. I turn and watch as he walks towards me in his crisply pressed white linen pants and multicolored Hawaiian shirt. His hair appears to have a bit more sheen in it tonight. I sometimes wonder how much hair product Gerry uses to keep it so firm. He's much better at it than I am.

"Genie! You look spectacular. How do you like the dress?"

"I love it. I can't thank you enough."

"Seeing you in it is all the thanks I need. It really suits you. You look beautiful, Genie," says Gerry as he looks me over from head to toe. I am feeling a little uncomfortable. As much as I want to look up into his eyes, I'm afraid to. I thank the Lord that he picks up on it. He asks, "Would you like to take a stroll along the lagoon before we go?"

As much as I want to, I don't want a repeat performance of earlier in the day. I can't endure having some ghost ruin my night. But how am I going to say no without sounding as if I don't want to be alone with him? A stroll would be lovely, but I suggest an alternative.

"I hear the grounds of the *lūʻau* are spectacular. Maybe we can grab a drink there, and you can give me a tour at the same time."

"Why didn't I think of that? Splendid idea," Gerry agrees. "Let's go." He takes my hand and leads me to the car. "I'd much rather be away from the prying eyes of staff anyhow. You know how employees can be."

Of course I know how they can be—I'm one of them, and I'm questioning his motives right now. Does he not see this stunned look on my face? "I sure do know how it is."

"It's not the same, Genie. You must realize that I've become quite smitten with you?"

I honestly don't know how to reply to that. If I say yes, I'll sound arrogant. If I say I haven't noticed, I'll be a bit of a dimwit. But I choose to match him. "I've come to be quite fond of you, too." That one simple compliment justifies his giving my hand a squeeze as he drives. What I wasn't expecting was Deborah whispering in my ear.

"Oh, Genie. You know what he expects from you?"

I must have jerked, because Gerry asks, "Are you okay?"

Probably looking like a lunatic, I reply, "I felt something on my shoulder—sorry, it kind of startled me." Meanwhile I keep the lie up by swatting at an imaginary object, hoping to be able to take a swipe at Deborah without making Gerry suspicious of my actions.

"I can stop the car if you need a minute?"

"No, keep driving, it was probably just a bug of some sort," I laugh.

"Okay, we aren't far from the *lū'au*. I'm sure it's nothing a Mai Tai can't fix," says Gerry as he looks over at me and winks.

Gerry parks the car. Before he can come over to my side, I open the door and get out, half hoping I can slam the door before Deborah has time to follow me. I'm not certain on the mobility of ghosts. I pray I don't slam the door on her, which I don't think I did. No … I'm sure she'd have screamed. That's if they actually feel pain. I realize I know nothing about ghosts. Then again, why would I have needed to before now? My Lord, I'm really sounding batty, but I truly hope she'll sit in the car until we finish our dinner.

"Genie, you seem a little preoccupied," Gerry says. "I'm worried that you've been working too hard."

"It's nothing, I swear. I just want everything to be ship-shape back at the resort." I hate lying to Gerry, but what choice do I have?

He takes my arm as we walk through the parking lot, making our way to the front gate of the grounds. "It'll be fine. You seem to have everything under control. Come now. Tonight is about you having some fun. No talk about work, promise?"

"Pro—promise. Sorry, I had a hiccup." In reality, what I have is Deborah whispering in my ear. She made it out of the car.

"Of course he doesn't want to talk about work," she whispers. "Why would he buy you that beautiful dress if he wanted to discuss work? He can't wait …"

I slip my arm out of Gerry's hold. "Would you mind pointing me to the ladies' room, please? I'll only be a minute."

"Sure, it's just past the entrance. Come. I'll take you."

After entering the washroom marked *wāhine*, woman, I stand defiantly waiting for Deborah to speak first. When she doesn't, I say, "Lookit here! If you want to be my friend, you will get back in that car, right now. Do you hear me?"

"Well, well, well. The lady does have a temper."

"What? You've been badgering me since I arrived. What is it that you want?"

"I want your help."

"With what?"

"I want my land to stay in my family."

"What?" I say. "And how am I supposed to accomplish that? This is too much for me to understand right now. I need to get back out there before I get fired on grounds of lunacy. You know? Mental instability? Ring any bells?"

She booms with laughter. "Oh, dear Genie. I knew why I liked you right away. It's your flare for the dramatic. You will come to realize that we are similar in so many ways. Now please, can you use my name when you speak to me? Remember, I can also pick up on some of your thoughts. Not nice to call me an old woman. Even though I am."

I'm about to have myself committed if she … Deborah … doesn't stop. I have no choice but to say, "Okay, I'll make you a deal. You quietly go back to the car and sit there until we're done. I don't want to hear from you for the remainder of the night. Not here, nor back at the resort. Just give me this one night. We can discuss me helping you in the morning. Am I making myself clear?"

"Quite."

"That's it. The cat got your tongue now? You had so much to say earlier."

"I don't need your harshness, thank you very much. I will go back to the car and wait for you there. Tomorrow, we will speak."

Great. Now I'm feeling bad for snapping at her. "Listen. I apologize for being short with you, but you must realize that having a conversation with a ghost is not normal."

"But you *are* having a conversation with a ghost," says Deborah with a hint of innocence. "By the way ... would you be so kind as to bring me back some *kalua* pig?"

"Some what?"

"For heaven's sake. It's the pig that you'll be eating at the *lū'au*. The one that they will be removing from the ground."

I draw a deep breath and let out an even deeper sigh—the nerve of her! She leaves me no choice, and just when I thought we had a deal. I can tell dealing with her won't be an easy feat moving forward. I don't dare mention anything to Gerry, as my mental state will definitely be questioned. It's not as if I'm not questioning it myself. How did I go from being CEO of one of the biggest oil companies in the world to speaking with a ghost within a few short months? Something is just not right with this picture. No wonder Gerry made me an offer I couldn't refuse. I'm living in the tropics for free, with a salary to match my previous one, except this time around I have my own personal ghost as a bonus—who'd have guessed? I wonder if she's ever spoken to Gerry. Maybe that's why he doesn't want anyone in the room. Why else?

I exit the restroom and see Gerry waiting for me at the ticket counter. He's wearing a fresh floral *lei* and holding another in his hands for me. As I approach, he places it over my head and it gently cascades around my neck.

"Now that completes the outfit," he says, kissing me on the cheek. "Come. I have our tickets. Let's go and get us a Mai Tai before dinner. I'll give you a tour of the grounds."

"Sounds like a great idea," I say. But before we go anywhere, I feel Gerry's arm wrap around my waist. I'd be lying if I said I minded, because on the contrary, I welcome it. His touch sends a tingling rush through my entire body—something that hasn't happened in a very long time.

As we approach the bar, I can hear a familiar voice. I don't turn around, as my mind has already been playing tricks on me. I'm not sure I'm ready for a male ghost, but while the bartender mixes our drinks, I hear the voice getting closer and closer. I turn to look, and it's Dean. I can't believe it. I stare at Dean and then Gerry, realizing he's set up the entire night to surprise me. I run to hug Dean.

"Well, look at you. Not gone more than a few months and already you've forgotten your Texan ways," he laughs. "This tropical look suits you."

"Oh Dean," I cry. "It's so good to see you. Why didn't you tell me you were coming? I'd—"

Dean stops me before I can say another word. "What kind of surprise would it be, if we'd have told you? Gerry tells me you've done wonders with the resort, so I wanted to see it with my own eyes."

I look at Gerry. "How long have you known about this?"

"I won't admit to anything," Gerry chuckles. "Come on. Let's get our drinks and find ourselves a seat."

Gerry knows the owner of the family-run business and got us front row seats. We have a choice of picnic tables or beautiful handcrafted blankets supplied by local artisans. I choose to sit at a table because I couldn't really shimmy myself down to sit on the ground in such a tight-fitting dress. I've never experienced having dinner with my feet in the sand—it feels good to kick off my high heels and play in the soothing, warm crystals.

"So, Dean? When are you going to ask me if you were right about this move?"

"I don't have to. I can see it in the glow of your skin. Seems to me someone found the ignition spark," says Dean, winking at me.

"Oh, you," I say, blushing. I don't want Gerry to know that my flame had burnt out. I wonder if the two of them have spoken about it. I'm not going to worry for the time being, as I'm distracted by the sound of beating drums. They are sending a lovely echo throughout the lush garden. Gerry informs me that it's time for the *imu* ceremony, which will be followed by a lighting ceremony. Not sure what it all means, but I will watch and learn.

As the drums relent to a softer beat, two young men appear wearing sarongs and holding conch shells, while a narrator tells of the unearthing of the pig and the significance of each horn's blowing. He continues, as the horns are blown four times to give thanks. Both young men face the mountains, then turn to the ocean, and then in the directions of the rising and setting sun. Once they are done, each of the men sets his shell down and retrieves a rake to clear the sand which forms a mound atop the *imu* or pit. In less than five minutes, the roasted pig—or *kalua,* I should say—is removed and brought to a huge table where the chef chops it up to be served for dinner. The aromas don't take long to reach me, and my hunger has suddenly escalated.

I look to Gerry and Dean who are engaged in conversation. They don't even notice the four young men who've run out with lit torches. They begin to light all the tiki torches that have been placed around the grounds. Another mental note: remove existing outdoor lights and have them changed to tiki torches, ASAP. What was Gerry thinking? How could he not have a lighting ceremony at the resort? This could be an everyday affair. What a wonderful tradition. I sit back and admire the traditional clothing. The men are all wearing the same green banana-leaf-patterned sarong. They've accessorized it with black beads around the neck, and the *pièce de résistance* is the fresh floral crown on their heads. I'll have to learn what the accessories are called in Hawaiian. Maybe I'll ask Deborah. I feel a whole new excitement bubbling within me. I can't wait to get started on my plans for the lighting ceremony.

Having been distracted by my own excitement, I notice Gerry and Dean again. I'm quite sure that there's an inside joke behind their laughter. "Would you like to share?" I ask.

They are both getting up from the table. Gerry reaches for my hand. "Come. Let's go and get another drink before the food is served."

"I think I'll just stay here, if you don't mind. I'm quite enjoying the scenery," I respond. I swear I'm going to be struck by lightning. I've lied, yet again. I don't want to get a drink, because I've noticed where the pork station has been set up. I decide to saunter on over, because I'm feeling bad for leaving Deborah in the car. She must be starving.

When I open the car door, it doesn't take Deborah long to appear. For the first time I can fully see her. I crack a joke to lighten any tension that may be lingering between us. "If I knew bringing you food would reveal your full identity, I'd have done it sooner," I offer jokingly, which spreads a hint of a smile across Deborah's face.

Deborah extends her hand to take the plate. "Thank you, dear. I meant it when I said I like you. I haven't been visible to anyone since I died," she admits.

I watch as she takes a bite of food. She looks up at me, which causes a sudden pang of warmth between us. As much as I should get back to the *lū'au*, I figure a couple more minutes won't hurt.

I tell Deborah, "The ceremonies were so beautiful. I've never seen anything like it. I'm going to get Gerry to have a lighting ceremony at the Coco Palms. What do you think?"

"I think you're a smart woman."

"Then, why so gloomy. What is it?"

"I always get choked up by the sound of the horns blowing."

"I wasn't even aware that it was possible to use shells as an instrument. They have such a lovely sound."

"Yes, they do. They would blow them to let the locals know when I was coming down the path of the Wailua River. I wasn't joking when I told you I was the last of the royal family to reign over this land, or did I tell you that already? You know at my stage in life I can be a bit forgetful."

"I believe I came to that conclusion in a roundabout way," I say as we both giggle like old college friends would do. I watch as Deborah devours her meal. "I take it you haven't eaten in a while? Would you care for more?"

"I'm good for now, dear, thank you. You don't want to know how long it's been. It tastes divine," she says, licking her lips. "I've always loved the *kalua* pork, but my favorite dish is *lau lau*."

"*Lau* ... what?"

Deborah roars with laughter. "Somehow it doesn't sound the same with your English. What is that accent you have? Or do you have a speech impediment?"

"You don't like my Texas drawl?"

"Is that what you call it? Well, not to worry. I will get accustomed to it."

I have to admit that I find the woman just as charming as she is unbearable, but I must get back before the guys notice I've been gone too long.

"Listen, Deborah. I'll be by first thing in the morning as promised."

"Okay, dear," she says with a melancholy tone.

"What is it?"

"I don't think Gerry is good for you. Just stick to your work."

"I'll take your advice into consideration, but let's not forget that you promised you'd be good for the remainder of the night."

"I'm a woman of my word. Don't you worry."

Great! Anytime someone says don't worry, you know you should worry. "Okay then, I'll be off," I say, but I can see Deborah pouting. She couldn't possibly expect me to stay with her, or could she? What have I gotten myself into?

CHAPTER EIGHT:
Abby
(2015)

I decide to book an early morning appointment with my therapist. It's been almost nine months since I started seeing her. To be exact, it was two weeks after I got blindsided by Noah's disappearance. I fully understand what people mean when they say that life would be easier if their ex were dead. Don't get me wrong. I'd never wish death on anyone. But the wondering and the anxiety I feel would have been different. There isn't a day that goes by when I don't ask myself what he's doing, or where he is. I still can't come to terms with why he up and left. What did I do to make him leave? I could go on and on, but that's what my therapist is for. She's supposed to try and help me figure these things out.

It was on my mother's urging that I first sought help. Maybe I should back up a bit. When Noah left, you could only imagine the shock. I got home late from work, but that wasn't anything unusual. What was odd was the fact that I had five missed calls from Noah that day, but he hadn't left a message—that was not like him. Unfortunately, I hadn't looked at my phone until my day wrapped. I'd been in court all day, and right after that I was stuck in meetings with Stan. When I did try to call Noah on my way home, a recording came on and said the number was not in service. I figured he may have lost his phone and canceled his account.

I unlocked the apartment door and stepped in. It was pitch black inside. It's amazing how our natural instincts work. I didn't need light to know that something felt off. An uneasy sensation started to flow through my entire body. I flicked on the light in the foyer, and as I opened the coat closet, the emptiness inside started to make my insides quiver. All of Noah's things were gone. I automatically ran to the bedroom. On my pillow was a note. Not a lovely farewell letter neatly tucked into an envelope—this was a tiny page ripped from my grocery pad in the kitchen. It read: *Please, don't be mad at me for leaving. It has nothing to do with you. This is my journey— one I couldn't possibly expect you to understand. I hope that one day you will find the love and happiness you deserve. Noah.*

How could a man I thought I knew so well leave me this way? We had one of the most amazing relationships, or so I thought. We prided ourselves on the fact that we were soul mates. Our chemistry was never off. Even after two years, we both couldn't keep our hands off one another. We were almost always in sync. Yes, of course we had our own personal differences, but nothing that warranted his leaving me. When we looked into each other's eyes, there was genuine love and passion there. And that's what makes his disappearance so hard to accept.

That night, I didn't know what to do besides call my mother. I remember her answering the phone and me blubbering uncontrollably, "Mom ..."

"Abby! What is it? Are you okay? Is Noah hurt?"

"Mom ... he's gone."

"What do you mean he's gone? Did he have an accident?"

"No," I said, sobbing my eyes out. "He's left me."

My mother's silence spoke volumes. I could feel the horror through her extended silence. In the background I heard Dad asking her who it was.

I snapped, "Mom! Please, please don't say anything to Dad. Please, promise me."

You see, my dad is a private investigator. I'm sure you're wondering why I wouldn't have wanted to have him find Noah. Well ... let's just say Dad voiced his unsolicited opinion once too often. He told me that a man who doesn't discuss his family or where he's from is definitely hiding something. With hindsight, I guess he was right, but that's not the Noah I thought I knew.

I could hear my mother telling Dad that it was one of her friends from bridge. She said she'd explain as soon as she hung up. I hated having my mother lie, but my thinking wasn't rational. Don't get me wrong. I love my Dad to bits.

Since Noah's leaving, there isn't a scenario that I haven't thought of. I went as far as wondering if he'd left due to a terminal illness which he couldn't bring himself to tell me about. Otherwise, who does something like this? Not to mention that he couldn't even sign the note *Love, Noah*. That in itself was a deep sting.

I had my full-blown meltdown the minute my mom stepped into my apartment that night. I couldn't regain my composure. Before her arrival, from what I can remember, I felt frozen. It's as if I was afraid to move within my own apartment. I made Mom promise me that she wouldn't mention a word of Noah's disappearance to Dad, at least not yet—it wasn't something I wanted to deal with. In order for her to promise me that, though, she made me a deal. I was to seek help from a therapist immediately. I didn't want to talk about it. I shrugged it off and thought she was being ridiculous. As days passed, I couldn't bring myself to leave my bed, and that's when my mother showed up at my apartment again, with Dad in tow. Let's just say he wasn't interested in finding Noah. My parents were worried about me. At first I was furious with Mom for breaking her promise, but after a few weeks had passed, I understood her concern. My mind had been so clouded by sorrow that it didn't leave any room for logic. I thank my lucky stars for my mom and my dad.

I reach my therapist's and climb the four levels to her office. Exercise relieves my anxiety a bit, and I would rather walk up than ride an elevator, which makes me feel claustrophobic. I make it to the reception area on time. Dr. Iris, as she likes to be called, opens her door just as I'm about to sit down.

"Good morning, Dr. Iris."

"Hello Abby. Please, come in."

I take a seat in my usual spot, which is on the three-person sofa. I sit upright today. Usually I am relaxed and have my legs curled up to my chest. Being the last patient of the day has its advantages. I have time to go home and change into my comfy clothes first. Today, for the first time, I'm in a business suit—another reason why I'm forced to sit properly.

"So, Abby, why the switch in appointment?"

"I have a confession to make and I didn't want to wait another moment. I haven't been totally honest with you. You see ..."

I can feel my heart pounding. It feels as if it's going to leap out of my chest.

"Take your time. Gather your thoughts."

I do as she instructs. I take a couple of deep breaths. When I feel ready, I say, "Let me start with the fact that I haven't thrown everything out that belongs to Noah, as I said I had." Even as I hear myself say the words, I'm embarrassed to have lied. I feel weak and liberated at the same time. "I have a few things he left behind tucked away nicely in a box. No, not entirely true. His monogrammed towels are still hanging on the towel rack in the bathroom. I face them every day. Along with his pajama bottoms which are still on the bathroom hook."

I stop talking. I can't bring myself to look up at Dr. Iris. I'm not sure if I should mention that his hairbrush is still in my bathroom, along with all the dead hair. I decide it's not really relevant. I did say I haven't thrown some of his things out.

"Do you know why you felt the need to lie to me?"

"Yes. It makes me feel weak for not getting rid of his things."

"I'm here to help you, so you know that when you lie it's counterproductive?"

"I get all the logic, but when you suggested I get rid of his things, I couldn't erase him entirely out of my life. I'm ashamed that I still hang on to these objects."

"What is it about purging his things that makes you feel sad?"

I can feel my eyes starting to sting. I'm telling myself not to cry, but I can't answer truthfully without getting emotional. She keeps asking questions. "Do you feel that purging makes the relationship feel as if it never existed? Or … is it the hope of seeing him again?"

Oh, great. I didn't want to ruin my makeup before work. Why can't I be stronger when I talk about him? How can I still be a ball of mush after all these months? I need something new in my life.

"Abby?" I can hear my therapist asking. "Can you answer my questions?"

I take a deep breath. "They're the only things I have of his. As sad and angry as I am, I loved Noah. I feel that throwing away his stuff …" I can't continue. I'm blubbering like a big baby. Dr. Iris gets up to push the tissue box closer to me.

"Take your time. You're doing great. You may not see this as a breakthrough right now, but it is."

She knows damn well what is triggering my emotions. Sometimes therapists piss me off. They think they're being tricky in getting us to answer with just the right thing they want to hear. I have to regroup. I'm getting angry with her, again. I hate that I feel anger towards her during my sessions.

"Abby. Maybe you'd like to reflect on what you're really mad at. Is it something in the relationship that made you insecure, maybe?"

"No! Absolutely not, I'm a confident woman. That is … until this happened."

"Could you be mad because you didn't have control over the outcome?"

And there it is—like a heated dagger running straight through my heart. I don't like to lose control over anything. I'm telling you, they always have the answers. Why have I spent almost nine months doing this if she already knew? I answer, "Yes. I've never been dumped by anyone. I'm not saying it to be arrogant. I don't have the coping skills to deal with a breakup that I didn't initiate. But more than that, this is abandonment. At least with a breakup, I could have asked him what went wrong."

"I know we've discussed this many times, but you need to keep channeling your energy into something productive. Something which will make you feel good about yourself. You need to stop looking in the rearview mirror. I know it's difficult, but I'm confident you'll get there."

Why is she telling me this again? I just wanted to come clean. I swear sometimes I feel better before I walk in the door. It's like seeing a zit on my face, and by the time I finish picking, it's become a massive sore spot.

"How is work going?"

"Work is fine. I'm quite busy. Well ... maybe I could be busier. I think that taking time off made Stan lose a little faith in me."

"Could you sit and discuss it with him?"

I think about it for a few moments. I'm not sure, but I find myself saying, "I think I will talk to him when I get to the office. Just making that decision has made me feel better." Then I tell her, "I'm sorry for lying to you. It's been weighing heavily on me."

"I appreciate your honesty."

"Dr. Iris? I know you don't like to give me any false hopes, et cetera, but you must see that I'm doing better."

"I see a gleam in your eye when you talk about work. I believe you genuinely like the work you do. But you need to work on the anger."

Damn! She noticed. Good thing she's not a mind reader. God only knows, maybe she's capable of that too. "I agree." That's all I can muster.

"You've come a long way, Abby. It's okay to have raw emotions. Just think where you were months ago compared to today. I know I said don't look behind you, but this is one time when it's okay to look in that rearview mirror. It's a positive. Don't be so hard on yourself."

"Thanks, Dr. Iris. Again, sorry for lying, and for my anger."

I leave her office and start walking to work. Looking back at my relationship with Noah, I know who I'm mad at. It's me. I'm mad at myself for not pressing him on certain issues. I'd get so caught up in our physical attraction that, I now realize, we really didn't have a lot of important discussions. I'm embarrassed to say that I don't know much about him, besides that he lived in New York. I met some of his colleagues, but never close friends. We were both so busy with our careers that it didn't matter. We barely even argued—silly things like toothpaste on the sink, or leaving the top off the peanut butter jar, but nothing major. That's why his leaving still doesn't compute in my brain.

I make it back to my office, but before I put my purse down I already hear Stan's footsteps approaching. He walks in.

"Morning, doll. I've been waiting for you."

"Stan, it's not even office hours yet."

"You practically live here. I was half expecting to see you sleeping in your chair," Stan says, laughing. Subtle he isn't. "Do you remember that snowstorm when I asked you to fill in for me in Jersey?"

Oh Jesus, please help me. I just had a therapy session to feel better. Last thing I need is to think back to that night. *Stay calm*, I tell myself. It's one of the many personal mantras I chant internally.

"I do. What's up?"

"They finally signed on. We got their business," says Stan with grand enthusiasm.

"Congratulations on bringing them onboard."

"This isn't just any client. We need to seal this deal for them. It will be one of our most lucrative deals, if you get my drift." And just like that he switches gears. "How are you, by the way? I mean, really, how are you?"

"I'm fine."

"I've noticed you've been doing some excellent work, but ..."

"There are no buts, Stan, I'm fine, truly."

"Great! Because I want you to work on this case with me."

I feel as though my ears are deceiving me. I have to get him to repeat what he just said, in order to make sure I heard him correctly.

"Don't move, doll. I'll be right back." I watch Stan walk out the door. He comes back in with his arms full of files. As he's dropping them on my desk he says, "Get familiar with the project. We've got two weeks before the Baker brothers from Kelly Corporation come in for a meeting."

"I don't know what to say, Stan. Thank you for giving me this opportunity."

"Think nothing of it."

Somehow there *is* something to think about, though. Stan has that old, familiar look in his eyes. That look is what earned him the nickname, "The Shark," not that he knows we call him that. Everyone who works for Stan knows he has no scruples when it comes to getting lucrative accounts. He can sniff out fresh, rich blood as easily and silently as a shark looking for its next meal. I know I should be happy that he chose me, but my gut feeling is to question his motives—or maybe I've just got trust issues in general, especially since Noah's departure.

But enough with the negative thoughts, as Dr. Iris suggested. In order to celebrate, I'm going to treat myself to some shopping therapy. There's nothing like a few new outfits for a temporary high. I can even change the apartment up a tad. Today is definitely looking up, for the first time in a long while.

CHAPTER NINE:

Genie

The morning after the *lū'au*, I show up to Room #256 as promised, not knowing what to expect from Deborah. I can't say that I'm not nervous, because I am. I figure a basket full of baked goods and freshly squeezed pineapple juice might put me in good standing. I'm hoping she won't ask me to hurt anyone. My worries about her expectations of me kept me up all night. If she hasn't succeeded in over a hundred years to reclaim her land, how can I possibly be of help?

With every step I take, the pineapple juice on the tray sways back and forth, ready to come over the edge like a tidal wave. I will my hands to stop trembling. I'm not sure if I'm more afraid of confronting a ghost, or having Gerry find out that I'm about to betray him yet again by entering Room #256. I've become so fond of Gerry that I don't feel right going behind his back, but what choice do I have, with this apparition constantly breathing down my neck?

I give a gentle knock. I don't want to disturb the neighboring guests. I can hear faint shuffling sounds coming from inside, but none are approaching the door. Either she hasn't heard me, or … she's had a change of heart about seeing me. I decide to let myself in with a spare key I found at reception. Gerry had the key tucked away in a small white envelope. I don't think he'll notice it missing, seeing as he never goes in the room—so he says.

I put the tray on the floor and slide the key into the keyhole. I gently turn the key and pop the door ajar— enough to be able to push it open. I bend down to retrieve the tray, and as I stand I give the door a slight shove with my hip. After removing my shoes and walking into the main living quarters, I can't believe my eyes. The room is stunningly beautiful. It doesn't resemble the décor of the other rooms whatsoever, and it's nothing like the way Gerry described it. It has Old World opulence. This elaborate room is far from a disaster.

Seeing the room brings a tightness to my chest—the kind you get when you catch someone you like kissing another person. My thoughts are running rampant. Maybe Gerry saved the room for his own personal trysts. It would make sense. On second thought, no, it couldn't be. I saw his face the day I arrived. He turned chalk white when the door opened. But maybe there was someone in there waiting for him and he didn't want me to find out! Note to self: stop making yourself crazy, and ask

Deborah if she has scared Gerry off. Also, ask why the room is not as Gerry described it. But then again, knowing how she feels about Gerry, why would I believe anything she has to say?

I put the tray down on the oversized wooden table, which has six chairs tucked under it. A minute later, Deborah emerges from the bathroom—a room I'm now dying to see, but it can wait.

"Good morning, Deborah. I apologize for letting myself in, but you didn't hear me knocking."

"Good morning, dear. I did hear your knock. I was just testing to see if you had the gumption to let yourself in."

What? I have to give my head a shake. I don't know if I should be mad, or laugh at her brutal honesty. Why is this woman playing mind games with me? What could she possibly want with little old me?

"It's very kind of you to bring me such lovely treats."

"I wasn't sure what you like for breakfast ... and ..."

"I love most things. Let's face it, in the position I'm in, I'm lucky if I get real food every few decades," she laughs.

I feel my face getting flushed. How can this little old apparition in front of me be intimidating as hell, and humorous at the same time?

"Come," she says, gesturing for me to sit next to her at the table. "Please, join me for breakfast. By the way, I loved the *kālua*-style pork last night, thank you."

"You're most welcome. If there's ever anything—"

She doesn't let me finish my offer. Right away Deborah goes into a litany of things she'd like. I stop her in mid-sentence. "Hold on, at least give me a paper and pen. That's if you have any."

"I do," Deborah says, walking over to her desk, which is pushed up against one of the two windows. I get up and follow her. I stop in front of the window while she rifles through a drawer. The panoramic view is breathtaking. All the rooms in the main building are oceanfront, but because of the architectural angle, this is the best view by far, and I have seen every room. Deborah retrieves the paper and pen and we head back to the dining table.

"What I'd like you to do is get me some *lau lau*. I haven't had it in … it's too long to count," she says as she fans her hand beside her cheek.

"Some what?" I ask. Does she really expect me to understand what that is? "Are we still talking about food?" Stupid question. Why did I ask it aloud?

She is roaring with laughter. I stay composed and ask how to spell it. I can tell by the look on her face that this isn't going to be a spelling bee. I quickly realize that this woman has no tolerance for inane questions. To avoid losing my own dignity I say, "Never mind. I will get you some *la*—" Damn, I forgot how to pronounce it. "Next item."

"Just the *lau lau* for now, dear. I'll write the other things down later. In case you may be wondering what *lau lau* is—though I'm sure you already know …" (She looks at me with a smirk. I'm sure she's waiting for me to flinch, but I don't) "… it's a pork dish."

I say nothing, just nod my head in acknowledgment. I see that she and I are going to butt heads on a competitive level. But as odd as it may sound, there is something about her that makes me feel warm and fuzzy. I truly want to get to know her, and I believe she feels the same about me. After a half hour of sitting and chatting with Queen Deborah, I feel a strange loyalty to her. So much so, I decide right then that I will never breathe a word about my knowing her to Gerry. Never. I think we all deserve to have one personal secret—especially if that secret could make me look certifiably *lōlō*.

I sit with Deborah for hours. We watch the sunrise as I tell her about the lighting ceremony I'm going to implement at the resort. I'm explaining how it'd be nice to incorporate the old world into the modern day of the 1960s. I may be reading her wrong, but I could swear that Deborah's eyes start to glisten.

"I didn't mean to upset you," I say, hoping that she'll open up.

"I'm not upset, dear. Over the past hundred years or so, I haven't come across anyone like you. Everybody wants something, if you know what I mean. Take Gerry, for example. He just sees this as an investment, but you … I can already see that you're genuinely interested in the history. You are pouring your heart into not only this resort but also the land itself. I can help you make this resort successful again. I truly can. Who else knows it better than me? After all, I owned the land and it's been in my family for generations."

"I'd love it if you could share some stories with me."

"Maybe another time, seeing as you have to get to work. I'll leave you with this bit of my past: I should have listened to my parents and not married that rat who was only after me for my family wealth and title. He was and still is a monster. It's because of him that the property left my family's possession. He stole it. One day when you have time, I'll tell you all about him," says Deborah as she picks up a hairpin off the table and places it in her perfectly coifed bun. She continues as she walks over to a mirror on the wall and looks at her deeply lined features. "Gerry may own the property, but I promise you, I'll get it back one day. For once I'm not saying it with harsh feelings towards Gerry. The circumstances presented themselves, and he jumped all over it. Any smart businessperson would. I'd rather Gerry than someone else."

"I'm not quite sure what all this means," I say, "but I'm sure you'll explain it to me when we have time."

"My family deserves their land back, Genie. I'll stop at nothing to see that they get it."

Oh my Lord. Is this woman talking about violent acts? Does she expect me to kill Gerry?

"Why do you do that?" she asks.

"Do what?"

"Your face shrivels up to the point where I can barely see your eyes. You did it the first time I opened my door. You also did it yesterday on the way to the *lūʻau*. I'm not out to kill anyone, for Heaven's sake, if that's what you're thinking. You need to take hold of yourself."

"But … you just said …"

"I know what I said. I don't want to harm Gerry, even though I can't stand his womanizing ways, but again, you probably think that it's none of my business."

"Well … it's not."

"But *you* are my concern, Genie. If we are to be friends, friends watch out for one another."

"You don't have to worry about me. I'm a big girl."

"Oh sure, that's what they all say," the Queen mutters under her breath. "That's why by the end of their stay they're all in tears."

"Do you really think that I didn't hear that?"

"I intended for you to hear it."

I keep chanting to myself, be the bigger person. Don't let her see you sweating the small stuff. I ask, "What is it that you want from me? And don't beat around the bush. I'm not as soft as you may think. Actually, let me cut to the chase. I'm an intelligent businesswoman and I was offered this job to help save the resort. So, whatever it is you need help with, be honest."

Deborah claps her hands three times. "Bravo, dear. I knew you had it in you. Maybe I'm hard on you about Gerry because you remind me so much of myself, and I'll leave it at that ... for now. On to more important matters, which also involve Gerry. You see, I know this is an investment for his retirement. I don't begrudge him that, but what I want is for you to tell me if and when he's thinking of selling. I want this coconut grove to be back in the hands of my family. Where it rightfully belongs. I also need your help with some other matters, but I don't fully trust you as of yet."

"Oh, my Lord, you don't trust me? Are you joking with me right now?"

"No. Why would I joke?"

"Never mind. Tell me how I fit in?"

"I will help you with whatever it is you need," she says. "The resort's success is beneficial to all three of us. But … the only thing I won't do is give up my room. No one is to enter … besides you, of course. You will never give this room to anyone, understood?"

"That's a given. Gerry would kill me if he knew I was in here. Since we're on the topic, what have you done to scare Gerry off so badly?"

Deborah can't catch her breath, she is laughing so hard. "I will save that story for another time. I think you best get going. You don't want to spark any suspicion. By the way … come back later, or whenever you have time. I can give you some pointers about past ceremonies and things we used to do on the land. I'm not sure if you know this, but those cottages in the back—I had them built when I moved back here just before I died. They are very special to me."

"I can't wait to hear about them."

"I do need one thing before you go."

"Name it," I say.

"I need you to believe when I say I'm not here to hurt you, or Gerry. If I wanted him gone, I'd have found a way—believe me. I like that he's got this place up and running again. I admit that he's a good investor. I just—"

"*No*. No more about Gerry. Let's stick to our business together."

And just like that, she goes about eating her baked goods, looking like she doesn't have a care in the world. I can't wait to come back and find out more about the old days. She's definitely a knowledgeable spitfire.

I start walking towards the door. "See you later."

"Later, dear. Thank you for my goodies."

And just like that, a bizarre friendship has begun to take shape.

CHAPTER TEN:

Genie

It's been two years since my arrival in Kaua'i. In the past eight months bookings have been steady and revenue is up. We still aren't at full capacity, and I don't think I'll rest until we're booked well into the coming year. In order to do that, I need to come up with a new plan. I decide to enlist the help of Gerry and Dean. Over the years the three of us have met many people from around the world. We need to try and attract a different echelon of guests.

I was notorious for my boardroom charts over the years. I liked to map out the demographics of where the company had been and where we needed to expand. For the Coco Palms, my chart reveals that we need to expand beyond North America. I need to somehow try and grab the attention of the rest of the world. What would make them want to travel the distance to Kaua'i?

Each night I make my rounds to ensure that all the tiki torches are lit along both sides of the lagoon. It's my nightly fixation; I can't stand to see one malfunctioning. At the same time, I make sure all the outdoor speakers are working. Soft romantic music can be heard, whether one is taking a romantic canoe ride under the moonlight, or simply strolling the pathways.

It's a beautiful starry night as I make my way back to the main building. Gerry pleasantly surprises me. "I knew I'd find you out here," he says.

"Hi," I say. "I thought you were having dinner with some friends?"

"I changed my mind. How about you have dinner with me?"

"I can't—"

Gerry looks at me with raised eyebrows, which means he's not taking no for an answer. I've seen the look before. I wait for him to speak.

"How about a stroll?" he says. "We can walk back together."

"Sure," I say. It's not as if Gerry is a total stranger to me. We have had our private liaisons, but never anything deep. It's all ... how should I say this? It fulfills our needs. But tonight, he has a different look in his eyes, one I've never seen before. Strolling along and talking about how things are going, he stops in his tracks.

"Hear that? I love that song. Give me your hand."

I giggle like a teenager as he pulls me in close to him. We begin to dance. When the song is done playing, I'm ready to pull away, but Gerry suddenly kisses me. There is more to the kiss than any other we've shared. Unfortunately, it comes to an abrupt halt when I spot Deborah. I know she doesn't think Gerry is good for me, but must she ruin my night? And just like that—it's as if she read my mind—she disappears, which I'll make sure to tell her I'm grateful for.

I suggest, "What do you say we head back inside and have dinner, I'm starving."

"Sounds like a great idea," says Gerry as we stroll along the cobblestoned path. "Genie, listen. I love this song, don't you?" he asks. "Perfect for a slow dance by the lagoon," he says, pulling me in tight. "What do you say?"

I rest my head on his shoulder while he sings the song softly in my ear. When it finishes we look into each other's eyes and kiss. I love looking into his face as the tiki torches give off shadow from palm leaves.

"I have to be honest," I say, "I've never heard that song before, but it's lovely."

"Genie! Where have you been?"

"I guess I've been busy working."

"Okay, that's it. Tomorrow I'm taking you away from all this. You are officially taking the day off. No ifs, ands or buts out of you."

For once I don't argue. I merely ask, "The song—what's the name of it?"

"Sleepy Lagoon, by the Platters," Gerry says as he squeezes my hand. "You must give it a listen when you're alone. Beautiful words, which I hope you will remember me by."

The next day we start out bright and early. Seeing as I haven't seen much of the island, Gerry suggests taking me to see some of the most famous landmarks on Kaua'i.

"How are you going to be excited about the island if you've only seen part of it?" he says. "Today I'm taking you to a couple locations, but first we're going to start with the Nā Pali Coast."

I wasn't aware that there are only three ways to get there and none of them involve a motor vehicle. Sometimes ignorance is quite blissful. As he explains the different modes of transportation, which are air, sea and land (hiking rough terrain, of course), Gerry keeps going on about how one needs to be athletic and able to survive all the elements that Mother Nature might throw our way. What the hell does that mean? Plus, it's a three-day hike, or something like that. This is supposed to be a day off. That type of hike is too much for me, let alone him. I'm pretty sure Gerry doesn't have an athletic bone in his body.

I throw caution to the wind as he keeps talking and play "Eeny, meeny, miny, moe" in my head to make a decision. I'm only choosing between helicopter and waterway—something he doesn't need to know. I end up with air. Not the worst choice—plus, we'll be flying by helicopter, which I've done many times in the oil fields. I just don't like it when it feels like you're nose-diving.

Gerry keeps me entertained in conversation as we drive to get our helicopter. I board without asking how long a ride it's going to be.

The mountainous coastline is unlike any mountain range I've ever laid eyes on. Jutting straight up out of the ocean are these majestic, jagged cliffs. I feel as if I could reach down and prick my finger on them. They have to be thousands of feet in height. The further in we fly, the more spectacular the color becomes. The red Hawaiian dirt is exposed in places, but right next to it is the lushness of emerald-green land. I'm having difficulty describing how tiny it makes me feel. I realize just how insignificant we really are compared to the wonders of nature. And just like that, it hits me. I have found the answer to how I'm going to generate more money for the Coco Palms.

Gerry was right—without him even knowing, he's solved my problem. How could I have been excited about the island, or try to sell it full-heartedly, when I didn't even know it? I stay focused for the remainder of our trip, but in the back of my mind, all I can think about is getting back so I can work on a new marketing strategy.

Gerry asks, "Are you okay?"

It takes me a minute or so to answer him. I'm not sure if I want to divulge my thoughts for fear of jinxing things. Instead I say, "I'm more than okay. Do you think we can get the pilot to fly a bit further into the cliffs?" I decide I want to keep things to myself, at least until I have something tangible. After our tour of the cliffs, Gerry has the pilot take us over Waimea Canyon. My brain is in overdrive.

In the days and weeks following our excursions, I work hard on new strategies to bring in more revenue— but most of all, I want Hollywood to take notice. If they take notice, then the entire world could see us—just as the world has seen Waikiki and Honolulu, on the island of O'ahu. I need them to come over to our lush Garden Isle and take notice of Kaua'i.

Four months have passed when things begin to happen. I'm in my office when a call comes in from one of the top movie production companies I've contacted. I nearly faint when they give me the news. My heart is about to pound straight out of my chest. When I hang up, I run as fast as I can to the main reception hall to see if Gerry is still having breakfast. He's sipping his coffee as I approach him huffing and puffing. I say with grand excitement, "Gerry!"

He gets up right away and offers me a seat.

"No. I don't want to sit. I have something to tell you. You won't believe it."

Gerry throws the napkin he's holding on the table. He takes my arm and walks me towards the lobby, away from the guests having breakfast. "Are you okay?" he asks.

"I'm fine. Gerry, I did it. I got their attention."

"Who? Who are *they*?"

"Hollywood."

Gerry has no clue what I'm referring to, but then again, how could he? I haven't told him what I've been up to. I take his hand in mine and squeeze it tight as I jump up and down. "Gerry, one of Hollywood's biggest stars is coming here. He wants to film his movie right here at the Coco Palms. Isn't that exciting?"

"Are you serious?" he asks. "I don't know what to say. That is fantastic news, Genie. You're a genius. Who, when …?"

"Elvis. Elvis Presley!"

"Go on! You're kidding me, right?"

"Why would I do that? Oh my Lord, Gerry. Do you know what this means?"

"Yeah! It means we are going to be in pandemonium. Jesus, Genie. I can't believe it. I need a second to digest this," says Gerry as he looks in my eyes. He's behaving as if I'm going to tell him it's all just a bad joke.

His excitement and fear of what's to come has him squeezing my hand so tight that I finally tell him, "Gerry, you need to let go of my hand, I can't feel it. By the way, don't you have a meeting to get to?"

"Yes, but—"

"No buts," I tell him. "This is real and I need to start planning." Before I can say another word, I'm being twirled around in Gerry's arms.

"God, Genie. You are the best thing that has ever happened to me."

"Gerry," I say calmly. "Do you think you can put me down? I don't need all the guests to see the color of my underpants, if you know what I mean?"

Gerry laughs as he kisses me. "You are a genius. Okay, I'll be off. If you need anything, you know where to reach me."

I nod because the reality of it all is setting in. I know it's going to take an army to get things organized, but that isn't the biggest thing worrying me. What's got me going batty is the fact that I have to tell Queen Deborah that I need her room.

I am late bringing Deborah her breakfast, but over the months, as the resort's become busier and busier, it's not unusual to be late every now and then. I'm so nervous to approach her that I make it a little too obvious when I walk in. I stupidly say, "Good morning, ma'am," as I place her breakfast down in front of her. "Did you have a good night's rest?"

Oh great, what's with the scowl on her face?

"Not so much. I'm feeling a bit uneasy. I can't quite put my finger on it. Almost as if an intruder is about to descend on my land."

"They're just dreams, Deborah." I can barely look at her for fear that she can read my mind. My body's getting flushed with waves of heat.

"Dreams?

Great, as if her eyebrows weren't furrowed enough when I first walked in.

"Who said anything about dreams? What is wrong with you?" Deborah asks. "I'd say you look like you've seen a ghost, but we are well past that stage, aren't we? Are you ill?"

"No," I reply as I stare out the window, wishing I were floundering in the ocean, rather than having to tell her …

"Why aren't you looking at me when you speak? You know it's very rude."

I turn to look at her. "I'm sorry ma'am, I'm just a bit preoccupied."

"What's with the ma'am? Genie! Snap out of whatever it is, and just tell me before you drive me mad."

"Well … you see, I … I need this room."

Deborah starts to laugh uncontrollably. But when she notices I'm not laughing along with her, she becomes agitated, which is the reaction I was expecting.

"You can't be serious," she says. "Have you gone mad?"

"No. You see ..."

"*No.* I don't see. No one enters my room, and you know that. I thought we had an understanding."

"But Deborah—"

She cuts me off right away. She is fuming mad. "First, it's ma'am, now it's Deborah ... try using my proper title."

Somehow this last statement makes me snap out of my fearful state. I retaliate with, "Oh, I see. You want to play this game again. I thought you'd matured since our first meeting. Your Highness, may I have permission, please, to use your room for a short while?"

"NO."

"Come on. I'm begging you, please. At least hear me out. I promise you will love the reason for my asking, and plus, I'll give you a room just as lovely."

"Really? There isn't one just as lovely. If there is one, give it to whoever it is that's coming."

"I reckon I can't."

Deborah gives out a sarcastic "Hmmm." I move closer and look her straight in the eyes. "Please, Deb—sorry—Your Highness."

"Cut the gibberish and go back to calling me Deborah—even ma'am sounds better. Come now. Spit it out. Tell me who deserves this room?"

"The King. The King himself will be filming here. Isn't that exciting?"

Her facial expression is anything but excited. I believe if she were capable of shooting fire out of her nostrils, this would be the time to do it.

"The King? Why would that excite me? He had me banished from my own land. Plus, have you forgotten he's tried to kill me? Your request is preposterous."

I give out a nervous chuckle, which is not pleasing to the Queen at this moment—so much so that she tries to pound her fist on the table, which makes me chuckle even more as her fist disappears into the wood. I keep telling myself to stop giggling, but her failed attempts are hilarious.

"No. You don't understand," I say. "Not that king. The King of Rock and Roll, Elvis!"

"For Heaven's sake, why didn't you just say his name in the first place?"

"Urgh. You drive me mad."

"Really? I drive you mad? After you laugh at my expense."

"Come on, you know it was funny."

I see she's not going to budge. I clear my throat and make sure I'm not wearing even the slightest smirk on my face. I need her on my side, especially today. I mentally tell my stomach to stop the butterflies from fluttering. My nerves are getting the better of me, but I know I just need to get the words out.

"What do you think about Elvis staying here?" I ask.

"I agree to letting Elvis stay with me."

"No! No! No!" For God's sake, this woman is going to be the death of me. "You are not in the same room with him. Out of the question. You are going to another room," I say firmly in the hope that Deborah will take me seriously. "Come now. You said you want this resort to be a success. What happened to helping me out?"

I hear Deborah give out a sigh before responding, "Fine, but under one condition."

"And what may that be?"

"You must let me come in here at least once. I want to hear Elvis sing."

"And how will I do that? Command him to perform for me? That's ludicrous."

"You're an intelligent woman, you'll figure it out."

Out of frustration, I say, "Fine, fine, fine. Have it your way, but there better not be any pranks coming from you. Now, you promise me you'll behave."

Deborah lifts her right hand up to her heart. "I swear."

"You can put your arm down. You know as well as I do that that won't convince me. Please, Deborah, I am begging you to behave."

"I will," says Deborah, giving out an unconvincing guffaw. What choice do I have but to trust her? "Remember Genie, no one besides the King and I get this room. Is that understood?"

"Fully. I promise I will make it up to you for being so generous. I know how much this room means to you."

"Remember, I want to hear him sing. That's all I want, dear. That's all," Deborah says as she turns to eat her baked goods.

"You will. I promise you that. Now, you will promise me not to sneak in here, right?"

"You know something, dear? You really should learn to speak proper English," she says with a snicker.

"Don't try and change the subject. You know as well as I do that Gerry will be furious when he finds out I've given this room to Elvis. I'll have some explaining to do, so cut me some slack. I beg of you, don't make matters worse for me," I say with my hands clasped as if I were praying.

"Gerry, Gerry, Gerry. Who cares what he thinks? He was nothing before you arrived and—"

"Deborah, please. Not today."

"Fine. But don't say I didn't warn you about him. That man should be proposing to you. And I'm not talking a business proposal."

"Yes, Deborah, I know what you're referring to. You see, Gerry just ain't—"

"Don't you dare tell me again he ain't the marrying kind. There you go, now you've got me speaking your bizarre language. Stop with those words."

As I roll my eyes at Deborah, she asks, "Why are you still standing? Sit. Tell me more about Elvis's arrival."

She's too much to bear at times, but I do care for her, so I patiently explain, "The plan is, he'll be filming part of the movie here on the island, in Cottage #25. I believe the title of the movie is *Blue Hawaii*, but it could change— that's what I've been told. Originally I was going to give him that cottage to stay in, but it suited their filming. Plus, Elvis specified an oceanfront view, and what better view than this?"

I can tell Deborah is satisfied—indeed, thrilled—with my explanation, as she doesn't protest any longer. I finally leave her room and start preparing for the mayhem that's to come.

CHAPTER ELEVEN:

Abby

For the first time in a week, I'm getting home at what most would consider a regular supper hour. On my way, I stop in at the deli to pick up a large chicken Caesar salad. Every weekend I keep promising myself to make home-cooked food, but I never seem to get around to it. This past weekend my excuse was working on the files Stan had given me on the Hawaiian property.

As I eat my supper, I flip open my laptop and start researching. I'm curious to find out more about the Baker brothers. I scroll through screen after screen of straightforward land acquisitions by the older brother, Charles. What I'm looking to know more about is their background—as in who and what their family life is about, which speaks volumes about a person's character. I also like to get a feel for the type of social media they generate. Not that most things on the Internet are true, but with succesful land developers, surely there has to be some kind of record.

Two hours into it, I pour myself a glass of wine. Not sure why I hadn't thought of it sooner. By the umpteenth land deal, I need to switch gears. I close the screen down and grab the file labeled Coco Palms. I type the name into the search engine. I didn't expect to find so many articles. Most are about the devastation that Hurricane Iniki brought upon the island of Kaua'i back in 1992. Oh my, here's a coincidence—it happened on September 11. That just gave me goosebumps. After finishing the article, I realize just how little I know about our fiftieth state. As I read on, I can't even imagine what it must have been like to be without power for months in some of the more remote areas. I click on the next article, which is solely about the Coco Palms. When I blow up the photo and take a closer look, I understand why the place is vaguely familiar to me. I had no idea that this particular resort was used to film *Blue Hawai'i*. It was my maternal grandmother's favorite film. There wasn't a sleepover that she didn't put it on as we'd snuggle together and eat popcorn.

I dial my mother. "Mom?"

"Are you all right, dear? What's wrong?"

"You won't believe this," I say. "I'm researching for a new case Stan has given me and it's in Hawai'i. You will never guess where the property is." Of course, I wasn't really asking her to guess, because I was dying to tell her. "It's in Kaua'i, the Coco Palms. Ring any bells?"

Before my mother answers I hear her give out a surprised squeak followed by a deep breath, so deep I feel my lungs fill up in empathy.

"Oh my God!" she says. "That was Mom and Dad's favorite place. They vacationed there many times."

"I had no idea they vacationed there. I only remember it because Grandma used to play the movie every time I stayed over. I used to think Grandpa was sick of seeing it, because he never watched it with us," I laugh. "She'd gush over Elvis every time. Maybe Grandpa was sick of that." I can hear my mother's laughter as I recount the stories of my sleepovers.

"Bless her heart. Yes, Mom was a huge Elvis fan."

"Tell me more about the resort. Did you ever go with them?"

"I wish, but no, I never went. To be honest, I never took much interest. I'm ashamed to admit this, but we didn't discuss things the way you and I do. A much different era! Also, Mom had a very different relationship with you, which was nice to see."

"I for one enjoyed her lighthearted side."

"Hindsight, I wish we'd have had more of the lighthearted conversations. It was always a bit too regimented—but as I've said, a different time. That's life."

I hear a sniffle and suddenly feel horrible for upsetting my mother. "Oh Mom, I didn't call to make you sad or ..."

"On the contrary. I'm thrilled about your news. This is fantastic, truly it is. I'm just wishing I'd have gone with Mom, but at least I'll get to live my past through you. So, what's happening with the Coco Palms? I haven't thought of that place since the last time your grandmother went there, which was the year after Dad passed. I remember—it was a year or so before that storm hit the islands, and Mom's first time traveling alone."

"I just finished reading about that hurricane. I had no idea this place existed, let alone the devastation of that storm. Get this—the Coco Palms has been sitting in ruins since 1992. No one has ever restored it. How bizarre is that?"

"Quite. Eerie, in a way," says Mom.

Mom saying the word eerie has sent a shiver down my spine. What's wrong with me? There's nothing unusual about people wanting to acquire land. But at the same time, I look around my apartment as if expecting to see someone. Jesus, I've never been known to be frightened of much. Now Mom is asking me again if I'm okay.

"I'm good," I tell her. "As I was saying, I've stumbled upon the Coco Palms because we have a new client—I should say *clients*. They want to purchase the land. I'll know more in a few weeks when I meet with them."

"You'll have to keep me updated. This is quite intriguing."

"I most definitely will. It makes work that much more exciting, knowing I have a little bit of history with Grandma. I'm thrilled that Stan chose me for this case."

"That's fantastic, honey. I'm really happy for you."

"Thanks, Mom. Talk to you later, and give Dad my love."

"I will when he gets in."

"It's late. What happened to him slowing down?"

"He is—well, the Paul version of slowing down," Mom laughs.

I feel a whole new sense of excitement flow through my veins. I shut down my computer. I decide to grab my stack of files and head to the bedroom. I promise myself I'll only look at two, but I get carried away, only realizing it when I look over at my phone and see that it's four AM. It's painful knowing I have to be up in two hours.

As the days go on, so does my research. I start to get a good sense of the stumbling blocks which have been preventing the redevelopment of the Coco Palms. There seems to be a ton of problems—everything from descendants who claim to be the rightful owners squatting on the land, right down to getting permits for demolition and building. I'd venture to guess that these issues are just the tip of the iceberg. It's become apparent that over the years many different buyers have put their best foot forward, but something, or someone, keeps stepping on their toes. I'm realizing that Hawaiian real estate is tricky to acquire. But I can't see the local Heritage and Cultural Association not wanting such an iconic landmark rebuilt. What is really going on? The only person who can answer that for me is a gentleman by the name of Kanoa Kahala, who heads the Heritage and Cultural Association. He's been the voice of his people for the past ten years.

I get that they want to preserve the land, but the Coco Palms is a preexisting resort. I can't put my finger on why they wouldn't want to have their island benefit economically from rebuilding. I fully agree with the association's mission to declare the structure a heritage building, but with heritage status comes a ton of regulations, and this is why real estate developers hire lawyers like me to litigate. This is not going to be as cut-and-dried as Stan would like me to believe. With the information in these files, I really need to speak to Mr. Kahala. If anyone can give me more in-depth information, it's him.

I decide to place a call to the Heritage Association today, seeing that our meeting with the brothers from Kelly Corporation is rapidly approaching. To be more accurate, it is first thing in the morning. I'm not sure where the past two weeks have gone.

I arrive at the office bright and early. The only downfall to having these new clients is the fact that it keeps reminding me of that fateful snowy night when I met Noah. It never fails to send a shiver up my spine. I try to regain focus as I dial the number to the Heritage office. The third ring leaves me listening to an outgoing message. I realize that the office isn't open due to the time zone. My phone begins to ring and I see it's Stan.

"Hey, doll. Just wanted to let you know that our meeting got canceled."

"Oh no, why?"

"No idea. They said they'd be in touch. Seeing as they aren't coming, I'm going to a few outside appointments I'd previously scheduled. I'll see you tomorrow."

I have enough work to keep me busy. As I pick up the file on the Coco Palms, yet again, I can't keep my mind from wandering. I wonder what my life would be like had I not gotten into the cab that night. I was at a happy station in life, not looking for love, because my first love was my job. It allowed me to have the apartment address I'd been working so hard to get, even if it didn't have the second bedroom, but at least it was mine. My job also motivated me to keep pushing for bigger and better things, which brings me to my designer wardrobe. Maybe if I didn't spend so much on clothes, I'd have that second bedroom. Anyhow, falling in love was not part of my plan, at least not until I was more financially stable. It just hit me, like a surprise meteor crashing into earth. That's exactly how I would describe the moment I first laid eyes on Noah.

Since his disappearance I've beaten myself up with questions. Was I too picky? Did it annoy him that I liked expensive clothes? Was I too pretentious? Did I not love him enough? Maybe I didn't give him enough attention. I sure thought I did. I don't know. All I know is that no amount of therapy can stop me from missing him. I go through moments of hate and then flip on a dime, crumbling into itty-bitty pieces. I ache all over from his absence. I wonder if he misses me. Why would he? He's the one that left. And that, right there, is what hurts the most—being abandoned.

I just about jump out of my skin when I see Stan standing in front of my desk. "Jesus, Stan. I thought you said you weren't coming in?"

"I was halfway down the street when I got a call. I came back to call you into a meeting. It's urgent. Let's go. My office."

I follow Stan like a lost puppy. He asks me to take a seat, then sits down behind his desk and stares at me as if he's about to fire me. Don't be crazy, I tell myself, why would he fire me? I'm doing an excellent job. Okay, I did take some time off. Snap out of it! It's hard to stay focused on Stan's face, as he has two large stacks of files on either side of his desk. For a brief moment I got a glimpse of him as Moses in the middle of parting the sea.

"Hey!"

"Sorry, Stan."

"Have I got your undivided attention?"

"Yes," I say and sit up as straight as I can. I tell myself to stop imagining Stan in fictional form.

"I need you down in Kaua'i. I just got a call from Charles Baker, the eldest of the brothers. It appears that the reason they aren't here is because they're still in Hawai'i. Something has gone awry with the land deal."

I'm stunned and speechless. I mumble, "Uhhhh … are you coming to Kaua'i with me?"

"No," he says. "I'll dial in, we can conference. I need to be in court. I'm trying that discrepancy over the empty lot on … Anyway, how fast can you pack?"

"When am I going?"

"As soon as I get Mindy to book you a flight."

"Oh my God. Okay. Well, can you fill me in on what's happened?"

"It appears that something's gone wrong with the Heritage Association. This Kanoa Kahala is making a stink about preserving certain areas of the land—the building, for one. The Bakers were under the impression that they could demolish and rebuild, but that's not

Kahala's intention. He says his people will never tear down the Coco Palms. It also appears that the Bakers might not be as close to acquiring the land as they thought. Kahala keeps coming up with different regulations that were implemented God knows when. This guy is a real hardnose."

Stan seems pretty ticked. I'm not sure I want to tell him that I tried to get in contact with Mr. Kahala earlier. I'm sure I'll be meeting him soon enough.

I have so many thoughts rushing through my mind. I need to call my therapist and let her know I'll be going away.

"How long will I be gone?" I ask Stan, who is fuming and stomping his feet like an agitated child. He's going to wear out the carpet.

"However long it takes you to see this through. I don't know. There is one thing, though. Don't fuck up. This land deal will have you seeing six figures. So, don't screw this up whatever you do."

I wish I wasn't standing in front of Stan with my mouth wide open, because I can feel my jaw literally drop. Could I have heard him correctly? That is a ton of money. What do I have to do to get that kind of money? Obviously, I'm not going to earn six figures for easy work. Oh, God, what is Stan getting us into, or me for that matter? I need to call my mother back. I can't have my parents worrying about me.

"I'll talk to Mindy about times of departure," I tell Stan as I exit his office and head towards her desk. Mindy is our office manager and assistant. I've never been able to tell Mindy's age, as she looks like she hasn't slept in years. She's always got a tissue box next to her and sniffles constantly. I've never known Mindy to be healthy, but I have to hand it to her, she is one of the most pleasant people I've ever met. "Hey Mindy. I guess Stan mentioned I need a flight to Kaua'i right away?"

"Yes. I have three flight times for you. There's one leaving tonight at midnight, or you can take either the six or ten AM tomorrow morning."

"I'll go for the six AM," I tell her. "Thanks, Mindy. If you could forward everything to me, that'd be great. I'll be leaving the office soon. I need to pack."

"Will do," she says as I start to walk away. "Hey, Abby. Bring a little sunshine back for me." I look back and smile at her.

On my way home, I call my parents, but since there's no answer, I leave a voice message telling them I'll text once I land in Kaua'i. I leave another message for my therapist to cancel my appointments until further notice. I'm sure she's going to think I've relapsed, but that's not the case. I haven't felt this excited in a long time. I'll send her an email from the airport to reassure her I'm doing okay.

Since I'm sitting in traffic, I decide to try the Heritage office. I would really love to speak with Mr. Kahala before I get there. Scheduling a meeting would be even better. Unfortunately I have no luck on either count.

CHAPTER TWELVE:

Kanoa Kahala

"Nani. Do you have the latest bid from Kelly Corporation?"

"Got it right here, boss," Nani answers as she shakes her head at me—followed by a "tsk" to show her disapproval.

"I know, I know. I promise I will get my papers organized," I say, laughing. Nani is relentless when it comes to badgering me about my messy desk. Of course, having the huge heart that she does, Nani is always itching to clean it up herself, but she knows better. I need my things to be exactly where I put them, and no one is to touch them. But I always appreciate her offers.

"Look at it this way," I say to Nani. "If I were perfect in everything I do, what would I need you for?"

"Oh please, my list would go on forever. Now get out of here," she says in her usual playful tone. "If you don't get moving, you'll be late for your meeting."

I kiss Nani on the cheek as I grab the file out of her hand. Nani isn't just any ordinary personal assistant. She is a longtime loyal friend who helps me out on my pro bono work for the Heritage and Cultural Association, which is something that we both hold very dear to our hearts, seeing as we are fellow Kaua'ians.

Nani and I first met in grade school. At the time, I was shy and quite a bit more reserved than Nani, but then again, most people are. I remember the day when this beautiful girl with eyes as dark as cocoa beans walked straight over to me and said, "Aloha. Do you want to be my friend?" I was taken aback. I looked around. I could see the other kids staring at us. Nani asked me again, except much louder, "Well, what are you waiting for—do you want to be my friend or not?"

I couldn't resist. And that's how it all began. We lost touch for about ten years when I went off to college in Honolulu and, immediately after graduation, ventured off the islands and onto the mainland, where I worked for almost five years. It wasn't until I came back to Kaua'i to start my own investment firm that I bumped into Nani again. She didn't hesitate to take me up on my offer to come work for me. I can't even think of another person I'd rather spend my workdays with. Yes, she can be a pain at times, but I'm quite certain that she sees me in the same light.

Today I have a one-hour window of opportunity to meet with Ken and Charles Baker from Kelly Corporation.

This is a special case for me. I'm not only working on behalf of the Heritage Association, but also a dozen investors who are interested in bidding on the property. This isn't my first meeting with the Bakers, but I can tell you that this will definitely not be a cordial one. Every time I think we've come to an understanding, these two want to pull the wool over our eyes.

It all started when the Coco Palms property was put up on auction for the umpteenth time. Two city slickers stride in from New York and start making all sorts of demands. For one thing, I don't care how rich they are, or how many other acquisitions they've made. What these two don't get is our property laws, which are slightly different than on the mainland. I'm not sure which of them has trouble reading, because it's stated that the original Coco Palms may not be torn down. Granted, it hasn't been designated as a heritage building, but I've been working on it for years, in hopes that we get our approval before the next bid.

Our saving grace is that the last bid Kelly Corporation won was forfeited. I found a loophole in their offer. It appears that they lied about having no lingering lawsuits against their company. And for this reason, their bid was thrown out. Had they been honest and disclosed everything, they may have become the new owners of the coconut grove property. The Hawaiian gods are definitely on our side. *Mahalo* to our ancestors, as they look down on us and protect our land.

If I'm going to be truly honest, I hate these two pompous assholes I'm about to meet with. I've seen their type over the years. They don't care whom they step on in order to get what they want—but they don't know me. I'll do anything within my legal power to stop them from acquiring Kaua'ian soil.

As for the investors I've rounded up, the majority are wealthy businessmen spread across the islands. Four of the guys are childhood friends of mine. We were all born on Kaua'i, and our families have been here for generations. A couple of the guys are not in the millionaire category, but I couldn't leave them out. Our family roots mean everything to us; so much so that I've been working hard to make the money for those who can't come up with it quite as easily. I'm lucky to be in the business I've chosen, and helping my close friends gave me the drive to stay away from Kaua'i as long as I have in order to make money.

My friend Sam is one of the investors. We were in our last year of college when we had our first talk about the Coco Palms. We were driving to the North Shore on the island of O'ahu. At the time Sam was in a civil engineering program at college, while I was studying economics. Together we thought we'd solve the railroad problems that have plagued Hawai'i, but I soon realized it wasn't a grand passion of mine. I left it to Sam. As we drove to Hale'iwa we started talking about Kaua'ian history. One thing led to another, and Sam told me that the land was up for sale. He'd been talking to his parents about it the night before. They mentioned that the locals were very upset about the passing of the current owner.

"Who was it?" I asked Sam.

"Her name was Genie Gartner. Her husband passed away years before her and left her the entire grove. She'd retired from managing the Coco Palms a few years before Iniki hit. Too bad she hadn't sold it before the hurricane."

"Do they have children?"

"No. It appears she didn't even have a will."

"That's crazy. How could she not have had a will?" I ask.

"Beats me, man," said Sam as we pulled into the parking lot.

"*Makuahine* said there's at least a dozen squatters on the land ever since it went up for sale. Got the locals protesting and causing a real jam-up on the highway."

And just like that, it happened. I couldn't stop thinking about the Coco Palms. I spent the entire day riding the waves and thinking about what I could do to help the people of my island. My passion was preserving the coconut grove on which the Coco Palms rests.

As usual, Tweedle Dee and Tweedle Dum are late for the meeting. These guys have balls to keep pissing me off. You'd think with the bid falling through they'd humble themselves just a tad. A waitress comes to the table to ask if I'd like anything. I tell her to come back in a few minutes, and then I see the older brother approaching me.

"Mr. Kahala. I hope you won't mind, but it will be just the two of us. My brother is attending to other matters."

As if I give a shit. He's probably sucking back his mini-bar. "Not a problem. Can I offer you a coffee?"

"No, I'm good."

I wave the waitress back over. I'm not going to take up her table without ordering something. "I'll have the lunch special with a cup of coffee, *'olu'olu.*" I look over at

Charles to make sure he's definite he doesn't want something.

He says, "I'll have the same."

As we eat our lunch, which I do rapidly, Charles says, "I just want you to know that I've contacted a new lawyer. One who can help us out of this minor glitch we are experiencing."

Minor glitch my ass. Who's this guy kidding? I answer, "It could tie you up for quite some time."

"No. My lawyer should be arriving any day now. I'm told that it shouldn't take too long to fix the problem."

Is he baiting me? I'm sure he wants me to ask his lawyer's name, but I don't. I'm not giving him the satisfaction. "You do what you feel is necessary."

"Where does this leave us?" he asks.

"I guess you'll have to wait and see what your lawyer tells you."

I leave the café and head back to the office. My focus is on getting the Coco Palms designated as a heritage building. I've worked too long and hard to let it slip because of my animosity for the Bakers. We are so close to accomplishing our first major goal … fingers crossed.

CHAPTER THIRTEEN:

Abby

Once I get home and focus on my schedule, I realize I've got just enough time to pack a bag and tidy up some things around the apartment, and if I'm lucky steal a couple hours of sleep.

Looking in my closet I have no idea what to pack, but that's also Stan's fault for not giving me a timeline. I'm figuring I'll be away a week or ten days, tops. I'm going on the fact that Stan hates compensating me for expenses, so I can't imagine him footing the bill to keep me in Hawaii.

I decide to take a basic black suit, which is always a sure bet, and a light textured summer linen. I throw in a bunch of bathing suits, casual dresses, and of course, five pair of shoes. Okay ... add another five pair of sandals. I figure I can always pick up some clothes if I need them, but I'm quite fond of my shoe collection. I quickly throw in some toiletries and try to get a few hours of sleep, which I know will be next to impossible.

I hear a beep on my phone. It's Mindy; she's sent me my airline ticket. Oh wow, I see she's got me booked in a premium seat. Oh God, hold on a minute—I see why I'm going in luxury. There isn't a stopover until Honolulu, which means I'm on an eleven-hour nonstop flight. At least the short flight to Kaua'i will be getting in around five PM, just before sunset. I've never been partial to driving around unfamiliar territory in the dark.

I suddenly feel like a toddler who needs his or her special blanket as it sucks its thumb. The N.K. monogrammed towels are my security. What's one trip? I get out of bed to get the towel out of the dryer and into my suitcase. I promise I'll get rid of it when I get home. I know it's not logical, but I never said I was logical about all things.

I arrive at JFK at four AM. I didn't want to chance getting stuck in traffic and missing my flight. I guess there wasn't really much chance of that happening, seeing as I barely slept. The reality of going so far away is getting the better of me. It's not as much the distance as it is the feeling of being on an island in the middle of nowhere, surrounded by water. For God's sake, listen to me! I live on an island—what is wrong with me? A chat with my therapist right about now would do me some good. But to my credit, my island has easy access to neighboring places. I'm not thousands of miles away and stuck in the Pacific Ocean.

I go through security and head to the magazine stand. This anxiety is nothing a few fashion magazines can't fix. I sit at a quiet table facing the tarmac while I sip my coffee and flip through the pages of *Vogue*. It's not the type of magazine I want to lug with me—way too heavy. I'll leave it for another fashionista to look at. Halfway through the double issue I hear a ping on my phone. It's a text message: *"Haters not welcome."* What the hell is this about? It can't be for me. Someone probably punched in the wrong number, and I don't recognize the caller. I finish scanning the fashion pages just in time for boarding. I take my carry-on and purse, and head to the gate.

What have I got to complain about? I'm in the very first seat in one of the new reclining pods. It's perfect. On the seat I find a blanket and pillow with a box lying on top of it. I put my phone on airplane mode and slip it into my purse. I take the items off the seat and sit down. As I buckle up and wait for the passengers to finish boarding, I take a peek in the box. There's a sleeping mask, miniature toiletries, slippers, a comb and a pen. Oops, I dropped something. It's earplugs for the in-seat tablet. Suddenly the thought of an eleven-hour flight is starting to feel better. I'll have to remember to buy Mindy a special souvenir. This is beyond any expectation I may have had. In all honesty, I figured I'd be sitting in Economy.

I take my phone back out to schedule a reminder to pick up a gift for Mindy, when I notice another text from the same number. *"Beware of rough waters."* Okay ... this really isn't funny, especially since I'm about to be flying for hours over endless miles of water. My panicking has me taking the phone off airplane mode and punching in a reply: *"Whoever you are, this isn't funny! Bloody coward!"* But it comes back with a red x and says undelivered. Damn! I'm being stupid. The text is just a bad coincidence. I need to stop thinking about it. But I can't help wondering ... why now? No, there's no way the message is intended for me.

I try to avert my attention from the text and focus on positive things, such as my luxurious amenities. But my fear of flying is coming to the forefront. I'm now kicking myself for never mentioning it to Stan. As if it would have made a difference. He'd have had me out of town every chance he had; that's just the kind of guy he is. I can handle short flights, anything under two hours. I'm actually okay once I'm airborne—it's the takeoff and landing that have me sweating like a bandit. Oh good, a new distraction: champagne.

I sit quietly sipping my champagne as I rifle through a list of available movies. The menu card seems to be jumping out at me in 3D. I close my eyes and try to quiet my mind. The wheels aren't even off the runway; I need to breathe if I'm to survive eleven hours in this sardine can. Of course, thoughts like that aren't helping. I silently pray as I did as a child. I hope I still have some pull, seeing as I gave up going to church years ago. Maybe I should promise to go back. *No,* I tell myself ... don't make promises you can't keep, especially to the big guy.

The flight attendants are super-friendly and attentive. So much so that the young woman working in my section must have noticed I was nervous. I feel her gently tap my shoulder to inform me that I am wearing the complimentary eye mask upside down. She helps me adjust it and says, "Just let me know if there is anything you may need. Don't hesitate."

Typical me, I tell her I'm fine and then, as soon as she turns to walk away, I find myself tumbling out of my seat. She runs back towards me as I sheepishly smile and say, "Sorry, I'm looking for the tablet." How was I to know it was inside the round cylinder to my right? I thought it was strictly for ornamental purposes. The attendant smiles and goes back to work, as I take the tablet out and recline my seat. Time to chill out and watch a movie. I click on *Fifty Shades of Grey*. Is it weird to want to watch that? I haven't read any of the books. I'm going solely on the actor's looks right now—he's pretty cute.

I'm ashamed to admit that I panicked for nothing. My flight is uneventful, thank God. After watching five movies and not doing a stitch of work, I've arrived. I can't remember the last time I've been so relaxed. Who'd have thought? I can barely sit still for a couple of sitcoms on quick flights. I can't thank the big man above enough for getting me here. I'll make sure I thank the pilot on my way out. After all, he is the one who landed us safely.

While we all wait for the door to open, I think back to my only tropical vacation, which was with Noah. It was our first Christmas together. He'd been working day and night. I was lucky if we got to spend six hours of waking time together during the week. To make up for it, he surprised me with airline tickets to Barbados—one-week all-inclusive. We were staying in our own private villa. The only problem for me was the flying time. That was my very first flight over two hours. Happy to report I survived the entire flight. It was hard to think of anything else when Noah was by my side. Except when it came to the landing.

I'd gone to get my nails done two days before departure. I usually just had a paraffin wax manicure and fresh polish applied. I figured since we were going to the tropics, I'd opt for a sexier look. I decided to get acrylics. Let's just say that the majority of the tips ended up on the floor of the plane. That's how hard my grasp was when the landing felt like sitting on a teeter-totter. I'll never forget the look on Noah's face. It's the same look a parent gives their child when they're choking. I just remember my arms flailing and reaching for my armrest over and over. I must have looked like Big Bird flapping his big yellow wings. Yes … I had a yellow ruffled top on. Bright yellow. After that ordeal, we took vacations that were driving-only.

I'm on a thirty-minute connector flight to Kaua'i. It feels like we just took off and the pilot is already announcing the start of the descent. Looking out my window, I start to feel anxious again. I guess I was expecting the same highrises I'd just seen landing in Honolulu, but this is completely different. I'm sure that nestled somewhere on this volcanic rock below us are houses, but it's hard to tell from up here. This is one of the most beautiful sights I've ever seen. It's surreal for me to think that millions of years ago these islands were formed by volcanic eruptions. It's truly something to marvel over. Listen to me … my logical side is functioning. And we've landed safely, yet again.

"Hurray!" I say out loud. Yes, I'm one of those people that clap.

Seeing as it's five PM, Hawaiian Standard Time, I need to get moving before the sun disappears. I walk as briskly as I can with my bags in hand to catch the complimentary shuttle, which will take me to the rental car office. I walk in and make it to the front of the line. The agent is smiling from ear to ear as she greets me.

"Aloha, and welcome to our beautiful island. Is this your first time here?" she asks, busily tapping information into her computer.

"Yes," I say. "Yes, it is. I'm hoping to get to my hotel before sunset."

"I guarantee you'll be out of here in five minutes."

I feel relief. She's going to get me going before it gets dark. I hope my trembling voice didn't give me away. "Does the car have a built-in GPS system?"

"No, but I can rent you one. In my opinion you won't need it. If you have the app on your phone, it will be good enough. Plus, I'll give you a couple maps. Chart out your own adventure. This really isn't a complicated island to get around."

I take her word for it. She seems very sweet and genuine. She begins highlighting a route on a map. "Your hotel is five minutes away. When you leave here you'll take the first right at the lights, then continue straight, until you see a sign for your hotel. Trust me, you will be looking at that sunset from your balcony," she says, smiling.

"Thank you so much."

"My pleasure. I hope you'll enjoy your stay."

I find my way with no problem at all. Within a few moments I'm checked in and standing right where she told me I'd be, on my balcony, overlooking the mighty Pacific. I watch as the last speck of sun makes its way behind the horizon, leaving bright flames of orange and red with streaks of yellow.

Feeling jetlagged and famished, I decide to order room service. By the time I place my order and return to the balcony, it is pitch dark, except for some strategically positioned tiki torches. The swaying flames give off a soothing aura of light that could put me to sleep, except that the rumbling roars of the ocean have me on high alert. It's daunting to hear the thunderous, crashing waves as they sweep ashore amid the blackness of the night. I swear I can feel the more ferocious waves shaking the ground all the way from my balcony.

I get about four bites of food down and push the plate aside. Guess I'm not as hungry as I thought. Running hypothetical scenarios all day long has exhausted me. I've gotten too deep into my own head. Maybe a couple more sips of wine will help with the reality of being thousands of miles from the mainland. If only the ocean would calm down a bit, I'd calm down along with it. I sure hope it's not this loud every night.

I turn on the television to try and redirect my thoughts—only to catch the weather report. Why are they reporting that a hurricane is on the path toward making landfall on the Hawaiian Islands? Oh please, say it isn't so. My God, my palms are sweating. I want to run, but where to? I grab my key and go down to the lobby.

I get out of the elevator. Good—no one is with the concierge. "Excuse me," I say to the gentleman.

"Yes. How may I help you?"

"I was just watching the weather report and they're calling for a potential hurricane coming this way." As I get the last words out, I remember about the text. *Beware of rough waters.* This is what the warning was about. But who sent it to me? Could it have been the airlines?

"Are you okay, Miss?"

"Where does one go for shelter from the storm?"

"Higher elevation. You'll survive a tsunami up there—well, depending where you go. Check the literature in your room. It will give you all the steps that need to be taken."

Oh my God, did he just say tsunami? Please don't let me die this way. I promise I'll start attending church services again. I can see the concierge's lips moving, but I don't hear a thing. I'm stone deaf. The lights have gone dim. Is the wave already coming? Can't be—they said it's hours away, didn't they? But why am I suffocating? I can feel my air supply getting sucked out of me like a high-speed vacuum. The water is rising above my nostrils, even though my neck is stretched as far as it will go. As I give one last breath, my body jerks upward. I don't know if I'm dead. I can hear garbled, tinny voices. I keep closing and opening my eyes. Nothing looks familiar.

Except, I hear the rumbling of the ocean. I finally gain some perspective. I realize I've fallen asleep in front of the television. I am drenched in sweat. I grab the remote and try to find a weather report. A beautiful young woman in a floral dress is smiling and reporting that it's going to be eighty-four degrees by mid-morning, and pretty much the same for the next seven days, with some intermittent showers.

I sit and watch the weather channel for two consecutive weather updates, just to make sure that there's no hurricane coming our way, nor a tsunami. I can't remember when I've been so scared. I look up towards the heavens and catch myself mouthing, "Thank you, God."

I get up off the sofa. It's eleven PM—I can't believe I've been sleeping so long. I walk to the entrance where the bellman dropped off my bag. As I pass the credenza, I see a bunch of magazines—the typical hotel information package. I open the package, and there it is in bold, red lettering: *Evacuation route in case of a tsunami or a hurricane.*

CHAPTER FOURTEEN

This can't be happening. How did I manage to sleep in? Shit! I missed my meeting. This time change is getting to me, and it's only day one. I quickly reach for my phone to call Charles Baker.

"Damn!" I say out loud. My phone isn't working. I try the landline and there's no dial tone. I'm beyond frustrated. I run to the bathroom and turn on the shower. I need to get out of here and find my clients.

My first stop is the concierge's desk. Of course, he has no explanation as to why neither of my phones work. He's had no complaints from other guests, and he assures me that the internet and wifi are working just fine.

"Miss, I can lend you a phone if you'd like."

"No, thank you," I tell him. "Maybe you can direct me to the closest cellular shop."

It was nice of him to offer me a phone, but I can't jeopardize any information getting out on this land deal. Stan would have my head on a silver platter. He may anyway—once he finds out I missed the meeting. My only saving grace right now is that he can't yell at me on my phone. I take down the name of the cellular shop, which apparently is close to where I'm heading.

I hop in my car and get on the highway in the hope I'll find them still at the Coco Palms. My gut tells me it's a slim chance, but it's only a ten-minute drive from where I'm staying and it could save my ass. It's extremely hard to keep my eyes on the road, once the ocean appears in clear view to my right. Someone else must have thought the same thing, because suddenly my front view becomes a sea of braking red lights. Oh shit, what now? Traffic is at a dead stop. Minute after minute we don't move an inch. I try to keep myself calm, I could be stuck in worst places, but I can't get the clients out of my mind, or Stan's angry face if he knew I was running late.

Thirty minutes later, we've moved less than ten feet. I want to cry. I really just want to sob like a baby with a heat rash, because that's how my body is feeling after sitting for over an hour with scorching sunrays beaming into the car. And like everything else that's gone wrong, so has the air conditioner. Not that I'm partial to air conditioning in general, but under these circumstances, I'd sit on a block of ice. My left arm has gotten the brunt of the sun. I put my suit jacket back on, but unfortunately, I chose to wear the black suit ... that's what happens when one rushes and isn't thinking.

I finally arrive at the Coco Palms. I try to tug my blazer off, but my left arm is stuck to the lining. It's drenched in sweat. I finally manage to pull it off with the sleeve turning inside out. I throw it onto the passenger seat in frustration.

I notice there aren't any other vehicles in the vacant parking lot. Since I missed the meeting, I really should get back in the car and head to the phone shop. But curiosity gets the better of me. I walk towards the fence, which is half broken down. A slanted sign hangs in the center of the fence stating NO TRESPASSING. Police tape has been put up to keep trespassers from getting through the gaping holes which are obviously the work of vandals. I stand staring as I contemplate whether to enter. After all, I am—or was supposed to be—here to meet some clients, which technically means it's not trespassing. I try not to think too much about the smaller print on the sign, the part indicating that prosecution will be to the fullest extent of the law. I'm sticking with the fact that I'm looking for my clients. It's legitimate business, I convince myself, and climb through the broken fence.

As I walk I struggle to keep the dry red dirt from getting all over my feet, but no such luck. What makes it even more difficult is the unkempt vegetation. There are palm tree leaves strewn everywhere. Mound upon mound of nature's debris. I feel like I'm trying to trek through a jungle—not that I ever have, but I'd imagine it to be like this. I keep looking down in order to avoid tripping on the exposed tree roots. Some are as thick as tree stumps. I've never seen anything like it.

About three hundred feet away I can see the Coco Palms Resort. As I reach what may have been the main entrance, I feel something land on my shoulder. I let out a deafening shrill, only to realize that it's a piece of tree bark. The lack of sleep has made me jittery. Well, actually, this place is making me jittery too. Having seen enough, I make the conscious decision to come back another time when the Bakers are here.

As I turn to head back to my car, I spot a shadow on the second level. Someone is up there. It's too tall to be an animal, but looking at the size of the vegetation around here, anything is possible, I suppose. Who knows what's in this empty shell of a structure? After all, it has been sitting dormant for decades. It's all looking quite creepy, and the swaying lamp in the open window is freaking me out to a new level. I can't get out of here fast enough, but I don't seem to be going anywhere fast. Damn, why did I have to wear these stupid heels?

I no sooner ask myself than one of my heels gets stuck in the red dirt like a garden marker. Shit! This is one of my favorite pairs of slingbacks. I try to pull the heel out, but I can't get a good grip on it. It's in too deep. I bend down and try to dig the dirt with my bare hands. I manage to loosen the heel and give it a forceful pull, but the strap breaks. I give up. I not only forfeit an expensive pair of shoes, but my three-day-old manicure is shot to hell. I get up and start wobbling as fast as I can to the car. Like an idiot, I make the mistake of looking back. I know I shouldn't look upstairs, but I do. And there, looking at me, is a silhouette of what I perceive to be an old woman.

I feel every hair on my body tingling as if an electrical current is ripping the hairs from my skin—again, not something I've ever experienced, but if I had, I'm sure it'd feel this way. Do I even need to ask myself what she's doing up there? Maybe she's homeless? NO! It's me, and

I'm fucked in the head. I'm supposed to be here, because I'm a bright young woman, and now I find myself thinking that a shadow is homeless. I blink, trying to erase her from my mind. It must have worked—she's no longer up there, but then, why is the ceiling lamp swaying? She must have bumped it, because God knows there definitely isn't a breeze out here at the moment. I'm becoming so agitated by this day that my inner Sarah Connor starts to come out. You know, Linda Hamilton in *Terminator*. I'm pumped and ready to take on this property. I say out loud in the general direction of my shadowy friend, wherever she is, "You listen to me. I didn't come all the way out here to be intimidated by you or anyone else for that matter. You have no idea who you're messing with." Okay, I may have wanted to leave out the last part.

I finally reach the car and climb in. I'm about to shut the car door when a thunderous laughter vibrates around me. And just as I'm hoping and praying that whatever it is I've seen is still up there, instead of down here, I feel her breath on my shoulder.

"Don't be a coward," I say. "Show your face, woman." Again, she laughs at me and I feel her swoosh by me. "You're starting to tick me off. If you don't have anything to say, I'll be seeing you later."

"Oh, I have plenty to say to you," the invisible presence replies. "I'm just not sure where I want to start."

I can feel my stomach doing flips. Is this phantom out to kill me? I need to get away, but I instinctively say, "How about starting with why you're following me?"

"Because I know why you're here. Let me say this to you, and I'll be loud and clear: No one takes this land away. If you so much as attempt it, you'll be sorry beyond —"

"Please, don't make me laugh. What can a ghost possibly do to me?" Even as I ask the question, I know I should be running, but it seems I can't keep my mouth shut. "It's been a pleasure, but I have bigger fish to fry."

"I'm warning you. Don't test the land or you'll be sleeping with the fish."

Oh no, here comes Sarah. I find myself back out of the car, standing where I believe the voice is coming from. I say, "Why aren't you showing yourself to me? Don't talk the talk if you can't live up to it." I may sound tough, but her voice seriously had me shaking in my one high heel.

"Don't you dare test me, young lady. You are trespassing on my land. Just remember that. No smartass lawyer from the mainland is going to take away what is rightfully mine. Understood? You have no idea the types of people you're dealing with. And for the record, don't say I didn't warn you."

I'm confused. Is she the bad person, or is she referring to others? What the hell is going on? "If you are so quick to threaten and warn me in the same breath, why aren't you showing yourself to me? Who are you?" Did I really just utter those words? Am I so jetlagged that I'm hallucinating this woman's presence? I get back in my car, shaken to my core, but my adrenaline is pumping at full throttle. I refocus and start driving, trying to make my way to the nearest cellphone shop.

Of course, as randomly as everything else that's happened so far, my phone miraculously begins functioning again. I notice my message light flickering. I pray that it's not Stan. I punch in the code and then skip through at least ten messages before getting to one left by Charles Baker: "Hello Miss Parker, I'm not sure if your flight has been delayed, but my brother Ken and I have been waiting for you at the Coco Palms for over a half hour. Unfortunately, we have other meetings to attend to. I hope that you are safe. Give me a call as soon as you get this. Regards, Charles." At least he wasn't pissed off. I dial his number and reschedule a meeting for late afternoon. In the meantime, I'm in desperate need of food and shoes. Maybe a clean outfit wouldn't hurt, seeing as I have more red dirt on me than the ground does.

CHAPTER FIFTEEN

I couldn't be more pleased about rescheduling my meeting, which will allow me the time to run into the ABC convenience shop I'm approaching. Hobbling along on one high heel is not ideal; maybe I can find a pair of sandals in here. Upon entering, I realize I won't be coming out with anything more than casual sandals that don't match my suit, but being picky is not an option right now.

"Great," I exclaim aloud. "Just what I was looking for, bright neon colors. Are we back in the eighties?" After about ten minutes of searching through the racks in the fragrance-laden shop, I spot an elastic tube dress. The fabric is navy blue with a subtle hibiscus floral pattern. "Definitely not my style, but at least it has some straps. This and a pair of island slippers in navy will do for now. I can always run back to my hotel to change after I grab a bite." As I talk to myself while staring at myself in the mirror wearing what may be my new ensemble, a saleswoman approaches me.

"Is there anything I can help you with?"

"I'll take everything I'm wearing, and these," I say as I hand the woman all the tags off the clothes, plus a box of chocolate-covered macadamia nuts.

"Glad you found what you were looking for," she says as I follow her to the cash register. While she rings in the purchases, I spot a stack of local newspapers. I pick up a copy and lay it on the counter.

"Can you add this also?"

The woman looks at me with a wide, proud smile and says, "Ah ... yes, our beautiful Kanoa. We so love our boy."

"Excuse me?"

"I'm sorry. I thought you were purchasing it because of Kanoa."

"Kanoa?"

"Yes, Kanoa Kahala. He is our native hero."

"What exactly does that mean?"

"Kanoa is the boy who helps preserve our heritage," says the woman. "That will be fifty-six dollars and fifty cents."

My hands are trembling as I hand the woman my money. I grab the paper to take a closer look at the tiny photo. I'm in complete shock as I ask her, "Does he go by any other name?"

The woman appears to be confused. "Not that I know of. I've only ever known him as Kanoa. He is native Kauai'ian."

I take my purchases and proceed to the exit, only to find myself on the sidewalk staring down at the photo in the paper. Not sure if I'm feeling faint from the photo or from lack of food. I realize I haven't eaten and it's already noontime—food is much needed. I keep getting a waft of delicious food aromas, but I believe it's just my hunger making me hallucinate, until I look down the street and spot a lineup of people waiting in front of a shop called Pono Market. If this many locals have lined up for lunch, the shop must be doing something right. I walk down the street and join the others.

The long lineup moves along faster than I expected, and suddenly I'm at the front, caught off guard by the many lunch selections in front of me. I recognize a couple of dishes, such as *poke*, but they must have a dozen different varieties. I swear I can feel sweat beads starting to form on my nose from being overwhelmed. I hate holding up lines, and just as I'm thinking this, a beautiful young woman enters the shop. I watch and listen as the older woman behind the counter says to the younger woman, "Aloha, Nani, always a pleasure to see your smiling face."

Nani replies, "Aloha Auntie, I believe those bags are for me?" Auntie doesn't have a chance to respond, when the guy behind the counter says to Nani, but eyes focused on me, "Hey Nani, give my best to Kanoa."

As the older woman is retrieving the bags, I make eye contact with Nani, who walks towards me, and it's too late to look away. She asks me, "Would you like some help translating what the dishes are? Seeing as our good friend Makani has lost his tongue," and then laughs.

"Yes, thank you. It's so kind of you. I'm Abby, by the way."

"Nice to meet you, Abby. I'm Nani, and our smitten boy behind the counter is Makani." We both giggle, while Makani blushes and serves the people in front of me.

"Would you like me to explain some of the dishes," Nani asks, "or ..."

"Oh please, don't hold the line on my account. I will eat whatever you choose, I'm famished."

"You sure?"

"Yes."

"We'll have the *lau lau* plate," she says to Makani and then looks back at me. "What would you like to drink, Abby?"

"I'm fine with water, thank you."

"If you're going to be staying around these parts, you may want to say *mahalo* in place of thank you."

"Well then, *mahalo* for ordering my food. I promise I'll be better prepared the next time I come in. I swear I was literally having a dialogue with myself to take anything just to move it along, and then you rescued me. The aromas from this place caught my attention from way down the street."

"I hear you," Nani says. "I've been coming here my entire life. I guarantee you will like what you're getting. Are you here on vacation?"

"No, business."

Nani starts to dig into her purse. She pulls out a business card and hands it to me. "If you want to have coffee or lunch, maybe even a tour of the island, give me a shout. I'd love to show you around."

"That's so sweet of you."

"Think nothing of it. I'm proud to show off our island. Sorry, I have to run. Just came to pick up food for a working lunch. It's been a pleasure meeting you, Abby, and welcome to Kaua'i."

"*Mahalo*, Nani. Lovely meeting you."

As Nani walks away from Abby she stops at the checkout counter and asks, "Auntie, please put Abby's lunch on our tab."

"Oh, no," I exclaim. "I can't let you do that."

"Island aloha," says Nani as she crooks her head around some of the other customers. "Until we meet again."

As Nani grabs her three bags from Auntie and leaves the market, I can't help but laugh a little inside. This would never happen in New York City, such a kind act from a total stranger. But then again, if it did, I wouldn't be the type to engage. I'm running out of hands, so I throw the business card in my purse without looking at it.

There are only two tiny tables, but lucky for me, one is about to become vacant. For a brief moment, Nani had me forgetting about the face I'd seen in the paper—but then again, I know I'm being silly. Don't we all have a doppelgänger? As the table clears, I sit down and lay the paper next to my lunch plate. Feeling ravenous, I pop open the lid of my styrofoam box. I recognize the *poke* and take a bite. The *Ahi* tuna is like butter gliding through my teeth. I devour it so quickly that I'm ready to get back in line for more. It is absolutely divine. Looking down at my container, I'm not as confident about the other choice Nani made. For one, I don't recognize anything besides the rice, and I can't stop staring at the giant green ball of something on top of it. It looks like overly steamed spinach. As hungry as I am, I push it aside for a moment and turn to the paper again. The face staring up at me is much too familiar. How can this Kanoa Kahala look identical to my Noah? Could Noah be of Hawaiian descent? No! I'm sure he would have mentioned it.

I turn the paper over. The face is starting to make me anxious about setting up a meeting with Mr. Kahala. I tell myself it's just the way the photo was taken; there's no way it's Noah. This guy's a native Kauaiʻian stranger, not Noah. I really think lack of sleep and jetlag are playing tricks on me, but this wackiness is a whole new realm, even for me. I need to stop this obsessing. I'm sure the woman at the counter would have known if Mr. Kahala went by any other name.

I look back down at my food because the aroma is so inviting, but the only thing I dig into is the plain rice. Maybe Noah was right when he said I am a bit of a picky eater. I never realized it until now. Before I can swallow, I hear a voice behind me. I turn to look. It's an elderly gentleman tucked away in the corner.

"I see you're not touching the *lau lau*," he says. "You'll be hooked after the first bite."

I smile at him and ask, "What exactly is it?"

"It's pork steamed in taro leaves."

"So, it's strictly pork and greens on rice?"

"No. It is chunks of pork with one piece of salt fish wrapped in taro leaves. *Ti* leaves are used as a cooking vessel for the steaming process—but not as in tea leaves which one drinks. They're discarded before serving, so you are safe to eat. Try it. I guarantee you will love it. Plus, the taro leaves are very nutritious. Quite similar to spinach, but better in my opinion."

I keep playing with it as if I'm about to eat it, but I can't muster up the courage to bring it to my mouth. Instead I ask the elderly stranger his name.

"Mike," he replies. "What's yours?"

"Abby, Abby Parker."

"Well, Abby Parker, very nice to meet you."

I find myself turning my chair sideways slightly in order to see the man. He's very old, I'd venture to guess in his eighties. Now that I can see his sweet, humble face, I decide to take a small bite of the *lau lau*. The warmth of his eyes makes me feel as if I've been covered by a cashmere throw on a cold winter's night. As I chew my food, my taste buds make contact with something that tastes entirely different than what my brain was expecting. I look over at Mike, who's smiling.

"I knew you'd love it."

I can't respond, as I've already shoveled another mouthful in, and then another, until I finish the entire portion. I catch myself saying, "This could easily become my new food addiction."

Mike laughs and slowly pries himself up with the help of his cane.

"Are you leaving?"

"No," says Mike, "I want to introduce you to something. If you will sit tight for a moment, I'll be right back."

He shuffles over to the cashier. I can see them chatting as Auntie hands him something. He approaches my table and places a cellophane-wrapped package of desserts in front of me.

"It gave me great pleasure to see how much you enjoyed our local food. I thought you might like to try some of the in-house desserts. They're baked fresh every morning, by Auntie and Makani."

I'm so taken aback by the generosity of the locals that I temporarily forget about my meeting, which is coming up in a few short hours. I debate whether to take the desserts to go. I really should get back to my hotel and change into proper business attire, or … should I stay and have the old man join me? What's happening to me? I'd never consider such a gesture back home. I'm usually all business, but how can I eat and run? Plus, my meeting has been rescheduled to a local Starbucks, which I noticed is just down the road. It's walking distance from where I am at the moment. One meeting without a suit won't kill me, or will it? The Baker brothers must be used to more relaxed island attire. I know I'm trying to convince myself, but there's something about the old man, and I don't want to disappoint him by running out.

I receive a call from Charles Baker at the exact moment I've decided to stay for dessert. I excuse myself and take the call outside.

"Miss Parker, as anxious as Ken and I are to meet with you, we must attend to an urgent matter. We will be flying back from Oʻahu first thing tomorrow morning. There's no way we can make our afternoon meeting with you. How about we stick to our original meeting place for tomorrow?"

"The Coco Palms?"

"Yes, we will see you there at ten AM sharp."

I hang up the phone and go back into Pono Market. Our coffees have arrived. I sit down to enjoy the fabulous desserts that Mike has bought.

"Sorry about that," I tell him, "but I missed my meeting earlier and there's been some rescheduling issues."

"Not to worry," says Mike. "I'm not going anywhere too fast."

Normally I hate talking to strangers, but there is something magical and endearing about the people I've met so far—especially this old man. Something about him makes me want to reach over and hug him like I used to do to my teddy bear when I was a kid. There's also something I'm dying to ask him.

"Please take this the right way, but ... is Mike your real name?" Obviously, I've asked a funny question. He is laughing aloud.

"No. My Hawaiian name is as long as the name of our state fish, the *humuhumunukunukuapua'a*. My native name is Kaleikaumaka. My teacher was the first to call me Mike, and it stuck with me. My parents weren't happy about it, but that's how it is and I'm still Mike."

"Your native name is lovely."

"*Mahalo*, that's very sweet of you to say. So, Abby, where're you from?"

"New York City."

"You've come quite a distance. I take it it's your first time, seeing as you weren't familiar with our cuisine."

"You'd be right. I don't know why I never thought to come sooner. I'm really looking forward to exploring the island. Seeing as my meeting has been pushed to the morning, I might head back to the hotel and go paddle boarding."

"Sounds like a brilliant idea. Best to take in every moment of the natural wonders God has bestowed upon us," Mike says as he drinks his coffee. Why do I suddenly feel like a louse? I know why. Because here I am sitting in front of one of the sweetest people I've ever met, and I don't have the guts to tell him what my work entails. I suddenly feel that it's time for me to go, even though I love his company. I can't have silly emotions cloud my judgment. But Mike beats me to the punch.

"Well Abby, it's been an absolute pleasure meeting you, but an old man like myself needs to have an afternoon nap. I welcome you to our island and hope to see you again. I wish you a pleasant stay."

"With the island spirit that you and Nani have shown me, it's already looking up. Maybe I'll see you tomorrow. I just may be back for lunch."

I watch Mike struggle to stand and as much as I want to help him, something tells me to leave him be.

"I'll be here," says Mike with a warm smile.

I go back to my hotel. I need to get a meeting with Kanoa Kahala as soon as possible. Just as I'm about to dial his number, I realize I've forgotten the newspaper back at Pono Market. Damn! I'll just have to get another when I go back out. On my third attempt to reach his office, I decide to leave a message, seeing as no one is picking up.

I make my way down to the beach. The sun is beaming bright over the calm waters. It's a perfect afternoon for paddle boarding, plus I haven't been on a board since Noah and I vacationed in the Hamptons. If my memory serves me correctly, it was one of my last summer vacations with him.

Even though the ocean looks calm, I decide to pay for a one-hour refresher course. Best to be on the safe side. After the way my day started, why tempt fate?

After my lesson, I venture out on my own. The view at Kalapaki Beach is exhilarating. My mission is to paddle out to the mountains, which are straight ahead from where I'm standing. I can see tiny white specks of sailboats in the distance. The beach is bustling today and there's a lifeguard on duty. I figure if I get into trouble, someone will surely notice me, but I'm not feeling as confident about going as far as the mountain range. I play it safe and paddle around the perimeter of the beach.

I happily get on my board and start to paddle out. Not more than thirty feet out, I feel something brush up against me. If I weren't out on a paddleboard I'd have sworn that someone was standing next to me. I tell myself to remain calm. I don't need to be slipping off my board. I slowly try to turn around and head back to shore, but something is preventing me from doing so. I can hear a male voice, but there isn't anyone around. He says, "My ex-Queen warned you, didn't she? You're a silly girl not to listen."

I frantically jerk around and lose control of the board. Before I know it, I'm in the water. I can feel a force dragging me under. I try with all my might to pull my body up, but it's as if my limbs are entangled in seaweed. Every time I feel a bit of relief from the downward force, I quickly break free and pop my head up for air, but something keeps dragging me under. As I fight for my life I feel as weak as a ragdoll.

CHAPTER SIXTEEN:

Kanoa

Back at the office Nani arrives with lunch for all the investors who are seated around the boardroom table. She places the bag on the credenza.

"Nani, don't bother getting plates," I say, standing to get the bag of food. "I'll just pass these around. You of all people know we're island guys at heart."

"Okay boss, whatever you say. I'll be at my desk."

As I pass the food around, my buddy Keanu asks, "Did you guys hear that the Baker brothers have gotten some big-shot lawyer from New York?"

"Really," I reply. "Do you know who it is?"

"No, but I hear it's a woman."

"I had a meeting with Charles and Ken last week—they never mentioned it."

Keanu laughs, "Maybe because they know how much you can't stand them."

"Trust me brother, I'm not exaggerating when I tell you all that these two are bad news. Anyhow, I guess I'll cross paths with her soon enough. I don't care how many lawyers they hire, because we won't let them take advantage of us."

"Hear, hear," the men reply.

I clear my throat and take a deep breath to refocus. "I'm sure you must all be wondering why I called this meeting. For a change, I have some good—no, let me rephrase, I have *great* news, but first …"

I leave the boardroom to retrieve two bottles of champagne and ask Nani to come join us. This will be as big a surprise for her as it will be for the investors.

Keanu says, "Oh, fancy, champagne with our *lau lau*. Did you win a lottery?"

"Funny, brother." I pop the corks and Nani takes over the pouring duty from me. I'm sure she's just trying to save me from spilling it everywhere. I have a bit of a chuckle inside; this woman knows me better than anyone. I watch until Nani has distributed the last of the glasses before continuing my speech. Nani is about to leave, but I grab her arm gently and give her my glass as I pour myself another. I say to Nani, "I need you to hear this, since you're a big part of my life."

I turn to the investors. "If you'd all be so kind as to raise your glasses. As of ten o'clock last night, the Coco Palms has officially been designated a heritage building."

Cheers can be heard from around the table. Guys are whistling with joy. But the happiest of all is me, who is being squeezed tight by Nani. Nothing gives me more pleasure than to see my people this happy. It's been a long time coming.

The celebratory meeting with the investors comes to an end after about thirty more minutes, as everyone has busy schedules. I'm helping Nani clean up, when a brilliant idea pops into my head. "Hey, Nani, how about we finish cleaning and hit the waves. How long's it been since we …?"

"Have you lost your mind? How about you start cleaning up that pile of papers that's consumed your desk for weeks."

"Seriously?" I reply. "I don't want to think about paperwork right now. It's taken years to win this battle— can't you just humor me once?"

Nani drops what she's doing. I figure I'm getting somewhere with her, but then she blurts out, "I appreciate it, but no."

"Then you're fired."

"Ha ha ha, yeah right. What would you do without me?"

"Nani, don't make me go there," I laugh. "Come on, Nani, it'll be like old times. Just you and …"

"Okay, okay, fine. But why do I feel like I'm about to regret this decision?"

"Because you've always been the suspicious type, that's why."

Nani and I arrive at Kalapaki Beach, where commotion in the parking lot prevents me from even turning off the road. Nani looks over at me and says, "Probably another drowning."

"Let's hope not. I really don't know how many more signs we need to put up to warn people about the strong currents."

"You know as well as I do that no amount of signage matters to some people. They think they're strong swimmers and nothing will happen to them."

"The locals should know better, but even they cross the line at times. Tourists, on the other hand, see the islands as paradise—which they are—but the beauty distracts them from the dangers of our waters. Mother Nature will always win out here."

"So true."

There's no way I can get into the parking lot due to the crowd that has gathered around the first responder's vehicle. I suggest to Nani, "Why don't you hop out and I'll go park this thing up one of the side streets?"

"Great idea. You see? This is why you're my boss," Nani says as she opens the van door and jumps out. "Why don't you leave the boards with me?"

"I don't have any. They're all at the house. We'll rent."

"Okay, now you've pissed me off. What a waste of money."

"Nani! Get a grip. We're supposed to be celebrating, plus it's my treat. Now shut the door and let me—" Before I can finish speaking, Nani slams the door. There isn't a day that goes by that I don't shake my head at Nani, but … I love her.

I find a parking spot a few streets away. When I return on foot, Nani is waiting on the sidewalk. I see her looking in the opposite direction. I yell, "Nani, over here." Her head twists around and she spots me waving. She begins to run towards me. I pray she doesn't trip. I'm always concerned for her well-being because Nani approaches everything in life at the speed of light. As she stands in front of me gasping for air, I ask, "Any news on what's happened?"

"Apparently a woman paddle-boarding fell into the water. Bystander saw everything. Said it was calm waters and out of nowhere he could see her struggling on her board, until she went over. He said she seemed to keep getting dragged under. Maybe the undercurrent was too strong for her. You and I both know that even though the waters look calm above, underneath is a different story."

"Maybe she had a cramp or something," I say.

"Yeah … I guess."

"I hope she'll be okay. Anyway, enough of that, I'm glad she's alive, but how about we go get us some boards? We came here to have fun. And don't say a word about the cost of renting—got it?"

Nani mimes zipping her mouth shut and throwing the key towards the ocean. Fat chance. I've never seen Nani silent for more than thirty seconds. Even that is too long. I always know something is up if she's silent for any longer. I laugh aloud without letting her in on the joke. I take her hand and start walking.

"You know I don't usually waste my money," I tell her. "It's just that we both deserve a break. I don't even do spontaneous that well, isn't that what you always tell me? Humor me just this once, *makuwahine*. Just say *mahalo*."

Nani shoves me like she used to when we were kids. *"Fine, mahalo."*

"I guess you found the key?" I laugh. "Seriously, Nani, you deserve it. I know I should do things like this more often. You're not only a dear friend to me, but you also work very hard. I don't ever want you to think that I don't notice. I appreciate everything you do. So *mahalo* to you, my dear friend."

I can see tears starting to well in Nani's eyes. She stops and hugs me tightly. I'm about to kiss Nani when out of the corner of my eye I see the back of the ambulance door open. The paramedics are helping a young woman out of the vehicle. I quickly let go of Nani and run as fast as I can towards the ambulance. The crowd has left me struggling to get through. The person I think I'm seeing would never be on this island. I feel helpless watching as the paramedics escort her into the hotel and she disappears from my sight. I stand dumbfounded, until Nani catches up with me.

"What's wrong?" asks Nani. "You look like you've seen a ghost. Are you okay?"

"I … I'm not sure. Maybe my eyes are playing tricks on me, but I really don't think so. I know it's her."

"Who are you referring to?"

"The girl in the ambulance."

"Who is it? Do we know her?"

"You don't, but I certainly do."

"Well? Spit it out. Who is she?"

As much as I want to say her name, I can't. It's almost as if saying her name would make it a reality—as of right now I'm just guessing it could be her. I finally answer Nani before her piercing eyes burn a hole through me.

"I think it's my ex-girlfriend. I couldn't get close enough, but I'd know her anywhere."

"Oh my God. What is she doing here? Do you think she's here to see you?

"*No*, definitely not. Keanu mentioned a female lawyer from New York that's going to be working on the Coco Palms property. I bet you it's Abby. That's why she's here. She's going to be fighting us for the land."

"Did you say *Abby*?" asks Nani with a shocked look on her face.

"Yes, Abby. Have I not mentioned her name before?"

"No, and I wish you would have. I met her at Pono Market earlier, when I went to pick up lunch."

"What? Why didn't ... never mind, I realize you wouldn't have known who she was."

"No, I didn't, but I have to admit, she seemed quite nice."

"She is. That's not the issue, it's a complicated situation."

"Well, get inside and go find her," Nani commands.

As much as I try to argue all the reasons why it wouldn't be a good idea, I can't win, nor have I ever with Nani. My head feels like it's in a vise.

"Okay, let's go," I say, looking at Nani.

"What do you mean let's go? No!" she says firmly. "You get yourself in there."

"I can't. I don't think it will go over very well, especially the way I left. I need to think about this, but I'd like to make sure she's okay. Maybe you should go in there and check on her."

"Are you insane? No. I'm not getting caught up in your mess. Like I said, she seems like a very nice person. You get in there and fix whatever it is that needs fixing. You know it won't be easy, but do you really want to wait until you have to go to court or sit across a boardroom table from her? Just get the initial first meeting over with right now. No matter how bad the outcome, you will be relieved. Right?"

"Logically, yes. Morally, yes, but ..."

"No time for buts," she says. "Get moving and give me the keys. I'm sure you can get yourself back."

"Before you go, tell me a bit about seeing Abby. How'd she seem?"

As soon as I say the words out loud I realize how self-absorbed I've been never to have mentioned Abby's name to Nani. I look at Nani moving her lips as she's talking to me, but I feel like I'm underwater in my own muffled world.

"How'd she seem? Confused about lunch?" laughs Nani. "I didn't really focus too much on her. I noticed she was having trouble with the food choices and Makani was no help. He was too busy drooling over her and holding up the line. Better watch it, boss—our boy may swoop right in."

"Don't be ridiculous," I say, a bit too sharply. I find myself bubbling with pangs of jealousy and protectiveness towards Abby. "How'd she look to you?"

"It was only a couple minutes. Like I said, she seemed very nice and I was extending a helping hand as I'd do for anybody. By the way, I had Auntie put Abby's lunch on our tab. Listen boss, the sooner you get going the better the chances are of seeing the girl. I have a ton of things to do back at the office. Surfing can wait for another time."

As much as I want to make sure Abby is okay, I'm not looking forward to our first encounter. I can honestly say I'm petrified. I haven't felt this scared since the day I found out my parents had passed. I can feel my stomach heave the same way it did that day. I'm starting to perspire. I keep telling myself to man up and face the music. I take a couple deep breaths to take away the weight I feel on my chest. I start walking towards the entrance to the hotel. Before reaching the door, I see Abby sitting alone under a shaded table on the *lānai*. With every step I take, my legs become less and less cooperative. I'm about to turn around to leave, when Abby turns and sees me. Her face is ashen. I'm not sure if it's from her accident or seeing me.

"Well, if it isn't Mr. Kanoa Kahala, or should I call you Noah King? Which are you today?" asks Abby in almost too calm and sarcastic a tone. Not that I blame her, but she's definitely not shocked to see me. Could she have known I live here? It's not the reaction I was expecting.

"What?" she asks. "Cat got your tongue? Surprised that you've been found? Trust me, I haven't been looking for you, if that's what you're thinking."

I'm feeling small and sheepish. "No, I wouldn't have expected you to be looking for me. I'm sorry ..."

"Please! Don't. If you dare give me some half-assed apology right now … I'll be liable to say things I really don't want to say."

I know I need to stay strong, but seeing Abby so vulnerable, all I want to do is wrap my arms around her and tell her that everything will be okay—but I can't.

"Can I at least sit down? I'd like to make sure you're okay. What happened? Did you …"

"Please, stop! I just want to be alone. Obviously, you know what that means, seeing as you left me all alone before."

I decide not to utter another word. I see the hurt and anger in her eyes. The hate in them is palpable, but I can't fault her, can I? I did a shitty thing and deserve anything and everything that Abby is throwing my way. Had the situation been reversed, I'd have been devastated. Decimated. I left in the only, shitty way I knew how. It was a stupid move and one I can never take back—what's done is done. I will never expect her to understand my reasons for my actions. I stand for a few more awkward moments before Abby asks, "Tell me, why did you change your name? Who are you?"

I sit, without asking again for permission. I don't want to draw any more attention than is needed. I don't recall Abby having a loud voice, but somehow one has presented itself here, along with the hardened way she's staring at me. I'd be lying if I said I haven't missed her. She looks as beautiful as I remember. Sitting across from her I can feel my body trembling. I know I still have feelings for her, but I need to keep them bottled up.

"I didn't lie about my name. I used Noah King because it's the American translation of Kanoa Kahala, that's all." I wait for her to say something, but there's no response. She just keeps staring at my face as if I'm a total stranger. I guess in her eyes I am. "Abby—"

"I swear I won't be responsible for anything that comes out of my mouth if you continue."

"Listen, I realize that you almost drowned out there. I just want to make sure you're okay. That's all."

"The paramedics took care of that. I don't need your concern. That'd be quite hypocritical coming from you."

"I deserve that."

"Noah, or should I call you Kanoa, Mr. Kahala, whoever the hell you are, I truly don't give two shits what you want. You made your bed, now lie in it," Abby says. She stands to leave, but I can see her knees buckling from under her. I quickly stand to catch her. The touch of her skin against mine is like the rush of burning wildfire. Our eyes connect for a brief moment. I know she feels the same as I do, but Abby quickly shoves me away. She regains her strength and turns to leave, but not before saying, "I'm here to do my job, which you know I do damn well, so I'd watch myself, Mr. Kahala."

As if the Coco Palms property wasn't a huge thorn in my side to begin with, now all I need is my jilted ex-lover to fight me over the land. Just fucking great.

CHAPTER SEVENTEEN:
Abby

Oh my God. What are the fucking odds that Noah and Kanoa are one and the same? This is insane. I keep telling myself to walk straight as I leave him standing at the table. My human side wants to look back, but I can't. I'm already so overwhelmed with all the events this day has brought, and Noah is the last straw. I need to call Stan. There's no way I can work on this case. As tough as I acted back there, I don't think I can take seeing him on a regular basis. Part of me wants to rip him apart. But another part, the Abby who still clings to his monogrammed towel, wants to wrap her arms around him and pretend that we just met, even though that's entirely delusional.

I keep walking and finally make it to my room. I head straight for the balcony, where I can still see Noah outside the entrance; he's in the exact same spot where I left him. I watch him as he stares out at the ocean. I wish I'd had the energy to listen to his explanations, but I couldn't. It's tough enough seeing him; I can't have him clouding my mind and my judgment, especially when I'm here to work.

I don't want to remember watching Noah's lips uttering apologies. Right now, all I want to remember is how they felt against mine when we were together. It's so hard to wrap my mind around how he just threw it all away. And now, I find out it was because of this land deal—nothing like coming in second to land. It's insane, but at least it wasn't another woman. I don't know what's more insane—being dumped for land, or speaking to an old woman whom I believe to be a ghost. As if that's not enough, her ex-husband, who is also a ghost, throws me off my paddleboard. Yup! I'm definitely the loony tune here. How has my therapist allowed me to go on like this? Why couldn't this all be a bad dream like the tsunami? My random thoughts come to an abrupt halt when I hear a knock at my door.

"Madame? Hello, it's hotel services. We've come to make sure everything is fine. Would you mind opening the door?"

Oh God, what if this is another ghost trying to kill me? I look through the peephole, and it's two of the hotel staff that I recognize. I open the door and right behind them appears Noah.

"Sorry to disturb you, Miss Parker," one of the staff members says, "but after what happened to you earlier, we wanted to make sure that you're okay."

"Thank you for your concern, I truly appreciate it. Besides feeling a bit tired, I'm doing fine."

"Well then, we will leave you, but should you need anything, don't hesitate to call us directly," the young woman says as she hands me a business card. "We'll leave you and Mr. Kahala to it."

"Oh no! Please take him with you," I say, and the staffers look back at me as if I've lost my mind. Noah says something to them as they take one final look at me and walk away.

Noah turns to me. "Please, let's go inside, where we can talk privately," he says as he points into my suite. I could have stood there and argued, but I decide to hear him out. Other people shouldn't have to endure listening to our battle.

"Don't think because I let you in that you've won this round. I did it to let the two innocent parties off the hook. You have people wrapped around your finger, don't you? Is there anywhere you go that you don't use your charm? Hell, earlier I thought the older woman at the ABC shop was going to jump out of her skin with all the praises she sang for you."

"Are you done?"

"No. Actually, yes, I'm done. I have nothing else to say to you," I say nonchalantly, until I notice the monogrammed towel on the sofa, which I'd used to wipe my face earlier. I quickly dive face down onto the sofa like I'm tackling a wild animal that was trying to escape. Now that I have a tight grip on the towel, I'm not quite sure how to get rid of it. I decide to stick it under my shirt. I can hear Kanoa asking, "Are you okay?"

"Yes," I shriek. "Can you please turn around, I think I've ripped my blouse." As I watch him turn, I make a run for the bedroom and throw the towel under the bed. I walk back out but forget one thing.

Noah asks, "I thought you ripped your blouse?"

Oops, I can't think of everything. I'm really feeling overwhelmed now. Get a grip, Abby. Don't show your weak side. Be strong, girl. I finally answer, "I noticed it was just buttoned up wrong. No big deal." I fiddle with the buttons on my blouse.

I look at his face for signs of uncertainty, but I think he bought it. Well, maybe not—he's no dummy.

"Abby?" he asks as he walks towards the balcony then turns to look at me. "I don't want to stand here making excuses for why I left. I know it was a dumbass move. Believe me, if I could take it back, I would, but I can't. I also know that saying sorry a million times won't cut it. All I can give you is the honest-to-God truth of why I left."

"Why would I believe anything you have to say? You could have picked up the phone and told me. At least you could have put my mind at ease. Have you any idea how it feels to be abandoned?"

"You're absolutely right, I could have. It's not as if I haven't thought about it at least once a day, but I kept rationalizing the outcome, which I now know is irrational. I know I hurt you, but the one thing I'm not is a liar. I haven't lied to you about anything."

"Really? How about your name, for one?"

I watch him as he searches deep within for an answer. He looks the way I imagine I do when I'm trying to convince my parents I'm okay when I'm not. His eyes keep shifting sideways nervously.

"Listen," he says, "I didn't know that things between us would get serious so fast, and when they did, I never found the right time to tell you my authentic name. I guess in that respect I was a coward. I didn't want to have to deal with all the other questions that would follow."

"But you must have known that you'd dump me sooner or later?"

"No. I never thought our relationship through to that extent. I was deeply in love with you. I know that's hard for you to believe, but I know what I felt for you. I'm just trying to say it's never too late to right a wrong. I need you to know my reasons for being in New York and for leaving."

"You had nine months to reach out, but instead you chose to stay silent. You're only eager to explain now because I'm standing in front of you. Oh, and let's not leave out the fact that I'm here to fight you for your precious land. You've got two minutes, then I want you out." Oh God, why did I say two minutes? It makes me sound like such an unreasonable twit. No, I have every right. I'm hurt and he needs to acknowledge it, damn him. I need to stop having feelings for him. He motions for me to sit next to him on the balcony.

He asks, "Can I order you up a drink, maybe something to eat?"

I stare blankly at his face.

"I'm not looking to stay, I just want to make sure you're okay. Sincerely, that's all."

"I'm fine, except this island is far from feeling like paradise."

"What happened today would make anyone feel jaded," he says, "but if you stay long enough, I guarantee you'll change your mind. It truly is paradise when approached with caution."

"I have been cautious, but I won't be here long enough to do much exploring. I'm here for one thing, and I'm sure I don't need to tell you again what that one thing is."

My truth has changed Noah's demeanor. I can always tell when he's got his back up against the wall.

"Maybe this isn't the best time," he says. "I'm glad you're safe, Abby. We'll save our talk for another time."

As much as he pisses me off, I want to kick myself. I wish he didn't look so damn good. Maybe my memory is starting to betray me, but I don't remember Noah looking so buff. He's always been fit, but ... damn him, why is he looking *exceptionally* fit? Maybe it's the tan.

"Whatever you think," I say.

"Abby. Let's just get one thing straight. I don't care who the lawyer is that will be working on the Coco Palms case. I'll never stop fighting for this land. I'll take down whoever I have to."

"Then may the best man win," I say with defiance in my tone. So much so, Noah storms out of my room without so much as a goodbye. But then again, it's his nature, isn't it?

CHAPTER EIGHTEEN

The next morning, I arrive at the Coco Palms ten minutes earlier than scheduled. I don't get out of my car until Ken and Charles Baker arrive. I really can't put up with any more shenanigans, not today.

We all get out of the car and exchange pleasantries. Right away Charles comes across as the dominant player of the two. I'm not sure of my feelings towards Ken. I hate that I assess people so quickly. Some would say I'm judgmental, but I say I know what I see, and this guy is odd—but time will tell.

"Good morning, gentlemen. Sorry about the delay."

"No worries," says Charles as he shakes my hand. "Traveling abroad isn't always predictable, something like this property," he laughs. "We need to get our bid in on this piece of land. I want the papers signed, sealed and delivered."

"I don't think the bidding is your only hurdle, unless you're willing to restore the main building. The Heritage

Association is your roadblock. I'm sure you've heard that they've passed a bill to declare the Coco Palms a Heritage site. This property is not zoned for condos, nor will it ever be. The main building has to stay."

"Yeah, right," Ken exclaims. He looks at his brother. "This is the lawyer we were waiting for? Seriously?"

"Excuse me!" I protest.

"He didn't mean that," Charles says, trying to cover up his brother's rudeness.

"No, I did mean it," Ken spews.

I can feel the rage building up inside me, but I have to remember that he's the client. Stay calm, Abby.

"As of yesterday, the property has been declared a Heritage site. You're welcome to call the Heritage Association yourself, Mr. Baker," I say, looking directly at Ken. "Yes, we can try to get it reversed and take it back to court, but that would take years, and in the end, I guarantee you, it'll still remain a heritage site."

"What kind of lawyer are you?" asks Ken.

I take a moment to digest his inane question. I want to burn him like I'm a dragon about to be slain, but I keep my flame-shooting nostrils on pause and reply, "I'm a damn good lawyer. That's why I'm telling you the truth. Now let's discuss what your intentions are, going forward. Shall we?"

Charles replies, "All right, let me give you a quick tour and then we can go to our temporary office and iron out the details for the upcoming bidding war."

"Charles," I say, "if you don't mind, I've already seen the property—well, part of it. It's best we move along and start brainstorming over the details. It's not as clear-cut as it may appear, as you well know. There's more to this than just coming up with the best bid. The land laws are different out here, but I'm sure I don't need to preach that to you. After so many failed attempts at acquiring the land, we want to take our time and do it right."

And just like that, they agree, and I'm spared any further ghost antics. That doesn't mean that my eyes missed the lamp swaying on the second floor again. I need to stay focused. I can't let Coco Palms ghosts, nor ones from my past, get the better of me. The real incentive, though, is knowing that Stan will kill me if I don't come through on this deal. Maybe kill is too harsh a word, but I'll definitely be fired.

Sitting around advising the Bakers at their temporary office space isn't exactly a hard task to do. They've leased an oceanfront home and use the screened-in lānai as their boardroom. I feel much more at ease in these surroundings as they tell me more about Mr. Kahala. I continue our meeting by asking, "So, you're telling me that two years ago Kanoa Kahala stopped your bidding process over a technicality?"

"That's right," Charles replies. "This guy is a viper. I swear he lives and breathes the Coco Palms. I can't make a move without him knowing within a split second."

"What exactly happened? And start from the beginning. I need an accurate account, details."

"I'll do my best. The first time we went to bid on the property, it was a bankruptcy sale. Different from the private sale it's up for now. I was told we put in one of the highest bids. Of course, we won. When it came time to get demolition permits, we were told that our deal wasn't legal. After much digging on Kahala's part, it appeared that the engineer I had hired was a fraud and all the blueprints he'd provided us with weren't legit. You'd think it'd be a matter of getting a new engineer on the case and rapidly solving the issue, but no. The winning bid was forfeited, and the land went to the next highest bidder. The guy that bought it died, and here we are yet again, two years later."

"Why didn't I see any of these issues in your records? I thought we had an understanding that everything was to be full disclosure."

"I just told you about it."

"I had to drag it out of you."

"It's irrelevant at this point. What does it matter?"

"It matters to me in court. How do you expect me to defend your interests?"

There's a deafening silence for an extended period. Finally, I break the ice. "Listen, Charles, I need to know every detail. What might seem irrelevant to you could be of significant importance in the case. Look at the proof. A small detail about the engineer you hired became known. Now some would say that's a big deal, but ... "

"Okay. Point taken."

I obviously struck a nerve, but he needed to feel that pain.

My initial one-week stay quickly turns into an indefinite one. Every day we find ourselves challenged with yet more roadblocks. The date for bidding submissions has been postponed for two weeks, which brings my stay to three weeks at the minimum. In the meantime, I've been working around the clock with time to spare only for quick dinners and sleep. I've seen Noah at the courthouse a few times, but we've kept our distance from one another on a personal level. I can't say that my mind hasn't wandered to thoughts of him, but they are fleeting, thanks to my heavy workload. I'm also working remotely on other files.

The only people I have had the pleasure of seeing are Mike, Makani and Auntie. I've made sure to get up early just so I can spend an hour having a chat and coffee with Mike each day. Talk about an exceptionally interesting man. The other person I'm dying to connect with is Nani, but since she works as Noah's assistant, she has to be up to her ears in administrative work. I decide that once the bids are in, I'll reach out to her.

After a month of back and forth and making sure that no legal detail has been overlooked, the Baker Brothers have their bid in. I tried hard to convince them to increase their offer, but at the end of the day, it's their money. I'm here strictly to help them with the legal challenges. Personally, had I footed the bill to have me come all this way, I would have taken my advice. At least it would put their mind to rest knowing they had a better chance to seal the deal. Doesn't make any sense as far as I'm concerned.

Before leaving for the day, Charles says, "Well, I know it's premature for celebratory drinks, but is anyone interested?"

Of course, Ken is the first to agree, but then again, Ken looks like he's always a bit boozed ... just my opinion, or else it's a coincidence that his cologne resembles alcohol. The truth is, I want nothing to do with these men on my free time.

I'm feeling rather tired and in all honesty, I'd rather be alone. I say, "I think I'll pass, gentlemen. A little R and R is what I need right now, but we will be in touch. Other parties still have until end of day to get the bids in and then it's the weekend, so if you should need me for anything, you have my number. Remember, we still have time for amendments."

"There won't be any need for adjustments," both Ken and Charles say. For the first time the two are in sync, so much so that it sounds contrived. Or maybe it's because I don't really like either of them that I find most things they do suspicious. If I had to choose one of the evils, though, I'd take the older brother, Charles. At least he's business savvy.

I can't tell you how great it feels to have a few days off. Maybe I can finally explore the island a bit. There's no harm in trying Nani, so once I've left the Bakers' office, I decide to dial her number.

"Aloha. May I please speak with Nani?"

"Speaking."

"Abby here, the girl that almost drowned. The one you saved from having a lunch order disaster!" I can hear Nani laughing on the other end of the line. "I hope I'm not disturbing you. I know that you've been quite busy and …"

"This is perfect timing," Nani says. "So nice to hear from you, Abby. How've you been?"

"Overworked and exhausted, as I'm sure you are."

"I hear you. To what do I owe the pleasure of your call?"

"Well … if I remember correctly, you offered to show me the island, so …"

I never got to finish my sentence. "I'd love to show you around Kaua'i. When were you thinking?"

"Oh, sometime, as in yesterday," I say jokingly. "Whatever suits your schedule? I have a few days off and if that doesn't work, I'll work around another date."

"What about first thing tomorrow morning? Let's say nine?"

"Yes! Sounds perfect. I can't wait."

"How about I pick you up, seeing as I'm the guide," Nani suggests.

"Great, but only if you let me pay for gas."

"We'll see. Okay, tomorrow it is. I have some paperwork to tidy up, and *à demain*, as the French say."

CHAPTER NINETEEN

Seeing as I have the afternoon free, I take my chances and stop by Pono Market. Sitting in his usual spot is Mike, and I walk up to him. "What would you say to a walk in the park with me?"

"You don't want to be hanging around an old man on such a beautiful afternoon."

"Says who?"

I look around to see if anyone is objecting to Mike coming with me. But it appears that not one of the customers has even acknowledged our presence.

Mike laughs. "Okay, but I warn you, I'm not the quickest walker, as you can see."

"I don't care," I say. "We'll stroll. There's no rush to get anywhere. Let's just enjoy each other's company and the fresh air. I can sure use the sunshine."

"Well, when you put it like that, what can I say?"

"Yes?"

"Yes, I'd love to. *Mahalo*."

"My pleasure. If there's anywhere you'd like to go, I'm up for anything."

I can see Mike contemplating his decision. His brows are almost one. He finally looks up at me. "I'd love to go to the Coco Palms. I haven't been there since Hurricane Iniki ravaged the property in 1992. I hear the terrain is quite rough, but I'd really love to see the lagoon again. At my age, you just never know when you'll get another opportunity. Just thinking about it makes me miss my dear friend Genie."

I feel as if a hot dagger has been plunged into my stomach. I just put in a bid to have the property taken away from his people. What the hell kind of monster am I?

"Abby, are you all right? We don't have to—"

"No! Don't be silly. I'd love to take you there. I know exactly where it is." I can't lie about everything. In all fairness, I haven't exactly lied; I've just omitted telling him my reasons for being here. (Spoken like a true litigator.)

As we drive down the Kuhio Highway, Mike inhales the fragrant floral air that makes its way through the open windows. He must have been such a handsome young man, as he is still very handsome with his platinum-white hair and dark skin. I'd say his skin is three shades darker than Kanoa's. I notice how brightly Mike's eyes shine for such an elderly man.

"Being from New York, I can't tell you how apparent the floral aroma lingering in the air is," I say. "As soon as I got off the plane, it hit my nasal passages full force. I don't know if you've ever been to downtown NYC, but it's not quite the same as here. How should I put it without sounding as if I'm bashing my city ...?"

Mike laughs. "No worries, child, I get what you're trying to say; and no, I have not been to NYC. Our boy from the Heritage Association, Kanoa, worked there for a few years. He has told me all about it."

I slam the brakes a little too hard at Mike's admission to knowing Noah. I apologize profusely for just about knocking his teeth onto the dashboard.

Mike goes on. "Kanoa said it was tough to eat in certain outdoor areas as he walked the streets. The pungent smell of rotting garbage and sewage would take him by surprise every time."

Boy, do I remember that well. He couldn't eat a hotdog or sausage from a street vendor without gagging at least once. I learned after a few occasions that it was best to eat indoors, or else find a spot that was odor-free and not move until we were done eating. I'm not sure if I should admit to knowing Kanoa, or just let it be for now. I choose the latter.

As we're getting out at the vacant parking lot, I'm nervous that the grounds are too rough for Mike. Also, we really shouldn't be trespassing. Maybe if we get caught, I can get out of it by pretending that he is one of my clients. My entire cover would be revealed, but it's a chance I'm willing to take. It may be an easier way of letting Mike find out why I'm here.

Stupid thought, Abby, and you know it. I will tell Mike the truth. Maybe I'll do it today.

I hear Mike say, "Abby, what's happening over there? You're so quiet."

"Sorry, Mike. I have a lot on my mind."

"I promise you, once you see where I'm taking you, everything in that busy mind will be put to rest."

Mike is already ten steps ahead and making his way to the main building, or what is left of it. Mike maneuvers with his cane like a martial arts stick-fighter. He swings that cane left and right to clear whatever is in our path. "It may take a bit of time to get to the lagoon, but it will be worth it." He makes a sudden stop and stares up at the building.

"Bringing back some memories?" I ask.

"You have no idea. The best years of my life were spent here."

I'm a little shocked at his admission. I had no idea that the Coco Palms itself was of such significance to Mike's life. Oh God! I'm feeling like a bigger louse than I already was. Thank goodness the bid is already in, or else I'm not sure if I could have gone through with it.

"It breaks my heart to see such a beautiful place sitting lifeless," he says. "To think of all the wonderful memories it holds for so many people around the world! I'm not sure what pains me more, the fact that it's a constant reminder of years gone by, or the fact that one day soon condos will be taking over what was once the most luxurious, sought-after getaway. All I know is that I'm lucky to always have the memories of years past locked away in my mind and heart. No one can ever take that away from me."

I look at him as glistening tears escape his eyes and make their way down to the red dirt he's standing on. My heart is breaking. I want to tell him that condos will never be erected, but I don't. I wonder what it is that has him so emotional—it can't just be the building. I'm not sure what to say. But then a wide smile spreads across Mike's face. We continue walking.

Mike stops again, right in the center of the main entrance, where the once-famous gigantic seashell hung. He says, "If only these walls could talk. It'd be better than any book or movie that's ever been made about the Coco Palms."

"I bet it would. Are there any stories you'd be willing to share?"

"Yes, of course. I would be honored, but for now, I'd really like to make it to the lagoon, if you don't mind."

I don't have time to respond. Mike is already turned around and walking towards the back of the building. For an elderly man with walking limitations, he sure has some pep in his step. I follow, and Mike starts to open up about the last owners of the resort before Hurricane Iniki hit.

"Genie was a dear friend of mine. I'll never forget how she took this hotel and turned it into one of the most famous resorts in the world. That Genie was a real class act."

"Was she your girlfriend?"

Mike bursts into laughter. "Funny you should ask. Most people back then thought that we were an item, but we weren't. I truly loved Genie as a person, but she only had eyes for one man, and that was Gerry—Gerry Gartner. The man she ended up marrying. You see, he owned the Coco Palms but couldn't make a go of it. Then he hired Genie, and his world changed."

"Business savvy, was she?"

"Genie was one of the warmest and most genuine people you could ever meet. I'd have never thought she was a shrewd businesswoman, but under that exterior was a woman with fire in her belly. We became the best of friends. We were one another's confidants. I have to admit, had Gerry not been in the picture, I would have definitely wanted to date Genie, and I believe she felt the same. When we looked at one another there was an underlying spark we both knew existed, but we were on different pages in our life."

"That's so nice, Mike."

"I trusted her with my life."

"I sure hope I find someone I can trust one day."

"You will, dear. You need to be open to know when that person comes along. Don't be like me. I opened up to Genie when it was too late."

"But I thought you …"

"I'm giving you a condensed version. I spent one too many years of my life pining over a woman who was unattainable, and those were the years when Gerry made his move on Genie."

And just like that, Mike closes down the personal side of the conversation. I don't ask any more questions. I can see the hurt in his otherwise joyous, bright eyes.

"Mike?"

"Yes."

"I have something I need to tell you. I feel as if—"

"Sorry to cut you off Abby, but we've reached our destination."

Amid the broken cobblestone pathways and overgrown vegetation is one of the most beautiful lagoons I've ever seen. "I can understand why you wanted to come out here," I say.

"You have no idea. Back in the day, these pathways were littered with people, not debris like they are now. I'm not sure what I liked better, watching the double-hulled canoes go up and down during the day or the tiki torches that lit the paths at night."

"Wow! It must have been gorgeous with the torches."

"It was a place where lovers would walk for hours and steal kisses. It was an age of innocence. The lagoon is also where Gerry proposed to Genie," Mike says. "They ended up getting married at the Chapel. Same place where Elvis filmed *Blue Hawaii*. Where Elvis and actress Joan Blackman descended off the double-hulled canoe, followed by many wedding guests walking along the cobblestoned pathways. The chapel was situated right here at the start of the lagoon, except now you're seeing nothing more than a hollow structure. Did you know that Elvis vacationed here many times with Priscilla? It was their paradise getaway, as they liked to call it."

"That's so fascinating. Did you ever meet him?"

"Oh yes. He was here for extended periods while filming *Blue Hawaii*. Thanks to Genie, I got to hang out with Elvis on many occasions. He was such a loving and kind man, shyer than one would expect. You should see the suite he stayed in while filming—it was the best one. When he came back with Priscilla, they'd rent out the cottage out in the back, the same cottage that was in the movie. It gave them more privacy, you know, away from the main building and guests. Those were the days. It was really a spectacular time."

"You know my grandparents also vacationed here a few times, but then my grandfather passed, and ..."

"I'm sorry to hear about your grandfather, dear."

"Thank you. They are both together now, so I'm sure they're happy wherever they may be. Tell me, what was Elvis like? How did he ever come to film a movie out here?"

"That was our mastermind, Genie. In order to get worldwide exposure, she thought she'd put a proposal out to General Parker, Elvis's manager at the time. He refused, but when Elvis caught wind that the General had turned it down, he was furious. Elvis had a real fascination for the Polynesian culture. General Parker said it was too far and it wouldn't be worth the expense, but Elvis dealt with the problem directly and said he was doing it with or without Parker, so Parker came up with a movie script, called *Blue Hawaii*, and the rest is history.

"The funny part was the day Genie got the call. I swear I could hear her screams all the way to my home. I for one am forever grateful to Genie and Elvis for putting not only Hawai'i on the map, but especially the island of Kaua'i. It got overlooked before his presence. People naturally gravitated to the island of O'ahu. At the time our island was much more primitive, but Elvis has changed us forever. That's the story, in case you were wondering why there's still such a strong Elvis influence on the island."

As I listen to Mike, I can tell that his breathing is becoming a bit labored. I suggest we take a break.

"I think that's a good idea. *Mahalo*, dear. I'm not sure I can go any further, I'm sorry. I'd love nothing more than to stroll this entire lagoon with you, but just seeing it ..."

"Please, don't apologize. This is great." I look around to see if there's anywhere to sit.

"Come. Let's go take a seat over there," Mike says, pointing to a massive tree trunk with his cane, and I take his lead as he looks lovingly across the lagoon. I sit next to him and put my arm around him for comfort, as I can tell memories are flooding his mind.

"Oh dear," he says. "You're such a sweet young lady. Genie would have loved you." Mike continues without so much as a slight flinch as he says, "Rumor has it that our Queen lingers on the grounds."

"And this doesn't bother you?"

"Why? She's one of us. This was her land. I should be honored by her presence. I've never met her, but Genie confided in me one day. She told me that she used to have daily visits with the Queen. At first I thought Genie must have been hallucinating, but over time, I came to understand how strong-minded some of our ancestors can be, and the Queen was a force to be reckoned with. Genie wasn't hallucinating. Queen Deborah did exist, and still does. Yet another story for another time," Mike says, looking quite tired. If anything, I feel better at hearing that Deborah is a real presence. It means I wasn't going crazy.

Driving back to my hotel after dropping Mike off, I call Stan, but he isn't picking up. I feel an urgent need to tell him about what I've been thinking. By the time I get back to my hotel, though, that sentiment has escaped me.

What was I thinking? Stan would kill me for getting soft-hearted. He wouldn't understand. He'd serve me my head on a silver platter if I backed out. I give my head a shake and tell myself to toughen the hell up. Instead, I place a call to my therapist. We've had a few chats since I first spotted Noah. There's no way I'd have lasted this long without her guidance. Thank God for FaceTime and Skype, but the HST doesn't always make for the best time of day. I always settle for whatever timeslot Dr. Iris can give me.

My phone rings that night at three AM. I thought I'd turned my ringer off before heading to bed, but obviously I didn't. Who in the hell is calling? Oh shit, it's Stan. I better put on a chipper voice. Not sure that I actually have one; I need to make sure I don't sound too phony.

"Hey Stan, how's it going?" Okay, that was all wrong.

"Jeez doll, I thought you'd be a bit sleepier-sounding than this," laughs Stan. He's the type of man that laughs at his own jokes. "So, tell me. How are things going? Happy with the bid you guys submitted?"

"Personally, no I'm not, but you taught me to fight as hard as I can and if the client won't listen, there's not much else I can do." I disclose the amount to Stan, but he doesn't seem surprised. And why would he be? Of course, the Bakers have spoken with him. "I think they bid way too low. Should something go wrong, I think you should put someone else on the case."

I'm sure the other guests sleeping in the hotel can hear Stan's protest through the phone. "What? Have you lost your fucking mind? I sent you down there and you want to pull out? What the hell are you telling me? Are you having another breakdown?"

I know how Goddess Pele feels just before she's about to erupt. I, too, feel the rumbling of fire deep in my belly. How dare he bring my breakdown to the forefront?

"No, Stan, and by the way I resent that."

"And what are you going to do about it? You will stay put, you hear me? I personally trained you here at Brickman and Brickman. Don't you dare disappoint me."

Disappoint him? Doesn't he realize that right now he's flowing down a stream of molten lava in my head? OMG! I need to stop these thoughts. I swear Stan is the worst thing for me, but I also know which side my bread is buttered on right now.

"Hear me out, before you say anything more, please."

"This better be good, doll."

"You see, the head of the Heritage association, Mr. Kanoa Kahala, is my ex-boyfriend Noah King, remember him?"

"So? What's that got to do with anything?"

"I just think that if something should go wrong, I'm not sure I can fight this fight, not against Kanoa Kahala. I think you'd be better off with someone who doesn't know him on a personal level like I do."

"This is ludicrous!" yells Stan. "You will stay until the ink has dried on the contract. Do you hear me?"

The better question would be, is there anyone who can't hear him? He sounds like a male banshee, if there were such a thing.

"Listen," he says, "and listen closely. You come back before the ink is dry and I swear you won't have a job to come back to."

"Got it. Sorry for being honest and telling you that my heart might not be in for another round."

"Fuck your heart. Maybe you need a reminder about the six figures you'll be getting for winning this case. How's your heart now? You make sure Kelly Corporation signs that dotted line. Understood?"

"Clearly. Been a pleasure as always, Stan."

"Likewise, doll."

Bastard. He knows I need my job. I have my apartment and other expenses. I could turn to my parents, but I swore I'd never do that. I told myself early on that I wanted to be independent and make it on my own. Right now, Stan is truly living up to his Shark nickname. He's exactly like a shark circling the waters around me. He has me right where he wants me. I could always find a new job, but who would hire me after Stan drags my name through the mud? I can just see it: *My best lawyer walked out in the middle of a high-profile deal because she's an emotional wreck.* Yeah, that would definitely not find me employment any time soon.

That's the problem with New York. With the masses of elite cliques, a person can only succeed if she's capable of staying in the good graces of her peers. That is exactly what I've always feared the most, a bad reputation.

Since I'm awake, I go to the credenza to grab a sheet of stationery paper. I decide to scribble down all the incidents that have taken place since my arrival. Should anything happen, at least it'll be documented. Something bizarre is definitely happening thanks to this land deal. Who knows what these apparitions are capable of?

I may be tough in a courtroom, but my soft side has me questioning my morals. I've chosen my salary over ancestral land, land that generations of people have worked very hard to acquire and keep in the family. It hasn't helped watching Kanoa plead his case for his people, his face full of compassion and pride. What does my face have but eyes that twinkle at the thought of earning a lucrative salary and getting revenge on Noah? I have a strong work ethic, but I also let Stan intimidate me. If this bid doesn't go through, I'll have to think long and hard about my options. I have some life-altering decisions to make.

The more I think about my conversation with Stan, the odder it seems. I can't put my finger on it, but why didn't Stan react when I mentioned Kanoa's name? Normally he blows his top at the chance of anything personal jeopardizing a case. He was definitely mad that I mentioned wanting off the case, but he didn't flinch about Kanoa. Maybe I'm just overreacting. Oh well, questions for another day. Right now, I need sleep, or I'll be a basketcase for my sightseeing with Nani.

CHAPTER TWENTY

It's a bit difficult getting up, but I make it outside for nine AM sharp. I see Nani pulling into the parking lot of the hotel. I'd wave at her, but I'm carrying two cups of coffee. No worries, though—she has spotted me.

"Good morning, Abby, and *mahalo* for the coffee."

"It's the least I can do," I say as I hand her a cup and walk over to the passenger side. "*Mahalo* for taking the time to show me around today. I can really use the company."

"It's my pleasure. I feel the same way. I'm sure you've been as cooped up as Kanoa has on this land deal."

"I sure have. Sad to think I've been here a month and barely seen the island. I've visited a few places around my hotel, but that's about it. I also wasn't expecting to be here this long. I'm not complaining by any means—who wouldn't like to work from here? I'm getting quite spoiled waking up to such beautiful ocean views. Mind you, it took me almost two weeks to sleep properly."

"Really? What's been the problem? Sorry … stupid question. Of course, the near-drowning incident."

"Yes, the drowning, but mostly it's being so far away from the mainland that has gotten the best of me. I haven't had reason to give it much thought until I actually found myself here."

"It's so funny. It's not something I ever think about. But I see your point. Glad you're feeling more comfortable."

"I am, except for … nah, forget it," I say, shaking my head.

"What is it? Tell me."

I take a deep breath of the floral air as we drive. I fill my lungs a second time before answering, especially knowing how it's going to come across.

"You'll think I'm crazy."

"Is it Kanoa?"

"No," I say. "Well, yes. No. Noah is part of the angst I feel, but it's something entirely different. It's something I saw and felt, or I think I did."

"What, a ghost?" laughs Nani.

"Yes," I reply, a little too excitedly. "I believe I've seen a ghost. I also believe one tried to drown me."

I look over at Nani, expecting to see a look of shock at my admission, but instead, she's as cool as a cucumber.

"I'm not surprised. I've heard of others seeing ghosts. It only seems to happen when there is something stirring with foreigners attempting to take our land, or interfere in our culture, if you know what I mean. Many have made claims about ghost sightings, especially over at the Coco Palms. Nowadays you can Google it."

"Oh sure, why didn't I think of that," I laugh sarcastically. "Who thinks to Google ghosts at the Coco Palms?"

"You, as soon as you get back to your hotel," she snickers.

"You're right." Wish someone had told me this sooner. "As if it wasn't bad enough thinking I'd seen a ghost when I spotted Noah's face in the local paper."

I can't help but notice displeasure on Nani's face, the same expression a person has when they've just poured a glass of sour milk.

"I hate to be so forward," she says, "but can we just call him by one name? I have always known him as Kanoa, and this Noah business—not cool."

"Tell *him* that."

"Oh, believe me, he's heard my take on it. I don't know the situation, but I just wish you two could at least sit down and talk. Why waste so much energy on negative things?"

I've already realized that Nani is not the kind of person who lets you get away with blowing smoke up her you-know-what. So, I tread cautiously. "I don't want to get you in the middle, but he's the one that abandoned me."

"I'm not defending him by any means. It was shitty the way he left you, and believe me I'd be just as pissed as you are. But won't your life be even worse if you leave here without any resolution at all?"

I can feel my heart sinking to the ground at Nani's question. She's right—I can't imagine getting back on a plane without at least seeing Noah, if not talking to him.

"You're absolutely right. I think we both deserve proper closure."

I see Nani smiling. By closure, I didn't mean dating him again, so why is she smiling? What does she know that I don't? I'm getting into my head again—stop!

"If there is one thing I could change right now," I say, "it would be working on this land deal. I just hope you understand. I have a job to do. It's nothing personal about the people."

"Of course. I totally get it. How about we change the subject? I'm just as uncomfortable as you are talking about it. Tell me about your ghost sightings."

"I think there's one looking over my shoulder whenever I set foot on the grounds of the Coco Palms. Actually, I believe there are two ghosts. Good and evil, except the evil one seems to travel, whereas the other is only at the Coco Palms."

"Interesting," Nani replies with skepticism in her tone. I look over at her.

"You're mocking me, aren't you? By the way, where are we going?"

"Sorry. I should have asked you straight away what you'd like to do, but the ghost got the better of you."

We both burst out laughing.

"I know," I say, "it's stupid, but …"

"I believe you, Abby. I'll tell you a true story, but first, how are you with heights?"

"I'm good," I say, trying to keep my voice from quivering. I'm not partial to heights, but I also don't want to sound like a wimp. After all, how high can it be? (Who am I kidding? A stepladder is too high for me.)

"Okay, great," she says. "I'll take you to Waimea Canyon. You may know it as the Grand Canyon of the Pacific." Nani hands me a brochure.

"Can't say I've heard of it, but it seems lovely." Grand Canyon of the Pacific, oh God, what have I agreed to? I can barely look at *photos* of the Grand Canyon without quivering. Breathe, Abby, breathe.

"Abby? Are you okay?" she asks as she looks over at me.

"I'm good. You know, just overthinking things."

"You mean your relationship with Kanoa?"

"We don't have a relationship," I say.

"No, maybe not now, but you did. It must have been hard to see him again. It's okay to talk about it. I won't tell Kanoa."

I'm not one to share my feelings outside of my parents and my therapist, but Nani for some strange reason feels like a sister, even though I barely know her—not that I know what having a sister really feels like. "I'm not sure it's a good idea. I realize that you two are very close."

And just as I've said the words out loud, I wonder just how close they are. Is there something going on with them, or is she a past lover? Abby, *stop*, just try and enjoy the day, I tell myself.

"It's up to you," she says. "I'm here if you need a friend. I've known Kanoa since we were kids."

"I'll keep that in mind, but for now, maybe you can share that ghost story with me. The one you were going to tell me about earlier."

Nani doesn't skip a beat. "There have been many sightings, but this one in particular happened to a potential buyer. I'm referring to the Coco Palms. This guy had gone out for a morning snorkel and almost drowned. Witnesses speculated that his equipment failed, but it turns out that it was perfectly fine. He was one day away from taking possession of the land."

"I don't understand. Maybe he wasn't breathing properly or something."

"No, that's not it. He said that he had an eerie feeling the entire time he was putting his equipment on. It was as if there was a presence next to him but he had trouble explaining it. He told the authorities that he had tried his mask and snorkel before fully submerging into the water. It's a ritual of his. Everything seemed to be working fine. It's not as if this guy was an amateur snorkeler; he was seasoned. Had the best equipment money could buy. Supposedly he'd been to some of the most dangerous snorkeling sites in the world."

"Where was he snorkeling?"

"Lydgate State Park."

My eyes widen. This was most definitely not a dangerous area. Nani must have gotten it wrong.

"I was just there yesterday," I say. "After my near drowning I asked around and was told to go there because of the manmade stone wall."

"So, you see what I'm saying. How does a seasoned snorkeler, an adrenaline junkie, almost drown there?"

"I have to admit that even in that contained area, those undercurrents are strong, but I know what you're saying. The day I was paddleboarding I didn't even feel strong undercurrents. I literally felt as if I kept getting dunked under by someone."

"This is how this guy explained it. I, myself, believe it has to do with the Coco Palms. I have always thought that place was haunted. There's a lot of unfinished business with these ghosts."

I take a deep breath. "After a month of being here, I believe there is something going on on this island. Either that or I've gone totally mad. Just the other day I walked back into my room after my morning workout and the atmosphere had a thick eeriness to it. I had ordered room service to arrive when I got back. I heard a knock and when I went to open the door, I couldn't move. It's as if my feet were stuck in quicksand. I just remember thinking, *Yell, yell at the ghost, and be as intimidating as he is.*"

"Why did you say he?" she asks.

"Because this is definitely a male ghost. My female ghost is at the Coco Palms."

I can see Nani smirking, but I'm dead serious. I ask, "You don't believe me?"

"On the contrary. I absolutely believe you. I just didn't take you for a believer in ghosts."

"Listen, I wouldn't preach this to my colleagues. They'd think I was bonkers. I know that the day I was out paddleboarding it was the male ghost. He's evil and out to kill me. And as crazy as it sounds, the lamp-swaying female ghost has nothing on this guy."

"You're not crazy by any means. I can't say I've personally experienced these same issues, but there is a myth about Reverend John Lydgate. He was a civil leader in the Wailua area, where he still has many descendants. They say that his spirit is there to protect the land and the children who swim within the stone wall."

"Are you pulling my leg?"

"No. I'm being serious. I don't know that it's true, but I have to say it's something I believe in. What people don't understand is that they are trespassing on ancient sacred grounds. We should be honored to enjoy what the island has to offer, but when people get greedy, the ancient descendants roar."

"Okay, as if I wasn't freaked out enough. At least it puts my mind at ease that I'm not nuts for spotting a ghost on the second floor of the Coco Palms."

"You are definitely not *lōlō*. Something or someone does live on the grounds of the Coco Palms. I'm telling you, Google it."

"Thank God I didn't feel anything unusual while I was snorkeling at Lydgate yesterday. If anything, it felt extremely peaceful."

"Very strange. Considering the bidding doesn't officially close until later today."

"Jesus, Nani, what are you trying to say?"

"Watch yourself, that's all."

"Tell me, did the snorkeler back away from the deal?"

"Word on the street was that he was no longer interested and retired. The excuse he gave was he wanted to spend more time with his family," Nani says with an eyeroll.

"No one from these parts believed him. The guy was wise to retire. You see, the entire Wailua area was the birthplace of royalty in ancient Hawaiian times.

Hawaiian belief is that the land is never to be in the possession of *haoles*, non-Hawaiians. Queen Deborah was the last reigning queen here on the island of Kaua'i. The Coco Palms property was her land until she died in 1853. Her ex-husband, the King, took her land away from her for a few years and had Queen Deborah banished. Somehow, she managed to regain her possessions. To this day, no one knows where Deborah is buried. Her remains have never been found."

I feel my anxiety rising as Nani keeps talking a mile a minute while taking hairpin curves along a never-ending mountainside. I happen to look out the window to my side, where an opening in the bushy vegetation gives me a clear view of just how high up in the mountains we've driven. A sign appears indicating we are about a half mile from our destination. We talked so much that I missed most of the scenery getting here, except for this half-hour mountain climb. I can tell it is nothing to Nani, but even the word canyon has me anxious. Suddenly, her cell phone begins to ring. I envision us plummeting to our death as Nani reaches to answer the phone, so I snag it from the console where it's resting and say, "Hello, Nani's phone, Abby speaking."

"Nani have you on the payroll?" a very familiar voice says back to me.

I struggle to get the words out that are swarming around my brain like worker bees. I feel as if I'm about to pass out. I can hear Noah saying my name over and over.

"Sorry, I …"

"Are you okay?"

"I'm fine," I say in a not-so-convincing, trembling voice.

"Nani got you on the payroll?" he jokes again, sounding about as nervous as I'm feeling. "Where is Nani?"

I look over at Nani as I cover the phone's speaker with my hand. "It's Noah."

"Tell Kanoa that I'm just getting to Waimea Canyon. He'll have to leave a message with you."

I clear my throat before getting back on the phone. I reiterate what Nani has told me and use his Hawaiian name for the first time.

He remarks, "That sounds odd coming from you. Don't get me wrong, I like it, it's just odd."

I try to loosen up, responding in a joking manner, "You think it's odd for you?"

Kanoa suggests that Nani call him back later, and I tell her this while I still have him on the phone.

Nani asks me to put it on speaker. She yells over, "Come by later. We will have dinner together. I'm not taking no for an answer." Then she asks me to take the phone off speaker before Kanoa has a chance to reply.

I say into the phone, "Do you need me to repeat that?"

Kanoa laughs, "No. I heard Nani loud and clear. By the way, why Waimea Canyon? You're petrified of heights."

Great, just what I need, Kanoa remembering something about me that I thought he'd forgotten. I try to whisper, but it's nearly impossible. "It'll be fine."

"You haven't mentioned your fear to Nani, have you?"

"That's right."

"Abby? Just concentrate on the beauty of the canyon," he says. "Don't ever look down. When you get to the lookout, keep looking ahead at all times. You will see a waterfall amongst the mountains. If you're lucky, it's rained up in that area and there could be water overflow that will look like more waterfalls. It's spectacular, but as I mentioned, never look down, or that can throw your balance off—otherwise you'll be fine."

"Like they say in these parts, *mahalo*. I really should be going. Is there anything else you'd like to relay to Nani?"

"No, I'm good. Have fun and remember what I told you."

"I will."

Nani parks the car. She looks over at me. "Think you'd like to come back down to earth?"

"Sorry, Nani. I . . ."

"No need for explanations," she says playfully. Even as I mentally process his real name, I have to admit it suits him better than Noah—but I can only say that because I now know his real identity. I'm grateful for his pep talk, but I hate feeling vulnerable.

Nani and I start walking toward the lookout point. With every step I take, I can feel my stomach churning. I can't seem to quiet down my fearful brain. I try to keep going over what Kanoa told me, but the anticipation of the unknown is getting to me. As we climb the path towards the lookout, I cling to the railing for dear life.

The railing would make it hard to actually fall, but I know what lies on the other side. We finally make it to the lookout point, and I follow Kanoa's instructions and spot the waterfall. He is absolutely right. I can also see another little runoff waterfall. As I'm processing these beautiful natural wonders, I forget for an instant and happen to look down—and there's no turning back.

"Abby! Are you okay? My heavens, your face is yellowish-green."

I try to muster an *I'm okay,* but I'm afraid I'll be sick if I dare move my lips. My hands are clinging to the railing for dear life. I've got such a tight grip that my knuckles are white. I hear Nani telling me, "Abby, let go of the railing. Come on. Let's get you down a bit further." She tries to take my hand, but I can't let go.

"I can't move, Nani," I cry.

"Yes you can. Come on. Give me your hand. I'll stand by your side and block the view."

Nani can't pry my hands off the railing. A bystander notices what's happening and offers to help, managing to free my hands. Before I know it, we are back down the ramp and away from the panoramic view of the canyon. I do recall the beautiful scenic colors of bright red, deep green, and yellow, but that's about as much as I saw. I want to thank the man, but I have no energy. Nani does the thanking and then turns to me and takes my arm. "Come, we need to get you to the restroom."

I try hard to put one foot in front of the other, but I can't. Unfortunately, at that moment I spew my breakfast like a volcanic eruption. I can feel Nani taking hold of my hair. She pulls it back away from my face, standing with me until I finish. She wipes my face with tissues from her handbag, then suggests, "Come this way. Let's go sit at that picnic table over there."

Once Nani gets me settled, she walks over to a concession stand where a young man is selling refreshments. I am mortified at what has just taken place. Nani acts as if it's not a big deal. I have managed to slump my head onto the picnic table. I watch Nani sideways as she walks back with two cans of ginger ale in her hands.

"Here you go, sweetie," she says, handing me a pop and a bag of ginger chews. "These should help your queasy stomach."

I slowly raise my head off the table. If I jerk too much I'll be sick again. I take the ginger ale and begin to drink. "Thank you, Nani. I'm so sorry for everything. I didn't mean to ruin the day."

"The day? We just got started. Come now, drink up, we have so much more to do, but not up here," laughs Nani.

"I can't, Nani. I feel like I'm dying."

"It will pass in a little while. Try to drink all your ginger ale. I promise it will help."

I do as Nani instructs. After about twenty minutes of silence and resting my head, I feel better. I ask, "Do you think we should start to make our way back down?"

"Only if you're sure you're okay. I'm fine with sitting here for as long as it takes."

"I'm good."

"Okay, as long as you promise me that you won't look over the edge as we drive."

"I promise I won't get sick in your car."

"If you do feel anything coming up, open the window and aim outside. We don't have anywhere to pull over for about twenty minutes. Make sure you aim far enough out so it doesn't come back in."

"Trust me, after that explanation I will stay seated and meditate. Maybe a barf bag for backup might be a good idea." We get back in the car and I decide to recline my seat; that way I can close my eyes. I pop a ginger chew and stay quiet. After about fifteen minutes of silence, I can feel myself coming back to life. I put my seat up slightly. Nani looks over at me and tells me that my soft-pink pigmentation is back. Success.

CHAPTER TWENTY-ONE

The sign reads KAUA'I'S BIGGEST LITTLE TOWN, HANAPĒPĒ. "That's an odd description," I say to Nani.

"Don't blink, because you'll miss it. I figured coming to the island's art capital is a better option than you going out on a catamaran to the Nāpali Coast."

"Agreed. I'm not even sure exactly what that is, but anything involving a catamaran and waves right now would not be a great idea. This is a much better option."

We both laugh; like most things, it's always funnier after the fact. Nani parks the car. She's a trooper to want to continue with our sightseeing tour.

As we stroll the main drag, I realize that Nani wasn't kidding. Besides a few small eating establishments—and I mean small—almost every storefront is an art shop. "How did Hanapēpē become the art capital?" I ask.

"At one time Hanapēpē was booming economically with plantations. Over the last century, its population has dwindled significantly. The buildings, as you can see, have turned into shops and art galleries. When Hurricane Iniki hit, all of these shops were affected. Most had to start from scratch."

"Don't take this the wrong way," I say, "but this place has a sort of an eeriness to it."

"I agree. I'm sure if the walls of these plantation homes could speak, they'd have a lot to say. The seaport isn't far from here, and believe it or not, this street was the place to be back in the day. I still hear tales being told by my *Kupuna* of how the seamen used to come here to spend their time off."

"I'm sure these ghosts have some fascinating stories, but I'd rather they told someone besides us," I say as my eyes scan the buildings from side to side. Something is giving me an uneasy feeling, but it's nothing like the sense of danger I felt on my paddleboard—it feels more like a lamentation, if that even makes sense.

As we continue to walk, we stumble upon a quaint bookstore, a confectionary shop and an old movie theater—but the rest is art shops. Just how much art is needed on the island? It has to be a tough way to make a living. I sometimes feel as if Nani can read my mind.

"Most of the people from this area have relocated closer to Lihue. It cuts down on travel time, depending on where their jobs are situated. I mean, I'd never live out here and work in Kapa'a. The traffic would drive me *lōlō*, but there are families who do it every day. You've experienced how unforgiving a two-lane highway can be."

As Nani keeps talking I spot a quaint shop reminiscent of a sprinkle doughnut, except its sprinkles are faded. "I'm sorry for interrupting, but that little shop tucked away over there," I say as I point towards it. "Would you mind if we go in? There's something about it that I'm finding intriguing."

"I've been here so many times. I don't know why I've never noticed it. Lady, you have laser vision," Nani says as she follows me. "It's not some ghost that's leading you there, is it?"

"It's not its bright colors, so something has caught my attention," I say jokingly.

Nani's phone rings. She stops to answer it, waving for me to go into the shop so she can take the call. Upon entering, I'm greeted by a jovial elderly woman.

"Welcome, please take a look around. Let me know if there's anything I can help you with."

I give the shop a quick scan. My attention is focused on a collection of portraits displayed at the back of the room. I say, "What a lovely shop you have. Maybe you can tell me a little bit about the artist you have displayed," I say, pointing to the paintings.

"Oh yes, aren't those lovely? I have to tell you that I'm selling the entire collection as one, no singles. They're too beautiful to separate."

"I have to agree. Who's the artist? A local?"

"Yes and no. An anonymous donor from the Bay area in San Francisco shipped the collection here. Claims she once lived on the island. Said she was born and raised here, but she didn't give me her name. She just goes by her initials on all her paintings."

"How intriguing. These are absolutely breathtaking," I say as I scan each painting closely. "It's too bad people can't tell her what wonderful work she's done."

"I tried to track her through the courier she used, but she covered her tracks. She made it quite clear that she doesn't want to be found. Very bizarre, if you ask me, but it's an artist's right and I appreciate her art and her decision."

Because of the anonymity of the artist, the shop owner assumes that I'm not interested, but this intrigues me even more. "How much for the set?"

"Oh goodness," says the shop owner. "When I tell most people that I know nothing about the artist, they turn away. You're the first to show such interest, and for that I'll give you a fair price."

I have to say, I think she more than gave me a deal. I'll give the largest and most exquisite piece to my parents. Between their NYC penthouse and the Hamptons house, this piece would suit either. I make arrangements to have it shipped to them, but as for mine, I ask, "Would you mind holding on to these until I leave the island? I'll pay for them now, I'm just not quite sure when I'll be returning to New York."

"Of course, I'd be more than happy to keep them here."

I also buy a painting for Mindy—not the same artist, but something I think will suit her workspace perfectly. After all, she did say to bring back a bit of sunshine.

I turn one last time to wave goodbye to the lovely shop owner. Nani is coming up the front steps of the shop as I open the door to exit. I can tell that something is bothering her. "You won't believe this," she says.

As I'm about to ask her what's happened, I can feel my phone vibrating in my bag. I open it and it's Stan. I need to take it, so I excuse myself.

"Where the hell have you been?" he yells. "I've tried to call you a half-dozen times."

"Sorry, I must have been out of cell range."

"Out of cell range! What am I paying you for? Where are you?"

"You know where I am, Stan—what's up?"

"The sale of the Coco Palms has come to a halt. I just got word that the owner has decided to delay the cut-off date."

"What?" I ask. "How did you hear about this? Why? When?"

"Don't know all the details. Appears there's been a drowning in the family."

Holy shit! I can feel my eyes widen and every hair on my body standing at attention. I avert my eyes to Nani, who obviously got the news while I was in the shop.

Stan is still yelling through the receiver. "Call the Baker brothers, they need to know. I've had trouble contacting them."

"They could be in flight. They were going to Oʻahu today."

"I don't care, find them!"

I know it's not polite to secretly swear at your boss, but my brain is spewing out curse word after curse word. If only I could tell him I quit. Do I really need this crazy stress? Yes, I do, unfortunately; I have bills. I swear that when I get back, I'm looking for a new job. Note to self!

I hang up. Nani and I look at one another. "Now what?" I ask.

"We wait. Kanoa said they found someone floating facedown by the ocean's edge. An early-morning jogger found the body. They haven't released more details."

"Do I dare ask where?"

"Guess," Nani says, with the same eyeroll as when we were discussing Reverend Lydgate earlier.

"Oh, come on."

"Afraid so."

"This is really *lōlō*!"

Nani nods. "Not much we can do about it. Come on, let's keep going. We can't let it get us down."

"Nani, I'm petrified, and being thousands of miles away from home is getting to me."

"Listen, why don't you come stay with me? Before you say no, think about it. Tonight you will be my guest for dinner. Decide then."

My brain has stopped computing. I just want to run back into the shop, grab my paintings, and head for the first flight home.

"Abby! Did you hear me?"

"Yeah," I mutter, but I'm not sure what I'm agreeing to.

For the next hour we enter every shop on the strip. By the time we finish, my arms are full of bags harboring everything from t-shirts to spices and all sorts of lovely scented soaps. I need to bring this floral scent home with me.

"I'm exhausted," Nani says as we place all the bags in her Jeep.

"Let me buy you lunch," I say. "Let's go somewhere where we can kick back and soak up the sun."

"Got just the place, but I'll sit in a shaded area, if you don't mind. Too much sun isn't good for your skin—you know that, right?"

I have to laugh. "No worries," I tell her, as I pull out some SPF 50 face protector and start applying it. "By the way, how'd Kanoa take the news?"

"He's pretty bummed, but not as much as you. He feels bad for the person that died, but elated that Kelly Corp. is railroaded, yet again."

After about fifteen minutes of driving we arrive at this place called Lawa'i, in the southern part of the island. Nani pulls up along the street and parks her Jeep. We walk over to a restaurant called The Beach House. The scenery is exquisite. Nani says, "This place is first class. Wait until you taste the food. Just go light on the Mai Tais; they're quite potent. Since I'm driving, I'll stick to virgin Mai Tais."

We have the choice of being seated indoors or out, and we choose to sit outdoors, which looks out onto the ocean. The view is of the never-ending ocean and horizon—absolutely spectacular.

"You should get Kanoa to take you here for dinner," Nani says. "The sunsets are breathtaking. You'll see people start to gather every night along the stone wall and the street."

"Thanks for the tip, but I'm not sure Kanoa would be my choice of a dinner companion. You can't have a relationship with me for two years and think you can just abandon me."

"Listen, I get what he did was horrible—and believe you me, I've told him as much—but can you really go home and not have hashed things out with him? How will you ever be able to move on if you don't get closure? I'm not asking you to go back out with him, but do it for you. I'm a woman, and you can't tell me that you don't have a million questions that you need answered."

"You're right, but will I get honest answers to my questions?"

"I believe you will. Kanoa may have made one of the dumbest mistakes of his life, but a liar he isn't."

My Mai Tai arrives just in time. Somehow it's easier to talk about someone who's just died than face conversation about Kanoa. I know that Nani means well—and she is right. I do want to face him at some point. I'm just not sure what the right timing is.

By my third Mai Tai I'm feeling nothing but relaxed. The ocean waves crashing up against the rocks have me in Zen mode. I love sitting back and watching people swimming and having fun—it's just what Nani and I needed today.

"I'm so glad you brought me here, *mahalo*. I almost wish I were staying at that hotel and waking up to this," I say, pointing towards an oceanfront complex.

"If you have any more drinks you may be staying there," laughs Nani.

"I'm good, no worries here."

Nani whispers under her breath, "Yeah, that's what they all say."

195

We sit and chat for another hour or so, and then Nani informs me she needs to get home. "*Mahalo* for lunch," she says. "It's been such a fun day."

"It's the least I can do, and I had a fabulous time, minus the death and my vomiting," I say as I try to stand.

"Yeah, just as I thought. Will we need to go over the rolling down of the window and barf bag again? You know where to aim, right?"

"Oh my God. My head is spinning."

"Come on," Nani says as she takes my arm and intertwines it with hers. She guides me over to her Jeep and buckles me in. "Would you like your head up, or shall I slant the seat back?"

"Maybe staying upright would be better." Nani hands me a cold bottle of water. "Where'd you get this?"

"Around these parts, we have one another's back," she laughs. "The waiter handed it to me."

CHAPTER TWENTY-TWO

Hearing a loud bang, my body instantly bolts upright in the car seat, causing my eyes to open wide. I get a sudden whiff of something sweet.

"Oh, hi sleepyhead," Nani chuckles. "Have a good nap?"

"Please tell me I haven't been sleeping the entire time?"

"Afraid so—I even did my groceries. Sorry, but I had to leave you in the car. I know what you must be thinking, but no worries, I knew you'd be safe; plus I parked in the shade with the windows down."

"What must you think of me? I'm not usually such a trainwreck. I'm so sorry. I've been a bit of a mess ever since I saw Kanoa again. By the way, where are we?"

"First of all, I don't judge—well, I try not to—and secondly, we are back in Kapaʻa. This is my home."

I unbuckle my seatbelt and look around. "That smell, what is it?"

"Pineapples. Why don't you go take a walk around the field? Give me ten minutes to bring these bags in and start supper, and then I'll come join you. I guarantee you'll love it down there. And by the way, welcome to my *hale*."

"Thanks for having me. Is this land all yours? Oh my, look at that mountain range."

"All mine, thanks to my parents. They passed the land down to me. At one time, this was my great-grandfather's sugar plantation. If you look over there"—she points—"you'll see approximately ten acres of sugarcane that my husband harvests. That mountain range straight ahead is better known as the Sleeping Giant. If you look closely at its formation you can make out the Giant's head and you will see his body dips in at the waist and continues. He looks like he's sleeping."

"Yes! I see it. That is spectacular. Wow, Nani, this is breathtaking. You mentioned husband? I didn't know you were married." All this time I assumed there could be something between her and Kanoa. Not that I should care in the least, but I'm sort of relieved Nani is married.

"I'm married, all right. My inlaws live in Hanapēpē. After all the excitement today at the canyon and the death notice, my personal life seemed too boring to mention. My husband's ancestors come from a long lineage of sugarcane plantation owners. Unfortunately, they sold the land back in the fifties. That's what happened to most Hawaiians."

"What do you mean?"

"Foreigners started coming in and making land deals. Let's just say the deals didn't really benefit native Hawaiians. If you stick around long enough, you'll see what I'm referring to. You'll get a wider perspective on the importance of the Coco Palms—but we don't want to talk about that property anymore today, right? Personally, I'm glad my husband's passion for harvesting has never left him. He decided to give up his desk job after a year into it. He's now able to keep the tradition going for the next generation."

"That's really great. So, you don't mind if I take a walk around the grounds? I've never seen anything like this. It's so lush. Let's be honest, I don't actually know what a sugarcane plantation looks like."

"By all means, please, go ahead," she says as she starts to unload the grocery bags.

"Sorry, that was so stupid of me. The least I can do is help with the bags."

"No! I insist. Now go."

I start to make my way down to the fields, which smell delectable. I'm starting to understand why Kanoa couldn't handle the smells on the streets of NY. I have to admit, he was quite a trooper coming from this. I'm not sure I'd have been so tolerant. It makes me realize that being born and raised in NY, I know nothing besides the sounds of sirens and overpopulated chatter, and the smells, which aren't always that appealing. No wonder my parents escaped in the summer. The Hamptons were my parents' survival, as they liked to call it. I can feel my lungs come alive now, the same way I used to all those summers in the Hamptons, minus the pineapples.

I stop in my tracks as I look towards the Sleeping Giant. As I've gotten closer I can makeout the forehead and chin. The mountain range has a soothing aura about it, definitely not what I've been experiencing with these so-called apparitions. I want to curl up on the lush green range and have a nap myself, it's so inviting.

It's amazing what a couple extra weeks on the island has done for my paranoia. If I stop and think about it, of course I'm still fearful about being so far away from the mainland, but it's not at the forefront of my thinking any longer. I feel free out here. I find myself daydreaming of what life could have been like had I met Kanoa here in Kaua'i. Maybe I'd have been more carefree. We could have had a beautiful place like Nani. I suddenly realize how dangerous my thinking pattern is becoming. I tell myself to stop it. As I walk on, with every few steps a waft of sweet-smelling air brushes up against my cheek. I'm enveloped by the sweet aroma of ripening pineapples. After maybe half an hour, I finally reach the pineapple field. I can't believe my eyes. "Holy shit!" I say out loud. "I had no idea pineapples grew this way."

"Where did you think they grew?" a male voice says from behind me, and I turn quickly and see Kanoa standing there. How did I not hear his footsteps? I'm left gasping for air and holding onto my upper chest with both hands. It takes me a few seconds to shake myself out of my startled state. "Shit, Noah ... Kanoa ... you just about gave me a heart attack. You need to stop sneaking up on me."

"Sorry. It wasn't intentional. I thought you heard me coming. I did call your name. I assumed you were ignoring me."

"I was deep in thought."

"I know that now—sorry."

As much as I want to snub him, I can't.

"What do you think?" he asks.

"About?"

"The pineapples. I heard you say that you didn't think this is how they grew."

I start to giggle from embarrassment and lack of knowledge. "Give a city gal a break."

Kanoa starts to laugh along with me. "You thought they grew on trees like coconuts and bananas, didn't you?"

"Don't be a smarty pants."

"I'm not. It's what a lot of people think."

"Okay, guilty as charged. I thought there was such a thing as pineapple trees. You'd think at some point in my life I'd have seen photos, but it's just another thing I take for granted. I have to admit I'm learning a few things out here. Okay—don't judge me—but why are they golden colored? I always thought they were greenish-yellow."

"Golden means they're ripe and ready for picking. The green you're familiar with is for exporting purposes. Pineapples are picked before they're ripe, and shipped out. They will ripen a bit more before reaching their destination, similar to bananas. It gives them a longer shelf life. Here they are fully sun-ripened on the plant and ready to eat. It makes them that much sweeter. Have you tried one?"

"No."

"What? You've been here a month. How is that possible?"

I can't believe Kanoa and I are having a conversation, let alone one over something as silly as pineapples. Who the hell are we? It's actually nice not to be bickering for a split second, but I don't want to start sliding down a rabbit hole. Also, it's hard not to notice what a gorgeous specimen of a man he is. I find myself watching as he cuts open a pineapple with his Swiss Army knife; I didn't know he carried one. For a moment I see the same sweet guy who offered me that first sip of water on the night we met. Without my anger bubbling over and blinding me, I can see the Noah I fell in love with. As I watch him, I remark, "I remember you cringing every time I suggested we buy a pineapple. Makes sense now why you had them juice it for us."

"Wait until you taste this," he says as he cuts a piece off. "You tell me if it has the same flavor."

As he gets up and comes towards me, I catch the scent of his cologne. He's still wearing the one I bought him.

Is this just a guy thing to do, wear your old girlfriend's gift so as not to waste? Or did he wear it as a reminder of me? Dangerous thinking, Abby! I need to switch gears.

Before I can have another neurotic thought, I feel a juicy piece of pineapple against my lips. The juice is dripping down my chin as I bite down on it. I can feel my heart fluttering with Kanoa standing so close to me. He needs to back up. Being the consummate gentleman, Kanoa wipes my chin with the back of his hand. The scent of the sweet pineapple mixed in with his cologne has my knees quivering. I feel like a fawn trying to stand for the first time away from its mother. But I know I have to run. I need to move away. For a split second we gaze into each other's eyes, and just as quickly we both step back a few inches as if we've been zapped by a taser.

With my knees still weak, I can hear voices coming our way—it's Nani. She is yelling at someone and it's not long before that someone is standing right in front of us.

"Aloha, Uncle K," says a wee little toddler. Kanoa bends down to pick her up. He kisses the tiny tot on the cheek.

"Well, if it isn't my favorite girl."

"Uncle K, is this your girlfriend?"

"Kai!" interrupts Nani.

Kai looks startled. I try to put the little one at ease by asking, "You want to know something?"

"Yes. Tell me," answers Kai.

"Say please," commands Nani, as she tries to catch up with Kai.

"E'olu'olu," Kai replies.

Nani and Kanoa both try not to laugh, but Kai is way too adorable. Nani wasn't expecting Kai to say please in Hawaiian.

I say to Kai, "Not too many people know this about me, but my middle name is Ky. You see, when I was born, my mother wanted to name me Kylie, but my father preferred Ky. They decided that my second name should be Ky. I believe mine is spelled differently than yours."

Kai's eyes are filled with enthusiasm, the same look a child has upon seeing cotton candy for the first time. Still in Kanoa's arms, she's flailing her own arms with excitement.

"Did you hear that, Uncle K? Your *wāhine* has the same name as me. She sure is beautiful, Uncle K. Don't you think?"

I can feel the blood rushing through my veins faster than usual. Somehow, I don't get the feeling that Kanoa feels as uncomfortable as I do, but Nani apparently does. She steps in: "Okay, Kai, come with me."

Kai won't have it. She latches on to Kanoa's neck for dear life.

Kanoa waves Nani away. "That's okay. I think we should all go back to the *hale*. I was just getting some pineapple for Abby to try. She's never seen our golden pineapples."

Kai giggles in his arms. "You're funny, Uncle K." Then she looks at me and asks, "Do you know what Kai means?"

"No, I haven't a clue. Do you?"

With a bit of a lisp, Kai replies, "It means ocean. My mommy said she named me Kai because I am from the ocean. Right, Mommy?"

"That's right, baby."

Nani winks at me and whispers, "Let's just say she was conceived on a romantic evening by the ocean."

I laugh. "She's a doll, Nani."

"Well, if you like this doll, come on up to the *hale*, because I have more."

I look over at Kanoa for confirmation as we all head back up the hill to the *hale*. He laughs, "This is why I could never ask her out. The *wāhine* has been having babies all her adult life."

Even though Kai probably has no idea what we're talking about, she joins us in laughter. Her giggles are definitely contagious.

"Just how many children do you have?" I ask Nani.

"I have three brothers," responds Kai.

I stand with my jaw open. Again, I look at Kanoa for affirmation.

"It's all true," he says. "You know I don't poke fun about serious matters."

"Uncle K, are you and Abby going to have babies?"

Nani leaps as fast as a cheetah upon hearing Kai's question. She takes hold of Kai and pulls her away from Kanoa's arms.

"If you two will excuse us, I have something in the oven," Nani says as she sprints away with Kai. We can hear her telling Kai not to ask so many questions, but Kai just keeps on asking. I can't remember when I've laughed so hard, especially in Kanoa's presence.

"In case you didn't know," he says, "*wāhine* means girl or woman. Some people like to call their significant other *wāhine*."

"Is my ignorance that apparent?"

"No. Actually, yes," laughs Kanoa. "You still scrunch your nose when you haven't fully comprehended something."

I'm not sure if I want to laugh or cry at such a sentimental gesture. I'm afraid I'll have to tell Nani I can't stay for dinner. Sitting at the same table as Kanoa may not be such a smart idea.

"Listen Abby, if it makes you uncomfortable, I'll make an excuse about dinner. I'll just grab what I came to get and be gone."

Great, he beat me to the punch. Now I'm just going to sound like a whiny baby if I agree that he leave. I catch myself responding, "We're adults, we should be able to act like two civilized human beings for a few hours," but I tell my logical side not to let down its guard.

"I hope in time you'll forgive me for the way I left," he says, staring me directly in the eyes, like a man that means what he's saying and knows the pain he has caused. "It never had anything to do with how I felt about you—please believe that much."

"Uncle K, are you coming in?" yells a well-timed Kai from inside. "Don't forget to bring your *wāhine* with you."

Who am I to ruin a little tot's supper? I graciously say nothing and proceed to go inside, but not before Kanoa adds one last thing as he reaches for my hand. "I should go. I don't ..."

The touch of his hand sends tingling sensations throughout my body. I hate that he still has such an effect on me. Part of me wishes he felt the same. I want him to be aching for something he can no longer have. Hiding my inner pain, I say, "We both stay, or Kai will be disappointed. As for the Coco Palms, I think we both know where we stand, right?"

"Right."

And just like that, we and our unresolved issues are thrust into an amicable dinner.

CHAPTER TWENTY-THREE

I tell myself that I can't go another day without telling Mike the truth about why I'm in Kaua'i. The Baker Brothers won't be back until later in the day, so I have plenty of time set aside to see Mike, no more excuses. I need to be upfront. As much as I try not to get emotionally attached, Mike is just one of those people— I can't help but have feelings for him. He seems like a grandfather figure to me.

Our coffee time together will be a bit different today. Mike has invited me over to his *hale*. I pull onto Mike's street, where he's waiting for me at the end of his property. He steadies himself with his cane while he waves.

"Good morning, sweet Abby."

I quickly get out of the car before he needs to take another step. I run to give him a hug. "Morning, Mike. This is a lovely area. You really aren't far from the Coco Palms."

"And yet, I haven't been there in years." He leads me out to the *lānai*, where he's laid out a scrumptious breakfast.

"Oh my goodness, Mike. You shouldn't have gone to all this trouble."

"My dear, it's my honor. Please, sit."

"Before I do, I have something I need to tell you."

"Abby, if it's about the Coco Palms property and your job, I already know," says Mike with a genuinely loving smile on his face. "Don't fret. As I told you from day one, sweet Abby, the man above, he sees everything. You are my friend, as I believe I am yours. I have the utmost faith in my friends."

I feel my eyes stinging. How can this gentle old man have so much kindness in his heart for me? "Mike, I consider you my friend also, but friends don't lie to one another. I should have been honest with you."

"Then let's consider it a delayed truth and not speak of it again. Don't put such a heavy burden on your heart. Why don't you sit and enjoy this lovely food? If you'd like, I'll tell you a bit of what life was like at the Coco Palms. Remember, it's good company that brings us peace in life, and I believe that's what you and I are, good company," smiles Mike.

And without another word we both help ourselves to the buffet Mike has put out. There's an assortment of fresh tropical fruit and juices, pancakes with coconut-flavoured syrup one of my favorites, *loco moco*. I look up at Mike as he makes himself a plate and realize I don't have anywhere near the level of inner peace that he does. It's not anything he's said, but rather, my own feelings about my job and the land. I bet every wrinkle on his face represents memories that I am here to take away. As Mike places a hot cup of coffee in front of me, he says, "Went to the coffee plantation first thing this morning for some fresh-ground coffee."

"It smells lovely, *mahalo*."

"Relax and enjoy. Now, let me ask you, what would you like to know about the Coco Palms?"

"Oh my gosh, that's a loaded question. How about you tell me about one of your most memorable nights there."

Mike sits back, sips his coffee, and begins to tell me about the first time Elvis set foot on the property.

"Genie had invited me to a private *lū'au* that was being held in honor of Elvis. By this point Genie and I were thick as thieves. We considered ourselves to be the best of friends and shared our innermost secrets with one another. One of the biggest secrets she kept from her then-boyfriend and owner of the Coco Palms, Gerry, was the fact that she'd befriended a ghost. Don't get me wrong; at first, I thought maybe she was a bit off her rocker. But that night, I had the privilege of witnessing this ghost, which I'll get to later."

"Please tell me you're talking about Queen Deborah?"

"Yes."

"I may be as crazy as your friend Genie, but I do believe we've spoken."

Mike doesn't flinch at my admission. "Don't be afraid. She means well, but we'll talk about her a little later. Anyhow, Genie knew I'd been seeing someone, and she told me I could bring her to the *lūʻau*. I helped Genie with preparations for Elvis's arrival. I was in charge of making sure that the grounds were well secured. We didn't want fans crashing the *lūʻau* and putting Elvis's life at risk. The girls were just wild about Elvis. We had to get the police force and other security volunteers from the other islands during his stay."

"Did the resort guests know that Elvis was going to be staying there for the purposes of filming?"

"No, not at first. We were trying to keep it as private as possible, but it didn't take long for word to spread. Elvis also arrived with his own team of security men. The hotel guests weren't invited to the *lūʻau*. The guest list was limited to Elvis's entourage and a handful of staff members from the resort."

"Was Priscilla with him?"

"No. She vacationed the following year and a few other times, until she stopped coming. Let's just say for now that it was the beginning of the end."

"Oh my, sounds intriguing."

"Heartbreaking, really," says Mike.

He continues, "Anyhow, that night the champagne was flowing, and guests were dressed to the nines. Women were wearing gowns and long gloves, true to the sixties *haute couture*, but native Hawaiian women were wearing lovely sarongs and traditional *muʻumuʻus*. Every guest had fresh flower *leis* around their neck.

"Our hula dancers were spread out throughout the grounds giving dancing lessons, while tiki torches burned bright, illuminating the sky. The double-hulled canoes were out transporting guests up and down the lagoon, but the best was the moment of Elvis's entrance. At the stroke of ten PM, there he was, larger than life, standing on a double-hulled canoe in a bright blue shirt imprinted with white hibiscus flowers. The women tried to be discreet, but the shrills of excitement were echoing across the lagoon. I'm a man and I felt elated seeing him. He really was a rare specimen. Everyone loved Elvis. Sitting behind him on the canoe were our local band, The Hawaiian Beach Boys. They played while Elvis sang a mix of songs, but he started off with Hawaiian Sunset, followed by Can't Help Falling in Love, and ending it with Return to Sender."

"That is so surreal! My God, I wish my grandmother were here listening to you. She'd be tickled pink," I say, knowing how much she adored Elvis.

"She'd have loved his performance during the *lū'au*. It was impromptu. Genie had no idea that he was going to keep performing throughout the night. That's just the kind of warm person he was. I found him to be a very humble gentleman. It's not as if he was doing it to attract the attention of all the women. He struck me as being shy, not someone that was on the hunt for attention—it came naturally. I truly believe Elvis just wanted to sing, that's what made him happy."

"How was Genie throughout all of it?"

"Genie was a real trooper," laughs Mike. "I'm not sure who was more infatuated, her or Queen Deborah. This was the night that I finally came to believe Deborah existed. As Genie was thanking Elvis up at the podium and welcoming him to the Coco Palms, I could see her looking a bit frazzled. While she spoke, she kept looking off to the side. Maybe it wasn't apparent to most, but I knew her well. I excused myself from my date and got closer to where Genie could see me. When we made eye contact, I noticed she shifted her eyes to the left. For a split second, I could make out a faint silhouette of an old woman, but she disappeared from my sight in a flash."

"So, you think that was Queen Deborah?"

"I didn't at that moment, but once Genie came down from the podium, she told me that Deborah kept pestering her to ask Elvis to sing Are You Lonesome Tonight."

Both Mike and I crack up laughing. Mike's storytelling is so vivid, I feel as if I were there.

"Did you ever see her again after that?"

"I have sporadically. I know her spirit lives at the Coco Palms. Genie mentioned to me in confidence that Deborah wants her land back."

I can feel the hair standing up on my arms. What the hell am I mixed up in? I wish I had more time, but I need to get to my meeting with Ken and Charles.

"I'm sorry that I have to leave," I tell Mike. "Can we continue this story at a later date?"

"Of course, dear. You run. It's been a pleasure having you over. Please, feel free to drop in anytime."

"*Mahalo* for such a spectacular spread. It was all so delicious. I know where to come to get the best *loco moco*. I definitely won't be eating lunch today."

Half an hour later, as I'm about to step into Ken and Charles' office, I get a call that the bidding for the Coco

Palms is back on and bids are to be submitted by week's end.

"Gentlemen," I say as I step into the Bakers' office. "I have great news."

"We know," Ken quickly replies.

"Well, you always seem to know everything before any of us. How is this possible?"

Charles interrupts by pulling out a chair for me to sit in order to stop me from asking any more questions. These two are up to something, but what? I try to put these concerns in the back of my mind and drive on with my job. "I take it you know our timeline?"

"Listen," Charles says. "Let's not waste any more time. We are going back in with the exact same bid and not a penny more."

"Why? You know how I feel about it, and as your legal advisor, I believe you really should put forward a more solid bid."

"Waste of money," adds Ken.

"It's not a waste of money if you get what you want in the end. Paying me and not listening to my legal advice is the waste of money." For once they have nothing to say, but I can tell these two are not going to budge. "I'll get all the paperwork ready, and how about we meet here first thing Monday morning?"

"Just get the papers ready," Charles says. "You know the drill. Wednesday morning will suffice. We'll sign them, submit it and be done."

"We have to week's end, but it's your call."

Their silence speaks volumes, and Wednesday it will be. I leave their office and tell myself that they won't ruin my day. Instead, I place a call to Kanoa.

"Hi. I know I'm the last person you expect to hear from, but I'm wondering if you'd like to get together. I think we need to talk."

CHAPTER TWENTY-FOUR:
Genie (1969)

Queen Deborah spends most of her days reading. I bring her the daily newspapers and make sure to supply her with novels—pretty much any form of publication I can get my hands on. Deborah is probably one of the best-read ghosts, which is why I can't hide much from her.

As I walk in with her usual mid-morning snack and beverage, she asks, "So, why haven't you kicked me out yet?"

"What are you referring to?"

"Don't play coy with me. I know that Elvis is arriving today. Why must we play this game on all his visits?"

After all these years, I still can't help shaking my head at some of the things that come out of her mouth. I'm trying hard to set the tray down without spilling the juice. Deborah is relentless.

"Well?"

"Maybe I was trying to surprise you at the last minute," I say, knowing full well she's not going to buy my lame excuse.

And right on cue she says, "Rubbish! You don't have anywhere to put me. We are down to you wanting this room again. What's wrong with the cottage?"

"Well …"

"Well, what?"

"You see …"

"No, I don't see. I thought you put Elvis in the cottage when he's with Priscilla?"

"Just come stay with me, please. Don't make my life more difficult than it has to be."

"Tell me why?"

"I don't know. It's what he requested. Do you really expect me to intrude on his privacy? Never mind—of course you do."

"Oh!" says Deborah with the utmost defiance in her voice as she sashays across the room. "You think you know me so well."

"Yes."

"Then you should know that I'm not budging."

"Come on, Deborah. What have I ever done to you except be your friend and—"

"Yes, yes, I know. I just don't want to share your room. You know how I feel about Gerry."

I can't help but roll my eyes and take a deep breath. "Oh, for the love of God. Gerry is not going to come to my room while you are there."

"Well, how do I know that?"

"Because I'm telling you, and I think you know I have a bit more class than that."

"You're right. Class you have, but Gerry?"

I find myself walking over to the open window. Maybe a deep breath of floral air will calm me down. "Gerry has changed, and you know it."

"If you say so."

"I do, and I think you are jealous. I believe you are afraid that you'll lose me when Gerry and I marry." She'll never agree to stay with me now. So much for staying calm.

"Oh my!" she says. "Aren't we full of pepper today?"

"It's the truth, isn't it?"

"Why haven't you hooked up with Mike instead? What's wrong with you?"

"Mike is my friend and you know that. What's gotten into you today?"

Great, here comes the inevitable pout. "Nothing! I just think Mike is a good catch."

"You'd give your right eye for Mike and me, wouldn't you?"

"I'd give something."

"Then give me the okay and stay with me."

Deborah looks at me the way a mother looks at her child when she already knows the truth, but wants to drag it out of them anyway. Deborah is once again standing right in front of me and staring directly into my face. "Admit to me that you like Mike as more than a friend."

My head is about to explode. I swear if she wasn't already dead, I might kill her. Just a figure of speech, but she does try my patience. "Okay, fine, yes, if it were better timing, I'd say that Mike and I would make a pretty good couple. There. Are you happy?"

"Yes. And yes, I will come stay with you. I can't wait to see Elvis again. Did I tell you about the last time he was here?"

"Only about a hundred times. But please, feel free to refresh my memory."

"I know when someone is being sarcastic with me. That's fine, Genie. Have it your way."

"Oh, come on. You spew insults at me all the time. Why am I supposed to take it?" Never mind breathing fresh air from the open window—I'm about to jump out of it instead.

"They're not insults. I gave you a compliment. I said you're too good for Gerry. How is that an insult?"

"You undermine my intelligence."

"Fine!" she says. "Have it your way. I will not speak Gerry's name again."

"Hallelujah! Now I need you to drink up and eat your snack. We need to get you to my room."

"I'm not going," she says, staring off to the side, and now I'm looking at her as if she's a child who's dug her heels into the ground and won't budge no matter what.

"Why?" I ask. "I thought we were on good terms. What happened in the last second?"

"I want to see Elvis."

"For the love of God, Deborah, why must you be so difficult—and don't answer that. I will somehow get you to see him again. I was planning a surprise for you, but if I tell you, what kind of surprise will it be?"

"No surprises. Tell me."

This time I don't hide the fact that I'm rolling my eyes. I move closer to where Deborah is sitting and look her in the eyes so she'll know I'm not bullshitting her. "I've asked Colonel Parker if Elvis wouldn't mind performing a few songs down at the lagoon for you. Let me see, how does your birthday sound?"

"No! You didn't?"

"I have. Elvis won't know it, but he will be singing to you, so put your request in now."

"Oh, I think Elvis will know he's singing to me, don't you worry."

"I worry every time you tell me not to worry—and why must you ruin every surprise?"

"Genie, nothing has been ruined," she says, "you've made my day. No one has ever done anything remotely this nice for me. Let me give you a hug."

As we try to hug it out, Deborah keeps slithering around. I laugh. "Maybe hugging isn't such a good idea. I'll just take your word for it. I must get back to work. Remember, you are not allowed back in here. Got it?"

"Not even for a wee peek?"

"No!" I say. "That's exactly what I don't want. We don't need a repeat performance."

"But Elvis's bed is so comfy. In actuality, it is my bed."

"Deborah?" I say. I'm holding on to my stomach for fear of throwing up. The woman is literally causing me physical pain.

"Oh … all right."

"I mean it, Deborah. No lying next to him in the middle of the night. No surprise visits when he's changing."

"You take the fun out of being a ghost. And by the way, I don't take kindly to you making me out to be some sort of Peeping Tom."

"But that's how you behave."

"I just wanted to know what it was like to be in bed with Elvis. It's not as if he was naked."

"You still did something very unethical!"

"Oh please, have you forgotten my age? Not to mention I'm dead," Deborah says under her breath. "By the way, why hasn't someone thought of a female name yet? Peeping Tom. That's so ridiculous for a female."

"I know what you're doing. Changing the subject won't help your cause."

Deborah ignores everything else I have to say. She sits quietly and eats her snack like a child who is ready for mischief. The minute I walk out the door I know she is going to do whatever she damn well pleases. When has anyone stopped Deborah? And in classic Deborah style, she has one more thing to say. "You know there's been gossip about Elvis and Priscilla's marriage? Something tells me they may be coming for some damage control."

"I wasn't aware," I say. "How do you know?"

"Trust me. I know him better than you think."

"What are you referring to?"

"Let's just say that he may believe in ghosts."

"Deborah? You promised me you'd never make yourself visible."

"Did I say anything along those lines?"

I have to leave before my head explodes. Knowing Deborah, she is probably organizing a midnight rendezvous with Elvis. Sometimes ignorance is truly blissful.

CHAPTER TWENTY-FIVE:

Abby

With final bids in, I set up a time to call Kanoa. I want to see him before news comes back about the winning bid. I need us to be unbiased when we have the unavoidable discussion, which we've both been pros at avoiding.

Stan isn't always predictable. On our last conversation he informed me that I'd have forty-eight hours' notice as to my return to New York. I'm running out of time to try and put my mind at ease with Kanoa. I'd be an absolute liar if I said I wasn't feeling pangs of heartache, knowing I'll no longer see him. It wasn't supposed to be this way. No matter how hurt and angry I've been in the past, I know it's also a blessing that I found him—but I do need some form of closure.

Kanoa agrees to meet me at my hotel. At first I'm reluctant, until he suggests picking me up at ten-thirty AM for a little sightseeing. How could I say no to that?

I can barely sleep, thinking about seeing Kanoa outside the context of a work-related meeting. The only personal time we've had was dinner at Nani's house. In the morning I go for a workout. I've been trying desperately not to revive the butterflies that have been dormant in the pit of my stomach, but they are fluttering now regardless. After my workout I go for a swim.

Upon returning to my room I feel a presence, and not a welcoming one. I instinctively leave the door open in order to look around. Nothing seems to be out of place, but the eeriness is palpable. I am staring fear in the face, only I can't see anything. As I make a move to put my gym bag down in order to hold the door open, I see a sudden sweeping of the sheer curtains. Something has caused them to move. Whatever it is—is coming my way. I have two choices: run like hell or confront it. The latter seems to be the wisest, but before I get a word out, I feel something on my shoulder, which has me shrieking in terror.

"Abby! Are you okay?" Kanoa asks, grabbing my shoulders and looking into my face.

"I could have sworn someone was in the room," I reply with labored breathing.

"Stay here, I'll go look around," Kanoa offers as he lets go of my shoulder.

"Wait! I'm coming with you."

I walk quickly to catch up with him, taking two seconds to turn back around and shut the door, and that's when a deep male voice says, "Count yourself lucky this time."

I come to several moments later, staring up at Kanoa. I ask, "What happened?"

"I'm not sure. You tell me."

"Help me up. I think I'm okay."

"You just fainted," he says. "Obviously you're not okay."

"You'll just think I'm crazy."

"Try me."

"It's the same guy that threw me off the paddle board. I know it."

"Really?"

I know that tone all too well; he doubts me.

"See?" I say. "What was the point? You don't believe me."

"Let's just say I believe what I see with my own eyes, but obviously something has frightened you enough to cause you to faint. Whatever it is, it's not good."

"Thank you, Sherlock." I need to stop being so sarcastic, but he's frustrating the shit out of me at this moment. He's from these parts, why the hell can't he believe me? "Tell me about it. I'm a nervous wreck. I know how crazy it must sound, because it's still crazy to me, but you have to believe me."

"I believe every word you say. I know you don't make things up. If it's any consolation, I believe in good spirits, just not ghosts."

"Oh, for the love of God, it's the same thing. And if you're hoping to catch the essence of him, you won't because he's gone. This one is not a good spirit."

Kanoa is still holding my head up. I start to move and feel a bit lightheaded. He takes my hand and leads me to the sofa. "Please, try to rest for a few minutes. There's no rush—let's make sure you're okay. Maybe I should call a doctor to look you over?"

"You're being silly. I'm fine. Come on, it's not every day that a ghost tries to kill me," I say to lighten the mood. "Really, I'll be fine. Let's get on with the day."

"Okay, but you are taking it easy. Plus, since you extended the olive branch, I went ahead and prepared a little surprise for you. Let's call it a delayed welcoming and the start of many things to make up for. It's about time I properly show you my aloha spirit." We both laugh at the word *spirit*. "Bad choice of wording. If you're ready, let's get out of here."

"Can you give me five minutes? I was about to hop in the shower."

"Take your time, I'll be right out here," Kanoa says as he makes his way out onto the balcony.

"Help yourself to room service if you'd like."

I walk towards the bathroom, but I'm no fool. As much as I think my male ghost is gone, I stop in my tracks to make sure I can't feel his presence. I turn the shower on and let it run with the glass door open. He may be a bigger trickster than I give him credit for. I don't want to be enclosed in the shower when he tries to kill me.

I've never taken such a fast shower in my life. I take a towel and wrap it around my wet hair. As I throw my head back, I see someone in the mirror. "Jesus! Are you trying to give me a heart attack today? What are you doing in here?"

"I just wanted to make sure you were okay, that's all," Kanoa says as he stares at me—and why wouldn't he? I'm standing in his monogrammed towel.

As I'm about to ask him to leave, he asks, "Are those our towels from New York?"

Fuck! How was I to know he'd be in my bathroom? No matter what I say, it'll be a neurotic answer. He knows how much I loved our matching towels. He comes towards me.

"You're wearing my towel," he says as he takes a closer look.

I'm not sure if the temperature has suddenly risen, but I'm dying of heat. He reaches his hand out towards the towel. What the hell is he doing? He wouldn't dare, would he? We aren't exactly … he puts his hand on the towel. "It is mine," he says as he gives it a playful tug.

"You wouldn't dare!"

"Really?"

"Don't …"

"Come on, I'm just teasing you," he says as he turns away. "Just a little joke to lighten the mood."

Kanoa disappears into the other room, leaving me panting with desire. Bastard, I tell myself. I'm sure he's out there right now, laughing at me and my damn stupid towel. I quickly towel-dry my hair, throw on some clothes, and out I go. This time it's Kanoa who doesn't hear me. I find him standing on the balcony, staring pensively out at the ocean.

"Have you finally stopped laughing at me?" I ask.

"I'm sorry, Abby," he says, no longer in a joking manner. "That was insensitive of me. I didn't know how to react. It was a bad, thoughtless gesture. Believe it or not, I take our situation more seriously than I did back there. The sight of you in that towel brings back a lot of great memories. I truly wish things could have played out differently."

"Well they didn't," I say in a tone that's harsher than I intended. It's clear that neither Kanoa nor I are good at these talks. It's time to drive on and ignore what's just happened. I ask where we're going, but he insists on it being a surprise. As we're about to walk out the door to go down to the car, Kanoa turns and plants a sweet kiss on my cheek. I accept it as an apology and secretly enjoyed his touch.

As Kanoa drives, I recognize the way to Pono Market. He asks if I wouldn't mind waiting in the car instead of looking for a parking spot. He says he'll only be a few seconds. I agree to wait. In under a minute he's making his way back with a picnic basket in hand. He opens the hatchback and places the basket inside.

"Sorry about that," he says. "It wasn't ready when I came by earlier. They were up to their ears with breakfast plates."

"No worries, it's not as if I was waiting here forever. So where are we going?"

"Aren't you the nosey one?"

"I'm a little curious, but I can wait," I say. He knows I'm not partial to surprises. I need to know everything at all times, but I can see he's going to play this one out. After a few more minutes, we are passing by the Coco Palms when Kanoa makes a sudden turn and before I know it, we are parked in the abandoned lot.

I'm surprised he'd bring me here. "What's going on? Why are we here?"

"Mike told me about your visit to the lagoon," Kanoa says slyly, opening his door and coming around to my side. He opens my door. "I hear you were quite taken by it, so I thought I'd pack us a picnic lunch. It'll give us a chance to talk."

I'm not as surprised about Mike telling Kanoa as I am at the fact that Kanoa took the time to plan this. I can feel my emotions roaring through my body like a flash flood. I look over at Kanoa, unable to fathom the thought that I may never see him again once I leave the island. He's staring at me as he stands with the picnic basket in his hands. He asks, "Why the long face? Is it something I said?"

I can feel myself fighting back tears. I don't want to cry, and as fast as my wall was coming down it's making its way back up again. "No. It's nothing."

"That's a pretty sad face for being nothing. What is it?"

And his genuine concern is bringing my wall down again. "I just wish things were different, that's all. This entire land deal has drained me more than I ever thought possible. You're the last person I should be saying this to, but I hope Kelly Corporation doesn't win the bid. I honestly don't care about the money, but what I do care about is hurting Mike and your people. I feel like a monster now that it's all said and done." And just like that, I feel a tear roll down my face. "I can't believe I just admitted that to you."

The only part I left out is that I also felt bad for him, but I can't say it. I haven't forgiven him for leaving me. I don't get a reaction from Kanoa one way or another. It's hard to know what he's thinking. Instead, we start to make our way through the overgrowth and make small talk.

"I guess it's okay for you to trespass?" I say. "Who is going to get mad at Kanoa Kahala?"

"Do I detect a hint of jealousy?"

"No," I laugh. "I'm not jealous, but of course I'm envious. It must be nice to have so many people sing your praises."

"We both know that they're only referring to the work I do. I'm sure my people wouldn't be as understanding about the way I left you. We aren't that forgiving. Just because we live out here in paradise and everything may look like a storybook fairytale—trust me, we are human and face all the same challenges that life throws mainland people."

I let it go, because a more pressing issue has arisen. I can feel a cold breeze around my body, almost like a little funnel cloud.

"It's her," I say. "Every time I've been here, I feel it. She's here."

"Abby. There's no one here."

"It's her. I bet she smells the food. Last time I was here she asked me for some *lau lau*."

Kanoa looks like he's going to bust a gut. I don't think I've ever seen him laugh so hard.

"It's not funny," I say. "She did—ask Mike."

"Well, why don't we just leave a plate out for her? Great, now I went and ruined the surprise lunch I got for you. Mike told me how fast you ate your *lau lau* when he first met you, so I had Makani pack an abundance of it."

I feel a bit taken aback. I wasn't aware that Mike and Kanoa were this close. "Does Mike tell you everything?"

"No, I'm sure he doesn't. I've known Mike all my life and I barely know anything personal about him. He and my parents were the best of friends, but we all know he's a very discreet and gentle old man and leave it at that. I'm sure he just likes to share certain happy thoughts about you. Don't be mad at Mike for telling me things."

"I could never be mad at Mike. I've come to see for myself that he's one of the gentlest people on the planet."

"So? What do you say? Shall we leave your ghost lady some food?"

I'm not sure if he's being serious or just poking fun at me, yet again. I look into his dark eyes for the answer, but I'm not sure what I'm seeing. "You're poking fun at me, aren't you?"

"You could say that."

I know the Queen is around, because I feel the chilled air around me, but I stand proud and fearless. I'll show you, Mr. Kahala.

"Well why don't I ask her," I say to Kanoa. I clear my throat. "Hello … Queen Deborah. I was wondering if today was good for a visit. I brought you some *lau lau*." Suddenly I feel the cold air disappear. "I take it that means yes?"

I hear a faint voice in my ear. "Continue to the lagoon," Deborah says. "I will meet you there. You can leave the *lau*

lau on the double-hulled canoe. You'll know when you see it. Don't mind Kanoa. He doesn't believe I exist."

I hold my head up high and continue walking.

"What's the matter?" Kanoa asks. "Has your ghost friend snubbed you?"

"No. Just keep moving. I know where to leave her lunch."

"Who are you?" he asks with one eyebrow slanting upwards, looking quite serious. "Abby, stop walking, please. Look at me. Did I damage you to this point? Are you okay?"

"I'm fine. Well, I'm not fine about our situation. Of course I'm pissed at you, but I'm physically and mentally fine when it comes to … Oh hell, I don't know what I'm trying to say. It's all too much."

"How about we focus on us and what I can do to make things better?"

"Okay, but let's keep walking. I need to find a double-hulled canoe."

Kanoa shakes his head as if I'm a hopeless case. As we get closer to the lagoon, there's a bright reflection shining directly into my eyes. I look over at Kanoa; of course, nothing is happening to him. I can't even begin to understand why he doesn't see what I see. I start to follow the brightness, and there it is—it's coming from the canoe, which is right along the water's edge. I ask Kanoa if I can have a plated lunch from the basket. He hands it to me, and I take it over and place it on the canoe. Without a moment's hesitation, the canoe is floating down the lagoon as the bright light becomes less and less blinding. Kanoa is being a real trooper for not saying a word. He's busy scouting out a spot for us to sit.

"How's this for our picnic lunch? Do you like this area?"

"It's perfect," I answer as we avoid the entire subject of the canoe. Kanoa spreads a blanket on the ground and places the basket on it. He takes my hand and helps me to sit down. His gentlemanly way is one of the many things I loved about him. I wonder why I never told him as much?

CHAPTER TWENTY-SIX:

Kanoa

It's surreal seeing Abby sitting on the blanket in one of my favorite spots in the world. If only she knew how I've been beating myself up for the way I left her. What good would it do to tell her? I don't know what I could promise her—I know I'll never move back to New York. But then again, I can't presume that she's interested in me any longer. I hear her say, "Geez, what planet did you drift off to?"

I'm rummaging through the basket for the bottle of wine I asked Makani to pack for us.

Abby asks, "Don't you think it's a little early? It's not even noon."

I look at my wristwatch. "It's 11:45. I can drink alone until noon if you'd like?"

She chuckles, which is such a fresh change after the misery and grief I've caused her. I'm smart enough to know I've got a long road ahead of me to make amends with her.

"I'll join you," she says. "I think I can handle a glass, but maybe we should find a shadier spot. Sorry for being so picky, but I've learned that alcohol and strong Hawaiian sun are not my strong points."

She leaps up onto her feet and takes the blanket. She marches over to a tree that's long been fallen on its side. I watch as she drapes the blanket over the elevated branches. She yells over, "I think I'd prefer the shade, rather than sitting on this blanket, what do you think?"

I'm so happy to be with her that I just want to scream it out loud. She plants herself on the ground. There was a time when I didn't think Abby could ever be so laid back.

"I can go back to the car," I offer. "I'm sure I have some old blanket or shirt that you can sit on?"

"Don't be silly. I'm fine. Unless you want it?"

"No. I'm good," I say as I take the basket and our wine over to our new makeshift tent. "I always wondered if there was a Girl Scout hidden somewhere deep within you."

"Of course there is. I'll have you know I was one of the top cookie sellers."

"Why am I not surprised?"

"I was quite adamant about being a Girl Scout. I still have all my badges."

"I never knew this about you."

"It's become apparent that we don't know much about one another," she says as she takes her first sip of wine.

"Are you hungry?"

"I could be in a bit, but if you are …"

"I can wait," I say as I sit down next to her. We're both staring out onto the lagoon. "So, where do you think that plate of *lau lau* has floated off to?"

"Not sure, but I bet some hungry old ghost lady has devoured every single morsel."

"You must realize how nuts we sound, right?"

"Yeah, but I think I sounded even crazier about an hour ago," Abby says.

"True."

It feels really good to have idle chitchat together. Throughout all the meetings about the Coco Palms, I've always found myself feeling tense. I didn't want to step out of line and hurt Abby more than I already had, but I also couldn't be weak when it came to business. I don't think I was weak, but there were times when I caught myself drifting in memory as I looked at her across the boardroom table. If only she knew I never stopped loving her. I made a promise to myself years ago about helping my people, and it's something I don't take lightly. I should have known better than to ever get involved in a relationship, but I also didn't know I'd fall head over heels in love with her at first sight. I didn't think it was a possibility, as it'd never happened to me before. Again I hear Abby asking me something.

"Have I become so boring that you keep drifting off?"

"I'm sorry," I say with my jaw clenched. "It's been a long time since we've been alone, and I'm a bit nervous. I'm really happy you suggested we talk. You may not believe me, but I had every intention of doing the same. Today is perfect. I don't want a land decision to alter the way I'm feeling."

"Nor do I," says Abby as she twists her long hair around her finger. "That's why I called. Also, I could get a call from Stan asking me to get my ass back in a New York minute. And you know that's exactly how he'd say it—he's nuts."

"You don't really expect me to comment on Stan, do you?"

Abby knows how much I loathe the man. I only had to meet him once. I know Abby is worth so much more than to work for a guy like him. High salaries aren't always worth it.

"Let's not waste our time on Stan," she says. "I just want to get some closure. I need to know what I did to make you leave the way you did."

"It's not so much you as it is me. I didn't think you'd handle it well if I told you the truth, but with hindsight, I should never have assumed. I think we could have discussed it, but I fucked up, plain and simple. I did a really stupid thing, and there's no way I can take back the pain I've caused you, I know that."

"But I still don't understand. What about me made you feel as if I wouldn't understand?"

I have to tread carefully with this one. My answer could trigger an entirely different set of problems. Abby patiently waits for me to answer. I nervously take a sip of wine before saying, "I felt that you were too good for me. I figured that after the initial shock of me leaving, you'd stop caring."

"That's preposterous. How did you ever come to that conclusion? I adored you."

"But when did you ever tell me that?"

I can see Abby searching to say something. It takes her a moment or two before she says, "But I showed you in so many ways."

"Name one."

Again, she searches and searches within, but the vacant stare tells me she can't find an occasion. She finally blurts out, "We were so good together. I mean, we clicked from the first moment we met. You can't beat that."

"It's not about sex, Abby. I know what we had, and we still have a deep connection—it's undeniable—but I never felt like I measured up. I felt as though our feelings were more one-sided."

"What?" she says, in such a firm tone that it's as if my comment is beyond her comprehension.

"Yes," I say. "I always felt that I was just a stepping stone to something better for you."

"You're insane. What are you talking about? I was crazy about you."

"You keep telling me this, but why didn't you ever tell me before?"

I can see she's hurt. None of us like to hear our ex-partner's truths. She puts down her wine glass and gets up off the ground.

"Maybe we should go," she says, as upset as I figured she'd be.

I'm annoyed that she just wants to sweep it under the rug, after claiming that she could be called to go home at a moment's notice. "No, I don't think we should leave until we talk things through. You asked me a question and I answered. This right here is a good example of why I was afraid to tell you the truth. Will we ever really be able to discuss things?"

"You're right. I don't know what to say to you, okay?"

"Tell me what you're feeling."

"What good is it going to do? If you want to hear that I forgive you, then so be it. I forgive you for the shitty way you left me."

"Thank you, and I'm grateful for you. I also think we should forgive each other. It's a two-way street here. In all honesty, both our communications skills have been lacking. It's quite evident." I hate that I can see the hurt in her eyes. They are starting to glisten. "Abby? Can you please sit?"

"Sure," she replies. Not in a defeated way, but in a loving, caring manner. I take her hand and she sits back down. I put my arm around her shoulders and cradle her close to me as I brush her hair back and look at her. She complains a bit about her complexion, but to me it's as flawless as it's ever been. I forgot how much I loved her slightly turned-up nose and big brown eyes. She is the most beautiful girl I've ever seen, and just when I'm about to tell her what I'm feeling, she jumps up and yells, "There she goes. It's Queen Deborah, look!" I can see the double-hulled canoe, but that's all. Abby is going on and on about something shining in her eyes, but I don't dare question it. She turns to look at me. "You don't see her, do you?"

"Truth? No."

"I don't understand. You're crazy about this land, and how is it possible that you can't see her?"

"Maybe I'm not as determined to believe in ghosts as you are," I say. Deep down, though, I know there are spirits on this island, but now's not the time and place. "Lunch?" I offer.

"Good idea."

I hand Abby her lunch along with a cold bottle of water to keep her hydrated. I can't take my eyes off her as she eats. I remember every muscle movement in her face. "I know it takes time, but I'm wondering if there's a chance that you may one day trust me again? I'm more than willing to prove that I can be trustworthy. I'm just asking that we at least try and be friends. What do you say?" Even as I'm saying the word friends, I hate it. I don't just want to be friends, but how do you tell someone you abandoned that you made a massive mistake?

"What good is it going to do us? You live six thousand miles away from New York. I don't understand."

"I get that you're going back, but why can't we at least be civil and maybe call one another every now and then? I don't want to think that this is it. I want there to be hope that maybe we will see one another again." I reach for her hand. "When we're done lunch, let me take you on a proper tour of the property. I especially want to hop on that canoe. What do you say?"

"I say yes to being civil. I think I need to say that I forgive you for my own sanity, but I'm not promising that I trust you, because I don't."

"That's fair. We'll take baby steps."

"The canoe ride sounds like fun. See, I'm putting my best foot forward," Abby says in a light-hearted tone.

For the first time since she got to the island, I can feel us connecting. It takes all my strength not to reach over and kiss her. I'm dying to feel the touch of her lips on mine. I wonder if she feels the same. I can see a familiar twinkle in her eyes, but I could be wrong, and if that were the case, I'd feel like an ogre if I kissed her and she didn't reciprocate. Since we've agreed to stay connected even after she returns to NY, maybe I'll kiss her on the cheek after the canoe ride. *No!* I need to stop thinking everything will be okay. I'm setting myself up for a fall.

After the canoe ride has come and gone, I drive Abby back to her hotel. Just as I'm contemplating leaning over to kiss her cheek, she asks, "Would you like to join me for a swim?"

Hell yeah. I'm not turning down that offer. "I'd love to, thanks for offering. You've made me one of the happiest men on the island."

"You're crazy," she laughs. "If you don't mind, I just need to go back up to my room to change. Will you come with me?"

"Potential ghost fear?"

"Oh, you think you're so funny."

"Come on, admit it."

"Yes, of course, I'm petrified. It's not every day that I witness a blurry male ghost running through my body."

"Thanks for the graphics. You know, you could come stay with me. I have a spare room."

"Did you not hear me earlier when I said I need to learn to trust you again?" she replies, a bit more firmly than I would have hoped.

"I said I have a spare room," I say. "I'm not suggesting we hook up. Trust me, I know I fucked things up, but that doesn't mean I want you staying alone if there's something or someone putting your life in danger."

"So, you believe me when I tell you what I've experienced?"

"Yes, in the same way I believe the majority of people on these islands who believe in ancestral spirits. Who am I to tell anyone about spirits? All I care about is your safety."

"So what you're saying is that you're not a true believer?"

"Something like that."

Abby opens the door to her hotel room. She enters with trepidation. I take her hand to let her know she's safe with me. I check out her living quarters to make sure everything is intact. Abby suggests we have a cocktail on the balcony, and before we know it, we're watching the sunset and probably on our third drink. We never did go out for that swim; instead, we enjoy room service and a few more platonic hours together.

I offer to stay the night on her sofa. Abby doesn't refuse the offer, and I'm happy to know she feels safe with me. Who am I to question whether she felt the presence of an evil ghost? All I can go by is the fact that the Abby I know would never make such things up—it's definitely not in her nature.

Before we have a chance to finish breakfast, a call comes in about the Coco Palms. We've been asked to attend a meeting at the bank the following morning at ten. I feel both our demeanors change after the call, but I can truly only speak for myself. As much as I want to be with Abby, I feel an urgent need to get to the office.

CHAPTER TWENTY-SEVEN:

Abby

As I walk into the Bakers' office for our meeting, Ken walks past me without saying hello. He looks peeved, but what else is new?

"Sorry about that," Charles offers, with the fakest of smiles on his face. "Just a little family disagreement."

"By the looks of Ken, I'm not sure it was such a little one."

"Enough of him," he says. "Break it to me, where do we stand?"

"Two choices—you move forward with the same bid or, as I suggested, go higher."

"We're sticking to our guns. Let's just get the papers filed today and be done, once and for all."

I feel a headache coming on. I've never met a client that is willing to pay me big bucks but barely ever takes my advice. All I can do is shake my head and pray to the gods that this is it.

"Is Ken on board with your decision?" I ask.

Charles looks at me as if I have three heads for asking, but just as quickly forces a smile and replies, "Yes, most definitely. He's sick and tired of all the stalling."

"In all fairness, no one expected the family tragedy, so I wouldn't call it stalling—tragic would be more accurate."

"Not tragic. People should learn to swim."

"What? That's a bit harsh."

"Whatever, can we just get down to business?"

Wow. These two have even bigger sticks up their ass than normal—odd behavior for a couple of guys who are confident about their bid.

"Do you think Ken will be rejoining us anytime soon?" I ask. "I need him to sign the new contract."

"Leave it with me," Charles says as he tries to contact Ken on his cell. I take a seat and start doing my paperwork without saying another word. Can't wait until this entire ordeal is over.

As I'm working, my mind starts to wander. I keep thinking back to a few days ago when I went over to Mike's house to surprise him. I swear I saw Ken backing his car out of Mike's driveway. I wish I'd have questioned Mike about it, but something inside me didn't want me to be intrusive. I also thought it may have been a coincidence—just someone turning around in his driveway—but was it? Why was Ken leaving Mike's? None of it makes any sense. Mike has never mentioned Ken to me, but then again, why would he?

No time for any more thoughts, as the prodigal brother re-enters the building. "What have I missed?"

"Nothing," replies Charles sharply. "Maybe an apology to Abby might be nice."

I can see Ken's face scrunching up in anger. If there's one thing I've learned being around these two, it's how much Ken loathes Charles always telling him what to do. I look up from my papers. "No worries, let's get these documents signed so I can get them over to the bank." Which translates as, the sooner I get you two out of my hair, the faster I can get on with my life.

Thinking of going home has become a bittersweet thing for me. I want to get back to my own bed and routine, and especially my parents, whom I miss so much. I never knew I could miss them to this extent—so if any good has come from this trip so far, it's never to take my parents for granted, not even for a moment. But the difficulty lies with my heartbreak at leaving Mike and Nani, not to mention her kids and husband—and, most of all, Kanoa. Between Mike and Kanoa, I have so many unresolved feelings.

I snap out of my overthinking when I hear Charles in his office on the phone with Stan, arguing about something. Ken is in the same office I'm in, so I keep my head down, trying not to draw any attention to my eavesdropping.

Charles comes back into the room. I don't take notice until he asks, "Are the contracts ready? I need to be somewhere."

"Two more minutes," I reply. There is so much tension in the room that even a chainsaw couldn't cut through it. I put the papers in front of Charles, who has taken a seat across me. "Here you go, ready for your autograph."

Without so much as a blink of an eye he signs the forms, handing them over to his brother to sign. They both stand up, and Charles shakes my hand. "Thank you for everything. I know this hasn't been easy."

"We can both agree on that," I say half-jokingly. "I'll let you know as soon as I hear something."

Charles makes his way out of the office. Ken, who is still lingering for whatever reason, says, "So, I guess this is it for you. Are you heading back to New York?"

"Eventually. My return will depend on the outcome, I'm sure."

Ken stares at me as if he hasn't heard a word I've said. His stare is quite unnerving. I gather my papers and excuse myself. I really would have loved to ask what he was doing in Mike's driveway, but his daunting stare has me hurrying to exit the building. I head straight over to the bank to get everything handed in and beat the deadline.

CHAPTER TWENTY-EIGHT:
Kanoa

"Nani!" I yell from my office. "Where are the forms that we need to fill out?"

"I left them on the right-hand corner of your desk. You know the extremely large pile of files that you wanted to put away yourself?" Nani says as she steps partway into my office. "I don't understand why you won't let me file those for you."

"It's personal. I want to take care of them myself. Plus, I need them."

Nani comes straight over to grab the file I'm in search of and hands it to me.

"You're a lifesaver. Thanks, Nani. By the way, hold all calls. I need to focus on the Coco Palms exclusively—everything else can wait."

"Okay. Can I help you with anything?"

"If you'd be so kind as to take care of everything else, I should be okay. It'll give me the time I need to get this done."

Just as Nani is about to go back to her office, we hear the main door open. Standing in front of us are Charles and Ken. How dare they show up unannounced, especially at such a busy time? But this is nothing new for them. I think back to another unannounced meeting a year ago, when they both sauntered in like two proud peacocks thinking they could distract me from the very first bid. They had no idea who they were coming up against. In their minds, they'd already watched the ink dry on the Coco Palms land dead, and I watched it fail.

I remember Charles ignoring the fact that there were to be no condos ever erected on the land. This had been established in our very first meeting. He said, "Kahala, I think you'll change your mind about condos when you see how much it does for this tiny island."

Everything in me wanted to pop the guy in the mouth, but I've never been a fighter—the thought felt good, though. How dare he talk down when referring to our island, which I take very personally, not only for myself but my people? Before I had a chance to answer, I heard Ken say, "And then we can start putting them up everywhere, right Charles?"

I'd already had enough of the pompous asses, but I kept my cool. "You'll have to get past the Heritage Association first—and don't forget, gentlemen, I'm part of the Association."

And with that, our meeting ended, just the same way most of our meetings have ended.

Here I am faced again with these two snakes. Why are they really here? I quickly get up from my desk and nod for Nani to leave the room.

"What brings you two by? I don't think we have a scheduled meeting," I say sarcastically.

Charles replies, "Just wanted to let you know we have our bid in. No hard feelings, whoever should be the winner."

"That's quite noble of you, but what's the real reason you're here?" I ask suspiciously as Ken makes his way to Nani's desk. "Listen Charles, I know for a fact we no longer have anything to discuss, and I'm in the middle of something, so if you—"

"No worries," Charles says, extending his hand.

I can see through the doorway that Ken is asking Nani for something. I refocus on Charles and shake his hand, reluctantly. "Hate to rush you along, but like I said, I'm a busy man. Please make an appointment in the future."

"I won't be needing your services," Charles says, "but don't disregard me so quickly. You may want to partner with me some day."

"Don't bet on it," I say as I escort Charles to the main entrance where Nani is standing beside Ken, looking very uncomfortable. "What's going on here?" I ask.

"I asked your assistant if she wouldn't mind photocopying something for me," Ken says. "Our printer broke down."

"There's a UPS Store right down the street for future use," I tell Ken as I turn and walk back to my office. I feel relief when I hear the front door slam.

Nani enters my office. "Can you believe those two? They came all the way here to ask if I could photocopy some documents."

"Thank God we're almost done with them. Sorry you had to deal with that. If it's any consolation, you know how I feel about them. They're a couple of snakes."

"I know what you mean. I get bad vibes around them. No good *mana* when those two are around, so let's not dwell on it, I say," in order not to get Nani more worked up than she already is. I surpress my own hostile feelings towards them and focus on my own *mana,* spiritual energy.

CHAPTER TWENTY-NINE:
Genie (1989)

You'd think that after more than twenty years I'd have stopped feeling nervous about telling Deborah certain things, but I've realized that some things never do change. I used to dread telling her I needed her room to accommodate Elvis, but that makes this day feel easy. I know she won't take my news well, but life must move forward for all of us. I'm not getting any younger, that's for darn sure. She will have to understand.

I make my way to Deborah's room as I've done thousands of times before. I take a deep breath before I push her door open.

"Good morning, Genie."

"Morning, ma'am."

"Oh, oh. What's wrong? You only call me ma'am when there's an issue. What is it? You ill?"

"No, it's nothing like that."

I place the breakfast tray I'm carrying in front of Deborah, who is sitting in her usual spot at the head of the dining table. I'm not sure why, but today for some odd reason I keep getting a waft of a man's cologne. I look back at Deborah, who has already started to eat her morning croissant. I scan the room to see if anything is out of place, and just then, I get another waft. "Is someone here?"

"Whatever are you referring to?"

"You know what I'm asking. Don't play dumb with me."

"Yes, Elvis came for a visit."

"What? He's been dead for years. How is this even possible? Do you two belong to a ghost club?"

"Always the witty Genie—but today I'm hearing a hint of sarcasm. What is the matter with you? And before you answer, let me just say that Elvis has been visiting me for a while. That's what happens when you are a true believer."

I mutter under my breath, "Remind me not to be one."

"I heard that!"

I don't know how all this is possible, but I can't deal with it right now. I need to get things off my chest.

"Why are you so far away?" Deborah says. "Come closer. Pour yourself a cup of coffee and get whatever it is off your chest before I combust."

I look at Deborah and wonder if she's being sincere or just mocking me, but I decide to sit. I don't need coffee—I'm jittery enough—but I want to say what I came to say. "Gerry and I have decided that we're getting too old to continue this lifestyle. Gerry has decided to retire and asked me to marry him."

"Genie, tell me you're not leaving me? Please?"

"No," I say, "I'm not leaving, at least not yet. I've decided to continue on until Gerry decides to one day sell the place."

"Sell? No! You can't do that. Genie, you of all people know how much this place means to me."

"I know, Deborah, but that's why I'm telling you now. I don't plan on retiring for a couple of years, but I am getting too old and I don't want to stretch it out any further. If we can put our heads together, we can find a reputable buyer … you know what I mean?"

"Oh, Genie. I knew you wouldn't let me down, but for a minute I wasn't sure. Tell me, what's Gerry going to do with himself all day? Or do I even need to ask?" says Deborah as she smirks slyly.

"You're not going to start with your accusations are you? He's a changed man and you know that."

"You're absolutely right, he's changed. Who wants him now that he's an old bugger? Whether you believe me or not, I am happy for you. I'm happy that the womanizer has finally asked you to marry him."

"I'll take that as a grand gesture coming from you. I realize we've never been on the same page when it comes to Gerry, but besides that, you've been very good to me. I hope you know how much I cherish our friendship, even though I've questioned my sanity at times—especially when I first met you. In all the years, you're still my number one ghost friend."

"And I will take that as a grand gesture, seeing as I'm the only ghost you know—well, besides Elvis, whom you haven't actually seen in his ghost mode. If I could be serious for a moment, I want you to know how delighted I am that you'll be sticking around for a few more years. I don't want to think of the day I no longer see your smiling face," she says.

Her voice begins to crack. For the first time since we met, Deborah is expressing sincere, raw emotion. I didn't think she was capable of such a thing.

"There, there," I say as I reach for her hand. "Don't be sad. I'm not going anywhere just yet."

"Do you know what it was like not to have had a friend in the world—that is, until you and Elvis came along? Even when I was married to the King, my life was empty. And by King, I'm referring to my bastard ex-husband, not Elvis—just to be clear. Anyhow, he didn't love me. I knew he was after my family's land and money, but things were different back then. Women didn't have the same rights that modern-day women have. I married him because he'd convinced my family that he was an honorable man, but I don't think my family expected the rotten bastard to banish me from my own land. Once I was gone, they no longer had any right to the land, as I was the Queen. They had to endure watching him with every female who crossed his path. It was tough for them because he held the power. There wasn't a damn thing they could do. Even sadder is that those women didn't get to choose whether to be with him or not. He was rotten to the core and still is. A downright evil man."

"I'm so sorry, Deborah."

"Maybe this is why I'm hard on you when it comes to Gerry. I don't like some of the things he's done, but I know he does truly love you, and he's a good-hearted man. I know he's not an evil being like my ex-husband, but that doesn't mean I like his past womanizing ways. You notice I said *past*. I just give you a hard time about him because I have never wanted you to feel inferior to Gerry. Right now I'm also feeling sorry for myself. I don't want to lose you."

"Well, I'm not leaving today," I say, "so no more talk about it. Plus, who said anything about leaving Kaua'i? We might not be in this particular building, but I'll always be around."

"Music to my ears," says the Queen slyly.

"We've had some pretty good times, I have to admit—especially the times when Elvis visited. You're thinking about it right now, aren't you?"

I laugh as I watch Deborah with her mischievous smirk, quite reminiscent of the Cheshire cat.

"I am," the Queen giggles.

"Looking back, some of our escapades were pretty hilarious, of course in hindsight. In real time, you always had me on pins and needles when Elvis came here. You've still never admitted whether or not ... "

"A ghost never kisses and tells. I've told you once, and I'll say it again: what happens in Kaua'i, stays in Kaua'i."

"You're too much."

"Whoever came up with that silly catchphrase anyhow? Probably the same guy who made up Peeping Tom," she complains.

RITA D'ORAZIO

"I don't know who thought of them, but you've sure come to love them. You know, since Elvis's passing, it's been pretty quiet around here—but after smelling the cologne, maybe it hasn't been as quiet as I thought?"

"Still not telling," laughs Deborah.

We spend a good part of the next hour reminiscing about things that have happened at the resort. It isn't until Mike's name comes up that the Queen gets serious again.

"What is it?" I ask.

"I have something I need you to give to Mike."

"Mike?"

"Yes, Mike."

"I wasn't aware you knew him well."

"I'm full of surprises, Genie."

"What is it that you need me to give him?"

"I'll let you know when the time is right."

Gerry and I have agreed to a simple ceremony on the grounds of the Coco Palms, where we've witnessed hundreds of couples exchanging vows. What we aren't going to keep simple is the reception party.

We've decided to throw a reception party like no other, because for Gerry and me, it's also a celebration of our retirement—his sooner than mine, but that part is just for us to know, us and Deborah. This party will definitely be bittersweet. On one hand I'm over the moon to be getting married, even if it is at a much later time in my life (though love and companionship have no expiry date, I've learned). But leaving a place I've called home for the past twenty-seven fantastic years will not be easy. At least it's not happening as of yet.

I've been very fortunate to meet the most outstanding people from around the world. The only regret I have is that my career at the Coco Palms didn't start sooner in life. As for meeting great people, I'd have to say that my three favorites are still Gerry, Deborah and of course, Mike. Which brings me to the night of our party.

Deborah confides in me the day before our nuptials are to take place. She asks me to give Mike an ornate box, which she shows me when I brought her breakfast. She requests that I bring Mike to Room #256 in order to give it to him. In typical Deborah fashion, she doesn't explain why I can't bring it to my room and just hand it over to Mike. I have to follow her strict orders, which means I'm not to know the contents of the box—I am just the messenger.

Later that morning, Mike comes over to the Coco Palms to lend a hand, and that's when I ask that he meet me in Room #256 on the day of our wedding.

"I don't have a specific time in mind," I say, "but I'll let you know."

Mike stares at me as if waiting for me to say something else, but I have nothing more to add. He gathers his thoughts and says, "This is a strange request coming from you. You usually come right out and tell me everything. What is it? Are you ill?"

"No, I'm fine. Why is it that any time I do something the slightest bit out of character, everyone thinks I'm sick? I have something I need to give to you, plain and simple."

I know how crazy I just sounded, but Mike is the ultimate gentleman. He knows me well enough to know that the request is making me extremely nervous, which led me to my childish outburst. Mike graciously agrees to meet me in Room #256, whenever I see fit.

The next day, right after our wedding ceremony, while Gerry and I are mingling with guests, I excuse myself, as I don't want Deborah's request lingering over my head any longer. It's been putting too much pressure on what was supposed to be one of the most fantastic days of my life. I spot Mike and meet him in Deborah's room. Once we're in the room, Mike can't see Deborah, but I can, and she instructs me to take the ornate box and give it to Mike.

"By the way," Mike says, "this is quite a beautiful room. Isn't this the room that—"

Before Mike can say another word, I cut him off. "Yes. Gerry insisted that this room never be used, but I'll tell you about it another time. Right now, I need to give you this," I say as I hand Mike the box. He's about to open it when I yell, "*NO*, stop! Don't open it. I was given strict orders that you need to take it home and open it there. You are never to tell me its contents, or anyone else for that matter. Understood?"

Mike is wide-eyed at my outburst. I realize how crazy this must all sound to Mike, but he goes along and asks politely, "You do realize how nonsensical this is, right?"

"I don't expect you to understand, because frankly, I don't either. I'm just doing what I was instructed to—and please, I'm begging you, don't divulge the contents."

"You know I'm a man of my word. I'll do as you ask."

"Thanks, Mike."

"But I have a request. Can I at least keep it here until tomorrow morning? As you know, I'm staying over tonight. After all, I'm celebrating one of my dearest friends getting married. Who wants to go home early?"

"Of course," I say. "Please, not a word about this in front of Gerry."

"Genie! Stop worrying, I give you my word that nothing you have said will leave this room." Mike says. "I know what to do. I have always trusted you. If I didn't, don't you think I'd be opening this box right now? I'm curious to know where you got it, but I won't put you on the spot, so how about you trust in me?"

"You're right. You've been nothing but loyal and a very dear friend to me, and there isn't anyone I trust more than you. I guess I'm just really nervous. I know how important the contents are, or so I've been told."

"Got it," he says. "Now, enough about the box, how about we get back to the party? We have some celebrating to do."

"One more thing before you go. I need to tell you something that we don't want our guests to know, but you're not just any guest, you're one of my dearest friends. This is also a farewell celebration to the Coco Palms for me and Gerry."

"What? You're leaving?"

"Gerry is retiring, but he doesn't want to make a big deal about it. He decided he'll tell the staff on Monday, but he's done as of today. I will be staying on for a year or so; I'm not quite sure."

Mike hugs me with all his might. He simply says, "I'm happy for both of you if this is what you guys want. I thank you both for all the wonderful years and memories."

"Okay, you need to stop. It was one thing having mascara drip down my face when I was young, but this is unacceptable," I say to lighten the mood.

And just like that, no further words are needed amongst friends. Mike can't see Queen Deborah, who is sitting at the table wiping away her tears.

CHAPTER THIRTY:

Abby

I knew my days in Kaua'i were numbered, but I'd be lying if I didn't say how relieved I am to put the land deal to rest for the time being. I need to use this time to get things cleared up with Kanoa. I definitely don't want to go home without answers. I'm not sure if Kanoa has filed yet, and I don't want to disturb him, so instead, I dial Nani.

"Abby, *aloha*—I wasn't sure I'd ever hear your voice again," Nani says happily. "Listen, I have about another hour of work, but why don't I swing by when I'm done and we can go somewhere?"

"Well, the reason for my call is to ask if you'd like to go to a *lū'au*. I've never been, and I would love to take you and your family. It's the least I can do for all the generosity you've shown me."

"I don't know what to say. That's so sweet of you."

"Please say yes."

"Yes! The kids will be thrilled. James and I haven't been to a formal lūʻau in … actually, I don't know when the last time was. This will be so much fun. How did you manage to convince Kanoa to stop working?"

"I haven't. I don't want to disturb him. I'm sure he'll find me when he's ready."

"Abby! You know that boy will never be ready. Someone needs to give him a shove. I can see him from my office—would you like me to put you through?"

I can't help laughing. Nani is one of the most expressive people I've ever met. "No, that's okay, I'll let him finish up his work. By the way, I haven't picked a place. I figured who better than you to know where the best lūʻau is?"

"Leave it to me. I'll make the reservations. I'll text you the information. See you in about an hour and a half. *Mahalo*."

Kanoa

Nani pokes her head into my office. Even though the bid is in, I'm still knee-deep in work. Nani gives out a loud cough.

"Nani!" I ask. "What can I do for you?"

"Well, seeing as you asked …"

"As if I had a choice," I snicker.

"Can you take the night off?" she asks. "Please? I mean, I did attempt to go surfing with you when you felt the need, so the least you could do for a dear friend is take the night off."

"You're relentless. Nani, you know—"

"Don't give me any more excuses. Please? The bid is in. What is so urgent that you can't stop for dinner?"

"Nothing, except getting my desk organized. Aren't you the one that keeps reminding me of it?"

Nani, never one to be at a loss for words, is making odd, garbled noises, reminiscent of a toddler trying to get his first words out. I look up at her as she finally manages to articulate a couple of short sentences.

"It can wait another night," she says. "I need you to call Smiths."

"What?" I ask a little too loudly. "Are you *lōlō*? You want to go to a *lū'au*?"

"Is there something wrong with that?"

"Nani, seriously, what gets into you at times?"

"I think we should be out celebrating. Let's get out. It's time for some fun."

"I don't want to jinx things with the land deal. How about we wait for celebrations?"

"No," says Nani, also just a little too loudly.

I know she's up to something, but in all honesty I've always enjoyed her antics. I put my head back down as if I'm going to continue working; this way I can speed up what she has to say—it works every time. I laugh a little inside.

"There's always something in life to celebrate," she says. "Come on, please—Kai will be so disappointed if her Uncle K. ..."

"Okay, okay! You know that's emotional blackmail?"

Even though Nani has her back turned away from me, I can see her giggling shoulders moving. "No it's not," she says, "it's love. So, I'll leave you to make the reservations? By the way there will be eight of us."

"Eight?"

"Yes, and one more thing," she says. "You need to pick Abby up. I told her I'd be there in an hour or so, but I'm sure she won't mind the change in plan. Maybe you could go pick her up a bit earlier."

My head automatically starts to shake from side to side as it has many times with Nani but it's always out of love and affection for her nuttiness. "Oh my God, you are relentless. Is there anything you haven't thought of?"

"Yeah, yeah, get moving."

I work for another half hour, but I can't get my mind off Abby. I decide to take Nani's advice and head out earlier. As I get out of my car, I spot Abby on the beach. She's a vision as she strolls the water's edge in a long floral dress, one I've never seen before. Her hair is pulled back loosely with a red flower placed just above her ear. If I didn't know her, I'd think she was Polynesian. As I get closer, I can tell she's deep in thought. I'm not sure how to approach her without scaring her half to death, as I've done many times already. I walk behind her in hopes that she'll notice me. With every step I take the trade winds envelop me in the scent of plumeria and Abby's perfume, an intoxicating combination to say the least. She's holding her sandals in her left hand while keeping her dress hiked with her right. I watch as the warm ocean water splashes up onto her long legs. As I'm about to make my move to say hello, she suddenly turns and startles us both.

"Kanoa! What are you doing here?"

"Following you. And may I say you look exceptionally beautiful." I don't know what's got into me, but I finally lean in to kiss her cheek—and instead our lips lock.

"Sorry," I say. "I didn't mean to do that." I feel mortified because Abby isn't saying anything. It's as if she's looking right through me and thinking I am some sort of jackass.

"Nothing to be sorry for."

Boy, did I misread that one. "Abby ..."

"Let's not spoil the moment," she says. "I know this sounds crazy, especially coming from me, who still doesn't trust you—but knowing I'm going home soon, I want to take in as much of the good feelings as I can." And just like that, she kisses me. I can feel the familiar curve in the small of her back as I pull her in closer to me. I feel as if we're kissing for the very first time. Abby lets go of her dress to put her arm around my neck, and I think we both know we're treading dangerous waters. How I've missed the touch of her soft delicate hands.

"You do realize your dress is getting soaked?"

"It's okay," she responds. "But I do think we should get going. I don't want Nani and the kids to be waiting on us."

I take a deep breath of fragrant air—something I've learned not to take for granted, thanks to Abby. I look into her eyes. "You really do look beautiful. You should wear flowers in your hair more often. It suits you."

"I'd look like a *lōlō* woman wearing flowers in New York."

266

I can't help laughing. "Abby Parker, you are doing what you do best, deflecting from the fact that I paid you a compliment. I said you look beautiful and frankly, I wasn't suggesting you wear flowers in New York. As far as I'm concerned, New York doesn't exist right now."

"Well it does exist, but for tonight I'll agree with you. You have no idea how excited I am to be going to a *lū'au*. The closest I've ever come to one was watching an Elvis movie with my maternal grandmother."

"Hey, you wouldn't be making fun of Elvis now, would you? You'd want to be careful around these parts. Remember, he's a legend."

"What was I thinking? We should start our own Elvis sightings right here on the island."

"Don't joke about such a thing."

"Are you being serious right now? What, is the ghost of Elvis out to get me?"

"No, but the Elvis fans will. You know how much I believe in ghosts, but some say they've seen him on the Coco Palms property. Again, it's all hearsay. And let's be clear, I'm definitely not saying I believe in the sightings. As a fellow Hawaiian, I respect what Elvis did for our island. People around here worship him. So, ghost, or no ghost, he was real and his spirit lives on. Until someone proves it differently, I have no reason not to believe his spirit exists here."

"I'm not sure if you're pulling my leg," she says. "Are you?"

"I guess you may just have to stick around and figure it out," I say slyly.

"You think I'm *lōlō* every time I mention a ghost. Now I'm supposed to believe that you believe in the spirit of Elvis?"

"Just stating a fact, that's all."

As we walk along the beach to reach the parking lot, the scorching sun is still beaming down on us.

"Can you feel that?" Abby asks me.

"Feel what?"

"Cold air. It's circling around my neck. You must be feeling it. I can see goosebumps on you."

"No. I don't feel a thing."

"Yeah, me neither," she says and starts to walk faster towards the parking lot.

I'm not admitting to anything more. By the time we get to the car, we're both short of breath. Abby jumps in without waiting for me to open her door. I know that the incidences are no longer a coincidence. Something deliberate is happening.

"These happenings aren't things I'm willing to share with anyone outside of you and Nani. Kanoa? Do you think these oddities are happening again because of the bids on the Coco Palms property?"

"I honestly have no idea, because I'm not a true believer."

"Nani told me about the snorkeler who—"

"Don't!" I say. "Believe me when I say that these stories will drive you mad. It will stifle the way you go about your day, so please don't let it. Try to enjoy our beautiful island. Let it embrace you. If you're planning on going out in the water, don't go at it alone. Always make sure there's a lifeguard on duty, or me."

"Oh, so you're my big protector? Okay, here's one for you, how do you explain Queen Deborah at the Coco Palms?"

"I think you're better with her than I am."

Abby

Upon entering the gates, we spot Nani and James waving us over. They are chatting with the general manager, while the kids run around the thirty-acre complex. Playing isn't permitted in all areas, but Nani has warned their kids in advance, and they are well aware not to step out of line.

The *imu* ceremony isn't to commence for another hour. The guests can choose to take a tram to view the lush tropical gardens, or they can explore on foot. We decide to walk, since it'll be easier to keep an eye on the kids.

As I feel Kanoa reach for my hand, I let my guard down and take hold of it as we walk the grounds. I ask myself, what would be the harm?

I'm so full of shit, I know exactly what the harm is— I'm falling for him all over again, and I can't deny how the touch of his hand sparks a shivering sensation throughout my entire body. Not something I thought would ever be possible again, considering the pent-up anger I've felt towards him. Still, he's not off the hook yet, nor will I share just how excited his touch makes me, at least not for now.

"Have I told you how beautiful you look?"

I have to laugh. "Yes. A few times, but who's counting?" He leans over and kisses me on the cheek.

Nani yells from behind, "Okay you two, there are children in the vicinity." Nani is exaggerating, but she always means well. I know she'd like nothing more than for Kanoa and me to bury the hatchet.

We turn around, and James says, "Never mind them. Let's get our alone time before the kids come running back."

Their alone time is short-lived. Kai runs back first, spotting her Uncle K. She leaps so high it's as if she has springs under her shoes. Kai latches on to Kanoa's neck like those puppets with long arms and Velcro hands. She gives him a huge smack on the cheek.

"Uncle K, I'm so happy you came." Kai pokes her little head around to get a look at me. "Hi, Auntie A."

"Well, hello yourself, little one," I say as I extend my arms for her to jump into. Kai doesn't hesitate. She hugs me so tight that for a split second I have trouble breathing.

Kai whispers in my ear, "Mommy said to say *mahalo* for tonight's *lūʻau*, so *mahalo*, Auntie A."

I'm a sucker for the child. As I squeeze her tight, I tell her, *"Aʻole pilikia."*

Kai giggles and yells at the same time. "Mommy, Mommy. Did you hear Auntie A? She can speak Hawaiian. She said you're welcome."

"Impressive," says Nani, moving her eyebrows up and down at me with her signature wide smile. "You tell Auntie A. that if she stays with us long enough, she'll speak it fluently in no time. Probably better than some of the locals." Nani is adamant about not letting the Hawaiian language disappear. She wants her children to know all about their culture. She even has Kai enrolled in hula dance lessons.

Nani takes Kai out of my arms. "Maybe you should walk the rest of the way," she tells her. "It's not far to the ceremony."

We all return to where the *imu* ceremony is minutes from taking place, while James gathers the rest of the children.

As we walk, Kai is chattering nonstop. "Uncle K., will you bring Auntie A. to my dance recital?"

Kanoa, knowing that I will probably be back in New York at the time of the recital, says, "We'll see. Not sure of Auntie A.'s schedule."

Trying to rescue him from Kai's insistence on my attendance, I ask Kai, "What type of dance are you in?" Of course I'm already well aware, but I love her reactions to things.

Kai giggles as if I've just cracked the funniest joke. Nani winks at me as Kai starts to sway her hips back and forth. "One day I'm going to be in the show," Kai says. "Right, Mommy?"

"That's right, sweetie. You keep practicing the hula and you will be just like the beautiful dancers we'll see after dinner."

Within a nanosecond, Kai runs off as if we haven't been discussing a thing. She clenches her Uncle K.'s hand as we all watch the traditionally-dressed men come out to remove the roasted pig from the pit. Now it is Kanoa who is entertained by my reaction. He leans over and whispers, "Don't get any ideas. Those boys are probably married with three kids apiece."

I shake my head at him. "Ooh, imagine these muscular men in grass skirts cooking for me."

"What? Do you forget I did the majority of the cooking? I'm not chopped liver," Kanoa says jokingly.

"And when were you in a grass skirt?"

"I was referring to the muscular part."

"Okay, I give you that, but you'd look pretty hot in a grass skirt. Note to self," I say, "pick Kanoa up a grass skirt and arm bands!"

He gives me a gentle tap on the behind. "You'd better watch what you ask for."

"Oh, believe me, I'm watching."

"You're relentless."

"What are you and Auntie laughing about?" asks Kai.

"I'll tell you when you're older. How's that?"

"Okay."

I smirk and shake my head at Kanoa, but quickly turn my attention back to the two men, while a third blows the conch shell horn—an ancient tradition with various ceremonial connotations. I don't want to miss a beat, but Kanoa manages to get the last word in.

"If you think they're cute, wait until you see the rest of the performers tonight: men in grass skirts twirling fire as they dance."

"Are you trying to tell me you can fire-dance?"

Kanoa pulls me in tight with his free arm and whispers, "What if I say I can?"

Kai giggles. "You two are silly."

Thank goodness Kai has no idea how nervous her Uncle K. is making me, but it sure feels good to be on friendly ground. I've missed this part of our relationship so much.

CHAPTER THIRTY-ONE

Having trouble sleeping, I can't stop replaying the *lū'au* in my head, from the time Kanoa picked me up until he dropped me off. It was truly one of the best nights of my life, and soon I will have to leave. My memories of the night are interrupted by the sound of my phone ringing. I look at the lit-up panel and see it's Stan. He doesn't even start off by saying hello. He goes straight into a rant.

" Don't know how this happened, Stan. Do I think he could have upped the ante? Yes, of course, but we discussed this. At the end of the day, I can't torture our clients to make the decisions that we think are right. It is always their final call. It's their money," I say as I try to explain why the Bakers lost their bid.

"Well, it's money that you won't be seeing six figures of," screams Stan through the phone. "You'd best get your behind back here. By the way, doll, count yourself lucky that you still have a job."

Somehow, I'm not feeling lucky. I don't care about the money. What's bothering me is the fact that I have to leave Kaua'i, and that means leaving Kanoa. We still have so much to talk about. We've only just scratched the surface of our problems. I hate not winning a case for my client, but at the end of the day, Charles is a rich, selfish man who probably already has his sights on some other property. Who am I kidding? I don't feel sorry for Charles and Ken, because I've never trusted them. I just wanted my own selfish revenge when I found out I was up against Kanoa. The entire ordeal has been nothing but draining.

"Doll? You still there?"

"I'm here, Stan."

"Get back as soon as you can. No later than two days, you hear me? By the way, that two days includes your travel time, so it's best you get moving."

"I'll see what I can do, but I may be here a couple days longer. I have some things to tend to."

It feels so good to have said the words, whether Stan likes it or not.

"You have nothing to tend to, your job there is done. Do you hear me?"

Who wouldn't have been able to hear Stan? He is so bloody loud he could wake the dead.

I throw my cell phone on the bed out of frustration. I burst into tears knowing I have to leave Kanoa. After our *lū'au*, I've felt myself bringing down protective walls I'd built. We ended our night with a very passionate kiss, but that was all. And in typical Kanoa-and-Abby style, we let our physical beings take over instead of talking about our breakup. And here I am, no closer to closure, and very soon I have to leave. There are too many mixed emotions on all fronts. I pull myself off the bed and hop in the shower. I decide to give Charles a call and set up a time to meet at Starbucks.

An hour later he enters the coffee shop where I'm waiting, but I can't read his mood. Part of me is waiting for his anger to surface.

"Hi, Charles."

"Good morning, Abby. I hope you understand I had to call Stan on this one. At the end of the day, it is his law firm."

"Of course. I fully understand. I know saying sorry isn't enough, but I don't know what else to tell you."

"There's nothing to say," he says. "You were right. You told me not to lowball, and I didn't take your advice. Somehow, I didn't think a higher bid would have panned out in this case. Sounds like we've all been blown out of the water by whoever this private bidder is. Mr. Kahala isn't too happy today, I take it."

I ignore his last comment. "I'm surprised that the bank didn't contact me directly, though. That's a little troublesome, in my opinion."

"Well, again, that's sort of my fault. I badgered them into letting me know. I told them I'd be in contact with you."

I've pretty much stopped listening to Charles. I know a pathological bullshitter when I hear one. The only person I am genuinely feeling bad for is Kanoa. I know what the land means to him.

"I stopped in at Kanoa's office a few days ago," Charles says. "I wanted to make sure that there weren't any hard feelings. You never know. Maybe one day he and I can do business together."

"Maybe," is all I can muster, but giving it a second thought, I say, "Why would you go to his office? You know how he feels about you."

"We're all adults and it's just business. Anyhow, Abby, I can't thank you enough for everything you've done. Who knows? Maybe we'll meet up again on another venture."

I nod my head in agreement. I can't waste one more breath on him.

"Best I get going," he says. "We're leaving the islands on the next flight out."

We shake hands, and I walk Charles to his car. I think of calling Kanoa, but instead I hop in my car and head straight to his office. On the drive there, I try to wrap my head around the fact that I will have to leave soon. I'm feeling overwhelmed and torn, but somehow my emotions over Kanoa not winning the bid overpower everything.

I park my car and make my way to the entrance. I walk in, not expecting to see Kanoa sitting at Nani's desk. He looks extremely distraught. I'm not sure what to say at first.

"Hey! You're a sight for sore eyes," he remarks. "Guess I don't have to tell you the outcome?"

"I'm sorry, I know how much this meant to you."

"What's there to be sorry about? Maybe if I'd have listened to Nani, I wouldn't be in this predicament."

"What do you mean? What's Nani got to do with this? I heard that a private bidder won."

"The reason he or she won is because I forgot to file a document." Kanoa walks over to his desk and points. "You see, it was sitting right here under this pile, which Nani has repeatedly asked me to clean up. I still don't understand how it got here," Kanoa says, looking confused. "I know I had the paper in the submission package. That's why I can't understand how it ended up sitting right here," he exclaims, banging his fist on the pile. He looks at me. "Sorry for the outburst, but it's so frustrating. You know how often I check things. You've made fun of me for being so cautious."

"There's nothing wrong with being that way—I just like to tease you. But I do think the bank should have called you about it."

"They claim to have called. I can see the missed calls on my phone. What I can't understand is how I missed them. I never turn my phone off, especially after putting in a bid."

I really don't know what to say or how to comfort him, especially since I've been working for the enemy. What I'm having trouble comprehending is the fact that even though his desk is a mess, I know Kanoa well enough to know that nothing slips by him, ever. If he said he filed all the necessary papers, one can rest assured that he's not only triple-checked them, but he's also checked a fourth time for good measure.

"Guess I should be saying sorry to you for not winning," he says.

"This might sound really bad, but I'm happy those two didn't win. Not a good feeling for me as a lawyer representing a client, but knowing I can't be one hundred percent on my client's side makes me wonder if this is the career I really want. By the way, on another topic, Stan called, and I have to leave. He's expecting me back within two days. Of course, that includes my travel time. Have I mentioned what a dick he is?"

"I wish I had something encouraging to say."

It's not quite the response I'd been hoping for, but I know Kanoa isn't thinking straight.

"Sorry, Abby. I'm not the best company at the moment. I really appreciate you stopping by, even though it may not feel that way." He comes over to hug me, still holding the papers. "How about I pick you up for dinner? Would you be up for that?"

"Of course, but for now, why don't I stay here? I can help you out. I'm a pretty good file clerk. We all had to start somewhere. Remember?"

"It's a gorgeous day. You should be outside paddleboarding and taking in the beautiful sunshine. This is your last chance before you have to leave.

"I can't do that. We made a deal not to go out alone. So, if you're busy doing paperwork, this is where I want to be."

"Thank you, but seriously, if you want me to come with you, I will."

"No. You finish up. I have a few errands to run. I'll call you after that to see where you're at."

"That sounds like a plan to me."

As Kanoa kisses me goodbye, Nani walks in. She runs over and hugs me tight. "What can I say, Abby? My entire family had so much fun last night. *Mahalo.*"

"My pleasure, Nani. I'm just grateful to have shared such a wonderful experience with all of you."

"Kai hasn't stopped talking about it. She wants to know when you're coming by the house. She wants to teach you the hula dance."

"She is the sweetest child. I'm going to miss her so much." As I say the words, I feel myself starting to well up.

"There, there," says Nani as she grabs a tissue and hands it to me. "You sound as if you're leaving us forever."

"Well? Aren't I?"

Kanoa watches the two of us comforting one another.

"You don't have to leave if you don't want to."

Nani, being the hopeless romantic, is sniffling. That's until Kanoa turns around. "For the love of God, Nani."

"What?" she sniffs as she makes her exit. Seconds later, she returns. "Hey, I almost forgot to mention that you left the door unlocked last night," she tells Kanoa. "After the lūʻau, James dropped me off because we both forgot our house key. I keep a spare one here at the office."

"That's impossible. I know for a fact that I locked the door, because out of habit I have a need to check it twice."

"I don't know, boss. I'm just telling you what I found. I would have called you, but nothing looked out of place."

"Great, I forget to lock doors and misfile documents. None of it makes sense," says Kanoa as he looks at Nani then me. "I'm too young for dementia, right?"

Nani responds, "It could happen to any of us. Look at the bright side: nothing was stolen."

"As far as we can see at the moment. Who knows? Maybe I did get distracted. I blame you, Abby," he says jokingly to lighten the mood.

"Me! What do I have to do with it?"

"I believe I was in a hurry to come pick you up for the lūʻau. You got me so excited that I must have forgotten to close up."

I shake my head at him. "Yeah, right, great excuse. I'll see you later. Bye, Nani."

CHAPTER THIRTY-TWO:
Abby

I've run out of time. I need to get some answers before boarding a plane for New York, so I drive straight over to Pono in hopes of finding Mike sitting there; but instead, it's just Makani and Auntie. It saddens me looking at their bright, happy faces, which soon will be a distant memory. I put in my usual takeout order and make sure not to let on how sad I'm feeling inside. I've never been one for goodbyes, so I make sure to take in every little expression on their faces. I will miss them both dearly. It's too bad Mike isn't around, but on the other hand, I know for a fact the sight of his face would have me blubbering. Best to go see him at home. I leave with my takeout and venture off to my next stop.

Pulling into the barren parking lot of the Coco Palms for the last time also feels surreal. I get out of the car and make my way through the back of the complex. I owe it to myself to take in the beauty of the landscape one last time. I want to remember every detail of my picnic with Kanoa, which will comfort me for the long journey home. In case my ghost friend happens to appear, I have a bag with *lau lau* in it, just as requested. Okay, I may be a little late with it, but better late than never—I have had other things to tend to.

As I walk along the path, the sun is shining brightly through the tall palms, spreading its rays of light onto the lagoon. I stop to watch the numerous lily pads as they twist and turn on the water, each fighting its way around the other. They're like bumper cars trying to make their way to the finish line. It really is sad to see such a great property never being rebuilt; such a waste of lush waterfront property. I'm curious to know if the new owner, or owners, will actually rebuild, or if it will once again fall by the wayside.

Mesmerized by the twirling competition happening on the water, out of the corner of my eye I spot something gleaming. Its reflection is bouncing off the water directly into my eyes, making it difficult to see. I put my sunglasses on and move toward the moving shimmer. As I get closer, I realize that I'm standing in the area where Kanoa and I stopped to have our picnic. The double-hulled canoe is still rocking from side to side in its designated area. I can't understand how one section of the lagoon stays clear of all the lilypads. Scientifically, it's not possible. There are some odd forces present that no one is willing to talk about.

Once again, I feel an air of calmness at the Coco Palms. It doesn't last long, though. A rooster flies directly into my path. It almost gives me a heart attack, and I gasp for air as I try to calm down. The fowl couldn't care less about my presence, though, and we both continue on our leisurely stroll around the grounds. I've been told that the roosters are another significant sign left behind by Hurricane Iniki's flooding: roosters and chickens were set free from captivity in order to survive, and they have never been fenced in since. The locals see this as a sign from Mother Nature to give them their freedom.

I reach the end of the shimmering array of light and lose sight of it. After I take a couple more steps, I'm once again blinded by its glare. It's so hard for me to focus, I trip over a fallen tree branch and scrape my knee.

"Are you all right, dear?" asks the familiar voice.

I get up and look around, but I can't see anything, not even the shimmering glare. The voice asks me again if I'm okay. That's when I see a hair comb suspended in midair over the double-hulled canoe.

I hold up the takeout bag. "I'm sorry that I didn't bring this to you sooner, but at least you got some a few days ago. I just wanted to keep my promise to you, but I've been extremely busy. I didn't want to leave the island before you had one last *lau lau*."

The canoe starts to glide in closer towards me. As it reaches the water's edge, I see for the first time a beautiful elderly Hawaiian woman with a jeweled comb placed perfectly in her long white hair. I'm taken aback when she motions for me to get into the canoe. "Come, my child. It's time we had a heart to heart. Please don't be afraid."

I feel as though I'm losing my mind, but it doesn't stop me from getting in. She takes the bag I'm carrying out of my hands.

"Who are you?" I ask, as I watch the woman open the container with her *lau lau*. It's not as if I don't know who she is, but I need her to confirm what I think I know.

She acts as if I haven't said a word. She is too absorbed with the food. "Thank you, dear. You don't know what this means to me. Besides a few days ago, I haven't had any of this divine food since my good friend Genie died in 1999. Your generosity hasn't gone unnoticed. I think you could spoil me with all my favorite indulgences just as Genie used to. I haven't been able to trust anyone since her, so thank you, dear."

"Please tell me I'm not *lōlō*."

"You're not *lōlō*, dear."

"Good, because I didn't think that a figment of my imagination could eat food."

She roars with laughter. "You don't know how good it is to finally have a friend again."

"I take it this Genie you mentioned was your last victim?"

Why is she scrunching her eyebrows at me? I feel as if I've said something wrong.

"Oh dear!" she says. "Why must you use such a harsh tone towards me? Genie was my dear friend, not a victim. She's someone I trusted with my deepest secrets. You know, she used to run this place. Now look at it. I may have been wrong to think that I saw Genie in you."

"I'm sorry," I say, feeling horrible for using the word victim. "That was rude of me. I didn't mean to hurt your feelings. I'm honored that I remind you of someone you think so highly of. I'd love to be your friend, but I should know who I'm going to be friends with. Don't you agree? I've been assuming this entire time who you may be, but I haven't had a formal introduction."

"Excuse my manners, dear. The *lau lau* took over my senses. I was going to introduce myself, until I smelled the food. You see, I owned this land at one time. I'm Queen Deborah. Do you need me to explain further?"

I look at her, thinking she's joking, but her blank, stark stare unnerves me. I blurt out, "No! Your name is explanation enough."

"I take it that you've heard of me? I hope you haven't been listening to idle gossip."

I feel myself flinch, because I know damn well I've been listening to gossip, but I try to put it a little more diplomatically. "Let's just call them tales of the past. I've assumed up until this moment that you were the ghost I met the first time I was here. I figured I was right when you took the plate of *lau lau* I left you a few days ago, but one can't be too careful—there may have been two female ghosts out here."

"There's just me who is active," laughs the Queen. "Now tell me, what's this about your leaving? I need a favor from you; you can't leave."

What does she mean I can't leave? Is she going to try and stop me?

"I must get back to my job."

"No, you can't go just yet. I need you to do something for me; it's of the utmost importance. I need you to get to Mike. I had hoped you'd have stopped at his house by now."

I try hard not to make any body or facial movements that show I'm nervous that she's just said Mike's name. "As I mentioned, I've been busy working. Plus, how do you know I visit Mike at his house?"

"I'll fill you in when I know you better. And as for you being busy, yes, you've been busy trying to take the land away. I'll forgive you this one time, but let's get something straight. This land needs to be back in the proper hands."

"By proper hands, you mean you?"

Even as I'm speaking with the Queen I can't help feeling I'm now caught in the middle of something I didn't ask for. My eyes are shifting out of nervousness. I want her to stop talking in riddles—she's freaking me out—but she continues.

"You will figure that out, dear. You need to find Mike."

"How do you know Mike, besides him being a guest at the Coco Palms?"

"I see he told you he used to frequent my land. Let's just say I know him in a way that no one else knows him. I need you to find an antique box which is in his possession. You see, before my good friend Genie passed away, I had her give Mike a box that belonged to me. There were things in that box that no one but Mike should know about. Auntie has made reference to the—"

"Wait a minute. Whoa. You know Auntie?"

"Yes. She comes out here and clears the lagoon for me. Let's just say she became my friend through Mike, but I can't burden her with this secret. You see, Auntie is not as tough as Genie, or you for that matter. I only trust her with certain things."

"I can't believe what I'm hearing. Oh my God, someone pinch me. Please tell me I'm dreaming."

The queen leans over and pinches my arm. I squeak in pain.

"Ouch! What was that for?"

"I thought you wanted someone to pinch you? Who else was going to do it? I'm the only one here."

"It's a figure of … forget it," I say in frustration.

"Forgotten. Now, will you help me find the box? And before you ask me if you're going to die, my answer is no. Not if you're smart about it."

I lose my composure a bit after her last comment. Staring at her like a doe facing traffic, I blurt out, "Well, that's not very reassuring, now is it? Considering I've had some close calls since I've been here. Let me get this straight. What you're telling me is that there's a good chance I could get killed?"

"Precisely."

"Oh great. That just made my day."

"You've made mine too, dear. Thank you again for the food, even though it did take you a long time to bring it. Feel free to stop in more often."

I'm not sure about the Queen's brazen persona, but I can't dismiss her sense of humor. Who'd have thought I'd come across a ghost with such attitude? Unfortunately, it's going to cost me big dough in shrink bills once I get back to New York.

Deborah moves in as close as she can to stare into my face. She says, "You can't breathe a word of what I'm about to tell you to anyone," she says. "Do you understand?"

"I didn't tell anyone about our previous encounters," I catch myself saying with a trembling voice. "Well, that's not entirely true. I brought you up in conversation to see if others had ever heard of you still being around."

"I bet that made for interesting conversation. Please, do share some of their thoughts with me."

"I'd love to, but I'm pressed for time. Maybe on another visit."

"As you like, but please refrain from repeating this conversation, not even to your boyfriend," says the Queen, and I stare at her in shock. "Oh, you can wipe that surprised look off your face. I know you're in love with Kanoa. A blind person would see it. Now sit and let me explain a few things to you," she says as she takes another bite of food.

"Don't you think I should call the police if people are in danger?"

"No! Absolutely not!" she says. "This is a private matter."

"It's not that I don't want to help you, but you see, I'm leaving for home tomorrow. I don't have time to play sleuth. Plus, if I don't find Mike at home, I'm not breaking into his house to look for a box."

"I'm not asking you to break in. Where do you come up with these things? You're more like Genie than I even imagined," laughs the Queen.

"Well, she must have been an intelligent woman. Why can't you slither yourself into Mike's and get the box? No one would see you. By the way, why did you show yourself to me today?"

"So many questions at once. Which shall I answer first?"

"Let's start with why not get the box yourself?"

Deborah is staring at me as if I should know the answer. I try to quickly think of what I just asked her, but I still don't understand why she doesn't do it herself. I know she is staring at me with frustration as she answers, "It's not that easy. I can't carry certain objects. Yes, I may hold up a fork or a glass, but I can't drag a box with me. I'm not physically capable of doing that. Even us ghosts have limitations, you know. Please, dear, I wouldn't ask if it weren't of grave importance. Please, I'm begging you. And if you knew me well, you'd know that I don't beg for anything."

I'm feeling trapped, but I can't promise her much, seeing as I have to leave. Somehow, though, she gets to me.

"Okay," I say.

"Okay what? You will help me?"

"I will, but I have to go home first."

Shocked, Deborah asks, "What do you mean, go home first?"

"My flight to New York leaves tomorrow or the next day. My assistant needs to get back to me with the details. All I can promise you is that I will think long and hard about how I'm going to be able to help you, but I need your honesty about Mike. Is Mike's life in danger?"

"Yes, but only if certain people don't get what they are after."

"You're not going to tell me who they are, are you?"

The Queen shakes her head no.

"I didn't think so."

"You see? This is why I chose you, Abby. I've had my eye on you since you first came to the Coco Palms. You're a smart young woman. I also know Mike well enough that he'll try his trickery. He may hand them over something just to satisfy their greed."

"Earlier you said they might kill me, or is it Mike? I'm so confused."

"Dear, one thing I've learned in my long life is to always be prepared for the worst. You asked if there was a chance of being killed, and I said yes, if you're not careful. I think that's a logical answer."

My head is going to fall off, after the number of times I've shaken it in frustration. There's nothing logical about this conversation. I hear myself say, "I'll do my best, but with me leaving tomorrow, maybe you should let me tell Kanoa about this. I mean, who knows this island better than him?"

"No, no and no! Kanoa is the one person I absolutely don't want involved in this. I don't want anyone but you. I'm begging you one last time, please, Abby. Do you understand?"

"Loud and clear." I turn to step off the canoe, which has drifted back along the water's edge. I turn and ask, "Why me?"

"You'll know the answer to that, dear, if you are honest with yourself."

I'm left more confused than ever. I mutter under my breath as I descend from the canoe. "Why in God's name must she speak in riddles? Listen to me. I'm actually convinced that I'm speaking to someone, and I'm the nutcase that brought her food."

"You are speaking to someone," responds the Queen. "Why must you mortals act as if I'm deaf?"

I don't say another word. I walk as fast as I can until I get back to my car. I head straight for Mike's house.

This is all too strange. Why is Ken's car parked at Mike's house again? I barely believed Charles this morning when he told me his reasons for still being in Kauaʻi, but now that I think of it, he never mentioned Ken's whereabouts. Why were these two in such a rush to leave, and now, of all places, Ken is pulled over in front of Mike's house? Could he be the person the Queen was referring to when she said someone wants the contents of the box? None of it makes any sense.

As much as I want to call Kanoa, or better yet, the police, Deborah's words keep replaying over and over in my mind. I don't want to jeopardize anyone's life, so instead I reverse the car and park behind a huge wall of hibiscus flowers. Most of my car is shielded from view, but I have my eye on Ken, who I can see is staring directly at Mike's house. I keep my phone next to me in case I need to call for help. In the meantime, I sit and wait to see what plays out.

After an hour of sitting in my car, I see Mike pulling into his laneway. He gets out and walks directly over to Ken.

I can't believe my eyes. Mike opens a box—must be the one the Queen kept referencing—and removes something from it, but I'm too far away to make out what it is. He shuts the lid as he hands something over to Ken.

I'm just glad that Mike is safe. It appears that Ken got what he wanted, based on the wide smile that has spread across his face. I wish I knew what he was holding.

A call is coming in, and it takes my attention away from what's happening. It's Mindy with my flight information. She can't get me a flight until the day after Stan wanted me back. I can't say I'm disappointed, because it will allow me that much more time with people I've come to care about. I desperately need to use every minute to its fullest, and right now I need to get moving for my date with Kanoa.

CHAPTER THIRTY-THREE

I get back to my hotel to shower and throw on a crisp white linen dress. I figure it's a safe outfit, not knowing what's in store for the evening. Sitting with a heavy heart, I wait for Kanoa to arrive.

I ponder whether my job is really worth leaving Kanoa and the island without any form of resolution, but I know I must. I can't abandon the life I've built for myself in New York. My parents are there and they're the most important people in my life; I can't be this far away from them any longer. I feel the weight of the world on my shoulders all around. How can I leave the Queen after what she has requested of me? Will an extra day be enough to get more information out of her? Probably not, but before I have time to plummet into total panic mode, I hear a knock on the door.

I run with the anticipation of seeing Kanoa's face on the other side, but when I fling the door open I see only an empty hallway. I step out into the hallway and look up and down, expecting Kanoa to magically appear out of nowhere. I figure he's pranking me, but he's nowhere to be seen. After the day I've had, anything is possible. I walk back into my room, but I can sense a shift in the atmosphere. Even though nothing is apparent to the naked eye, I know I'm not alone. I have company—the unwanted kind. Thinking back to my conversation with the Queen, could the occult presence in my room be the corrupt ghost, the Queen's ex-husband?

Luckily for me, the next knock at the door is Kanoa, except I can't move as quickly as I'd like to answer the door. It's as if someone is tugging me back by the hem of my dress. I'll be damned if I'll let some evil spirit get the best of me. Bound and determined, my anger rises to a new level—one that might even be too much for the mighty Sarah Connor. Hearing Kanoa calling my name and not being able to reach him angers me even more. I free myself and run. I forcefully open the door and literally fly into Kanoa's arms.

"Hey! Hey! What's going on?" asks Kanoa in shock.

"Sorry," I shriek. "Phew. You know how it is with us women." Oh jeez, I cringe at my own stupid reply.

"I do? What's gotten into you? Plus, young lady, I have a bone to pick with you."

"Oh? What did I do now?"

"I thought you were going to call me after you finished running your errands."

"I did, didn't I? Time got away from me—sorry."

I can tell by Kanoa's smirk that he's not buying my excuses. "Abby Parker! Whose leg are you trying to pull?

There isn't a thing that slips by you. What have you been up to?"

"Got me. I got a little carried away with my shopping and …"

"Okay. I see you don't want to tell me. You weren't saying goodbye to some new boyfriend, were you?"

I jokingly shove him. "Okay. Now you're just being an idiot."

"Can't blame a guy. You have to admit your behavior has been a bit out of character."

I can still feel the unwanted force lingering in the room. I suggest we get going, but I can tell Kanoa isn't in a hurry. "Listen," I say. "I'm really sorry for what happened over the land deal. I fully understand if you don't want to go out. I know what that land means to you, and the misfiling —"

"Let's not talk about it. I've been beating myself up all day. It's something that I just can't wrap my head around. The last thing I want is to put a damper on the night. Let's just go out and be normal."

"Normal? What's normal on this island?" I ask in a half-joking manner. And just then, I feel the tension of the unwanted apparition leave the room.

"Abby? What are you looking at? Are you okay?"

"Yes, I'm fine. Before I forget, Mindy couldn't get me a flight for tomorrow, so it looks like I have an extra day."

"Seriously? That's fantastic news. That's definitely cause for celebration, but you never answered my questiong about what you were looking at."

"Nothing."

"Fine. Have it your way. So, what would you like to do tonight? It's entirely your call, because tomorrow, I'm going to take you somewhere really special."

"Oh! You've piqued my curiosity. Where are you taking me?"

"You'll have to wait and see, just be ready for five PM. Actually, we should spend the entire day together, unless you have other plans."

My mind races, the same way I flip through a fashion magazine. I can see all the faces of the people I've planned to revisit, but maybe I should just stick with Kanoa and the Queen. I'm sure I can run out early in the morning and have a quick visit with her. In the meantime, Kanoa and I have plenty to discuss.

"So, you're telling me that I have one extra day to change your mind about staying on the island and giving up your job?" he asks with clear optimism.

"No, not exactly, but I do have time to say that I'm truly sorry for you and your investors," I offer with only the sincerest, heartfelt sadness in my heart. I take Kanoa's hand in mine and continue, "Now that I've gotten to know Nani, Mike and some other folks, I can understand what the land means to Native Kauai'ians. I was naïve about that. When I initially saw you, I wanted nothing more than to see the land taken away from you. I'm ashamed to admit it, but I'm also not going to hide the fact. I was spiteful and in revenge mode. My heart breaks for you, but I'm gratefully happy that the Baker Brothers didn't get the land—which brings me to question whether I'm in the right line of work. I need to be in it one hundred percent for my clients. So, in a nutshell, I question the manner in which I let things get personal. For now I need a job to pay my bills, but I'll be thinking about things, that's for sure."

"I'm sure we could find you something in one of the law offices here."

"Come on. You know as well as I do that I'd never get the same salary."

"But having only two seasons will save you some money. We can make it work."

"Point taken, but ..." I can't finish my sentence. My emotions are rising to the top and getting the best of me.

"Hey, hey ... don't cry," Kanoa says as he gently brushes my hair away from my face.

"I can't help it. As much as I want to enjoy tonight, I'm feeling so damn stressed about everything. I know I'm here an extra day, but that's not a lot of time."

"Well, you'll just have to come back and visit. Soon! Hopefully we can arrange a trip every two months to start with."

"You're thousands of miles away. It's not going to happen that often, and you know it. We haven't even put a dent in talking about our breakup."

"We can talk about it right now. Plus, who says I won't come visit you? We will make it work, I promise. We'll figure things out as we go. I know you can't trust me right now, but I will prove to you that I'm still the guy you loved, just a much better version. So much so that I will pick a date right now and you can hold me to it. You watch," says Kanoa as he flips through his phone to open up his calendar.

"It all sounds great right now, but the reality is … I can't just get up and go. You'll realize that the distance between us will become an issue. Plus, you know I love New York. I love summer vacations at the Hamptons with my parents. It's just the three of us. I can't leave them. And let's not forget my job."

"And your job is the one thing that you're not sure about. Maybe there's no time like the present to make a change."

"It's too soon."

"Okay. I know we can't solve everything in a condensed timeslot, so why don't we at least start tonight. What do you say we order in? That way we won't be constantly interrupted and distracted by the serving staff. We'll have a romantic dinner on the balcony, while you listen to the waves and enjoy the burning tiki torches you've come to love so much. What do you say?"

"I think it's a great idea. Also, that was one hell of a sales pitch if I've ever heard one."

"That dress you're wearing is a distraction," says Kanoa as he makes his way over to where I'm standing. I can feel his warm hands as he places them on the small of my back. His touch has me quivering with desire. As much as I want to lean in and kiss him, my brain is telling me to step away. We've been down the physical road before and look where it landed us. I can't be swept up by the Kanoa tsunami, at least not just yet.

CHAPTER THIRTY-FOUR

Tonight, Kanoa is taking me to a fabulous restaurant in Poipu, on the southern tip of the island. He said he has a surprise for me and promised that we'll have a serious talk. It's best to be in public because behind-closed-doors privacy would land us in bed. There's no other way for us to talk about serious issues, as we've come to realize. I can't put all the blame on Kanoa—I definitely played a part in it—but first things first.

This morning, I'm heading over to have a talk with Mike and say my final goodbye. It won't be easy, but I need to see him one last time.

I arrive at Mike's house for what I thought was going to be a coffee, but he's put out a cornucopia of my favorite foods. I jokingly ask if I can take him home with me.

Mike replies, "I don't want to think about not seeing your beautiful face every day. I've come to love you like a daughter. I know how crazy it sounds, but I feel as if I've known you forever. You sure you can't stay a little longer?"

"I wish I could, Mike, but I really need to get back, but I promise I'll be back one day." I stop speaking for a moment because if I utter another word I'm afraid I'll be blubbering. Mike's face isn't helping keep my emotions from getting the better of me. The old man that I've come to adore with the soft, gentle soul is somehow looking much older this morning, or maybe I've been in denial about his age.

As much as I don't want to bring up the topic, I have to. I take a gulp of my strong coffee before saying, "Mike, what I'm about to say may shock you, but please know that it's out of concern for your welfare."

"What is it, child?"

"When I found out I had to return to New York, I came here unannounced hoping to find you at home."

"Why didn't you come in? Was my car not here?"

"Your car was here, but when I got to your front door, I saw you and Auntie. It looked like you were having a serious conversation. I didn't want to disturb you."

"Nonsense," he says. "You should have rung the bell. I know Auntie would have been thrilled to visit with you." Mike is staring at me waiting for an answer, but I take too long to reply. "Why the frown? You look troubled."

"I know this is none of my business, but I saw you two sitting in the living room with two boxes on the coffee table. I was told by a particular being that there are bad people wanting whatever it is you have in those boxes." I suddenly stop talking when I notice Mike is no longer eating. He looks agitated. No, agitated is not the emotion I'm seeing in his face—it's more of a worried look.

"Who is this person that told you about the box?"

"You said box, but you have two identical ones."

"Abby?"

"Sorry, that's me being a detective's daughter. I can't tell you who told me."

"Why? Because I'll think you are *lōlō* for talking to a ghost?" laughs Mike.

I'm not sure what to say. There's no point in omitting anything. Well, maybe just the fact that I saw him with Ken. It could make me out to look like I've been stalking him—or even worse, that I don't trust him. Lost in thought, I hear Mike say, "Abby, eat your breakfast before it gets cold."

I take a huge mouthful of food. Maybe it's best to eat and keep quiet for a while. I'll let Mike do the talking.

"Abby, I know that you visit the lagoon area. I may not have been down there for years, but I have my sources. I'm well aware that you visit the Queen."

My mouth is overstuffed, which has me chewing as fast as I can in order to answer Mike. I take a sip of coffee to speed up the swallowing process. After my final gulp I ask, "Why haven't you told me any of this before?"

"The same reason why you haven't fully disclosed your visits with the Queen to me," Mike says with his eyebrows raised. "Would you like to explain what the Queen is asking you to do?"

I'm at a loss for words. I can't look up at his face any longer. I'm feeling very uncomfortable and want to just say goodbye and leave, but it's too late for that. I'm about to say something, when Auntie walks into the kitchen. Was she eavesdropping? I really don't know much about Auntie, but what I do know is that she admitted to being the one who told Mike about my every move.

She says, "You see, Abby, I've been going out to the lagoon since Genie died. I clear part of the lagoon so the Queen can enjoy her canoe ride. I happened to stumble upon her one day and she befriended me, but I know I'll never be as close to her as Genie was, or you, for that matter."

"What has the Queen told you about me?"

"Absolutely nothing. I saw you there a few times as I was making my way to the lagoon. I chose to turn around and leave. Better question is, what has Queen Deborah told you about me and Mike?"

"All I know is that there is something in the box that she gave Mike, or you gave Mike, or maybe it was Genie? I don't know. I'm confused at this point as to who gave whom the box. She said the contents are very important and I know it has something to do with the Coco Palms. I swear that's all I know," I say as I throw my hands up in the air.

"Abby, don't be nervous," says Mike. "Auntie and I just want to make sure you don't get in over your head. We are worried for your well-being."

"Why? What do you know? Am I in danger?"

"Just don't discuss the box with anyone," Mike says. "It's of the utmost importance that the information in the box is kept secret. Auntie doesn't even know what's in the box. Well, in all honesty she didn't up until two years ago."

I don't fully comprehend the secrecy behind the box, but I know I don't want to discuss it any further—and nor do Mike and Auntie, judging by the exhausted expressions on their faces. I promise both of them that I won't breathe a word of it to anyone. They especially make me swear not to breathe a word to Kanoa, and I will keep my word on that. Auntie needs to get to work, so I offer to give her a lift, but I also have another agenda. Seeing as I have extra time, I want to make a quick stop to see Deborah.

Saying goodbye to Mike is even more difficult than I had anticipated. His confiding in me has made leaving that much harder. I try hard not to cry, but as Mike and I hug, I feel the tears drip onto my arm. I make sure to wipe my face before our eyes meet, but it doesn't matter, because I see a tear escaping from Mike's eyes and dropping to the ground. We are quite the pair. He holds my hand and says, "Tears of joy, dear. I wish you a safe trip and a speedy return to our island."

I stand speechless. I nod yes and turn to walk out with Auntie. Mike's fallen tears will be embedded in my brain forever.

The car ride to Pono Market from Mike's house is short, but long enough for Auntie to tell me what is on her mind.

"Abby, I don't know all the details of what has transpired between you and Kanoa, but I can't have you leaving without saying that I think you are making a terrible mistake."

"In what way?"

"I've known Kanoa since he was a baby and let me tell you, he's one of the finest young men you will ever meet. As a woman, I too would be mad about the way he left you in New York, but as a Native Kauaiʻian woman, I do understand his good intentions about the land. It's a terrible situation he put himself in, and you for that matter, but I know that he cares deeply for you."

We reach the market and within a few minutes Auntie will disappear from my sight and into her workplace. But before she leaves my car, I say, "*Mahalo*, Auntie. I will think long and hard about your words, but I do have to go back to New York for now. I don't know where life will take me, but I have come to understand what drove Kanoa to do the things he's done. I'm not saying I trust him fully—it's something we need to work on—but I do know we are doing better. Distance will be our enemy, though."

I feel Auntie's hand gently brush my cheek as she says, "Abby, there's no rush. There's no expiration date on true love." And with those wise words, Auntie gets out of the car. I sit and watch her as she walks through the doors of Pono Market. My heart is full of love, but heavy at the same time.

Lost in my own emotions, I start to drive away and realize I've forgotten to go in and pick up some *lau lau* for Queen Deborah. I hesitate to turn around because Auntie will know whom I'm buying it for, so I stop at another shop to get some.

When I reach the lagoon, I can see the sun reflecting off Queen Deborah's jeweled hair comb. Before she even reaches the water's edge, she says, "Why didn't you stop at Pono for my *lau lau*?"

Dumbfounded, I reply, "How did you know so quickly?"

"I can smell it. That's not Pono *lau lau*."

I'm hoping she can't see me rolling my eyes. "You've got to be kidding me."

"No."

"So, you don't want it."

"No, thank you, but I appreciate the thought."

I can't believe it. I have a new friend who's a ghost, and as if that isn't crazy enough, she is an extremely picky ghost to boot. "I'm sorry, it's just that I didn't want Auntie knowing I was coming out here."

"Don't fret, dear. I'm happy with all the other visits when you did bring me treats. Come, get on, and let's go for a little ride."

I can see Deborah's hand, and like a fool I try to take hold of it, only to slip and half fall into the water. I look up at her. "I keep forgetting that you're transparent."

"And I'm trying to forget that I've been dead for almost two hundred years," laughs the Queen boisterously. "I'm very happy that you came out to see me again. I just wish you didn't have to go back to New York."

"That seems to be the consensus on the island," I chuckle with a heavy heart. Somehow making a joke always softens the blow of reality. As we sail down the lagoon I ask, "Are you sure you can't tell me about the contents of the ornate box?"

"I can't. It's for your own good. Plus, things need to play out organically. I can't have any false or forced feelings. This may all sound crazy to you, but you just need to trust me, as I have come to trust you."

I want to reach over and hug her. I can't believe she admitted to trusting me. But lunging through someone's body is not something I want to experience. I'll settle for an air kiss.

"How long do you have?" asks Deborah.

"Do you mean left on the island?"

"No, how long is our visit for?"

"I was thinking an hour?"

"That's perfect. I regret not giving you something yesterday, so you can't imagine my delight when I smelled you coming. I don't mean smelled *you*—you know what I'm referring to."

"Yes, I think we've come to understand one another with fewer and fewer words."

"Yes, the mark of true friendship."

"So, what is it you want to give me?"

I watch as the Queen removes her jeweled hair comb from her long gray hair. "I want to give you this," she says as she places it gently in my hair. "Just as I had imagined. You know, you remind me so much of myself when I was your age. You look stunning with it. The jewels show up much better on your dark hair. I'm sure this is how Elvis had envisioned it on Priscilla."

"Elvis?"

"Yes. He gave me the comb as a farewell gift."

"As in, you never saw him again?"

"Not exactly. Seeing as you have time, I'll tell you a little story, because I know that you're not someone that would leak it to the press."

"Absolutely not. I'd never do such a thing."

"Have a seat, this will take a bit."

I sit down on the canoe as Deborah starts to recount the night she received the hair comb.

"It was 1969, and Elvis had brought Priscilla to Kaua'i with him. They were staying in Bungalow/Cottage #25, which was originally designed by me. Whenever he vacationed with Priscilla he chose to stay in the bungalow because it was harder for the press and fans to find them there. But first I need to back up a bit in my story. During the filming of Blue Hawaii in 1961, Elvis was staying in Room #256, which I promised not to sneak into, but I did, as Genie always loved to remind me," Deborah giggles.

"I honestly didn't think Elvis would see me, because there was no way I'd ever jeopardize his stay here, but he was the one who befriended me. Somehow, he had special powers with the afterlife. I'm certain that this is why so many people around the world still claim to have Elvis sightings. I didn't think anything could ever shock me, but his superpowers did. He even told me that he knew I was lying next to him in bed the first time he'd visited. I didn't have the courage to ever tell Genie— she'd have been mortified and too scared to ever give him my room again.

"Anyhow, Elvis and I became quite close— spiritually, not physically, as Genie accused me of. He said he looked forward to seeing me on his visits. I guess you could call me his spiritual guru. Anyhow, on one of his visits he was out by the lagoon singing for a private party. He was so happy to be arm in arm with his beautiful wife, Priscilla, as they strolled along the lagoon after the party. Earlier that day he'd told me that he was going to surprise her with a very special anniversary gift. Instead, he's the one who got the surprise. I call it more of a shock. When they went back to their cottage for the night, she told Elvis that she wanted a divorce. He told me it was as if he'd gone stone deaf after hearing the word divorce. Priscilla had found out about a few of his dalliances and wasn't willing to turn a blind eye any longer. She had also found someone else—except for Priscilla, it was more serious than just a fling. Elvis couldn't deal with it, which led Priscilla to fly home the next day without him."

"Oh my God! I can't believe it. I had no idea that this is where they ended their marriage. I thought they divorced in the seventies."

"Let's just say they stayed together for a few years longer—after all, they had a beautiful baby girl together—but the beginning of the end was in the sixties."

"Wow, very sad. I guess no one really has it all, do they? When Priscilla left the island, did Elvis stay on?"

Even as I ask the question I visualize a very somber Elvis sitting by the lagoon, wondering how life could have taken such a sad turn.

"He had contractual engagements to honor," Deborah says, "so he stayed a while longer. I'm sure he could have canceled them, but he was loyal to his fans—

just not so loyal to his wife, which is something he has always regretted. She was the one true love of his life; he told me so every chance he had. Anyhow, he flew to Oʻahu for a few days and then came back to Kauaʻi to gather his thoughts. On his last day he asked if he could stop by my room. I agreed and told him to stop in anytime, that I'd leave the door unlocked. I waited around most of the day. I figured he wasn't going to show because he hadn't been himself since Priscilla left, so I went out to the lagoon for some fresh air. When I got back, I found a box with a note leaning up against it. Mind you, I thought the jeweled box itself was the gift, until I opened it and there it was, the exquisite hair comb."

"So, he left you the comb that was meant for Priscilla?"

"Exactly."

"Wow! That's incredible. Are you sure you want me to have it?"

"Of course I'm sure. I know you'll cherish it as much as I have."

"But it must be worth gazillions. I can't take it. Plus, I'd be too afraid of losing it. It should be insured."

"It's priceless, but who's going to find out that it once belonged to Elvis?" the Queen says in a tone that makes it quite clear, yet again, that I'm not to repeat this to anyone.

"I promise I won't tell a soul," I utter nervously. "But, I still don't think I should have it."

"Nonsense. It's a gift and I expect you to wear it," says the Queen strictly. "You must never remove the comb, at least not until you come back to the island—promise me!"

This is one peculiar request, but what hasn't been peculiar about this entire journey?

"Abby? Are you listening to me?"

"Yes, of course, I've heard every word. I promise I won't take the comb off, but I do need to wash my hair and sleep. Besides that, I promise not to take it off."

"Just don't misplace the comb when you do remove it! And never remove it for long."

"I won't. My God, you make it sound as if it has magic powers," I say jokingly, but Deborah's expression isn't registering humor. "Does this comb ...?"

"Get going, I don't want to keep you from your date with Kanoa," says Deborah, another master of deflection.

"See! It's things like this. How do you know I have a date with Kanoa?"

"Well, what else would you be doing on your last night here? It only makes sense. Abby, you really are paranoid," she says with a naughty twinkle in her eyes. Her face glows with serenity, and for the very first time, Deborah's smile feels warm and sincere. Maybe I really do remind her of Genie and herself. I'm honored that she trusts me enough to give me her priceless comb, but I'm a nervous wreck thinking of its worth.

As I walk away, I still can't help think how ludicrous her request about the hair comb is. Of course I'm going to take it off. I can't be wearing it in my hair all the time— what if I did lose it? Maybe I'll keep it at my parents' place. They have a built-in safe.

After leaving the Coco Palms I make one last surprise stop to see Nani. Even though we said our goodbyes yesterday, I have to see her one last time, even if it's for just a brief moment. I know she'll be going home at noon to have lunch with Kai. As tough as it will be to have to answer all Kai's questions about leaving, it'd be tougher if I didn't see her.

CHAPTER THIRTY-FIVE

Kanoa calls just as I am leaving Nani's house. He asks if he can pick me up around two PM, saying, "I know it's a lot earlier than we'd planned, but all I'm doing is sitting here licking my wounds over the Coco Palms. It's draining me of positive energy when I could be spending my time with you right now."

"Hello, and what have you done with Kanoa?" I tease.

Kanoa doesn't take long to arrive at my hotel, but it's enough time for me to pack for my bittersweet departure. I open the door. "Hi, come in. Sorry I haven't changed yet; I was waiting to see what you've planned for us."

"In all honesty I didn't have any plans besides dinner, but an idea came to me while crossing the Wailua Bridge. You can't go back to New York without going for a kayak ride down the Wailua River. What do you say?"

"Sounds like fun. Would you mind if we pop back in here to change for dinner?"

"For sure, we'll definitely need to shower after kayaking."

On our ride to the expedition rental I tell Kanoa about calling my parents. "My mom was out today. It's funny to hear Dad answering the phone. Last time I talked to my mother she'd mentioned he was trying to work less. He's finally promised to spend more time at home with her. Mom's been retired for almost a year and has been trying to convince him to do the same."

"That's great, but I think it may take a little longer for your dad. Not sure it's in him to fully retire. I truly miss your parents. I know if I said give them my best, it wouldn't go over so well, but who can blame them. Looking back, if someone left my daughter the way—"

"Hey, hey, let's not make this into a heavy day, please. It was bad enough having to pack my suitcase and saying goodbye to my new friends."

Kanoa raises his eyes to look at me and smiles. "You're right. I'm sorry."

"I wanted my parents to know I'd be flying out tomorrow. But then you know Dad—he asks a million questions, and I told him a bit about the situation with the Coco Palms. I'd have never gotten him off the phone if I didn't give him something." We both find it quite hilarious because we know my dad never lets his detective guard down.

"Your parents were so good to me."

"I know Mom was, but I always found Dad to be a bit on the defensive."

"Maybe at first," he says, "but it's a parent's right. I know if I ever have children, I'll be no different."

"Well, Mr. Kahala, you think you'll have kids some day?"

"Yeah. Why? Is there something wrong with that?"

I can't believe how shocked he seems by my question. He never once mentioned kids in the two years we were together, but then again, neither did I. Maybe on the eve of leaving, discussing kids before getting to the root of what broke us up is not a good idea. I finally reply, "No, there's nothing wrong with wanting to start a family."

"Good, so we're on the same page."

I look over at Kanoa as he drives with his deadpan face. I can't help but wonder how this is going to transpire. One of us is definitely getting set up for a fall, if not both of us. Maybe he's convinced himself to stay positive today and avoid more talk of the past. The conversation comes to a halt as we turn into the kayak rental shop. I get out of the car.

"That's a pretty fancy comb you're wearing," he says. "It's so not you."

"You don't like it?"

"No, no, that's not what I meant at all. I think you look beautiful, as you do in everything. I've just never seen you wear an antique piece, that's all. I can see you wearing it with an evening gown, but a swimsuit—bit too ornate for rugged wear. Did it belong to your grandmother?"

And there it is, a question I'm not sure I should lie about. Do I offer up the truth? I'm always giving him a hard time about lying and it'd make me a hypocrite, so I say, "I got it as a gift this morning."

"Oh. That was nice of Nani."

"No, it wasn't Nani." I can feel Kanoa staring at me as if to say, *"Okay, then who?"*

"You mean when I joked about you having a local boyfriend it wasn't a joke?"

"No, now you're just being an idiot. I decided to go down to the lagoon, and I got it from …"

Kanoa stops dead in his tracks. He raises one hand and says, "No. No. No, no, not today."

With a reaction like that, what's a gal to do? I stare at Kanoa with a smile and a raised eyebrow. I shrug my shoulders at him and off we go to get our kayaks. Not another word is mentioned about the comb. I was told enough times by Deborah not to take it off, so he's going to have to live with my new look.

Thanks to both of us having such strong personalities, we quickly get into a new debate over who is going to lead in the two-person kayak. Seeing as we can't compromise on it, we each get our own single kayak.

Even after making the decision, Kanoa complains. "I don't understand why we need two—I said you should sit up front."

"But I know you want to show me where to go and I'd hate it if my view is blocked, so why should I think you'd be okay with it?"

"Abby, I'm much taller than you. I can see over your head when you're sitting. I could easily have navigated you from behind."

And with that, I find myself saying, before he pays, "I change my mind, let's just get a double kayak."

We could have opted to go in a group tour, but Kanoa says he's been up and down the river his entire life. That isn't his only reason. "We'd be with others for a four-hour tour and sometimes longer. I want you all to myself. It's our last day together. Plus, we can leave whenever we feel like it."

I'm not going to argue that point. "I'd prefer to be alone also, thank you." I had no idea it was going to be this long, but what better place to be? The girl at the counter hands Kanoa a packed picnic lunch, which he secretly ordered while I was changing earlier.

My decision to leave is becoming much more painful than I'd even imagined. The reality is setting in, but I try not to let it get me down. The sun is scorching hot and Kanoa, being the wiser when it comes to the outdoor elements, brought a tube of sunscreen with him, along with bug repellant and other survival goodies. I reapply sunscreen, realizing Kanoa is right—I don't know how to rough it. Back in NY, when he'd suggest we go camping in the Hamptons, I thought he was crazy. Being on the beach all day was camping enough for me.

After two hours of kayaking, we decide to stop for a bit. Kanoa jumps out of the kayak and offers to push me to shore so I won't get muddy. I think, no way, I want to show him I can do it. Of course, my exit out of the kayak lands me head first in the water—which by the way is quite refreshing—but I can see why he made the offer. Soon we're both thigh high in mud. I take it like a champ. I wash off as much as I can in the river and proceed to look for a shaded area to have a picnic.

I watch as Kanoa takes off his wet shirt and hangs it on a tree branch. His broad shoulders and ripped abs are making it hard for me not to stare. How I missed being wrapped up in his arms and pressed against his chest. Kanoa is the only man I've ever felt so much passion for, but on the flip side, it's also the one relationship that tore my soul to pieces. He finishes setting down a towel, then looks up and motions for me to go over and sit.

"How's this for a great spot?" he asks proudly.

"Fantastic. I can use a time-out from the sun's rays."

"Let me apply a fresh layer of sunscreen," offers Kanoa as he pulls the tube out of a waterproof bag— another thing I'd never think of. I am making a mental list of all the survival necessities.

"I just applied some, it's not necessary."

"You didn't apply any to your back. Come on, sit and stop being stubborn. You'll regret it when you can't sleep from water-blistered skin."

"Well, when you put it like that." I sit down on the towel and Kanoa straddles me from behind as he rubs lotion on my back.

After all this time on the island, it's not that I haven't thought about it, but we haven't made love. I didn't think we were in a particularly great place, but desperation and his touch are getting the better of me. All the what-ifs running through my mind have me wishing he'd just take me into his arms and make mad passionate love to me the way we used to. Then again, why do I need to wait for him to make the move?

I know why—because I'm scared to death of making a mistake, or even worse, being rejected. But when has love ever been logical or without pain? True love, that is? And just like that, I stop thinking altogether. I can hear Kanoa's breathing. The touch of his warm chest on my back has my heart practically pulsating out of my chest.

He whispers in my ear, "I've always loved you, Abby. I never stopped. I've missed you so much." He gently kisses my neck.

Every part of me wants to reciprocate the sentiment, but I'm frozen with fear. I don't want to take the chance and get hurt. I find myself saying, "I've always loved you, but look where it got us." He stops rubbing my back and turns me around to look at him.

"It got us here," he said, "where we are meant to be."

"But you had me in New York."

"I know, but what I didn't realize until I came back here, is that I didn't love myself any longer. I allowed myself to become someone I never thought I could be. I felt the walls closing in on me from all the pressure. I know now that it's pressure I put on myself."

"I must have been part of that pressure."

"Yes, but only because I wasn't honest about who I was—plus, you weren't the only factor. I felt pressure from my job, and not knowing if I could make enough money to have a chance to bid on the Coco Palms. I promised a lot of people things I was no longer sure I could deliver on, but when I did find myself in a position to pursue the Coco Palms, I didn't know how to tell you."

"You could have tried."

"I know that now, but everything looks better in hindsight, don't you think?"

"Not everything," I say as I gently kiss his soft, pillow-like lips. I fight hard not to give into the urge, but I can feel the protective wall I've built coming down bit by bit, the mortar crumbling. Kanoa tries to speak, but I hush him with another kiss, one that doesn't seem to have an end—that is, until I realize the comb is no longer in my hair.

"Oh my God!" I scream loudly. "My comb!"

My shrieking has left Kanoa wide-eyed and probably half deaf. He quickly gets up and starts to retrace every step we've taken. I watch as he runs through the shallow water to peer inside the kayak. He turns to look at me and shakes his head no, but his eyes don't fool me—they are gleaming.

I run towards him. "What's in your hand? Let me see!"

"What will you give me for it?"

He doesn't have to ask what I'm willing to give him, because I've decided it is time. Kanoa gently places the comb in my tangled, muddy hair. "Beautiful," he says as he pulls me in tight. "How about we continue our discussion?"

I have to laugh. "Sure, if that's what we're calling it now." The thing is, our moment of opportunity has passed. A group of kayakers has stopped in our shaded area. We decide to abandon it and start heading back towards the parking lot.

"Next time you're here," Kanoa says, "I will show you the falls and all the other sights. We really need the entire day, but this was a good start. I had a lot of fun. Thanks for agreeing to come out."

"Thank you for suggesting it. I had a great time, and I can't thank you enough for finding my comb. That was a close call. I don't know what I'd have done if you didn't find it."

Back at my hotel I have first dibs on the shower. It might take a while to get the tangles and dirt out of my hair since it's so caked on. I gently remove the hair comb and put it in my purse; this way I'll know exactly where to find it. Kanoa is having a beer out on the balcony, or so I thought. As I reach for the shampoo for a second round of washing, I feel Kanoa's hand on mine, which has me dropping the bottle and squealing from the soap stinging my eyes. Kanoa tries to calm me as he retrieves the shampoo. I can't keep my eyes open, because everytime I try to open them, the stinging pain automatically causes me to keep them shut. As I reach for a facecloth to wipe my eyes I hear the shampoo cap being flipped open. After wiping away all the suds from my eyes, I start to slowly open them.

Before I have a chance to say a word, shampoo and warm water are being gently massaged into my scalp, which I pray won't end up in my eyes again. After the best head massage I've ever had, Kanoa takes the hand shower and rinses out the shampoo. I can feel him slowly exploring my body as I remember him doing so many times before, but this is different. We are taking our time and absorbing every caress between us. It's as if we're exploring new things that we can hold onto when we're no longer together. I realize at that moment just how well I know him in certain ways. The feeling of my hands on his rock-hard thighs is something I never thought I'd experience again. Hearing Kanoa's moans of pleasure always got me more aroused than I'd ever been, and I think we used to have a pretty great sex life. We are both so eager to please one another that I gently remove Kanoa's hands from my breasts and whisper in his ear, "Let's not rush this," as I push him away so that I can look at his face with my eyes no longer stinging from soap.

Instinctively he swoops me up in his muscular arms and carries me to the bedroom, where we make love, not like it's our first time but like it's our last. There are moments when I don't know if I want to scream out loud in euphoria, or cry out from frustration.

We never do make our dinner reservation. It gets late and one thing leads to another, which means ordering room service. I'm not complaining by any means. We make love over and over, until we finally fall asleep in each other's arms.

I wake up thinking I've been sleeping for an hour, but when I check my phone it says six AM—that's when I notice an urgent message from my assistant, Mindy. The time of her message was ten PM, but I was otherwise occupied and had all notifications turned off. She was informing me of a flight change. I am no longer to depart at noon. The flight has been bumped up to seven AM, which doesn't leave me time to shower or have breakfast with Kanoa. I can feel my heart starting to pound and not in a good way. I slip out of bed quietly so as to not wake Kanoa. While I change into my clothes and gather my belongings, I think about waking him, but it would only make me late for my flight, plus why should I disturb his sleep? All we'd be doing is looking pitifully into one another's eyes and wishing we didn't have to say goodbye. My head is spinning. I honestly don't like any of my options. I opt to find a piece of paper and write Kanoa a note. I place it on my pillow and gently lean over to kiss his soft lips one last time. It may sound nuts, but I grab my phone to take a photo. This is how I want to remember him, with a peaceful, contented look spread across his handsome face.

I make it to the airport in the nick of time after dropping off the rental car. With every step I take, I can smell Kanoa's cologne still lingering in my hair. I wish the scent could last forever. I board my flight, and in about four hours I'll be connecting to New York through Los Angeles. I'll try calling Kanoa once I land at LAX.

CHAPTER THIRTY-SIX:

Kanoa

I open my eyes for an instant, thinking I heard Abby rustling about in the distance. It's still dark out, so I figure she's gotten up to use the bathroom, which is nothing unusual. I fall back to sleep, something I'm very good at. By the time I open my eyes again, I roll over to Abby's side, except she's not here. I notice a piece of paper on her pillow. Panic and frustration start to rise within me like bitter, burning bile. I don't need to read the note to know that she's gone. I feel as if I've been sucker-punched. As the question crosses my mind of how she could do this to me, I realize, this must be exactly how Abby felt when I left her. Did she just sleep with me for revenge? No. There's no way Abby would do that. She's not that type of person. I take the note and read it.

Dear Kanoa, I'm so sorry to leave this way, but when I woke up to use the bathroom, I noticed a missed message from Mindy from last night about a flight change. I debated whether to wake you, but I had less than an hour to get to the airport and return my car, plus I needed to get through security. I'm really sorry for the way I left, but I knew I'd never make my flight if we had to say goodbye in person. Please forgive me for leaving this way, but I'll call you as soon as I land in L.A.

P.S. I may not have told you this last night, but I love you, Kanoa Kahala. Xoxoxoxoxoxoxoxo...

And there it is. I feel so much better after reading the note. I try to dial Abby's number right away, but it goes straight to voicemail. I leave her a message saying, *"Good morning Abby, I'm sorry I missed you, but I just want to say that I love you too. I'm not just saying it because you did— I've never stopped loving you, and right now I'm going to hang up and see if I still have time to get to the airport to see you. I love you, Abby Parker."*

Abby forgot to tell me what time her flight was leaving, but I don't feel like wasting even one more minute to call the airport. I'm not that far away. I quickly get dressed and hop in my van. I'm hoping to catch Abby because I want to give her something. I had planned to take her out to a fine dining restaurant to watch the sunset last night, but we never made it. Since our plans changed, I was going to give it to her this morning during breakfast, but never in a million years did I think her flight would change. Things weren't supposed to turn out this way.

I drive as fast as I can, within the speed limit, to get to the airport. I'm feeling overjoyed and overwhelmed to know she still loves me. I can't believe this is happening right now. I also can't believe I'm crying. I haven't cried since the day my parents died, but at least these are tears of joy. I love Abby so much, there's no way I can lose her again.

I'm already approaching the airport intersection and still wiping the tears that are flowing down my face. I feel as if I'm going to drown in them. I come to a halt as I reach a red light. My window is down and the scent of plumeria makes its way in. It instantly reminds me of the night we went to the *lū'au*. Abby looked so beautiful with her plumeria *lei* around her neck. Every time I leaned in close to her I took in the fragrance. From now on I'll never think of anyone but her when I smell plumeria. Her face would beam with delight when she talked about our fragrant air.

The light turns green and I start to accelerate through the intersection. In a flash, tires screech and a horn from what sounds like a transport truck honks loudly. I can hear thunderous crushing metal, but I'm not sure what's happening. There are three more thuds, and the last thing I remember is being upside down in my van. I must have lost consciousness, but the one lingering smell is no longer plumeria, it's burning rubber.

CHAPTER THIRTY-SEVEN:

Abby

As soon as I land in L.A. for my connecting flight, I dial Kanoa's phone, but he's not answering. He has to be awake by now. I told him I'd call, why isn't he answering? I also know that I'm getting wigged out. A cup of coffee might help. Boarding is forty-five minutes away, which gives me plenty of time to fuel up on some caffeine.

I take my Americano to a quiet corner table. Sipping my hot coffee, I feel melancholy as I reflect on the past two months. I can't believe that such a small island has made such a huge impact on my life. As I raise my mug to take another sip of coffee, an old familiar draft appears out of nowhere. I keep telling myself that it's impossible. Being thousands of miles away from Kaua'i, and Deborah, there's no way that this could be happening. I chalk it up to my mind playing tricks on me from fatigue.

Also, it could be the air conditioner, which is always cranked up too high for my liking. I don't have time to finish my entire cup of coffee; I leave it on the table and proceed to the boarding gate.

As I get closer, I notice a swarm of people gathered. One woman in particular stands out because of the tight grip she has on her child's hand. Any tighter and it'll be turning blue. She stomps away, practically knocking me over, but slows down long enough to say, "I hope you're not on this flight, because it's been canceled." I don't have a chance to respond as she briskly walks away. I turn my attention back to the group at the departure gate. I can tell how pissed off they all are. I ask an elderly gentleman what all the commotion is about.

"Seems like there's some engine trouble," he laments. "We won't be going anywhere until morning."

"But this is morning."

"Try tomorrow morning," says the old man as he starts to walk away.

"Wait, wait, please. Do you mean to tell me that we are stuck here until tomorrow?"

The old man turns to look at me, and points his cane to the crowd. "Hey, if you don't believe me, you best get back in that line, but you'll be wasting your time. You'd be better off getting yourself another flight home."

"This is insane," I say under my breath, as the old man disappears into a crowd of passengers. Standing around, trying to figure out what I should do, I spot a couple of familiar faces. At first, I think I'm seeing things. I blink as one would do to readjust blurred vision, but there is absolutely nothing wrong with my eyesight.

There in the distance is my boss, Stan, and he's standing with Charles Baker.

What are they doing in Los Angeles? Why didn't he mention it when we spoke earlier? The day can't get any more bizarre, or can it?

As much as I want to confront them, it's best not to get noticed. Staying as far away as possible so they can't spot me, I stand back and observe their every move. Hopefully I can get an indication as to what they are doing together. Could this be a coincidence? They are buying airline tickets to New York, I think. They must be, because I'm sure they got bumped as we all did. Actually I have no clue. All I have is the questions swirling through my mind. Did they bump into one another, or was it planned? As I think back, nothing is adding up. Also, they are way too jubilant, considering they lost the Coco Palms deal.

Stan is sporting one of his signature facial expressions, the one some of the staff call the look of deceit. It's a smirk that makes his eyes squint, a slimy look in my opinion. I can't help but shake my head in disgust as I look at him. I try hard to stay out of their view, but I also want to get on that flight. I need to beat the huge lineup that's forming before tickets sell out. I try to get to the front of the line, incognito, when a woman faints— bad for her, but lucky for me. The crowd's attention is diverted. The woman is already coming to, and she seems okay, so I make a run for the line. I manage to get myself a ticket for a flight departing in an hour.

I head to the restroom so I don't have to use the plane's facilities. It still boggles my mind that people find it sexy to make out in a funky-smelling broom closet of a bathroom—not on this gal's bucket list.

As I'm washing my hands, I decide to splash some water on my face to freshen up, but before I can do that, I dig into my purse for a hair tie. To my surprise, I pull out the hair comb. Deborah was right—it's not hard to forget where I put the comb. It's been sitting in my purse since I fell in the mud. I'd totally forgotten about it.

I decide to place it in my hair for safekeeping. I wonder if that's why I was feeling the cold air earlier. Maybe it was Deborah's way of telling me to put it on. Oh my, I'm starting to sound like a complete lunatic. I pull my hair into a ponytail and tie it up. I reach for the comb but a sharp pain from coldness causes me to drop it in the basin. Something bizarre is happening again.

I need to be rational. I unravel paper towel from the dispenser to grab the comb. I give it a quick touch with my finger tip, and it feels fine. I make the conscious decision to wear it, as Deborah asked. I place it atop my ponytail and I'm not taking it off until I get home. Not sure what the coldness is about, but I'm sure Queen Deborah is sending me a message.

Feeling a bit more tranquil, I take my phone out and try Kanoa again, but it goes straight to voicemail. I'm about to turn my phone off when I notice a red flashing message light. I punch in my voicemail code and it's a message from Kanoa. After hearing his message, I feel a million times better. I put to rest my assumptions about him being mad at me. I can actually relax for a change. His sexy voice has me looking at the photo I took of him sleeping. God, he's such a fine specimen of a man, and one who just professed his love to me. I couldn't ask for anything more. I look at my watch, but I figure he must be in a meeting, so instead I begin to gather my things and leave the bathroom. I now know the meaning of walking on air, because that's how my weightless body feels.

I look for Stan and Charles, but I can't see them anywhere. The last thing I want is for them to spot me. I get in line and by the time I'm next to have my passport scanned for boarding, I hear familiar voices in the far distance. I don't dare turn around, but I could recognize Ken's voice anywhere. What the hell is going on? Why are the three of them together? They have all lied about their whereabouts. Why?

Walking into the offices of Brickman and Brickman the next morning has me feeling melancholy. In the five years of being here, I've never had the feeling of not belonging. If someone had told me that spending two months in Kauaʻi would have changed my outlook to this extreme, I'd have said they were crazy. I still haven't talked to Kanoa live, but I did leave him another sweet message. Our time zones do make it difficult, but I'll try again after work.

If it weren't for a few of my personal items around my office, I'd definitely say I was in a strange place. Here I am, impeccably dressed in a fresh designer suit for the first time in months, my hair and makeup are perfect, but somehow, I don't feel put together. The best way to describe it is an out-of-body experience—one that's transporting me back to simpler times across the Pacific.

Somehow the clothes and makeup aren't making me feel as good as they used to.

I place my briefcase on my desk, which has more files on it then when I was an actual file clerk. I take a stack of files and place them on the floor next to the garbage bin. I sit in my customized ergonomic leather chair, searching in my bag for my cellphone. I instantaneously pull my hand back out—it's throbbing with pain. Blood trickles from my finger. I get up to grab a tissue. When am I going to learn to just follow Deborah's instructions to never take it off? In all honesty, I didn't forget it was in my bag this time, I just didn't find it matched my outfit.

Remembering that Stan received a first-aid kit as a Christmas gift one year, I go into his office in search of a bandage. With every step I take toward Stan's desk, the air becomes colder. I gently place the comb on his desk while I reach for the kit. I clean my finger with peroxide and put a bandage over the wound. The last thing I need is for blood to seep all over Stan's desk. I replace the kit in its original spot and retrieve my comb, only to find that it has moved about twelve inches to the right. I try to stay calm, but as I lean in to take the comb, underneath it I notice a file of interest, labeled *TCP*. Could it stand for The Coco Palms? Before I have a chance to open it, I hear Stan's booming voice coming from the reception area. I take my comb and run into the kitchen, just as Stan walks in.

"If it isn't our island girl. When did the tide sweep you back home, doll?"

And just then it occurs to me. Stan wanted me back a day earlier. He didn't want to chance me seeing him with the Bakers. What's he hiding?

I reply, "I'm here, that's all that matters. If I had a witch's broom, I'd have made it back much sooner," I respond with a sarcastic smile.

"Well! Someone got up on the wrong side of the bed," Stan says. He reaches into a high cupboard for a coffee mug, and one comes crashing down on his head. He flinches with pain. "What the fuck! Doesn't anyone know how to put shit away around here? Fucking morons."

"Are you okay, Stan?" I ask, trying hard to hide my delight.

"Oh, you think it's funny. Lucky I don't fire you."

I walk out of the kitchen and head back to my office, saying, "Go ahead, Stan. I'm pretty sure it won't be the worst thing to happen today."

"You've come back with quite the attitude, doll. What's wrong, you realize that your Hawaiian boyfriend is a loser?"

Those are fighting words, which normally I'd ignore, but lack of sleep has me on edge. I turn around and go back into the kitchen blazing with anger. "Don't you ever speak about him in that manner again. Do you hear me?"

I storm back to my office, while Stan stands there like the buffoon that he is. He pokes his head into my office.

"I didn't mean to start the day off on the wrong foot, doll."

"Stop calling me doll! I'm not anyone's doll. I detest you calling me that. Don't you have anything better to talk about than the fact that I know Kanoa?"

"Okay, okay. You really need to lighten up, honey."

"You can't help yourself, can you? You put another man down, when you can't stop with the bullshit sexist names," I chuckle in disgust. "I've had it. I won't stand for your bigotry."

He shuts up. He's not as big an idiot as he comes across. He can always smell a lawsuit coming his way. He quietly slips out of my office and hightails it to his own. Within a minute of his exit, my phone buzzer goes off. It's Stan. "Can you please come to my office? We need to talk."

I don't feel like talking—I want to go for his jugular—but he is my boss and I have a job to do. Actually, the only thing keeping me from quitting isn't so much the money any longer, but that file that the comb was on. I walk into his office.

"Please, take a seat. We need to discuss your place here in the firm," says Stan. "After this Hawaiian fiasco, I think it best that I scale you back from some of the higher profile clients."

"Are you kidding me?"

"No, I'm demoting you."

Keeping the file in mind, I say, "You do what you feel you need to do."

"That's it?" asks Stan in shock. "You're not even going to question me on my decision?"

"What's there to question? You made it quite clear that if I have any thoughts on anything I'm fired, or did I read you wrong?"

"You're way too sensitive, doll. Sorry. It was a slip of the tongue."

I'd love to tell him where to shove that tongue. "No worries. What do you have in mind for me?"

"For today, while you get your head back on straight, I'd like you to finish up some of my paperwork. See these files on my desk? You'll also find another pile over there," he says, pointing to a stack on the floor. "Tomorrow we can go over some cases I'd like you to work on."

I can't believe my ears. I feel like a cop being thrown back into desk duty. I decide it's best to comply and keep my mouth shut. I'm not going to give him the satisfaction of witnessing my anger yet again. If he wants to play this game, I'm more than up for the challenge. He sits there, releasing his famous idiotic laugh. "Have a great day, Ms. Parker. I have meetings out of the office all day. I'll be leaving shortly, and this will all be yours," he says with arms opened wide, and laughing.

"I can't wait," I reply as I head back to my office with my mind racing all over the place. The confrontation with Stan makes me miss Kanoa that much more—not to mention Mike and Nani. Just the thought of little Kai is bringing tears to my eyes. I even miss my friendly ghost lady—and just like that the floodgates open, only to be interrupted by the buzzer, yet again. "By the way," Stan's voice says, "I forgot to mention, I'm giving a dinner party tonight. Don't be late, it's at seven. Formal wear, and do your best to keep your emotions in check."

He hangs up before I can get a word in. With Stan it's never an invitation; it's a command. Nothing like being ordered to have dinner with someone. That is pretty much the icing on the cake for the morning, but the cherry on top will be getting that file once he leaves.

CHAPTER THIRTY-EIGHT:

Nani

I've just fed the kids their breakfast and am about to join James outside for a coffee. I'm getting something from the bedroom when I turn and find James standing behind me, ashen faced. I look up at him and ask, "What is it? Is your *Makuahine* okay?"

James takes forever to answer me. I can feel the rush of fear gripping my entire body.

"No, it not *Makuahine*."

The thoughts going through my mind are like an accelerated movie reel. "It's Abby," I guess out loud. "Her plane has gone down."

"No honey, it's not Abby, it's Kanoa. He's been in a serious car accident. I just got a call from the police. We need to get to the hospital right away. I've already asked

Richard if his daughter can come over to stay with the kids. She will take them to school and watch Kai."

I feel as if I've gone deaf after hearing Kanoa's name. I'm praying that James will soon admit he's made a mistake, but it's not happening. He's rushing me along to get moving. I hear him say, "Honey, please don't cry. I haven't told the kids anything, you know how upset they'll be, please try and hold it together until we get to the car."

"I can't leave the kids," I say in a panic, but of course I do it anyway, because Richard is our next-door neighbor and an old childhood friend; his family is part of ours. I take a deep breath and try to compose myself. I need to kiss the kids goodbye and tell them to have a great day. That's about all the emotion I can muster right now. It's when I bend down to kiss Kai that I am barely keeping it together. I know how special her bond is with her Uncle K. Please, God, let Kanoa be okay.

James and I get in the car and head to the hospital. I finally find my voice to ask, "So Kanoa will be okay, right? I mean, if he's at the hospital, he's got to be okay." My tone is frantic. I'm desperately hoping I'll get some sort of positive affirmation, but James, never one to lie, gives it to me gently, but straight.

"No, honey, he's not okay. He's been seriously injured. Right now, he's in surgery. They don't know if he'll make it."

I feel myself becoming weak. I want to vomit, and I want James to stop talking. I fear if he says anything else, the situation will become even worse. I know my thinking isn't rational, but I need to be lied to for once, if that makes any sense. James is still talking and I've put him on mute. Unfortunately, I can still hear his muffled voice.

"We need to prepare ourselves for the worst, Nani. As bad as that sounds, I don't want you going to the hospital with false hope. The doctors are doing their best. That's all the information I have."

On our way to the hospital, we pass the scene of the accident and thank the Lord it's far enough away from us that I can't see much. James didn't take an alternative route because it would've taken us way too long. He tries to distract me, but I can see the mangled steel that was once Kanoa's van. Police cruisers are still at the scene, and the airport intersection has been barricaded. A small group of onlookers still remain on the sidewalk. James knows I'm not going to stop looking. "I can't believe that was Kanoa's van," I say.

"Sorry you had to see that, but there wasn't any other option."

"I know, honey. It's a miracle Kanoa made it out of that mess."

"They had to use the Jaws of Life to get him out. Apparently the truck driver escaped with few injuries. I didn't get this information from the police. One of my friends was driving home and was one of the first people at the scene. Until they pulled Kanoa out, he had no idea who'd been in the accident because he didn't recognize Kanoa's vehicle."

"What happened to the other guy? Where is he?"

"Down at the police station. Apparently he was DUI."

"That's just fucking great. Our friend is lying in a hospital because of this prick!"

"Nani, please, that is not going to do anyone any good. I know how you feel, believe me, I'm just as angry."

We are moments away from the hospital and I try not to think about this senseless person who has harmed my best friend. Instead I try to get ahold of Abby.

James says, "Honey, why don't we find out Kanoa's condition before saying anything to Abby? I don't think it's a good idea to leave her a voicemail; that would cruel."

"You're right. I wasn't planning on leaving her a message. I was hoping she'd pick up. I'm not thinking clearly. I just wish Abby were here right now. I miss her. You know, she was perfect for Kanoa."

"I know, sweetie," James answers as he slides his hand across the seat to hold my hand. "We're almost there, hang tight."

"I pray Kanoa will be okay," I say, my tears dripping down onto the car seat. "You know, this is entirely my fault. I'm the one who told him to follow his heart and kept badgering him about Abby. I know they were together last night. Maybe they had a huge fight just before she left."

"It's not your fault, Nani. Come now. Don't add to an already bad situation. This isn't the time for speculating. You had nothing to do with this. You hear me?"

"I hear you. I'm trying not to think the worst, but I can't help it. I don't know what I'd do without him."

James pulls up to the hospital and drops me off at the emergency entrance. I take off like a bullet through the oversized automatic sliding doors, while James goes to park the car. Given that I'm Kanoa's next of kin on paper, a nurse escorts me into a private room for a consultation with one of the surgeons. I don't have to wait long before the doctor on the team walks into the room to fill me in on Kanoa's condition.

"Please, doctor, just give it to me straight. Will he be okay?"

The doctor takes a deep breath and removes the cap on his head. "I can't say that he'll be okay. I can only tell you what we've assessed so far. The next forty-eight hours are crucial. We need his internal bleeding to stop. We are monitoring him to make sure that there is no swelling of the brain. You have to know that your friend is lucky to be alive. He has sustained multiple injuries. Frankly I'm shocked that he survived such a horrific hit. The gods were on your friend's side tonight."

"Does it look like the internal bleeding may stop?"

"Time will tell. If we can get through twenty-four hours, we are halfway home. As for the broken legs and pelvis, my team is working on him right now. Like I mentioned, it's the bleeding that could be fatal and we hope there's no permanent brain damage. Unless you have any other questions, I really need to get back to the O.R."

"I'm good, doctor. *Mahalo*."

"If there is anything, we will let you know."

"*Mahalo*, I'll be in the waiting room."

James makes his way into the hospital and finds me in worse shape. "As it appears right now, he has a slim chance of making it," I cry. "He's still in surgery. If they can't suppress his internal bleeding, he won't see the light of day. He has multiple fractures, including two broken legs and his pelvic bone. The doctors are amazed that he's alive from the impact the van sustained."

"When will he be out of surgery?"

"We didn't even touch on that. They're working on his legs right now, while another team works on controlling his internal bleeding. He's a mess. The doctor mentioned he might have brain damage. Looks like it's going to be a while, maybe you should go home and make sure everything is okay with the kids," I suggest.

"I'm not leaving you here alone. Plus, the kids are at school and Kai will be fine."

"I'd feel much better if I knew Kai was with you."

James holds me tight and kisses the top of my head. "We have a reliable sitter and you know that, so please stop worrying. Richard and his daughter know to contact us. They've watched our kids many times, so please, let's just stay here together?"

And with a nod of my head, I'm onboard with James' rational thinking. I'm so grateful to have him in my life.

CHAPTER THIRTY-NINE:

Abby

Thankfully my first day back at work is almost over. The last thing I feel like doing is having dinner with Stan and his disciples. No matter how busy and preoccupied I've been all day, I haven't been able to take my mind off Kanoa. All I want to do is go home, put my feet up, and have a long chat with him. But first things first, I need to get through this dinner. I'd feel ten times worse if Kanoa and I hadn't exchanged messages. At least it gives me a warm feeling hearing him say he loves me. Okay, I'm a bit of a sap. I've looked at his photo a few times today while replaying the message.

I look inside my tote bag to make sure the file I photocopied earlier is in there. On top of it is the shiny hair comb. I know I should be wearing it, but I don't feel the comb is appropriate for work. And speaking of work,

I don't need coworkers questioning me more than they already do. As I hold the comb in my hands, I admire its exquisiteness. I realize I'm being an idiot for caring what people think. It really is a stunning piece. I'll wear it moving forward, just not at my office. My phone rings and I put the comb down to answer. "Hi Stan. What can I do for you?"

"There's been a slight change in plan. Sorry, doll, but I need to cancel tonight's dinner. It appears that one of my guests of honor can't make it, so we'll reschedule. By the way, how did your day go?"

"Great," I say, grinding my teeth. "I'm all done. Now I can get back to my regular work, right?"

"With a slight change in client files."

"You're the one paying me the huge salary. Do what you see fit." I couldn't help myself. I know how to get under his skin. There's nothing Stan hates more than overpaying for any service, plus he also knows I have an ironclad contract as far as salary goes. I'm sure his mention of a demotion was just to get under my skin.

"We'll see in the morning," he says. "Get some beauty rest, doll. You looked a bit pale earlier."

Nothing will change this man—he is who he is. I'm just glad the dinner party is canceled. I grab my purse and out the door I go.

Stepping into my apartment, I start to feel tightness in my chest. I know I'm too young to have a coronary, but what if I am having one? Swiftly releasing my purse from my body, I go into the kitchen for a glass of water. The tightness hasn't subsided, so I slip into my comfy yoga pants and lie down on the bed. Coming to the realization that I'm not having a heart attack or stroke, I settle on a panic attack. I've had them before, but never did it feel like the walls of my luxury apartment were yearning to swallow me up. The lack of space is yet again leaving me gasping for air. Rushing to open the bedroom window, I try to fill my lungs with fresh air, but instead I get a mixture of street-food odors and sewage, which is making me nauseous. Has New York always smelled this way, or am I overtired and grumpy? What's happening to me?

I don't need anyone to answer that for me, because I know full well what it is. My heart has been imprinted with memories and surroundings with which this place can't compare. I'm back from being surrounded by lush vegetation and air that's filled with floral fragrances; of course I feel squished and nauseous in here. On the flip side, I hate that I'm being so harsh about a city that I call home and love so much; but somehow, my heart isn't feeling at home here. I know I just got back, but my heart is yearning for Kaua'i, and especially Kanoa. It's just past noon in Kaua'i—maybe I'll give him a quick call. I dial Kanoa's number, but once again it goes to voicemail. I tell him for the third time that I love him, which feels like the right thing to do, even if it is overkill. My therapist might beg to differ. That's the other thing; she may need therapy after I tell her what's happened.

I put my phone on the nightstand and take the file out of my purse. I'm about to open it when the apartment buzzer goes off. I walk to the kitchen to answer. A male voice blares through the speaker, but because of the static, it's a little difficult to make out.

"Who is this?" I ask.

"Ken, Ken Baker."

"What are you doing here?"

"Can I come up? I'd like to talk to you."

What could he possibly have to say? It's not like we are best buds. There's no way I want him in my apartment. "Just wait there. I'll be down in a few minutes."

"Okay, I'll wait for you on the sidewalk."

I go back to the bedroom and reach for my matching jacket. I'm not in the mood to change back into my work clothes. If it wasn't for my curiosity about how he knew Mike and what he wanted with him, there's no way I'd be doing this right now. I grab my purse and head for the elevator. As I'm getting out, the concierge, Giles, approaches me. "Good evening, Miss Parker."

"Hello, Giles. How are you this evening?" I reply as I move towards the front door. I notice that Giles keeps walking alongside me, which is odd, so I stop to ask, "What is it?"

"It's the gentleman waiting outside. I'm not sure how well you know him, but I wanted to warn you that he reeks of alcohol."

"I appreciate you letting me know. By the way, why is he waiting outside?"

"I asked him to. I didn't think it was good to subject others to his boozy stench. Maybe I should come outside with you. I don't get a good feeling from the guy."

"Thanks Giles, I should be all right, but I'd appreciate you keeping an eye on us." I laugh just to cover up my escalating nervousness. I'd like to know how Ken got my address.

"Of course, Miss Parker," agrees Giles.

I smile at Giles and proceed to walk out the revolving door. Ken is leaning up against the cast-iron railing of the brownstone next door. Upon spotting me he quickly stands up straight and shouts, louder than I'm sure he intended to, "Well, aren't you a sight for sore eyes?"

"Really, Ken? I didn't think you even liked me."

"Hey, no hard feelings. That's why I'm here. I want to apologize for my behavior."

"Really?"

"Listen, the whole Coco Palms deal had become a nightmare, and I took it out on you." Ken extends his hand, and I reluctantly shake it. "I hope we can be friends."

"Well, I'm not sure about a friendship, Ken, but we can have a working relationship, right?" Even as I say the words, I know I'd never work with this guy again.

"It's a start."

Giles's words are swirling around in my mind. I don't trust a word Ken is spewing.

"If that's all, I'll be going," I say as I turn to leave. Ken reaches for my arm, and a little too roughly. My facial expression turns to anger.

Ken quickly lets go. "Sorry. I didn't mean to grab you. It's just that … I was hoping to have a drink with you, or maybe a bite to eat, so we could chat."

"It appears to me that you've already had one too many drinks. Let's just leave it as apology accepted and call it a night."

"You're right. I probably shouldn't have any more alcohol. I was out celebrating with my brother. I admit,

I've had one too many, but I could use some food. What do you say? We don't have to go very far."

They didn't win the Coco Palms deal. What could they possibly be celebrating? Against my better judgment I hear myself say, "Okay, you've twisted my arm. I know a deli right around the corner and I could use some food myself, but I warn you, it's going to be a quick meal, I'm still jetlagged."

"What I have to say won't take long. I'm grateful for whatever time you can spare."

Ken doesn't see my eye-roll. I hate being judgmental, but I knew he was full of shit long ago.

I order a beer and a smoked meat sandwich. I find it amusing when Ken settles for sparkling water. "For a guy who has alcohol on his breath, you've surprised me yet again."

"Okay, guilty. Between you and your concierge, the message has come through loud and clear. I always drink too much when I'm around my brother," he says in an almost regretful, wide-eyed fashion.

"What were you two celebrating? I'd have thought you'd be a bit more upset over the Coco Palms."

Ken gives a peculiar chuckle but isn't willing to answer. Trying to provoke him a bit, I say unapologetically, "I never got the feeling that you and Charles were close enough to be drinking buddies. I always felt that he looked at you as the black sheep."

"What are you getting at?"

"What am I getting at? Why are you here? What do you want?"

"I already said, I was in the neighborhood, and I wanted to make amends. I know I haven't been that easy to get along with."

"A phone call or note would have sufficed. I don't buy what you're selling, Ken. Try answering my question about what you and your brother were celebrating and maybe I can warm up to the idea of trusting you?"

"Okay, I was just trying to be nice, Parker. If you must know the truth, I did it for my brother. It was his suggestion."

I stand up to leave, but not before throwing some money on the table. I don't want anything from this liar. Every ounce of me wants to ask about Mike, but I can't jeopardize things. Instead I leave without saying another word. I head to Duane Reade to pick up some toothpaste and a small carton of milk. Remembering that the hair comb is still in my purse, I rummage through to get it before placing the milk in my bag, but I don't see it. I could have sworn I had it in my bag.

I run out of the pharmacy as fast as I can and head back to my apartment. Maybe I placed it on the nightstand without thinking. My hands are trembling so badly, I can barely get the key in the door. I put my purchases on the kitchen counter and turn my purse upside down as I shake it to get everything out. Unfortunately, there's no comb in sight. I check to make sure there's isn't a hole in the lining, which for once would be a blessing. Turning my entire apartment upside down, I come up empty, when suddenly it hits me: I remember taking the hair comb out of my purse back at the office when Stan's call came in about canceling the party. How could I be so careless? There is no way that I'm waiting until morning to get it. I throw everything back into my bag, and out the door I go to hail a cab. When we reach my office, I ask the cab driver to wait outside for me, while I go in to retrieve the precious comb. I'll never forgive myself if it's gone. How stupid and arrogant was it of me to not wear it? I'm such an idiot. When will I learn?

Upon exiting the elevator I sense something is off. I've worked enough late nights to know that there are too many lights on, especially considering that they go into energy-saving mode at a certain time. Someone must have come in before me.

I walk into my office only to feel my stomach drop, just as it does in an accelerating elevator. Ken is there.

"What the hell are you doing in my office? How'd you get in?" I ask as I reach for my desk phone to call security.

"I wouldn't do that," Ken says as he moves closer to me. He takes the receiver out of my hand and slams it down. "I think it's best you walk out of here and pretend that you didn't see me."

I stand firm and say, "Like hell I will."

"Don't make this harder than it needs to be."

"I'm giving you the chance to turn around and walk away."

"Ha! You're giving me the chance? Who the hell do you think you are?" I reach into my bag for my cell phone to call 911, but Ken snatches the bag violently out of my hands.

"I'm not going to say it again, Parker. You need to leave. Pretend that you never saw me here."

"Or what, Ken? You going to kill me?"

The rage in his dark eyes answers the question without the need for words. My adrenaline is pumping full force, but fear is also setting in. I realize I forgot my cell phone next to my bed. Could this night get any worse? I ask Ken, "What the hell is going on? Why the dinner? What is it you're looking for in my office?"

As soon as I ask the question, a bell goes off in my head. I take a closer look at Ken, and there it is, in his left hand.

"Give me the comb," I say.

"Like I said, Parker, walk away."

"No!" I walk towards him to take back the comb. "What in God's name would you want with a hair comb? Tell me!"

"Abby, stop!"

"No, I won't stop. You are trespassing and stealing. Who put you up to this? Was it Stan? How else would you have gotten in here? You're the guest that couldn't make it to Stan's dinner, aren't you? What are you three up to?"

Ken pushes me aside as he bolts for the door. He's pissed me off so badly that I pick up the industrial stapler in front of me. I wind up like a pro baseball player and aim for his head. Of course, the stapler misses him by a long shot, but the loud crashing thud is enough to startle him. His bulging eyes are a good indication that I've infuriated him further. I try a different approach and calmly walk towards him. I put my hand out. "Give me the comb,

Ken. No one has to know that you gave it to me. Whoever sent you to do this is a lying cheat, and you know it. Give me the comb and walk away. I'll pretend that this never happened. You can just as easily tell whoever sent you that you couldn't find the comb."

"I can't do that, Parker. You don't understand."

"Maybe not, but I think I'm getting a clearer picture of who you are. Please, give me back what is rightfully mine."

Even though it seems I'm getting through to him, Ken keeps heading for the elevator. I'm definitely not going down without a fight. I want the comb back. I yell to Ken as he's walking, "You do realize that once you hand the comb over, they won't need you any longer? Did you also hand over what you stole from Mike back in Kaua'i? You're a puppet, Ken. That's all you'll ever be." I really have no idea what I'm saying, but desperation has the words flowing out of me like molten lava. I can't let Ken walk away. He turns abruptly, and runs back towards me until we are less than an inch from each other's faces.

"Don't you ever use that term again," he yells with clenched teeth. "I'm nobody's puppet!"

I'm not backing down, no matter how much Ken froths at the mouth. "Actually, you are, Ken. Why are you doing someone else's dirty work?"

He moves away from me, holding on to his forehead like his head is aching. He has slipped the comb into his pocket. There's an eerie silence. I don't want to make a wrong move. I'm trembling from fear right now, but I can't let him know that.

Suddenly Ken breaks the silence. "What the fuck?"

I can see him digging into his pocket. I have an idea what is happening. As crazy as it sounds, I know the comb is working its magic. Ken sticks his hand in his pocket to retrieve it, but he quickly withdraws it, only to find his left hand covered in blood. He screams bloody murder.

"Are you okay?" I ask, knowing that I don't sound genuine.

"Does it look like I'm okay?"

"Maybe you should take your pants off. Get a closer look at your leg."

"Good try, Parker. I'm not giving you this," he says as he holds up the comb, which I witness lodging itself deep into the palm of his hand. He is now squealing and flinging his hand to release the comb, which happens to land next to my feet. I bend down to pick it up. He's about to charge me when he sees that I have the phone receiver in my hand. I managed to punch in 911 while he was squealing.

"Walk away, Ken. I'll pretend this never happened. You so much as make a move towards me, and the police will be here in a nanosecond."

I don't think Ken feels defeated as much as fed up being his brother's shadow. Let's face it, this guy is more than capable of taking me down, even with all his throbbing pains and bleeding, but I think he no longer has any fight in him.

He looks at me. "We need to talk."

"Don't try and screw me over, Ken."

I watch as he puts his hands over his head in defeat and kicks my purse over to me. He is trying to prove that he won't do anything to harm me, but I'm still not buying it. He moves far enough away to let me have clearance to the elevator. I walk past him, press for the elevator to open, and get in. He hasn't moved an inch.

"If you want to talk, I'll meet you downstairs—I have a cab waiting," I say as the elevator door shuts without incident.

CHAPTER FORTY

I hop a cab and make my way to my parents' place. "Thanks for seeing me, Dad. I know it's late, but this couldn't wait."

"Not to worry," Dad says as he hugs me. "I was just finishing up some work. Your mother went to bed an hour ago, but she won't mind if I wake her."

"No, don't wake her. It's actually good she's sleeping. She might not like what I'm about to ask you."

"What's the pressing matter? I didn't think you'd have had time for anything, seeing as you just got back."

"It's a long story, which I'll explain fully later on. Right now I can give you a short summary of what I found out tonight, which I'm hoping you can help me with."

Dad's brows are furrowed as he asks, "Are you in some kind of trouble?"

"It's not that I'm in trouble, it's more a matter of wanting to help someone who might be in danger."

"Who might this someone be?"

I know darn well that Dad won't be thrilled to know I'm referring to Kanoa. And just as I thought, my father turns into the bull having a red cape fanned in front of him by his matador. He stomps his feet back and forth shaking his head.

"Daddy, please, hear me out before you go into a rant over Noah. Don't make any judgments until you hear the entire scenario."

"What could you possibly tell me that would make me want to help that man after the way he left you?"

"Once you hear the full story, you'll feel differently. There are things I didn't even know until tonight. So please, Daddy, please hear me out and try to keep an open mind."

I can feel myself holding my breath until my father, hopefully, says yes. I'm his only child and no matter what, I know he will trust my judgment and want to help me. He's always going on about how much he adores me.

"I need to know more," he says. "I can't help Noah after the pain he's caused you."

After an hour of talking with my dad and telling him what I've learned, I watch him as he stands up from behind his desk. He plants himself on the front edge of it, in order to face me. I'm sitting in one of the two huge leather chairs. The chair still gobbles me up just like it did when I was two years old. Which is pretty much exactly how old I'm feeling, facing my father.

"I'll help you out, Abby, but there is one condition."

"Name it."

"I don't want you anywhere near Noah, or Kanoa ... whatever the hell his name is."

"Have you not heard anything I've said? How can you make such a demand when I've told you everything that Ken has told me? How?"

"Because I don't trust Noah King."

"Then I guess we don't have anything further to discuss."

I get up and head towards the door. Looking back at him I say, "You know, Dad, I really thought that you of all people would understand. Sometimes I don't get you. You always say to come to you, and I never have because I want to stand on my own two feet, but this is different. People's lives ..."

"Fine, fine. I'll help you out, but don't mention his name to me, understood? Also, you are not leaving here without security."

I walk back to where my father is standing. "Thank you, Daddy. Thank you so much. I promise you won't regret this."

"I know I won't, because I'm going to arrange for a bodyguard to be with you starting tonight."

There's no point in arguing. In all honesty, I think I will feel better knowing someone is watching over me. "You know I'll pay you back every penny I'm borrowing. It may take a while, but I swear I will."

"I know you will, honey. I'm not worried about the money. I just want to see you safe and happy. That's all that your mother and I have ever wanted for you. You and your mother are all I have, nothing else matters," Dad says. "I need you to know that I trust your business decisions full-heartedly. It's the emotional side of this equation that I fear will cloud your judgment."

"That was the old Abby, Dad. I promise you, I won't let my feelings for Kanoa get in the way. I want what's fair for everybody."

I know my father can't fully comprehend my intentions after just an hour. Hell, I was in Kaua'i two months and my head is still spinning. My father has a driver/bodyguard at the house within the hour. It's almost midnight when I get back to my apartment with the bodyguard in tow. I make up the sofa for him to sleep on for the night. I know I'll have to arrange something much better for him tomorrow, since I don't have a concrete timeline in place just yet.

Once my bodyguard is settled, I go into my bedroom and close the door behind me. The day has turned out to be a much longer and more exhausting one than I anticipated. I'm drained both mentally and physically. I decide to run a warm bubble bath in hopes of calming down and getting a good night's sleep. While the bathtub fills, I return to my bedroom to retrieve my cell phone from the nightstand. I notice the battery is dead and needs to be charged. Damn, I so want to call Kanoa, and this would be the perfect time. It's about seven PM in Kaua'i. I can't exactly take a bath and talk on a plugged-in device—no, Abby, absolutely the stupidest thought to cross your mind. You'll be done your bath in about thirty minutes, I tell myself. I know I'm over-tired when I start talking to myself about irrational things. Instead, I grab the photocopied file, which I'm dying to read. I open the file and flip through the pages, momentarily forgetting I've left the bath water running. I run to turn it off and head back into my room.

I take my clothes off and drop them on the floor at the end of my bed. When I reach down to grab the papers, I notice that my cell has enough juice to light up the message icon. I decide to wait till after my bath to check the message, but when the phone rings a second later it overrules that decision. It's an unknown number. The last thing I remember after saying hello is hearing Nani's voice.

When I open my eyes, I find my bodyguard sitting next to me on the bed. He is talking on his cell to my father. Every word he utters is resonating in my head. I think I'm dreaming, until he says to my father, "I'll call you right back," then reaches for my hand and asks if I'm okay.

"Nice to see you're feeling better," he says. "Your father and doctor will be here soon. They're in transit, so try not to move."

"What happened?"

"I heard a loud crash and came running in. Apparently, you fainted."

As the bodyguard keeps talking, I try to get up.

"Don't move until the doctor gets here, please," he begs.

I nod my head in agreement to stay put. He continues telling me what happened. "I spoke with your friend Nani, who was still on the phone when you passed out. She told me about Kanoa. I'm very sorry, Miss Parker." And suddenly I feel my world go dark again.

My father must have arrived while I was unconscious, because I can hear his voice. I try desperately to open my flickering eyelids, but I can't keep them open. I catch a blurred vision of Dad sitting on my bed as the doctor examines me. Dad is on his phone. "Thank you, Nani," he says, "and please keep us posted of Kanoa's condition."

I finally manage to open my eyes fully and keep them open. This is how I know I'm not dreaming.

"Honey, I'm so glad you're okay," Dad says as he reaches for my hand.

"What happened?" I ask.

"You fainted. Do you remember having a conversation with your friend Nani?"

My father keeps talking, while my head is swirling around like a violent tornado trying to pick up everything in its path.

"Abby?"

I sit up slowly. "I'm okay, Dad. I need to go. I need to get to Kanoa. What if I don't make it in time?"

"Let's wait and see what the doctor says. Then we can decide if you're okay to fly. One thing at a time."

"Time is not on our side, Dad."

"I know, honey, but —"

The doctor interrupts. "You're good to go, but please stay hydrated. No alcohol on the flight. I'll give you a few sedatives to help you sleep. Only take one. Two will knock you out cold."

I can see the doctor's lips moving, but my conversation with Nani about Kanoa's car accident is in the forefront of my mind. My entire body is trembling. I need to get to Kanoa. I don't have time to sit around. The shock of it all leaves me in a daze. I watch as my father escorts the doctor out. I get myself out of bed and search for my clothes, realizing that my bodyguard must have found me naked on the floor. My father comes back into the bedroom.

"Against my better judgment I'm having my assistant book you the first flight out to Kaua'i. I'd come with you, but I'll stay here and take care of the matter we discussed." Dad looks over at the bodyguard, who is sitting outside my room. "And he's coming with you."

"*No*, Dad. I honestly don't need his services there. Please, no."

"I don't feel comfortable with you being on your own."

"I'll be fine. I just want to see Kanoa. Nothing else matters right now."

Dad knows not to push the issue any further. "Fine, he stays here, but you are going first class, no ands, ifs or buts, and here is my black card." He hands me his credit card. I'm reluctant to take it, but I know he won't back down and I don't have time to argue.

"Thanks, Dad. You can't imagine how much this means to me. I'm so glad I came to you for help. I truly appreciate it. I don't know what else to say."

"Say you'll be careful and please, call me for anything no matter the time of day. Make sure you let me or your mother know you've landed safely. I haven't told her any of this—as you can see, it's very late—but I'll fill her in as soon as morning rolls around."

Dad's phone begins to ring. He tells his assistant, "Get Abby on the red-eye to L.A., and first thing in the morning she can hop a flight to Kaua'i. Yes, that route sounds the most logical. Thank you. See you in the morning." He gets off the phone and looks at me. "Don't just stand there, get dressed."

One thing I'm not leaving behind is the hair comb. I put it in my hair, throw some essentials in my tote bag, and that's it. I don't need to pack a suitcase, all I want is to get to Kanoa. The bodyguard is taking me to the airport. I hug my father goodbye. "I love you, Dad. I promise I'll call as soon as I get there. Thank you, again."

"Hey, hey, no tears. You need to stay strong," Dad says as he hugs me back. "Now get going, you don't want to miss your flight."

Being at the airport is déjà vu. It hasn't even been forty-eight hours since I landed back in New York. Right now, all I want is to see Kanoa's face so that I can hold his hand and let him know he'll be okay. God, please let him be okay. As much as I want to call Nani, I hesitate ringing her. I'm over-the-top petrified of getting bad news. I can't help my brain from thinking the worst. These unproductive thoughts come in waves. I still think it best to just get moving without calling. I'm going to Kaua'i no matter what, so I'd rather stay with the thought that Kanoa will hang in and get better—he has to.

I board my flight, and as much as I love luxurious things, there's no way I'd ever fork out money for such an extravagant seat. Dad went all out to book me a pod. I have to admit, if ever there was a time for privacy, this is it. I appreciate not having someone's elbow jabbing into my ribs. Now that I'm here, it feels good to know I don't have to fear the nonstop chatterbox that sometimes sits next to me. Thank you, Dad!

I take my seat and try with all my might to stay positive about Kanoa's condition, but my human, weaker side gets the best of me. I knew I'd break at some point but didn't expect it to be this soon—we haven't even taken off. I see a flight attendant approaching, so I try to look through the welcome package that was on my seat. I put my head down and start taking out all the amenities in hopes that she will keep walking, but she stops at my pod.

She whispers, "Is there something I can get you?"

I quickly try to soak up my salty tears, which are starting to sting my entire face. I reply, "No, I'll be fine, but thank you."

"Would you like to talk about it?"

I find myself shaking my head no, because if I dare utter another word, I know I'll go into a full-blown, hiccupping cry. Trust me, I know myself. I had many of those cries when Kanoa left New York. I don't need to have a breakdown right here on the tarmac and chance them kicking me off. I try to compose myself the best I can and give her what I know to be the fakest of smiles. She smiles back at me in acknowledgment and gives me the privacy I'm craving.

"I'll be here if you need anything," she offers.

I try to get comfy and buckle myself in. I put the sleep mask to the side. I can see myself using it soon, but first I need to tell myself to breathe, the same way my therapist has instructed me to do so many times. As much as I keep trying to have logical thoughts, it's human nature to keep asking, What if Kanoa doesn't make it? Or is that actually a logical thought? All I know right now is that I can't wait to see him, and I will pray to whomever I must to get the result.

After what feels like five hours—in reality we've been in the air less than an hour—I find myself extremely restless. Maybe restless is the wrong word. I'm feeling extra frantic realizing I forgot to bring the photocopies with me. Rushing to the airport took precedence over everything. Thank goodness, at least I have my comb. Losing it is not something I want to face Deborah with. Acknowledging that there is absolutely nothing I can do at the moment, I decide that maybe it's best I sleep the entire way, so I take one of the sedatives the doctor handed me. I slip on my eye mask, and everything becomes as dark as the hole I feel in my heart.

CHAPTER FORTY-ONE

The flight attendant has difficulty waking me up. The sleeping pill I took has left me feeling a bit groggy. Mind you, I was a lot groggier than this when I connected in LAX. The doctor was right—the sedatives were just enough to give me the rest I needed.

I can hear the flight attendant's voice asking me to put my seat up for breakfast, but I can't see her. I finally realize I still have my eye mask on. As soon as I remove it, the brightness of the reading light above my seat wakes me up faster than a first sip of coffee—which I'm dying for, by the way, because the aroma of brewing coffee has spread throughout the plane.

We have forty-five minutes before we touch down in Kaua'i, where the sun will soon make its appearance for another spectacular day and surfers will start to take advantage of the waves from incoming swells, as others take to the beach for their morning walk or run.

Meanwhile, all I ask is that I find Kanoa alive. That will be the brightest ray of sunshine in my life.

As soon as we touch down, I try to call Nani, but it goes directly to voicemail. I don't bother leaving her a message, because in all honesty, I can't think straight and don't know what to say without blubbering at the mention of Kanoa's name. I've come this far and I need to stay strong, not only for myself, but for Kanoa and everyone else. I've been trying hard not to waste energy on negative thoughts; that's why I caved and took the mild sedative. I have to admit it's the first time I've ever taken one in my life. Even throughout the draining ordeal of our breakup, I never took anything to help with my sleep. It took lots of therapy and trying to think positively, which is what I'm doing right now.

I make it to the hospital and stop at the nurse's station. I'm not saying this in a rude sense, but my energy is already getting zapped out of me from the hospital smell. I don't know what it is, but it's as if my body weight doubles the instant I walk through hospital doors.

I'm told Kanoa is down the hall in the Intensive Care Unit. I give a sigh of relief knowing that he is still alive. I can literally feel the oxygen flowing through my body again. I couldn't have asked for anything more.

The head nurse, Luana, explains what's happened in the forty-eight hours since his accident. I know she is doing her due diligence, but I just want to see Kanoa's face. I need to feel the touch of his hand. Luana tells me he's still in a coma, but on the bright side, his internal bleeding is under control. As it turns out, the pelvic bone fracture is smaller than initially reported, which is also a blessing.

Luana continues, "When Kanoa comes out of his coma, he won't be able to apply any weight to the pelvic area, which shouldn't be a problem seeing as both of his legs have been set in casts. It's just something that will take a lot of getting used to, but I'm getting ahead of myself. One of his legs did endure a worse fracture than the other and required emergency surgery. A steel rod has been inserted. The doctors' highest priority is that Kanoa come out of his coma, because the longer he stays in it, the slimmer his chances of survival will be. Stable condition is all anyone can ask for at this point in time."

I'm not sure if it's the wafts of hospital air or the news that is making me feel faint, but I feel weak and about to pass out. Luana jumps out of her chair and runs around the counter to where I'm standing.

"I'm okay," I say as I hold onto the countertop. "I think I'm on information overload."

Luana gets a cold glass of water and hands it to me. "Come with me," she says.

I take a couple of sips. "Thank you."

"I know you want to see Kanoa, but I could offer you a place to lay down for a bit if you'd like?"

"I'm good, but thank you. I really just want to see Kanoa with my own eyes."

As we make our way to Kanoa's room, Luana tells me that she will have to make sure that Nani steps out of the room because only one visitor is allowed at any given time. She tells me that Nani has been at the hospital since she found out about the accident. When we get to the room, we find Kanoa alone and I'm escorted to his bedside. I'm so happy to see his face, but it's tough to see him attached to the ventilator. Between the breathing apparatus and his legs in casts, it's an overwhelming sight, to say the least. I keep repeating in my head how lucky we all are that he's alive.

I reach for Kanoa's hand, and tears start cascading gently down my face onto Kanoa's sheets. I didn't mean for this to happen. I take his hand in mine and bring it to my lips, even though there's an IV needle stuck in it. I kiss his forehead, more tears dripping down on him. I gently wipe them away and kiss him again, but without tears. I whisper in his ear in hopes that he can somehow hear me. "Kanoa, it's me, Abby. I came back to Kaua'i. I hope you can hear me. I want you to know that I'll be right here if you need me. I will never leave your side again. Can you hear me? I love you, Kanoa."

I sit down on the edge of the bed and keep hold of Kanoa's hand. After about ten minutes, Nani enters the room. I get up to greet her. We hug each other tight.

"Oh my God, Abby, it's so good to see you. I was really worried about you. I tried to call you so many times, but I'm sorry I never left a message. I figured once you saw my calls I'd hear from you."

"Great to see you too, Nani. There really wasn't time to call. As you know, after you spoke to my dad's bodyguard I wasn't doing so well. When you gave me the news I blacked out, but once the doctor gave me the okay, Dad had me on the first flight out. So I'm just as sorry for not contacting you; I really wasn't thinking straight. All I could think about was finding Kanoa alive. Until I saw his face with my own eyes, there's no way I could rest easy."

"I hear you. It's been tough even to try and go home for a quick change of clothes. James has been a saint taking care of everything at home."

"*You're* a saint. I know Kanoa would be mad at both of us for fretting, but he'd also be really happy to know you've been by his side."

"Thanks, Abby. It's very sweet of you to say that. I just hope he opens his eyes soon. Here," she says, handing me a bottle of cold water. "This place is so dry, I just stepped out to get these."

"Two-fisted drinker?" I ask as Nani holds two bottles of water.

We both laugh. It's good to lighten the heavy situation at hand. After we drink our water, I feel a bit more alive and convince Nani to take a break and go home. She looks like she's due for some rest. I tell her I'll call if there is any change in Kanoa.

I sit next to Kanoa and hold his hand for hours. To have his flesh next to mine is a blessing, but looking at his motionless body makes me anxious on so many levels. I don't understand why life has to put us through so many challenges. Our breakup is no longer the monumental disaster I had once thought it to be. Everything is irrelevant knowing Kanoa could easily slip away from me permanently. Every fiber in my body wants nothing more than to have him open his eyes. I can't imagine my life without him. I've been without before, and I hated it. The sheer thought of it has me sobbing quietly as I hold his hand.

I'm going on day three and still nothing has changed in Kanoa's condition. It's late afternoon and soon Nani will arrive with food and clean clothes, as she's been doing since I arrived. Nani has been an absolute lifesaver. Just when I feel hope dwindling away, somehow Nani's radar picks up on it even from afar. Yesterday I found myself losing hope after talking to Kanoa nonstop for what must have been hours on end. About to break down from feeling defeated, I got an encouraging text from Nani. I'm sure the sleepless nights at the hospital are making me lose my more positive side of things.

I speak to my father every night after Mom goes to bed. It's not that I don't want to speak to her, because I do when I get the chance, it's that we are trying to keep our investigation under wraps. Last night Dad told me what he'd found in the file.

"I'm not really sure what a lot of it means just yet," he said. "The way Stan worded his documents is a bit of a puzzle. I'll need some time to decipher his coding, but one thing I'm sure of is that there's more going on with the Coco Palms than Stan ever wanted you to know. Leave this to me, I promise I'll get to the bottom of it. I think you have enough to worry about with Kanoa."

"Thanks, Dad. I know how hard it is for you to work on something for a person you don't respect."

"Listen Abby, I don't dislike Kanoa. He pissed me off the way he left you. You have to believe I'd never want any harm for him. I hope for both your sakes he wakes up and you have the happy ending we all search for in life."

That was one speech I never expected to hear from my father's lips. It's moments like this that keep me positive. "You don't know how good it feels to hear you say that. Thank you, Dad."

"You're welcome, honey, and please try and get some sleep. You need to stay strong for so many reasons, and all good ones, remember that. Please promise me that you will shut your brain off tonight and get some rest. Maybe you should take that pill the doctor gave you."

I had to laugh at his suggestion. It wasn't going to happen, but I loved him for saying it. "Promise, I'll try. Please give Mom my love."

I'm so lost in thought over my conversation with Dad that I don't hear Nani walk into the room.

"I called your name a few times, but you didn't hear me."

"Sorry, Nani. I'm in my own world."

"I see that. I know I ask you this every day, but you sure you don't want to get out of here for a few hours?"

"No. I appreciate you asking, but I don't want to leave him," I say as I look over at Kanoa's lifeless body. I never thought it possible for someone to lie so still that not a single muscle flinched. "Do you have time to stay for a coffee?" I ask.

"I'm sorry, I can't, but I'll come back later. I know someone who would love to have a coffee with you, though. He's waiting outside. Why don't you go out and see who it is?"

I get up and practically run to the door. I'm thinking it's my dad; maybe he was fooling me by having me believe he was in New York when I spoke with him. I step out into the hallway, and there is Mike. I run and embrace him tight. When I step back to take a good look at him, I notice his eyes are bloodshot.

"Mike, my God it's so good to see you. *Mahalo* for coming."

"Dear child, there's nowhere I'd rather be. I'm so worried about you and Kanoa."

"Why haven't you come in? The nurses never mentioned you were here."

"I asked them not to. I just want to be close. You know, in case you may have needed me."

"How long have you been here?"

Mike hesitates. "Since it happened, but I always leave before you or Nani see me. I'm sorry, but today I fell asleep in the chair."

"Oh Mike," I say as I hold him tight and kiss his cheek. "Please, come in. You have nothing to be sorry for. I'm sure Kanoa would love to hear your voice."

Nani says her goodbyes, and I escort Mike to Kanoa's bedside. He sits down and gently takes hold of Kanoa's hand. I know they are close friends, but I wouldn't have expected the level of devastation I'm seeing in Mike's eyes. Tears cascade down his deeply lined face, lines that weren't as visible to me just a week ago. I put my hand on his shoulder for comfort. He pats my hand and leans his cheek on it.

"I never thought something like this would happen to Kanoa. Especially knowing the way his parents died," sobs Mike. "Never did I think I'd be reliving that nightmare. I have prayed and will keep praying that our boy comes through," he cries as he kisses Kanoa's hand. "Do you hear me, son? You must know how much we all love and miss you," he says to Kanoa. "I have so much to tell you. You can't leave us, Kanoa. You need to be strong for your parents—please, if you can hear me, please come back to us." Mike wipes away his tears.

I go to the sink and get Mike a cold face cloth. This poor man, I can't believe he's been outside the door the entire time. I hand him the cool cloth and offer to go get him a coffee and water. I'm sure his throat is constricted with fear and sadness—I know the feeling all too well.

"Thank you, child, that would be lovely. I'll be right here," Mike says as he holds on to Kanoa's hand.

Since Mike is with Kanoa, I thought I'd take advantage of a quick shower in the complimentary room the hospital provides for family members. When I return, Mike is bent over whispering in Kanoa's ear. I can't hear a thing he is saying. I'm pretty sure he's been talking to him the entire time I've been gone.

Mike stays long enough to drink his coffee. "I think it's best I get going. I hope you won't mind if I come back and stay this evening. I promise I won't bother you. I'll just sit in my usual spot outside."

"Nonsense, I'm sure Nurse Luana can arrange to have a lounging chair in here for you. Why don't I ask her?"

"I don't want to impose. I'm happy just to be near."

"You come back whenever you want. You must know you are always welcome," I tell Mike as we hug goodbye. "Take care of yourself—we need you around."

Feeling refreshed, I take my coffee and sit down next to Kanoa. As I'm about to take my first sip I think I can see his right eye flicker, but I'm not sure. I put my cup down and take his hand. "Good morning, I see you're just as popular as ever. You've got everyone in this—"

I cut my sentence short when I notice that both his eyelids have some movement. I don't wait a second longer before ringing for the nurse.

"Kanoa, can you hear me?" I say, crying with joy. "Baby, it's me, Abby. If you can hear me, squeeze my hand. Did you hear Mike? He was here visiting you."

Just like that, I feel his hand move in mine. I buzz the nurse's station again, but they're already running in. I don't have any more time with Kanoa, as the nurses ask me to step out into the hallway while they examine him.

I sit down in the seat next to the door, which until a few minutes ago I never realized had been occupied by Mike. I wonder if it was Mike who got a reaction out of Kanoa? It had to be Mike. I wonder what he said to him? Whatever it was, I'll be forever grateful.

I'd call Mike, but he doesn't have a cellphone, so instead I text Nani. She's back at the hospital within fifteen minutes. By this time, the nurses are pushing the curtains open around Kanoa's bed. I can see that his eyes are shut, but the doctor tells me on his way out not to be alarmed—it's normal to be tired once you've been through what Kanoa has. The brain needs to heal.

The doctor says, "He is out of his coma, which is the main thing. We'll be running some routine tests on him, which he's being prepped for as we speak, so if you'd like to have a quick visit with him before he's taken away, please do so."

I go to Kanoa's bedside and see him wincing in pain as he tries to move his body.

"Hi there," I whisper, trying to keep my happy tears from dripping on him. I can see him trying to process what is taking place as his eyes flutter like the wings of a butterfly.

"Why am I aching all over?" he asks. "What's happened?" I look over at Nurse Luana for a sign. She nods her head in approval for me to continue.

"You've been in a car accident. You've broken your legs, so they may feel weighed down due to the casts."

"A car accident?" asks Kanoa. I can see him trying to search for a glimpse of memory. His eyes are scrunched up, and I'm not sure if it's from pain or because he's thinking. "All I remember is the smell of plumeria that turned into a toxic burning-rubber smell. Didn't you leave for New York?" he asks, closing his eyes.

Nurse Luana comes over to Kanoa's bedside. She takes my hand and gently pushes me aside to check on him. "Don't worry. He will be doing a lot of nodding on and off today, it's normal after one wakes up from a coma. I should be getting him downstairs for his tests. We will be gone for a few hours, so maybe you ladies should go home and rest."

I look over at Nani who is still standing by the door. She knows I don't want to leave and says, "Let's go back to my place. I'm sure we can call the nurse's station in an hour to get an update."

"Yes," Luana says, "I'll let the nurse's station know that you will be inquiring about Kanoa."

We both thank Luana for her generosity and understanding. I kiss Kanoa on the cheek before we watch him being wheeled out. I'd be lying if I said I wasn't afraid of leaving him. I'd much rather wait in his room.

"Sweetie," Luana says, "I know you are worried, but you will be helping Kanoa by taking a break. A little mental rest goes a long way. I promise I will personally call you myself if there is concern about his state."

"Mahalo," I utter, feeling sad that I'm leaving, but I know it's the right thing to do.

"You good?" asks Nani, staring at me.

"I'm good," I hear myself saying. "I know we should get out for a bit."

Before I know it, we are pulling up to Nani's house, which makes me feel warm all over. She's also not far from the hospital, which is another reason I agreed to leave.

"I'm glad we came here," I say as I take a deep breath of the sweet air. "I feel like I've been on a never-ending rollercoaster. I'm sure you must feel the same."

"Until you got here, I was feeling that way, but I've been able to get more rest than you. It's really good having you back. You poor thing, I'm sure you didn't even have time to get over your jetlag."

"It's amazing what our bodies can endure. I feel physically strong; it's the mental part that's fatigued."

"Come on, let's go inside. I'll make us a good strong cup of coffee and something to eat. Kai won't be home for a few hours, so you can relax without her being all over you."

"It feels so good to be here with you. Just a few days ago I wouldn't have pictured myself standing in your kitchen this soon."

"Life's a funny thing, but I'm a firm believer in everything happening for a reason," Nani says, with an explosion of meaning behind the statement—which no doubt has to do with Kanoa and me.

"One step at a time," I say. I don't want to insult Nani, but I really don't know what my future holds at the moment.

We sip our coffees outside on the *lānai*. It feels good to have the sun in my face again. For the first time in a very long time, something inside me feels liberated. I don't know how much of it was confiding in Dad, and how much was having Kanoa come out of his coma, but it sure feels great right at this moment. And with that thought, I ask Nani, "Would you mind if I borrow your Jeep? That's if you don't need it?"

"Not at all, it's yours. James will be home with Kai soon, so if I need to go anywhere, I'll take his car. Are you heading back to the hospital?"

"Yeah," I say sheepishly. "You think I'm being crazy, right?"

"No, absolutely not. I totally understand. I'd be doing the same if it were James. I'm glad you got away for a bit. Please, don't feel you need to hang around here, I get it."

"*Mahalo*, Nani," I say as I hug her goodbye. "The coffee and *loco moco* was delicious. I was a lot hungrier than I thought. I owe you one, and it'll be my treat once Kanoa is better."

I place a call to my dad before entering the hospital.

"I was about to call you," he says. "How's Kanoa doing?"

"He came out of his coma a couple of hours ago. He's undergoing some tests right now."

"That's great news. I'm truly relieved to know he's on the mend."

"Thanks, Dad, it means a lot to me. So, why were you about to call me?"

"The codes in the file. I've done a thorough check and I'm currently working with our number-one techies, but if you have a moment, maybe you can take a look at some of the names. Something might sound familiar to you or make more sense, seeing as you work for Stan. It could jog your memory."

"About the working-for-Stan part," I say. "I'm leaning towards wanting to quit. And yes, before you say I have lots of responsibility and bills to pay, I need to keep my job, but—"

"There are no buts," Dad interrupts. "You have no idea how happy I am to hear you say this. Don't quit just yet, though. I need you to hang in until we can get more information, and don't tell a soul you're thinking of quitting, not even Kanoa."

"Okay, you have my word. Why don't you scan whatever it is you want me to see to my email?"

"I can't do that—it's the other thing I was going to mention. You will have to get yourself a new personal email. I don't want anything going through your work."

"Oh right, sorry, I'm not thinking. Okay, I'll do it when I get a moment. I'll text you the details as soon as I set it up."

"Great."

CHAPTER FORTY-TWO:

Kanoa

It's been over three weeks since the accident, and the good news is I'm finally getting discharged. Due to complications with my left leg, emergency surgery was needed, which prolonged my hospital stay. At least my right leg is healing nicely and in a half cast, which allows me to apply a bit of pressure—just enough to get me in and out of my wheelchair, though still with someone's help. I never in a million years would have predicted being in this situation, but things could have been worse. I'm a lucky man to be alive, and doubly so to have Abby and Nani by my side. Speaking of Abby, she'll be here any minute to pick me up.

My energy level isn't what it used to be before the accident, but the doctor told me that's to be expected. As I close my eyes to wait for Abby, I can hear Nurse

Luana's voice. She's standing at my bedside with a white manila envelope.

"This is for you, Mr. Kahala," Luana says as she hands me a sheet of paper. "It's your rehabilitation schedule. We suggest you don't miss any unless you have some form of infectious disease, understood?"

I have to laugh. Even though she's trying to be tough, she's a softie. "I won't disappoint you. No one wants to get better more than me. I can't thank you enough for taking such good care of me."

"You can thank me by having a speedy and full recovery. Also, maybe you could invite me to your wedding."

"I'm not getting married. Did Abby say we are?"

Luana laughs. "No, Abby didn't say a word. I know when I see a perfect match. Just don't forget me," she says as she places the envelope on the bed and squeezes my hand. "Take care, Kanoa. As much as I like you, I don't want to see your face here again."

"You and me both."

Within seconds of Luana leaving, Abby walks in, babbling a mile a minute. "I'm so sorry I'm late, but you'll never believe it."

"Try me."

"My mom and dad surprised me this morning. I had no idea they were coming. How great is that?"

"Great," I say, even though I'm a bit nervous about seeing her parents again. It's been a long time, and we all know the circumstances. "Where are they?"

"I just dropped them off at their hotel. They would love to come for a visit once you get settled, but Mom said there's no rush."

"They can come as soon as we get home. It'll be great to see them," I say, knowing that I really just need to get the awkward first meeting over with. None of us can move forward otherwise.

Abby helps me to the wheelchair and pushes me out to the parking lot. "I can't thank you enough, Abby. As I said before, I don't expect you to keep catering to me."

"Stop it, I'm doing it because I want to. Unless you're sick of seeing me?"

I watch as Abby puts my wheelchair in the trunk. "No, I'm not sick of you. If anything, I'm wondering if you'll be going back to New York with your parents."

"God, no. Where do you come up with these things?"

"I think it's weeks of being in bed."

Abby has been staying at my house since I came out of my coma. It was one thing to stay in a hotel indefinitely when her work was footing the bill, but it's such a waste of money now, when I have an empty house. It took a bit of coaxing, but she accepted my offer.

As I hold on to the front dash I ask, "Why are you driving so fast?"

"This isn't fast. I'm under the speed limit."

"You sure?"

"Kanoa, I'm sure. If I drive any slower the people behind will start getting more pissed off than they already are."

"Sorry. I guess I'm a little nervous."

"I understand your nervousness; I'd feel no different. Try not to worry, my goal is to get us both home safe."

We have about another five minutes to go, but I have to tell Abby what's been weighing heavily on me. I don't want to be a burden to her, and I most definitely don't want her staying with me out of pity. Like an idiot I blurt out, "Abby, I think you should go back to New York with your parents."

"What?"

"Keep your eyes on the road," I yell as she watches me instead of looking ahead. "Calm down and let me explain."

"Oh my God, could you not have waited to say something so shitty until we got home?"

"But it's not shitty, let me explain, please."

"Please do, before I combust."

"I appreciate everything you have done for me, because God knows I don't deserve it. You've been here now for almost a month, and I know what having a career means to you. I don't want to be the person that takes that away from you. I guess what I'm trying to say is that I don't want you to resent me by making you feel the need to take care of me."

"Are you done?"

"Well ..."

Taking hold of my hand as she steers with the other she says, "I was kidding. Please stop talking and listen. I'm here because I want to be here. No one is making me do anything. Do I miss New York? Yes, but I miss a lot of things and that's just it, it's things. My parents are my biggest concern. I hate being so far away from them, but you need to change your way of thinking, Kahala."

"But, what about your job?"

"But nothing. I'll let you know what I'm thinking about my job when I actually know. Does this suffice? Unless *you* want me gone?"

It's too late to answer, as we've arrived at the house. Thank goodness, because I was about to tell her that I'd planned on proposing marriage the night before the accident. I haven't wanted to tell her in the condition I'm in for fear that she'll say yes out of pity.

While I'm waiting for her to bring the wheelchair around, it isn't lost on me how hard she's been working on my behalf. It's not Abby that needs to prove her love to me; it's me that needs to step it up and prove it to her. I don't want to lose her again.

Abby is standing at my car window. She pokes her head in and asks, "What's going on in that head of yours, Kahala?"

"As much as I know you call me Kahala when you're pissed at me, it's a turn-on," I say teasingly, but with truth behind it. "I was thinking how beautiful you are, not just on the outside, but your entire being. I love you, Abby."

"I love you too, so no more talk about me going back to New York, okay?"

"Got it."

"Now come on, we need to go through the back entrance. I don't think I can lift you over that lip at the front door."

"It's nothing. I can tilt my chair back, no worries."

"No. We'll take the back way."

"You're the boss."

"Music to my ears," Abby laughs as she gives me a peck on the back of my neck. Little does she know that she's sent shivers down my spine. I wish I could pick her up and make love to her right now. Maybe not literally here at the side of the house—I don't have enough shrubbery, I laugh inside—but the backyard is private enough. The sun is perfect and—

"*SURPRISE!*"

Holy shit! I just about had a heart attack. "What's all this?" I ask, seeing Nani and James talking to Makani, while Mike is with Abby's parents. It takes a minute for the initial shock to wear off before I notice Sam and Keanu having a drink with the rest of the guys. I can't focus on everyone, as Auntie has made her way over to welcome me home. It's a lot to take in. "Are you guys trying to kill me?" I ask. "What a great surprise. Parker? So, this is why I couldn't go through the front door?"

"Got you," laughs Abby as she bends down to kiss me. She whispers, "We can all go inside. I've got the sofa ready for you to lay down on, if you want …"

I stop her from talking by kissing her again, but this time it's much longer. It was as if none of the guests existed for a moment.

"I want to stay right here in the fresh open air," I tell her. "Maybe we should go over and say hi to your parents."

"Too late, they're making their way over."

"Noah," Abby's mom says, dressed to the nines in a wide-brimmed sunhat and a dress printed with tiny flowers. "So glad you're finally out of the hospital. It's good to see you, it's been a long time."

"Good to see you too, Mrs. Parker."

"Oh Noah, call me Kate. There's no need to be so formal."

Abby, fretting and trying to not insult any of us, says, "Mom, his name is Kanoa."

"Oh, that's right. Where are my manners? Kanoa, it's a lovely name. You remember Paul," Kate says, stepping aside while Abby's father extends his hand to greet me. This is a real turning point. Shaking Paul's hand is the last thing I'd ever imagined doing again in my lifetime.

"Glad to see you're better, Noah. I think it'll take me a little longer to warm up to your new name. I'm sure you remember, but I'm not quite as sweet as Kate."

"Dad!" Abby exclaims.

"Best to be honest, don't you think, Noah?"

"Yes, of course, Mr. Parker. I'd like nothing more than to have a discussion with you and Mrs. Parker about what happened, but not today."

"Fair enough," says Paul. "And with that issue aside, I'm truly happy that you're alive and well, so welcome home. Now, Mike has been waiting to say hello." He steps aside to let Mike through.

Looking at Mike I notice he's lost weight and looks much older than before my accident. He shakes his head and smiles at me. "Oh, Kanoa, you'll never know how happy I am to see you back home. You had us all very worried."

I take his weathered hand in mine. "Thank you, Mike. I hear you had a few sleepless nights at the hospital. Why didn't you come visit once I came through? I'd have loved to see you."

"I knew that Abby was taking good care of you. I didn't want to be a third wheel."

"Mike! You could never be a third wheel, and by the way, *mahalo* for all your prayers. You are always welcome no matter where I am, remember that."

And just then an awkward flash goes through my mind. Did I imagine that Mike was talking to me while I was in a coma? I remember getting the feeling that maybe Mike had been in my room.

"We'll have plenty of time to catch up, son. I'll come see you now that you're home."

"I'd love that," I say, squeezing his hand. Mike has always been like a grandfather to me. I keep looking around for Abby, who has surprisingly walked away without any of us noticing. Maybe she's inside getting a welcome-home cake, I snicker to myself.

This has been one of the best days I can remember. It's great to see so many of my friends here. I'm sure Nani had a part in inviting all the investors. After losing the Coco Palms, the last thing I thought these guys wanted to do was celebrate with me, but I was wrong. It feels good to know that our friendships can withstand anything that's thrown at us.

There it is! I just got an instant flash of Mike again. What the hell is happening to me? I'll have to tell my doctor on my next visit. I don't think I'll burden Abby with it—she's got enough on her plate. And speaking of Abby, she has just reappeared, but she's talking to herself under my banana tree.

CHAPTER FORTY-THREE:

Abby

I make my way to the huge banana tree at the back of Kanoa's yard where I have spotted Deborah. I ask, "What are you doing here? I said you couldn't come to the party. Thought we had a deal."

Deborah rolls her eyes at me. "We didn't have a deal. You returned my comb, and I said I would keep it until you want it back. That's the only deal I recall making."

"I swear you will be the death of me. Do you know how crazy I must look right now talking to this tree?"

"Then stop talking."

I can't believe her right now. I don't want to get mad at such an old woman, but she's trying my patience. It's too beautiful a day to get wound up, I tell myself.

"I don't know how you got here, but don't you dare ruin this day for Kanoa, hear me?"

"Loud and clear. Now get back to the party and let me enjoy it."

I can't help but snicker. She definitely knows how to get to me, but that doesn't mean I trust her to stay quiet. "You promise not to make a peep, right?"

"What is it with you and Genie, always asking me to promise things? Yes, I promise. Now get back to your guests and let me enjoy the day."

"Okay. Look, I know I sound harsh, but I just want this to be a happy day for Kanoa. He's been through a lot."

"Say no more, child. I want his happiness also, so stop worrying. By the way, you must bring your parents to the Coco Palms. They seem like such a lovely couple. Treat them to a canoe ride."

"Deal. I'll bring my parents to the lagoon if you sit quietly and enjoy the party without any of your antics. Plus, as an added bonus, I'll put a plate of Pono's famous *lau lau* behind that bush over there," I say, pointing.

"Lovely," she says. "I'd be a fool not to accept that deal. You see, it's not that hard to get along."

We both giggle like school kids. "I have to ask. How did you get here?"

"A lady never tells."

"Fine, you'll tell me sooner or later. Enjoy the party. We'll talk later."

I start to walk away, but out of habit, I turn to see if Deborah is still there and sure enough, I see the comb—which throws me into panic mode. I run back over to the tree. "Why do you have that comb on? Kanoa and others will see it."

"No, they won't. They'll only see it if they believe in me. Okay, maybe Mike and Auntie, but they are used to me."

"You're sure?"

"For heaven's sake, yes. Sometimes you are overly exhausting. Now get on with the party," Deborah commands.

Kanoa is staring directly at me. Great, I've grabbed his attention, and not in a good way. Once we make eye contact he waves, but with raised eyebrows and a smirk, as if to say, "I know you're up to something." I ignore him for the time being, choosing to attend to my guests. I stop beside my parents and Mike, but the minute I show up, they drop their conversation.

"Am I interrupting?" I ask.

"No," my parents both say at the same time.

Their synchronicity has left me feeling a bit awkward. "I was thinking, Dad, maybe you and Mom would like to visit the Coco Palms property with me this week. I think it'd be fun for you to see what brought me here in the first place. And Mom, you can finally see where Grandmother and Grandfather vacationed. What do you guys think? Mike, would you like to join us?"

"It's definitely a sight to see," Mike responds. "I for one think it's a lovely idea."

"You should join us," I suggest. "I can stop by and pick you up."

Mike looks at Dad, as if he needs his approval or something. Either I'm super tired, or they are definitely projecting odd behavior. I excuse myself, as James and

Makani have come back with the food, and yes, it's from Pono Market.

I look over to see where Kanoa is. I notice he's looking a bit tired, but I don't want to make it obvious. It's so good to see him celebrating with his friends, but I do suggest to Kanoa, "I hate to interrupt, but I think we should get you inside on the sofa, where you'll be more comfortable. We can move the party indoors, if you gentlemen don't mind? What do you say?" I ask Kanoa.

His friends are all in agreement. Kanoa says, "Go ahead guys, get a head start, I may be a minute. Abby and I will be fine. We've got this, right?"

"We sure do," I reply as I start to wheel Kanoa toward the living room while his friends walk on ahead.

"I'm glad you came over," he says. "I was about to ask you to take me in earlier, but you were busy talking to that tree. Did it have anything interesting to say? Or, let me guess, your ghost friend likes parties?"

"You think you're so funny, don't you? Well, for your information, yes, she does. Don't ask me how she got here, because she won't tell me."

Kanoa bursts out laughing. "Really?"

"Kahala, why do you love me if you think I'm hallucinating or half nuts? I'll tell you why," I say playfully. "Because I keep a fire lit under you, that's why—and also because I know deep down you know Queen Deborah exists."

"Sorry I opened that can of worms. Come on, *wāhine*, let's get inside," he says as he taps my behind.

"You'd better watch yourself, buster."

"I'm watching, and I like what I see."

"You're insufferable," I remark as I push the wheelchair into the house.

"By the way, how long are your parents here for?"

"Two weeks. Do you think you can handle it?"

"I'll be fine, I've always liked your parents. I admit, I was a little nervous earlier, but they were both very cordial."

I stare at Kanoa as if he's lost his marbles. "Really, you think Dad was cordial?"

"Yes."

"Glad that's how you see it."

We make our way to the sofa, but Kanoa won't accept help from anyone. I'm very proud of his strength and courage on all counts. I can finally breathe a sigh of relief; I think he'll be A-OK.

Once Kanoa gets settled, I scout out my father. I need to talk to him, but not within earshot of my mother. I have to know what's been happening with Stan and the Bakers. Being by Kanoa's bedside has kept me out of the loop. I finally get a chance to speak with him, while my mother is outside talking to Auntie. Dad is getting himself some food. When he's done, we go off to a corner of the living room.

"If you're not doing anything tomorrow," he says, "your mother has booked an appointment to get her hair done."

"Really? Jeez, when did she find the time?"

"Apparently she did it online while we waited for our connecting flight at the Honolulu Airport."

Leave it to Mom, she has to be one of the most impeccably coiffed women I know.

"Let me check Kanoa's time for his first rehab session," I say. "I think it's in the morning, which means he'll be gone for a few hours. I'll let you know the exact time before you leave. I guess you won't give me a hint as to what you found?"

"Not now—it's not the place—but don't worry, it's good news for Kanoa, that's all I'll say."

"Really?"

"Yes, and I recall that you said something about quitting your job if things worked out. I'm telling you as a trusted and seasoned investigator, not to mention a loving father, I think you should quit first chance you get, and don't put it off."

"Come on, Dad. You've got to give me something. You can't just say quit your job without just a snippet of detail."

"That was your snippet, so take the advice. Okay, I need to freshen my drink. Is there anything you need help with, party-wise?"

"No, but thank you for offering. Tomorrow can't come soon enough."

The party winds down before sunset as Kanoa is feeling a bit tired. It was a fun day. My parents and Mike stay a while longer after Kanoa goes to lie down on the bed. I'm not sure when Deborah left, but it was nice to see that she kept her word.

CHAPTER FORTY-FOUR

I'm heading to the North Shore today to have lunch with my father. I don't have to pick Kanoa up until three PM, which gives me plenty of time for a visit. Plus, my mother had a change of heart and decided on a half-day spa treatment along with getting her hair done. Let's face it, she's staying in one of the most exclusive hotels in Princeville, which offers everything at her fingertips. If I know Mom, she'll be gone all day—and why shouldn't she? She deserves it. And it will give Dad and me the privacy we need.

I haven't seen the Nā Pali Coast yet, but I've been told that from the restaurant where we'll be eating lunch I'll get to see a glimpse of one of the most beautiful coastlines in the world. I've seen photos of the restaurant before, but nothing compares to actually seeing it live. As I'm standing on the patio mesmerized by the view, I forget to look for my father—that is, until I hear him calling my name. I turn and see Dad waving. He's probably ten feet in front of me, but my eyes are still projected across the Pacific.

"Hi, Dad," I say as I hug him tight.

"Hi, honey, isn't this one of the most spectacular views you've ever seen?"

"Oh my God! I don't even want to know how much this is costing."

"Let's just say it's not cheap," laughs Dad, "but I wouldn't have it any other way. Your mother adores it here and she deserves it for putting up with me."

We sit down facing the lush mountains of the Napali Coast. I order a sparkling water with lemon on the side.

"You sure you don't want anything stronger?" Dad asks with a tilted head and a slight eye-raise.

"Why, do I need it?"

"How about we have two sparkling waters and two white wines?"

"Sure," I say skeptically. He's got me worried. He obviously thinks I need a little alchol for whatever it is he needs to tell me. I wait for the waiter to leave so that we aren't interrupted.

"Tell me, what have you found?"

"First of all, I need you to stay calm. No matter what I say, I don't want you jumping to conclusions until you hear me out."

Here we go again. I hate when people tell me to be calm—that usually means I'm going to have a strong reaction, whether it be good or bad. I take a deep breath of the fresh, fragrant air that always seems to soothe me.

"Okay, give it to me," I say.

"Anyway, let's start with the man you work for. I found out that he's the mastermind behind this entire scam. My team found out that he'd been following Kanoa from the very beginning, before the two of you even started dating."

"You mean Stan set me up the night of that snowstorm?"

"No, he's not that magical. Neither Stan nor the Bakers had anything to do with that, but it played beautifully into their plan."

"I'm confused. Did Stan know Kanoa's identity?"

"Only when the Bakers signed with your firm. I should back up a bit. The only reason the Bakers signed with Brickman and Brickman is because they found out that Kanoa Kahala was the head of the Heritage Association—which led them to discover he was in New York under the name of Noah King. By this time, you and Kanoa had been dating. The Bakers knew the one obstacle that would stop them from building condos on the Coco Palms Property was the Heritage Association, and who better to defend them than the jilted girlfriend?"

"Oh my God. So when I bragged at the office about meeting Noah, Stan was all ears. He used me!"

Suddenly it feels as if I've gotten sunburnt, but I know it's my blood pressure rising. I swear I'm about to combust.

Dad reaches for my hand across the table, but I'm holding on to my head with both hands as if it's about to launch off my shoulders.

Dad gestures for me to give him my hand, which I finally do and he holds on tight to it. He continues, "Calm down, you haven't even heard the best part. I'll fast forward and skip the small details for now. The reason I didn't tell you this a week ago is because I didn't think Kanoa was strong enough. I didn't want him to relapse, and seeing that his leg …"

"Dad, it's okay, I get it."

"Kanoa was set up. We found a guy that'd been drinking with Ken at a bar in New York. Ken told this guy how he'd stolen the keys to Kanoa's office and made him think he'd forgot to file the submission form for the bid. He went into detail about how Charles was the one who'd initially seen the keys and ordered Ken to take them and make a copy. In order to make Kanoa think he'd left out the most important document, Ken used his spare to get in and out of Kanoa's office whenever he pleased. He was also the one that left the door unlocked the night you guys attended the *lū'au*. So, all that to say, Kanoa and his investors would have won the bid." Dad taps his forehead. "Oh, I almost forgot the most important detail. The silent bidder was Ken, under a new company name."

"This is insane. Is this witness reliable enough to be taken seriously in court?"

"That's the thing. His sobriety is questionable, so we need to find another angle to move in on these guys. We really should have pressed charges that night Ken tried to steal the hair comb from you, but it's not too late. I wanted to tell you in person and I was hoping you'd want to press charges."

"I agree, what are we waiting for?"

"Done. We have all the proof we need."

"Good job, Dad."

"You're welcome, but there's one other thing. "

I'm almost afraid to ask. "Which is?"

"I'm here to trail Mike. And before we get sidetracked, I need you to understand that you can't breathe a word of what I just told you to Kanoa. If you were any other client, I sure as hell wouldn't have told you any of this. I'm trusting you as my daughter."

"I swear, Dad. I won't breathe a word of it." I give him my Girl Guide salute, since he knows I always keep my promise as a Guide. We've done this since I was a little girl.

Dad laughs. He picks up his wine and makes a toast. "To concluding a portion of this case and looking forward to happy endings."

"Hear, hear," I say as I clink glasses. "If it's any help, I know Mike used to frequent the resort back in the day. I'm talking back in the early sixties and until it closed."

"Let's keep our eyes and ears open around Mike. I really like the man, and because of his age, I don't want to badger him."

"I agree. I love Mike. I don't believe he's doing anything wrong. He's the protective type, but what or who is he protecting?"

The waiter comes back to ask if we are ready to order our lunch, but Dad and I somehow order another glass of wine each. We ask for a couple more minutes to put in our lunch order. My head is swirling from information overload. It's all too surreal to wrap my head around at the moment.

"I have an idea," I say. "We suggested yesterday taking a tour of the Coco Palms. Let's do it and bring Mike, then maybe we can go out for lunch or dinner, depending what time we take our tour."

"Let's wait and see what your schedule is with Kanoa, and then call me. We'll figure something out."

"Sounds good," I say as we click our glasses of wine and cheer to tomorrow.

Later that afternoon, Kanoa is waiting for me outside the rehab center when I pull up. I want to tell him that he won the bid outright, but I promised Dad I wouldn't breathe a word. "I'm so sorry," I say. "I wasn't expecting lunch to be so long."

"Don't apologize, it's fine. I asked to be brought out here so I could take in some sun, it's all good," he says as I help him get into the car. "How was lunch?"

"First off, can I just tell you how spectacular the view was?"

"I knew you'd like it."

"Like? No, I loved it."

"Since you loved it, I have an idea. My rehab is scheduled for the early morning tomorrow, so why don't we take your parents and Mike on a catamaran lunch cruise, instead of the Coco Palms? I won't be able to walk, let alone wheel a wheelchair through those grounds. Why not show your parents the Nā Pali Coast? You can take them to the Coco Palms anytime. It'd be great to have everyone together—what do you say? And if you don't want to do the lunch," he continues, "we could take the later cruise and watch the sunset."

Kanoa seems like he's just had his spark re-lit, and I can't put it out. I want nothing more than for him to get back to being the happy-go-lucky person he was. "That sounds like a great idea—dinner cruise it is. I'll call Dad and let him know. Leave it to me."

CHAPTER FORTY-FIVE

M y dad agrees to the Nā Pali Coast cruise, even though Mom voices concern that she's just gotten her hair done. She wastes no time finding a solution, though. She runs down to the hotel gift shop and gets herself a silk scarf.

Meanwhile, Mike has asked Auntie if she'd like to join us for the dinner cruise, which I think is a great idea. But right now the only thing I can think of is being on such a long cruise. Ever since I had that horrible nightmare my first night here, I have followed the daily weather report. Swells have been moving in for a couple of days, but the catamaran company says they are still a distance away. They reassure me that they would never jeopardize the safety of their passengers or themselves. This gives me comfort, temporarily.

When Kanoa and I arrive at the catamaran headquarters to meet the others, I'm in full-blown scared mode. I decide to make the best of this trip by buying up all the ginger chews. The sales clerk suggest I buy the anti-nausea wristbands also. I'll do whatever it takes to avoid motion sickness.

Everyone has arrived: Mom and Dad, Mike and Auntie, and James and Nani. The Captain helps wheel Kanoa onboard. Once on, Kanoa's wheelchair is taken back down the ramp and left at the dock for safekeeping. The catamaran rides are usually open to the public, but when Dad heard about it, he made a phone call to the company and paid for a private cruise. He also called Nani and James to join us, which was a lovely surprise. Dad extended the offer for them to bring the children, but Nani said she wanted to enjoy a night without stress, which is understandable.

The first hour of sailing the ocean is uneventful. There is always hope of spotting spinner dolphins and, if you're very lucky, a whale, but nothing so far. Everyone seems to be relaxed and drinking cocktails, except me. I'll stick to my ginger ale and chews. I don't want a repeat performance of throwing up like I did on the Waimea Canyon trip. I seem to be the only person distracted by the swells. I watch as each one heaves and rolls itself under the catamaran—without even so much as a tilt. Nani has taken notice of what I'm doing. Before I know it, she's sitting next to me.

She says, "You realize that the longer you stare at those swells, the more likely you are to have motion sickness?"

I try hard to avert my eyes from the swells, but I just can't. "No, I didn't know that, but I appreciate you telling me. It's bizarre how it works. The water looks like it's about to slam right into us and instead, it gently rolls away beneath without any movement. It's astonishing."

"First time I saw it I was a little kid. After my mother warned me not to stare or I'd get sick, I've never looked again," Nani laughs. "How you feeling?"

"Good, but I've eaten a million ginger chews."

We sit and chat for longer than we realize. Nani points out that we're approaching the more colorful, jagged-edged cliffs that make up the Nā Pali Coastline. Upon seeing them, it's apparent how majestic they really are.

"I feel like an ant in this catamaran," I say. "These cliffs are insanely massive. I got a partial view yesterday from the hotel my parents are staying at, but nothing like what I'm seeing now. It's freaking me out how small our fifty-foot catamaran suddenly feels. Never mind that, I've never felt so small in my entire life!"

"Deep breaths, Abby," laughs Nani. "Not sure, but the captain may offer to let us snorkel, if you're interested? It will depend on the swells, but I'm no mariner, so don't listen to me."

"You and me both. I know very little of the ocean life."

Just then the captain's voice comes over the speaker. "We will soon be approaching where film production of *Jurassic Park* started in 1992. Unfortunately, when Hurricane Iniki hit, the production got moved to the island of Oʻahu for the final scenes. It's unbelievable how many movies and television shows have been filmed on our tiny island," the captain continues, listing a few of them.

I turn my head, when I catch sight of the haircomb. Deborah is directly behind me. Thank God Nani has just left to join James to view the coastline. I nervously turn to look at everyone onboard, but they are all too busy looking at the mountain range. Kanoa is standing up trying to stretch his legs. He is hanging on tight to the siderail, looking out at the cliffs while he chitchats with Mike and Dad. He's deep in conversation and doesn't notice that I've moved away from my seat to join Deborah.

"So lovely to see you today, dear," Deborah says. "You don't have to answer, as I know you'll look *lōlō* talking to yourself, yet again."

Let's just say it's a good thing the rest are mesmerized by the cliffs, because even the spinner dolphins below can see me moving my lips. I'm no Edgar Bergen.

"How'd you get here?" I ask.

"Auntie," she says. "Now stop talking. I promised Auntie I'd behave."

"As if that's ever stopped you."

"People do change," says Deborah as she shakes her head at me. "Seems to me you've changed your mind about our island, not to mention forgiving Kanoa."

"Okay, you win, as always. I'll let you do all the talking."

"First of all, I want to say that I admire the way you've been taking care of Kanoa. It's nice to see the love between the two of you. It melts my heart."

I pretend to move my head towards Deborah's face and say, "Is that a tear I see?"

"I thought you weren't going to say anything?"

"But you getting emotional is monumental."

RITA D'ORAZIO

"Stop it. You're going to make me blush," Deborah jokes.

The two of us continue chitchatting for so long that I fail to notice the moment when the catamaran turns to head back to port. We still have a two-hour ride back ahead of us.

The captain isn't able to get the boat closer to shore due to the rough seas, which rules out snorkeling. I can't say I'm disappointed. I'm not sure I'd have gone even if the ocean wasn't this rough. Soon dinner will be served below deck, and by the time we're done, sunset will be approaching. Everything is going smoothly.

"Are you okay, dear?" Deborah asks.

I'm taking my time answering. I feel I always need to be cautious with my words around Deborah. I finally say, "I'm fine. I just wish there was a way I could help Kanoa."

"What do you mean? You've been helping him since you got back."

"No, it's not about his recovery. It's to do with the Coco Palms. My dad has been helping me figure some things out."

Deborah rolls her eyes. "Dear, get to the point—maybe I can be of help."

"No, I don't think so."

"Don't make assumptions! Spit it out."

I decide to confide in Deborah about the way Kanoa and his investors were scammed. What I didn't realize was that this bit of information is music to Deobrah's ears. I shouldn't have said anything, because I promised Dad I wouldn't breathe a word, but Deborah is a ghost—what could she possibly do with the information?

The moment I've asked myself this, Deborah strikes. "Leave it with me. I know just what to do."

"No," I say. As I try to take hold of her arm, which I forgot is impossible. "I don't need you to do anything."

Thank goodness we've been called to have dinner—I can't deal with any shenanigans right now. I get a plate of food for Kanoa and myself and take it outside to the upper deck, where Kanoa sits looking out onto the water. The rest of the gang joins us once they finish their supper, and I thank the heavens above that Deborah stayed quiet. I'm feeling relaxed, which is more than I can say for the first three hours of the cruise.

A sudden loud thud causes the Catamaran to sway sideways. I hold on tight as I watch Kanoa slide down the bench he's sitting on.

"What was that?" I ask.

I no sooner ask than I hear the captain say, "For those of you who have been waiting to spot a whale, we have one right below us. I'm hoping he will show himself in a bit."

I no longer hear the engine. I turn to Kanoa. "Why isn't he moving away from the whale? Why are we stopped?"

"Abby! Take a breath."

"What if the whale capsizes us? I want to get out of here. By the way, where are the life preservers?"

I stand and approach the captain. "I need a life jacket."

"I can get you one," the captain says, smiling, "but you'll be fine, trust me."

After the captain's assistant gathers some life vests, I bring one to Kanoa. "Abby, I don't want a lifejacket." I keep trying to get him to wear one, but my words are falling on deaf ears. Let's just say, I'm the only one wearing a life vest. The captain makes sure his assistant leaves a few on the upper deck should the others have a change of heart.

Kanoa watches as I return to the captain at the controls. I ask, "Do you think we will be starting up soon? We really should stay on course."

"Don't you and your guest want to see the whale? Trust me, it's going to be spectacular."

Just then the whale makes an appearance, its tail rising out of the water and creating waves around it. The captain says into his microphone, "Everyone, look slightly to your left, the whale will come up again."

As soon as the words are out of the captain's mouth, the whale gives us a full view of its tail. The captain was right: it really is spectacular to see. Out of everyone here, I'm the most excited—go figure. I ask the captain, "Do you think he'll do it again? Was that a humpback?"

"Yes, it was a *kohola*. I'm seeing on my sonar that there's two more ahead. If we're lucky, maybe they'll entertain us with a few flips."

I'm so excited about seeing the whales turning and having fun in the water, I stay up front with the captain, forgetting about Kanoa and Queen Deborah for the moment—not to mention my fear of drowning.

Mom is trying to get a picture of the whales when she accidentally drops her camera into the ocean. What had been an uneventful afternoon is turning out to be an evening loaded with moments to remember. Soon the whales have come and gone, and the sun is slowly going down for the day. The cruise is now twenty minutes behind schedule, but the captain reassures us, "Sit back and enjoy the sunset. I'll have us back in no time."

No one seems too concerned about the fact that we are running late, except me. Why am I the one with all the issues? I whisper to Kanoa, "I hate when people say not to worry—that's when I start worrying."

Kanoa laughs as he puts his arm around me. "Come on babe, you were skeptical of the whales and look how much fun you had. The captain knows what he's doing— let him do his job. He's been doing this for most of his life."

"You're right," I say as I watch the sun change from bright yellow to a redder hue in a matter of seconds. After another minute has passed, I hear myself say, "OMG, I've never seen anything like this. One minute I'm seeing a ball of fire above the ocean and a split second later, it's as if it has fallen into an abyss. How did that just happen so quickly?"

"I take it you liked the sunset?"

"Liked it? I'm in awe and still can't believe what I just witnessed. I'll never get that image out of my head. The saddest part about this island is that the beauty of it all is so hard to explain to others. There isn't one perfect picture that can capture what it's truly like unless you see it with your own eyes."

"Glad you liked it," says Kanoa as he pulls me in tight for a kiss. He gives me a small blanket that's folded next to him. "Here, take this, it gets a bit chilly once the sun disappears."

Everyone is now huddled together taking in the moonlit ocean. Dad pops a bottle of champagne for one last toast. "I think I can speak for all of us. Kanoa, we are all very happy to see how well you've been recovering. If everyone would be so kind as to raise your glasses. Here's to Kanoa. May I—"

Before Dad can finish, Deborah's booming voice says, "Why don't you tell him why you are here?"

Everyone turns their head, realizing that it's no one in our circle that has spoken.

Dad replies, "Is this some sort of joke? Who are you? Better yet, where are you?"

Even the captain is freaked out, based on the shocked look on his face. He tries his handheld intercom control, but the voice is being projected over his system and he no longer has control of it. I'm mortified, because I know that I'm the one that leaked information to Deborah, never thinking that she'd use it. I stand up and approach my father, but it's too late.

"Well," the voice says, "if Paul won't speak up, I will. Let me start with you, Kanoa."

"Stop! Stop right now!" commands Mike.

"Well, finally, after all these years, I get a reaction out of you. Maybe you should tell everyone who you really are, Mike."

If jaws weren't dropping earlier, they are definitely hitting the planks right about now. I turn to look at Mike, whom I've gotten to know very well, and I've never seen him this shaken. I want to stand by Kanoa, and I know I need to tell my father what I told Deborah, but my heart right now is with Mike, and I run to his side. I whisper to him, "Come on, Mike, don't let her get to you."

"I must tell the truth," Mike whispers. "I've waited too many years. I am at fault here."

I have no idea what Mike is referring to. Obviously it isn't the same information that my father and I need to tell Kanoa.

Kanoa pipes up. "Okay, I've had enough. Who is on the speaker? Come out and show your face!"

Deborah responds, "If you believed in me you'd see my face, young man."

Kanoa looks over at me. He says in my direction, "This isn't funny. There's no ghost, I'm sick and tired of hearing about it, and we all need to regroup here. What the hell is going on? Paul, since you wanted to say something, please, continue."

"Mike, seeing as you're the eldest, you should go first," Dad suggests.

"No," says Mike shyly. "Please, Paul, go ahead."

I can tell that Kanoa is getting impatient with all the back and forth. He doesn't want to be rude, but he's reached a boiling point. Just as he's about to say something, Deborah beats him to the punch.

She yells, "For the love of God, someone say something or I will."

I decide to take charge. "It's all my fault. I asked Dad to help me investigate my boss, Stan, and my clients the Bakers. I had no idea what Dad had discovered until we had lunch yesterday. He came all the way here to tell me about it, and I just haven't had time to say anything because Dad needs more time." I look directly at Kanoa. "You were set up by Stan and his clients. The Coco Palms is yours. You and the investors won the bid fair and square. Ken tampered with your submission. He stole the keys to your office along with some of the papers. He went back after the papers were filed and planted the forms back on your desk to make you believe you'd forgotten to file them."

Kanoa is left speechless, as is Nani. He looks at my Dad, then me. "Are you sure?"

"One hundred percent," says Dad. "You and your investors are the rightful owners of the Coco Palms. I came here to bring you the news and to discuss taking legal action against Stan and the Bakers."

"Oh my God! I can't believe this," cries Kanoa with joy. "Wait until I tell the guys, it'll blow their mind." He looks at Mike. "Is this what you wanted to tell me?"

Deborah has given the captain back control of his PA system, and he announces that we've reached the port. It's time to disembark.

Kanoa asks, "Would you mind just giving us a few minutes?"

The captain replies, "I normally don't because it's against our policy, but it's okay as long as you understand that we are no longer liable should anything go wrong."

"No worries, we'll finish up our conversation and be out of your hair in a few minutes," says Kanoa. "So who was the woman speaking?" he asks, hoping that someone will answer.

Auntie speaks up. "Listen, this is no longer the time and place. You and Mike need to speak privately, and the woman is Queen Deborah, whether you want to believe it or not."

"You're right about one thing," Kanoa says, "this is no longer the time and place to speak—but Auntie, you of all people, I'd never have taken you for a ghost follower."

"Stop it," Auntie says sternly. "There are serious issues here. This is not a laughing matter. You need to talk to Mike, as I've already mentioned."

Kanoa turns to Mike. "How about tomorrow morning? Does that work for you?"

"Yes, that would be perfect. I'll make us breakfast. Everybody is welcome if you'd like."

Nani declines because she needs to be at the office, but the rest of us agree to meet at Mike's for eight AM.

As we disembark from the catamaran, Kanoa stops Dad. "Thank you so much, sir. I can't tell you what this means to me. I know I don't deserve everything that you've done."

"Let's just say that I don't want you to disappoint my daughter moving forward. All I want is to see Abby happy."

"You got it, sir."

Dad extends his hand to Kanoa. He says, "Enough with the sir. I liked it when you used to call me Paul."

And so Dad and Kanoa shake hands and descend the platform on a cordial note. I'm left trying to find Deborah, but she must have snuck into Mike's car already.

CHAPTER FORTY-SIX:

Kanoa

The shock of hearing that I won the bid takes a bit of time to sink in. It isn't until Abby is getting ready for bed that it all comes flooding in. My head feels as if it's going to explode. I need to get my guys in for a celebratory meeting. How am I going to fit rehab in along with everything else? And how can I forget Abby? Without her gut feeling about Stan and the Bakers, none of it would have come to flourish. I owe it all to Abby, who looks like an angel right now as she steps out of the bathroom.

"Kahala, I know that look," Abby says as she stops to spritz some perfume.

"Get over here, you. I can't believe you knew this yesterday. Just when I think you of all people can't keep a secret, you surprise me yet again. I can't believe you didn't even tell Nani."

"In all honesty, I didn't have much time. I only found out yesterday at noon."

"I know, but you were having your father investigate these dudes. I don't know how I'll ever repay you. You are truly my guardian angel," I say as I pull Abby into the bed to kiss her.

"I have something I need to tell you," she says. "I think this will make you really happy."

"You're pregnant?"

"Now you're being ridiculous. How can I be pregnant—I'm on the pill?" She shakes her head. "Stop talking, you got me off track. What I want to tell you is that I sent in my resignation letter late last night. Once Dad told me what had been going on, I figured we got what we needed and I never need to see Stan again."

"What! You're not messing with me, are you Parker?"

Abby slides her body as close to me as she can. She's kissing me in places where she knows I'll lose my concentration. "This is the only messing I want to do right now, Kahala."

We make love into the wee hours of the morning. I have trouble sleeping, so instead I stare at her until Abby rolls over and falls asleep. I know that there is no other woman on this planet for me. That's when I decide I want to give her the engagement ring I've been holding on to. I didn't think it was possible, but I'm feeling even more excited about proposing than before I had the accident. I want to live my life with Abby until my last breath on Earth. I should be exhausted after the day we all had, but I can't stop thinking about Mike, or that crazy voice that claims to be Queen Deborah. As much as I love Abby, how does she buy into the craziness? Can this apparition really exist?

No, it's only my exhaustion that's making me question myself. I keep telling my brain to shut off and go to sleep, but I'm not succeeding. I can't fathom what Mike has to tell me. Also, why would he have invited everyone for breakfast if it's a private matter? Maybe he wants to make me executor of his will or something. I know I'm grasping at straws, but what else does one do at three in the morning?

I can feel Abby's soft lips on my cheek. I think I'm dreaming until I hear her say, "Wake up, sleepyhead. We have a breakfast to get to."

"What time is it?"

"Seven thirty."

I'm so disappointed in myself for not setting my alarm. "Shit," I exclaim. "I was hoping to get up earlier, but I had so much trouble falling asleep."

"As much as you think I was in a deep sleep, I could feel you awake. I called Mike and told him we'd be about twenty minutes late, so no worries."

I have no words. Well, that's not entirely true. I have two options: I can either hurry up and get ready, or I can spend ten minutes doing something I should have done a long time ago. I push myself up and grab my walker. I head over to where I've been keeping Abby's engagement ring. There is no time like the present.

Abby walks back into the room holding a cup of coffee. "Why aren't you getting ready?"

"I'll be ready in fifteen minutes, but first I have something I need to ask you."

She hands me a steaming-hot cup. "Here, drink, it'll help you wake up."

I take a sip and place the coffee on the dresser. I take Abby's hand and say, "I'd get down on one knee, but—"

Before I have a chance to ask, Abby starts crying and says, "Yes."

I can't help but laugh. I take Abby's hand in mine. I look into her beautiful dark eyes as I open the box and place the ring on her finger. When I look up at her, I ask Abby, "Do you like it?"

"I love it," Abby says with tears streaming down her cheeks. "And I love you. When did you do all this?"

"I've actually had the ring for a while. I was planning on proposing before you left for New York, but we never made it to the restaurant and you were gone the next morning. But none of that matters—what matters is the here and now, and moving forward. So I'm now going to ask you: Abby Ky Parker, will you be my wife?"

"Yes! Yes I'll be your wife, best friend, and all of the above. I love you, Kahala."

"Okay, well, glad we got that out of the way."

I hold her tight, and we both take a moment to enjoy each other's company. Not to seem unromantic, but we need to get a move on. It takes me a bit longer to shower these days, but we make it to Mike's in the twenty extra minutes, like Abby predicted before she knew I was going to propose. It's these little things that mesmerize me about Abby. She's come a long way.

The entire car ride to Mike's, all Abby keeps doing is looking down at her ring, then putting her hand up to look at it from different angles.

"I'm sorry it wasn't the most romantic proposal," I say, "but I didn't want to wait another second. When I couldn't sleep last night I decided I'd do it before going to Mike's, because the last time I waited I ended up getting in a car accident."

"Stop thinking it wasn't romantic. What matters is that it was spontaneous and I wasn't expecting it. How much more romantic could it have been? I loved it."

We decide not to tell anyone until we've heard what Mike has to say. We don't want to overshadow his moment, so Abby decides to put the ring in her purse for the time being. We'll tell them all after breakfast, if we feel the timing is right.

When we arrive, everyone is outside on the *lānai*, where Mike has a table set up for breakfast. Auntie is there, helping, along with Kate.

Mike greets us and asks if we'd like to start with a cup of coffee. I watch as Abby walks off and says hello to her parents and Auntie. While I have Mike alone, I ask, "Is there something you'd like to tell me in private?"

Mike is fidgeting with the coffee cups. I place my hand on his to get him to leave the cups alone. He says, "I can't believe you picked up on it."

"I've known you for a very long time, Mike. You are one of my parents' oldest and dearest friends. I've never seen you this nervous. What is it?"

"Come with me to the living room, where no one will disturb us."

I follow Mike as he asks me to take a seat wherever I feel comfortable. I choose the sofa and ask him to sit next to me. "Mike, it's just me, Kanoa, you can tell me anything."

"I'm not so sure, son. You see, I came to learn something in 1989, when my friend Genie, whom I've told you about, gave me a box. One day she asked me to meet her privately, as she'd been instructed to give me an ornate box with documents in it."

"Where did the box come from?"

"From me," says the voice from the boat, as it echoes throughout the living room. I look towards the staircase, but Mike is looking directly at the front window, where the voice is really coming from.

"Come on Mike, what's going on? Who is this person?"

"It's Queen Deborah," Mike says. "I know it sounds insane, but her spirit lives on, and she's my great-great-grandmother."

"Your great-great-grandmother? How? Is that what's in the box, your birth certificate?"

"Among other things."

"So why does she keep hanging around?"

"Young man," Deborah says in a perturbed voice. "I'm not just hanging around like some bad disease. What Mike is having difficulty telling you is that you are his grandson. Tell him, Mike."

"That's okay, Madame, I think you've said enough."

I look at Mike and I know that what she just said is the truth. Mike's hands are trembling. Queen Deborah is about to say something else, when Mike stops her in her tracks by saying, "Madame, if you don't mind, please let me do the talking."

"How is this possible, Mike?" Even as I ask, I feel as if a tub of hot water has been thrown on me. My brain is jumping back and forth, showing me scattered images of my mother and father. Who is Mike referring to? "This is ludicrous!"

"No it's not," Mike says. "I'm not proud to admit my faults, but please keep in mind I thought I was doing what was best for everyone. You see, back in the day I was having an affair with a married woman. She used to come to the Coco Palms quite often. I loved her more than life itself, but when she decided that she was going to stay with her husband, I was devastated. I really thought that she and I had a future together. When I saw her for the last time, I didn't actually know it would be my last time, nor that she was pregnant with my child."

"Oh my God! I'm so sorry, Mike, but how does this make me Deborah's—?"

"Young man," Deborah pipes in. "It's not that difficult to put together."

Mike is getting agitated. "No disrespect, Madame, but I would like to continue without interruptions. As I was saying," he continues, "when I opened the box, it contained the baby's birth certificate."

"And it belonged to whom?" I ask with a scared, trembling voice. Of course I knew it had to be one of my parents, but I'm finding this all insanely bizarre.

"The birth certificate belonged to your father," Mike says, holding back tears. "I never told him he was my son, which I regret to this day."

"Oh Mike, I'm so sorry. I can't begin to know what it's been like for you," I offer as I lean over and put my hand on his. "Why didn't you tell anyone before today, especially my Dad? You two were good friends. You were friends with both my parents. Why didn't you ever tell them?"

"I was going to, I swear I was. But every time I tried, I froze. I didn't want him to hate me. I saw in his eyes how much he loved me as a friend. I didn't want that look to change."

"But my father may have had even more love in his eyes for you if he'd known the truth. Knowing my father, I'd guarantee it."

"I was going to, and God knows I tried many times over the years, but I always lost my nerve. This is why I had to tell you, especially when I saw you in that hospital bed. It brought back the horrible pain of losing your mother and father. I have beat myself up every day since their accident. I couldn't go another moment without telling you. Had I known I'd never see your father's face again, my actions would have been different. I can't change the past, but I can change the present and the future. You're my only family, Kanoa," cries Mike as he wipes his tears away with a handkerchief he's pulled out of his pocket.

I squeeze Mike's hand tight. "Mike, no one knew my father better than you. I bet he's got a smile on his face right now listening to us."

Mike gives me a smile. "I didn't want to rock his world, especially knowing how much he respected his adoptive parents. Part of me didn't want to take that away from any of them."

"As his son, I'm telling you that I couldn't be prouder of you. I can't wait for people to know that you're my biological *Kupunakāne*."

And that's when I hear sniffles, but they aren't coming from Mike. I choose to not say anything for fear that I may become a believer in Queen Deborah. Instead, I lean over and give my *Kupunakāne* a great big hug. "Come, let's go join the others. You and I will make time to catch up and speak further about years past, but mostly, I'm looking forward to things to come. I don't want to miss a minute of time we may have together."

We get off the sofa and are standing next to one another, but Mike is looking down, afraid of what I might do or say next.

"Mike," I say, "look at me. As sorry as I am for what happened to you, I am just as happy to know that you're my *Kupunakāne*. Do you have any idea how good it feels to know that I have a surviving family member?"

"Thank you for saying that, Kanoa. You have always been so respectful of others. I remember you being this way from the time you were a tiny tot. Your parents did a great job raising you. I love you, Kanoa," *Kupunakāne* says as he reaches for my hand.

I hug my *Kupunakāne* tight and tell him I love him, which is the truth. I've always had a soft spot for Mike, and now it will be even better.

Before we join the others outside to have breakfast, my great-great-great-great-grandmother gets the final say. Whether I want to believe it or not, I can hear her clearly.

"Wait right there, both of you," she says. "I have one thing to say. It appears that more than one of us in this *'ohana* has had illegitimate children. Now that you both know you are descendants of mine, use your title wisely. The Coco Palms property needs to be back where it rightfully belongs—with our family. I'm depending on the two of you to do that. Let your heart guide you in the right direction. I'm begging you, Kanoa. Let's make all these wrongs right. Please?"

I don't want to acknowledge her presence, but one thing I will do is respect my elders. I will honor everything she asks of me, but I refuse to answer her directly. Instead, I say, "I know what to do moving forward. I will honor our people the best I know how." I put my hand out, "Mike? Shall we join the others?"

"But …? What about the Queen?"

"No buts. We know what we need to do."

"Kanoa Kahala," Queen Deborah continues, "I have one last thing to say to you. No more illegitimate children, got it? What this land of ours needs is a happy family. If and when it happens, I will grant you my disappearance for good. I don't do much begging, young man, but for all our ancestors, I'm begging you, son, don't let that girl slip through your hands."

I promised myself I'd be respectful to my elders, and I hope that this will be my only time acknowledging the Queen. I look over at Mike, because I'm not sure exactly where the Queen is at this point, but I will address her this once. "Queen Deborah? Or what would you like to be called?" I ask out of respect.

Her voice sounds softer than normal. "I've always just wanted someone to call me *Tūtū*."

"Then *Tūtū* it shall be. So, *Tūtū* and *Kupunakāne*, I have some good news for you both. Before coming over here I proposed to Abby, but we were going to wait to tell everyone until you told us what we came here to hear," I say, staring at Mike.

"Oh, Kanoa," he says, "I'm so happy for you. I have come to love Abby dearly. Even when she was on the other side, I knew that girl had a heart of gold."

"That she does, *Kupunakāne*. And for once, I'm glad I went with my gut instinct. I'm glad I proposed to her earlier, without knowing anything about our lineage. Abby said yes to me—plain Kanoa, not the guy who's related to her ghost friend, the Queen."

I hear the Queen give out a chuckle. Part of me wants to laugh out loud also, but I need her out of our personal life. I don't want Abby to keep up with the ghost stories. Maybe I'm being unreasonable, but I see it as logical.

After Mike and I leave the living room to head to the *lānai*, I turn to look back, and there it is: the hair comb. I quickly blink to make it go away, but it doesn't. I'm not a believer, I tell myself over and over.

CHAPTER FORTY-SEVEN:

Abby

Quitting my job at Brickman and Brickman two years ago was the best decision I ever made. It allowed me to help Mike and Kanoa put Stan and the Baker Brothers where they deserve to be—behind bars. It was the final case of my career as a lawyer, and one of the most satisfying, even though I was only assisting.

Queen Deborah had been right all along. She said her ex-husband would do anything to get ownership back on the property. Not that he legally ever owned it, but when he had Deobrah banished soon after their marriage, he took possession of the land. So in his mind, he was always the rightful heir because of his marriage. Turns out that Deborah was also right about him being the apparition that kept coming after me. It's not that the Bakers or Stan knew anything about the Queen's ex-husband, it's just that the King finally had others chasing after what he wanted. He knew he could easily steal that birth certificate once it was out of the safety deposit box. Sounds absolutely nuts, but it's the truth.

As Mike and I prepared for the case, he told me all about his faith in Auntie.

"Of course there are plenty of people I trusted, but only one could handle what I needed to ask of them, and that was Auntie. I knew I could trust her with my life."

"How could you be so sure?" I asked him.

"Sometimes in life you just know. Even though Auntie and I aren't blood relatives, she is my 'ohana. It is Auntie who told me about this guy in Oʻahu who could replicate just about anything. She had seen him on a special investigative program."

"Did you go to Oʻahu with Auntie to meet him?"

"No, I was too nervous that I'd be followed. I knew how much that certificate was worth. Auntie and I agreed that I'd pay all her expenses for trips to Oʻahu and anything that was needed. I knew Auntie wouldn't misplace that certificate—plus, I had a bodyguard follow her. There's no way I'd risk her life. After she met with the gentleman that was going to replicate the box and certificate, Auntie opened a safety deposit box at one of the local banks in Oʻahu, where she stored the originals until two years ago.

"Once the replica of the ornate box was made," he continued, "Auntie flew to Oʻahu to retrieve it. Without her knowledge, Ken spotted her. I had no idea he knew her, until I realized he'd been following me for quite some time."

"Auntie must really love you for risking her own safety all these years. That's beyond the call of duty even for a true friend."

"Yes, she's always had my back, as did Genie; and I made sure to have theirs. I will always watch out for Auntie. It's not easy trusting people, but Auntie and Genie are like you. I knew when I first looked in your eyes that you were a good soul. Even when I found out you were working for the Bakers, it didn't affect how I felt about you."

Mike's admission that he saw the good in me made me cry. I love Mike as if he were my own grandfather. I asked something at that moment that I'd been dying to ask him: "Why didn't you just claim the land outright? Why wait and keep your birthright a secret?"

"After my son, Kanoa's father, passed, I couldn't bring myself to want anything to do with it. And for obvious reasons, I couldn't disclose this information to Kanoa. I wasn't sure how it would all go down. All I knew was that once I passed on, everything was being left to my grandson, Kanoa. It may seem odd to others, but it made sense to me."

"Fair enough," I responded and left it at that.

I'm sure by now you're all wondering about my engagement to Kanoa. Well, it's like this: we are still engaged, but not married. It was one thing knowing that Kanoa and the investors got scammed out of winning the bid, but finding out that Kanoa was related to the Queen put me in another mindset. I had to think long and hard about what this meant for my future. I had hoped that maybe Kanoa would come to live in New York for at least part of the year; but after finding out that Mike was his biological grandfather, who was I to take him away from his only surviving relative? By this point I had already been in Kaua'i for six months, so I told myself I'd try it for at least another six.

Not long after that, I opened up to my parents about my concerns. They had also been waiting to tell me something, but didn't want to jump the gun.

Dad said, "Since we've been there, your mother has done nothing but talk about visiting again. Not seeing you in New York has changed things. By the way, you're on speaker—your mother is right here."

"Hi, dear," Mom said, "I miss you so much. I've been dying to tell you my thoughts every time we speak, but your dad hadn't quite made up his mind."

"About what?"

"You tell her, Paul," she said.

I could hear them going back and forth. "Will someone tell me what's going on?"

Finally Dad came back on. "How would you feel if we told you we are thinking of moving to Kaua'i?"

"What? Are you guys serious about this?"

"Yes," said Mom and Dad simultaneously. Dad piped back in, "I thought we'd give it a try for a few months and if we like it, we will stay permanently. We decided to sell our New York apartment, but we'll keep the house in the Hamptons."

I could feel myself well up. This was the best news. I had to admit, as much as I loved Kanoa, I was feeling homesick. New York was the only home I'd ever had and I deeply missed my parents. I couldn't believe we would all be in one place as a family. I prayed to God they would like it, because that would be my determining factor in finally agreeing to stay here to live. I said, "You have no idea how happy you've made me. When can you come?"

"We've decided that if you're okay with the idea, we could be there in a few weeks."

And so, that made my decision to stay in Kaua'i that much easier. I hadn't realized how heavily it was weighing on me. I felt free for the first time in a very long time. I couldn't wait to share the news with Kanoa over dinner.

CHAPTER FORTY-EIGHT:

Kanoa

Finding out that we had won the bid was one thing, but the fact that Mike was the rightful owner put a different spin on the Coco Palms property. Here I found myself with a grandfather *and* a fiancée, and I was part of the lineage to acquire the land. It was a bittersweet feeling for me and not one I wanted to share with anyone, not even Abby. It tore at my heartstrings that some of my buddies wouldn't see a return on their investments.

Months had passed since finding out Mike was my biological grandfather. I'd regained full mobility of my legs, and started working out. I was the fittest I'd been in months. What I wasn't sure of was my future with Abby. I wondered how long before she got bored of Kauaʻi. Now that I had a grandfather, it changed things. I no longer saw myself living in New York for part of the year.

I asked myself whether Abby could really spend a lifetime on such a small, remote island. These issues were always at the back of my mind, so much so that it was stifling my productivity at work. Nothing was resolved until I got a visit one day from Queen Deborah, something I still haven't shared with Abby.

I'd gone out to the lagoon for some fresh air. I've always done my best thinking out there, ever since I was a kid. I soon saw a shiny object approaching. As it got closer, I knew it was my *Tūtū's* hair comb.

"Why so gloomy? Don't tell me Abby is going back to New York?"

I didn't answer her, because if I did, I'd have to acknowledge her existence. I sat quietly for what felt like an eternity, until she said, "Stop being a fool and talk to me. Did you not hear what I had to say to Mike about wanting a loving couple to take over the Coco Palms? Why has this property not started getting cleaned up? What have you been doing with your time? Answer me!" she demanded.

Like a coward, I turned around and left. I decided to go over to my grandfather's place.

Kupunakāne was outside pruning his mango trees. When he saw me, he put down the basket he was holding and dropped his shears into it. "Kanoa, what a lovely surprise."

"Sorry I didn't call first."

"Don't be ridiculous. You stop by anytime you like. What is it? You look bothered. Come," said *Kupunakāne*. "Let's get something to drink. We can sit outside, or would you prefer indoors?"

"The *lānai* is fine, but I'm good; I just finished a bottle of water on my way here. I came by because I have something to ask you and I hope you don't take it the wrong way," I asked. "Have you considered what you are going to do with the Coco Palms property?"

"Yes, I have. I'm glad you have finally asked me. I was waiting to see where your head was at, and Abby's also, for that matter. I wanted to make sure you two were on solid ground before I complicated things further."

"What do you mean?"

"Here's what I've been thinking about. I'd like to pass down ownership of the property to you, but there are a few conditions. You may not like what I have to say, but as your *Kupunakāne* I need you to do right by many people, including Abby."

"Tell me, what are your thoughts?"

"As Queen Deborah asked, you will honor the land and all our ancestors. You are to make all the wrongs right. We no longer will allow illegitimate children in this family lineage. Understood?"

I think this was the sternest I'd ever seen my *Kupunakāne*. For the first time, I saw my father in him. I replied, "Are you certain you want to do this? You know I could help you restore the Coco Palms along with the investors and —"

"I'm more than sure, but it's up to you to make things right with the investors. As the Queen stipulated, you will do right by everyone."

That night, Abby said she had something to tell me, but I asked if I could speak first. I said, "I had a talk with

Grandfather today. How would you feel about helping me renovate the Coco Palms Resort?"

"Are you serious?"

"Yes. I know you love interior design and you have just the personality to run this place. What do you say?"

Abby had her poker face on and took forever to answer. I really thought she was going to tell me I was nuts, but instead she said, "I don't have hotel experience, but I'd love to. I'll do whatever it takes to get the Coco Palms up and running." Her expressionless face changed into one wearing the brightest of smiles. She was elated, and it felt great to know we were on the same page. "I'm so excited, Kanoa."

"Me too," I said. "So much so that it also petrifies me."

"I know what you mean."

It's amazing how my breath was no longer labored. I could inhale and exhale without feeling like an elephant was on my chest. I took another breath and said, "You have no idea how happy you've just made me. You've been putting off our marriage and I really thought you might be thinking of going back to New York, even though you told me many times you weren't."

"Why didn't you ever say anything? I'm sorry about the marriage, but I just need to have the perfect time. I haven't felt the need."

I got up from the dinner table and kissed Abby. I felt like one of the happiest men on the planet. "I also want us to think about getting married—will you promise me that?"

Abby kissed me back, but she didn't seem too concerned about the marriage. I could see in her eyes that the wheels were already turning.

Abby cupped her mouth and giggled with excitement. "We'll get married when the Chapel is up and running. What do you think?"

"Really?" I said, surpised that she'd want to wait for the renovations. That told me that Abby was here to stay, and my heart was overflowing with joy. Just to reassure myself, I asked, "You're sure you want to get married at the Coco Palms?"

"Do you have a better place? Come on, this is perfect. It's part of who your are, and just think how thrilled Mike will be."

Abby didn't need to convince me any further. I loved the idea, but even better, I loved that she would be by my side every step of the way to get to our special day.

CHAPTER FORTY-NINE:

Abby

The moment has finally arrived. Tonight the Coco Palms will open, after more than a quarter century sitting in ruins. The devastation of Hurricane Iniki in 1992 has finally been put to rest. No one is happier to see this day take shape than Queen Deborah, whom I stop to check on. I bring fresh-squeezed pineapple juice as I always do, but today, I give it a spike of Prosecco, to celebrate the grand reopening. I let myself into Room #256, only to find Deborah talking to herself in the bathroom. I put the tray down and move closer to the bathroom door. I draw back suddenly, knowing I've intruded on something I shouldn't be hearing. Maybe it's my imagination running away with me, but I swear that voice sounds like Elvis. I don't have time to run before Deborah comes out.

"Good morning, dear. How are you this morning?" she asks in a chipper tone. "You must be so excited about tonight! I know I am."

I hand her a flute and take one myself. "Here's to the new Coco Palms Resort," I say, raising my glass. "We did it!" We clink glasses, but I can't contain myself. "Were you talking to someone when I came in?"

"No. Do you see anyone here?" asks Deborah.

"So you don't mind if I use the bathroom?"

"That's a silly question, why would I mind? Go use it, for Heaven's sake."

I really don't need to use it, but I walk in anyway. I shut the door behind me, and as Deborah said, no one is in here. I tell myself it's been a crazy two years of mixed emotions and hard work. It's like they say—you finally reach the finish line and that's when you come crashing. I'm sure fatigue is causing me to hear things; it's got to be. As I turn to walk out I notice something on the bathroom counter. I take a few steps closer and can't believe what I see.

It's one of Elvis's signature necklaces—the famous lightning bolt with the initials TCB for "Taking Care of Business." There's no way Elvis is here! "He's been dead ... let's see," I say to myself as I start to count on my fingers. What am I doing? Deborah's been dead almost two hundred years—could they be ghost buddies? I need to get a grip and a move on, as I've got a million things to do. Plus, Kanoa and I have a surprise for everyone later tonight. I can't start getting bogged down with other things. I join Deborah, who obviously isn't going to mention the necklace, and neither will I for that matter.

"My goodness," Deborah says, "I thought you'd flushed yourself down the toilet."

"You know how it is—opening jitters."

"Oh, dear, you'll be fine. The grounds look spectacular. You and Kanoa have done me proud."

"You just wait, we have a few surprises in store for tonight, but I best get going. We'll talk later."

What Deborah hasn't seen yet is Cottage #25. We've restored it to its original design, with a few modern twists. Of course, trying to find shell basins for these cottages has been quite the task, but it became my main focus until we got 350 of them. We thought we'd keep a few extra in storage. Getting these basins ready for installation took a good part of the two years, but so well worth it. Kanoa and I agreed that the basins were also our way of paying homage to Genie, who came up with the original concept; it's the least we could do. In all honesty, I don't think the Coco Palms would be as authentic without them.

In order to bring the bathrooms to a modern-day feel, we came up with a spa-type design. My favorite feature is the wall-mounted waterfall faucets above all the basins and bathtubs. Just hearing the water run gives you a feel of being in a tropical rainforest, especially when standing under the oversized rain-shower heads. Bringing everything together is the wallpaper we collaborated on with a local designer. All the walls are covered in oversized green palm-foliage print. We wanted to keep it simple and elegant, just like our amenities. We spared no cost in finding the finest face and body creams, with subtle tropical fragrances. Our bath products can all be found in our lobby souvenir shop. People love to take home a little piece of the island and none of these products can be found anywhere but here.

We experimented with Cottage #25 first. We wanted to make sure that the cottage Elvis and Priscilla visited would do them proud. We've even thought about turning it into a museum, something the locals would be proud of. Tourists could come and honor Elvis's memory. But we have to think about it, so #25 is still off our reservation system until further notice.

I know the Queen hasn't been in Cottage #25, because she'd stopped going after Hurricane Iniki. She said it was dilapidated and depressing and that it'd never be the same no matter what we did to it, but I hope that we can prove her wrong on this one thing.

As for Deborah's room, #256 in the main building, Kanoa didn't want to hear about it. I told him in no uncertain terms that it was never to be used by anyone but the Queen. When he wouldn't respond I said, "You just wait and see, Kanoa Kahala. One day you will be a believer. There are good spirits living amongst us." At first he'd get annoyed with me, but over time I've watched him become more lighthearted about my ghost encounters. He has started to laugh them off, especially when I said, "One day you'll acknowledge them, and be proud that we're surrounded with such good energy from past loves."

Kanoa's reply was, "You're definitely more Hawaiian than I am."

"Okay, have it your way," I said.

Before the opening-day ceremonies were to begin, I had a couple of workers do some last-minute checking on the gargantuan shell that we've suspended over the main entrance. I know it's safe, because we've spent a good chunk of our renovation budget working with a top-notch engineer, but one can never be too careful.

For a long while all we had were the logistics, and no shell. We were cutting it close to our renovation deadline and I was ready to scrap the plan, but Kanoa persevered and never lost hope of getting a shell of such magnitude. They aren't the easiest to come by, and just three months before opening day, Kanoa got a call from someone on the island of Moloka'i. Kanoa had the shell flown over to speed up the process. Let's just say that we went well over budget on the Coco Palms, but standing here today, it's overwhelmingly worth it. My heart is so full of love and pride for all the people of Kaua'i. I can say that I have a much better understanding of Kanoa's feelings about the land and his people.

It's a typical balmy day and Mike has arrived dressed in his Hawaiian best. The ribbon-cutting ceremony for the Grand Opening is scheduled for two PM, which gives Mike plenty of time to mingle. Kanoa has asked Mike to be the honorary ribbon cutter. None of this would have been possible had it not been for his *Kupunakāne*.

Before any of the renovations took shape, Kanoa had some huge decisions to make. It took over a month to get all the legalities and paperwork in order for the property. Kanoa felt he came to the fairest conclusion he could. He decided that we should be equal partners and owners of the resort, but I insisted that he always have the most shares and the final say in all decision making. After all, the land is part of his heritage, and I'm grateful to be part of it.

As for the investors, Kanoa saw fit to give them the option of either paying back the money they'd initially invested, or taking back a portion of their investment. This would allow him to disperse the remaining shares amongst whoever was interested. After weeks of deliberation, they all came to an agreement. They expressed that they'd like to be part shareholders in the resort itself, but not the land. They all agreed the land should stay in Kanoa's family for generations to come. They also stipulated that, should the hotel close for unforeseen reasons beyond human control, neither Kanoa or I would be liable to the shareholders. They are all confident that the resort will be around for many years to come, but no one can predict what Mother Nature has in store. She has struck before, but let's hope that raising the building will at least save it from potential flooding.

Most of the things that took place on the grounds have been impossible to hide from Deborah, but Kanoa and I did our best to keep another huge surprise from her. We will reveal it after sunset, during the tiki torch lighting ceremony.

I don't know where the day has gone, but it's already time for the ribbon-cutting ceremony, and I need to change into my new outfit which, may I say, I fell in love with as soon as I saw it. I chose a white sarong-style dress with a gorgeous tropical print in bright pink and green. My long black hair is up in what has become my signature style with a fresh flower over my right ear. Kanoa is right—there are times I look at myself in the mirror, and

I could be mistaken for a local, especially when I dress Polynesian style. I even find it hard to see the old Abby.

My parents have arrived, along with Nani and James and all the kids. Speaking of Nani, she will have a part in tonight's festivities. There is going to be a dance show later in the evening, which will portray the early years of Queen Deborah. Nani will be playing the role of the Queen. You can only imagine what it's been like listening to Nani practicing her lines. Sorry, I have to laugh; it's been quite entertaining to say the least.

The ribbon is up across the entrance to the Coco Palms, directly under the shell. There are hundreds of people standing outside to watch the ceremony. I have a feeling that there will be a lot of tourists taking pictures standing under the shell in the future.

The mayor has arrived to bless the land, as he did before we started demolition. I'm sure the mayor never thought he'd see this day. He'll be standing next to Mike, while Kanoa and I will be on the other side of them. Once the mayor gives his blessing, he'll step aside and hand Kanoa the scissors, which he then passes to Mike. Mike isn't one for public speaking, so he's just cutting the ribbon, and Kanoa and I will welcome the guests for refreshments on the lawn.

To commemorate the Grand Opening, we will be having an open house later in the week for all the locals, where they can see the new Coco Palms and enjoy a daytime *lūʻau*. This way the kids can participate too. But today's private Grand Opening party is strictly for close family and friends.

For the locals who were around in the heyday of the old Coco Palms, I hope that they will appreciate how we've incorporated our modern-day décor while holding on to touches of the past. By that I mean that we refurbished the entire reception and bar area to its original state, except Kanoa and I chose not use the original dark wood. We wanted to give it a much lighter and airier feel, so we went with driftwood, which has been whitewashed to give it a bright, outdoorsy feel. For the floor Kanoa left it up to me. I chose bright tiles that follow the coco palm theme, which gives the room just the right amount of pop. And spread throughout the reception area we have lovely oversized vases that are filled with fresh palm foliage and flowers.

I just hope that everyone loves the newly renovated Coco Palms as much as we do.

CHAPTER FIFTY

The day crowd has dissipated and the lagoon area will soon be busy with evening festivities. A luxurious white tent has been set up with a variety of my favorite island flowers cascading from the ceiling. Guests will enjoy a traditional *lū'au* feast, except it will be a sit-down serviced dinner with an open bar, and a chilled champagne fountain will flow throughout the night. I thought it best to place the fountain at the entrance of the tent, so guests will notice it upon entering.

Making sure people enjoy every aspect of our festivities is a must for me, and that's why I've arranged the seating so that everyone can enjoy the sunset and the tiki torch ceremony no matter what table they are at. I know I'm sounding a bit fastidious, but this Grand Opening is important to all of us. It's been long awaited, and I want it to be as great as I can possibly make it.

Guests have started to arrive for the evening. Most are taking advantage of the double-hulled canoe rides up and down the lagoon. As they walk along the pathways, we've made it possible for them to enjoy listening to local musical artists. The music will be coming from the ground speakers that have been installed throughout. Kanoa and I have hired extra hula dancers for tonight. We have asked that they be spread across the grounds to give guests private lessons. Sometimes people are shy to do it in groups, so we're trying to make things as laid back as possible.

It's an hour before sunset when an announcement comes over the speakers. It's Kanoa. "Can I have everyone's attention, please? I'd like to start off by thanking everyone for coming out to join in the grand re-opening festivities, but right now, Abby and I have a surprise we would like to share with all of you. We have one more ribbon-cutting ceremony, and we promise to be quick about it," he laughs. "If you would all like to make your way over to the lagoon, it'd be much appreciated."

Once the guests have all taken their places along both sides of the lagoon, Kanoa and I drift down the lagoon on one of the double-hulled rafts. We've practiced the timing umpteen times over the past couple weeks. What I especially love about the rafts is that we've decorated them with the same flowers we have in the tent. The only difference is that the platforms of the rafts are covered entirely with green foliage.

Kanoa is looking exceptionally handsome. He is wearing a *maile lei*, a fragrant island vine entwined with white orchids, which is traditional wear for grooms. I am standing next to Kanoa wearing a floor-length off-the-shoulder lilac gown—reminiscent of the gown actress

Joan Blackman wore in the final scene of *Blue Hawaii*. Around my neck, I am wearing a super-sized white *lei* made up of fragrant orchids, and my absolute favourite, white plumeria. I decided to wear a *maile* as well, similar to Kanoa's, as we stand side by side, making our way down the lagoon to where the old Chapel has been given new life. Kanoa and I have done an excellent job of keeping our nuptials under wraps. It's something we are gifting both Mike and Deborah with. It's our way of honoring Queen Deborah's wish of finally having a happy couple in her family. That's not to say that Kanoa and I wouldn't have gotten married at some point, but there's no time like the present.

As I look around to see if I can spot Deborah, I hear a change in the instrumental music we've chosen for our descent off the raft. I look at Kanoa for his reaction, but I don't think he's as concerned as I am. I swear I'm hearing a live version of the Hawaiian Wedding Song, except I can't see who's singing.

I've been around these ground speakers and testing them for months, so I definitely know the song isn't coming from the speakers. Keeping a smile on my face, so as to not look worried in front of our guests, I look at Kanoa and whisper, "Can you comprehend what's happening here?"

Kanoa shakes his head, but I don't need any further acknowledgement. I think I've spotted the culprit. I see Queen Deborah, and next to her is a silhouette that's a dead ringer for Elvis. As I stare a little longer, the silhouette becomes a bit more noticeable—so much so, the necklace I spotted earlier in Deborah's bathroom is in full view. The descending sun is shining one last ray of light on the famous diamond thunderbolt.

Kanoa squeezes my hand. He's finally become interested in what's happening. "Was the change in music your idea? What happened to instrumental only?"

"I'll have to ask Deborah," I say, smiling at my handsome groom. Little does Kanoa know that Elvis is actually singing! I'm not about to start to explain it, because we all know how that would pan out with Kanoa. Instead, I look straight ahead as we descend the raft. "We'll discuss it later," I say. "For now, how about we get married before something else happens?" I'm only half joking, because with Deborah around, the unpredictable is predictable.

We proceed to cut the ribbon draped across the Chapel entrance and invite guests to enter. When all the guests are seated, I walk down the aisle to the traditional wedding march with my father on one side and Mike on the other. This is a little surprise I've added for Kanoa— and now, to the surprise of both of us, a second song has been added. It is one of Elvis's favourites, The Wonder of You. I smile at Kanoa and he winks back at me; it seems Kanoa isn't really too concerned about song choices, but I must say, this song suits our personalities to a tee.

We didn't want our ceremony to go on and on, and after two rehearsals we've got it down to ten minutes. We don't want to bore our guests—we want them back outside enjoying the celebrations, because in all honesty, that's where we want to be also. We know we love one another; we don't need to drag it out.

After the initial ceremony, we greet all our guests as they exit the chapel. After we are done, I excuse myself from Kanoa and tell him I'll be back in a few minutes, as I need to take care of something. I catch up with Deborah down by the lagoon. She is in her usual spot, except this time Elvis is standing next to her, in full view for me to see.

"Congratulations, ma'am," says Elvis with his signature Memphis twang. "I hope our little surprise didn't ruin your plans."

I'm shocked and shaking. I try to extend my trembling arm in order to shake his hand, but remember he's a ghost. I hear myself say, "I'm speechless, I ..." Holy shit, I can't believe I'm star struck.

"I think what Abby is trying to say is *mahalo*," offers Deborah. All I can do is stare at him. I can't believe my eyes. He is wearing the exact same outfit he wore in the final wedding scene of his movie *Blue Hawaii*. What's even odder is the fact that Elvis looks to be the same age he was when he filmed the movie. To say I'm gobsmacked would be an understatement. How is this even possible?

It's as if he knows what I'm thinking. I hear him say, "I chose to stay in my happy years—a time when Pricilla and I were our happiest. I've never been the same without her, just in case you're wondering why I look this way. Priscilla was my one and only true love, and I messed it up."

I honestly don't know what to say. Every answer going through my mind sounds ridiculous. So I catch myself saying, "Well, sir. I hope Kanoa and I have done you proud. We wanted to honor your movie with our wedding."

"You have done me more than proud, Abby," he says. "This entire resort was one of my favorite places in the world. Priscilla loved vacationing here. I hope you and Kanoa enjoy it as much as we did. Like I said, it was the best time of our lives, and thank you for keeping my memory alive."

"Thank you, sir. It's been an honor. I know right now my grandmother is looking down on me and smiling from ear to ear. She was one of your biggest fans. If there is a chance that either of you bump into her, please let her know I love and miss her. And Deborah, whether you believe it or not, Kanoa wants nothing more than to honor your wishes, and hopefully he's made both you and Mike proud."

The Queen gestures for me to stand by her side and I do as I've been asked. She looks up at me with a warm smile. "He's done a fine job, dear, and now I'm afraid that I must honor my promise. I said that I'd leave if this day every happened, and it has."

Her smile isn't making me feel as warm and fuzzy as it was three seconds ago. I can't believe my ears. I ask, "What are you saying? You can't leave! We've only just begun."

"No dear, *you and Kanoa* have just begun. I'm tired and it's time to go, don't you think?" says the Queen as she looks over at Elvis.

Elvis seems to feel a bit differently than Deborah. "Maybe we can stay until the end of the night? What do you say?"

"Yes!" I cry. "Please, let's discuss this tomorrow, please? I beg you. Plus, you have to stick around a bit longer. We haven't fulfilled all your wishes."

"That's not true, dear, and you know it."

"What are you saying?"

"You know darn well what I'm saying."

"Deborah? How did you find out?" I whisper into Deborah's ear so that Elvis can't hear.

"Darling, you are glowing—plus, not to be rude, but that dress is a little snug in the bust area."

"Deborah!"

"Am I right?"

"Yes, but I haven't told Kanoa. I was going to announce it tonight after dinner. I thought the fireworks display would be the perfect setting. So you see, you can't leave!"

"I won't leave right now, but I made a promise to Kanoa and I am keeping it. I need to honor my words."

"Let me talk to Kanoa," I say. "Don't do anything until I talk to him—you have to promise."

"Dear, I already made a promise, now get on and go enjoy your wedding. If I haven't told you already, you look stunning. You're a rare beauty inside and out, Abby Kahala. I'm so proud of you, and just know this: you will make a fantastic mother." And just like that, the waterworks begin between Deborah and me. But Deborah, who can always compose herself quickly, says, "Go dear, before your groom starts to worry."

"Just one thing," Elvis says. "Would you mind if I sing a few songs?"

"Mind? It would be my honor. Oh! Before I forget, I do have another surprise for both of you, since the wedding wasn't a surprise," I say jokingly. "Why don't the two of you go down and check out Cottage #25? Maybe it will entice you to stick around."

"I agree with Elvis," Deborah says. "We will stay until the night ends, but I can't promise you anything more."

I'm not thrilled about Deborah's promise, but I'll take what I can get. I have time to persuade her further. As I go to find Kanoa, I still can't believe I met Elvis. My hands are trembling from the excitement. The moment I spot Kanoa, I hear Elvis start to sing Love Me Tender.

CHAPTER FIFTY-ONE

Our wedding is one of the most fun nights I've ever had. Throughout the early part of the evening I can see Deborah and Elvis. It's such a thrill to watch the guests dancing to Elvis songs—such a shame that they don't know he's performing live. After the ceremony, when I tell Kanoa about seeing them, I get nothing but an eye roll.

"Abby, can we have one night without ghost talk?"

"Come on," I say, "you know that wasn't the music we chose for our wedding. You have to admit, it was pretty authentic. Who do you think did that for us, if not Deborah and Elvis?"

"My *Kupunakāne*?"

"Well here he comes, let's ask him."

Kupunakāne is walking towards us beaming with pride. He looks so handsome in his white tuxedo jacket and black pants. "Congratulations, you two. Everything was spectacular. And Abby, can I say again how beautiful you look. I'm so proud of you both," he says as we stand in our group hug.

"You look quite dapper yourself, *Kupunakāne*. By the way, what did you think of the wedding song?"

Kupunakāne isn't answering. He looks at me, then at Kanoa. I ask, "Did you know about this?"

Mike'e eyes have finally stopped shifting. He stands firmly and looks directly at Kanoa. "I promised I wouldn't say anything, but someone had to set up a mic on Elvis. Sorry Kanoa, but Elvis and I go back a ways. It's been great to be around him again after all these years."

"Am I the only sane one, or am I the only crazy one for not believing all this?"

Kanoa puts his arm around his *Kupunakāne* and off they go to have a drink together. I figure this would be a good time to go up and see if Deborah is in her room. It's been a while since I've seen her and Elvis.

I decide to check out Cottage #25, since it's on my way to Room #256, but no one is here. I do notice a bottle of champagne chilling—which is odd, as we agreed not to let anyone use it—but of course I'd be happy if Elvis or Deborah wanted to stay here. Anyhow, I call out their names, but there's no answer, so I continue to the main building. I'm sure she's just taking a break; it's been a long day, and the night is just beginning.

When I get to Deborah's room the door is ajar. I gently push it open, and the only shimmer of light is coming from her desk lamp. I walk over to the desk and keep calling out their names, but no one seems to be here. As I turn, I spot an envelope addressed to me. My stomach starts doing flips, fear gripping my entire body.

I'm afraid to touch the envelope, as it may be a goodbye letter. I don't want to believe it, but a familiar box is next to it. My hands tremble with trepidation as I lift the lid—and there it is, her hair comb. I open the envelope and take the note out. I read every word over and over, three times. I stare at it as if the letters will jump around and place themselves in a way that isn't saying goodbye to me. I can't bring myself to believe Deborah would leave me this way. Why didn't she give me a chance to say goodbye? Right now I don't know if I'm angrier with her for not waiting until morning, or sadder that she's left me and I'll never see her again.

I read the note for the fourth time.

Abby dear, you, and Kanoa have done me proud, but I must keep my promise to Kanoa. Had he believed in me, it would be a different story, but that really isn't as important as the love the two of you share. Looking at both of you so in love makes me realize it's been a long time since I've felt such peace in my own life. Please promise me that you will always take care of one another, and know that I love you both so very much.

Also, there's nothing I've cherished more than the friendships I've had with you and Genie. Please, take care of yourself and know that you hold a special place in my heart. My disappearance is not to hinder your day, but to let you know how happy and proud I am of the love I witnessed at your wedding ceremony, between you and Kanoa.

Remember, no long faces. You and Kanoa gave me what I've been in search of for a lifetime, or maybe two lifetimes. Today was all about true love. Take care of each other and especially take good care of my unborn 'ohana member. Congratulations to both of you. I know you will both make superb, loving parents.

Love, Queen Deborah, your Tūtū.

P.S. Please, take care of Mike. Give him my love and a great big hug.

I gently pick up the comb and place it in my hair, while tears of joy and sadness sting my face. I turn the lamp off and make my way out of the room, but shutting the door behind me is a difficult task, as it brings everything I've come to know and love about Deborah to an end. The thought of never seeing her again is overwhelming. As I turn to walk away, I see Kanoa walking towards me.

"I knew I'd find you here. What's wrong? Why the tears?"

"She's gone," I say with a bit of a hiccup.

Kanoa is silent. His stare is one of familiarity. I know deep down he believes what I'm saying, but he's too stubborn to admit it. I don't know why he still has such difficulty opening up. The awkward silence lingers between us for what feels like a very long time.

"Would you like to show me the room?" he asks.

"No, I'm sorry, but not tonight."

He keeps looking at me, as if I'll change my mind. Instead, I reach for his hand and keep the note in mind: *No long faces.*

"Come on," I say. "I think we still have a few dances in us. After all, it is our wedding."

We dance until the wee hours of the morning, which I'd say is pretty good for a woman in her first trimester. It's now four AM, and I'm beyond ready to pack it in. Once we get to our hotel, I will surprise Kanoa with the baby news.

Walking towards the main building still wearing our fragrant *leis*, we stop to share a passionate kiss with the moonlight beaming down on us. Deep down I'm a bit peeved at Kanoa for not believing in Deborah, but my love for him trumps everything. I hear myself say, "I love you with every fiber of my body, Kanoa Kahala." In the past I didn't share such intimate thoughts with him, but this is truly a fresh start.

"And I ditto that, Mrs. Kahala."

"Boy, do I like the sound of that. Can you say it again?"

Kanoa holds me tight as I look into his moonlit face. He repeats, "Mrs. Kahala."

I pull him in as close to me as possible. I whisper, "Do you have any idea how sexy you are right at this moment?"

"Wow," laughs Kanoa. "I know what to say moving forward to get on your good side."

"You have no idea how much I want you right now."

"Good to hear, because I have a little surprise for you," Kanoa says as he heads in the opposite direction down one of the pathways. "Come with me."

I realize within a few moments that we are headed down to Cottage #25. Oh my God, it was Kanoa who decided to chill the champagne, for us. That is so romantic. I'm one of the luckiest girls in the world. "This surprise completes our Blue Hawaii wedding," I say.

"Abby Parker Kahala, you're a hopeless romantic. Who'd have thought?"

"You're laughing at me."

"No my love, I'm proud of you," he says. We stop in front of the cottage door and kiss before I feel Kanoa pick me up in his big, muscular arms, and he carries me over the threshold.

He puts me down, and as much as I love my wedding dress, it's feeling a bit snug. I say, "I know I'm about to be a buzz killer, but would you mind if I get out of this dress?"

"You realize I was just thinking the exact same thing, right?"

I'm so tired I kind of missed the joke.

"Here," Kanoa says as he turns me around. "Let me get that for you."

"Wait, let me take these *leis* off first."

"No. I want to see you with only your *leis* on."

"Well, when you put it like that, what's taking you so long to unzip?"

I can feel Kanoa slowly unzipping my wedding gown as he gently kisses my back. The dress drops to the floor as I step out of it. My considerate husband picks it up and places it on a chair close by. He turns to take me in his arms, and just like that the magic between us is the same as when we first met.

"I don't know what it is, but you are even more radiant than the day I met you, and I thought you were perfect," says Kanoa.

"I feel the same about you, Kahala," I say.

Our bodies are entwined in positions I didn't know were possible. Our honeymoon night has set a new bar for our sex life. I just hope that being pregnant doesn't diminish this completely. Maybe I need to stop Googling articles about what happens to the sex drive during pregnancy. I know I'm already more tired than I've ever been and it will only get worse, but I've also read that some women have a heightened libido—maybe that's what's happening to me right now. I'll take what I can get, because I'm definite that by my third trimester, rubbing my belly will be our foreplay.

I chuckle to myself, but I must have chuckled out loud unknowingly, as I hear Kanoa ask, "What's so funny?"

"Nothing."

"Really? What is it? Tell me," Kanoa demands as he starts to tickle me.

He knows I hate being tickled. This isn't how I want to tell him I'm expecting. Instead, I find myself blurting out, "Didn't I see a bottle of champagne chilling in the other room?"

Kanoa jumps out of bed as he makes his way to get the bottle. He reenters the room with a disappointed look on his face. "I can't believe it. I specifically asked the staff for a bottle of our finest champagne. Why in God's name would they put sparkling water in the ice bucket? I hope they don't do this with our guests."

I'm as stunned as he is, as I know I saw champagne earlier. My mind is racing, as I watch Kanoa put his pants on. He comes back to the bed where I'm sitting up, covered only with a sheet. He leans over and notices the hair comb I'm wearing.

He asks, "I thought you gave that back to *Tūtū*?"

I wish he hadn't asked, because I'd finally forgotten how awful I'd been feeling about Deborah leaving—but Kanoa keeps insisting on knowing why I have it.

"I found it on her desk tonight with a goodbye note. You can read it if you'd like, or I'll read it to you?"

"Goodbye note? Where'd she go? And by the way," he says, "you can read it. You know how much I love watching your lips …"

"Kanoa! Take me seriously right now. I'm very upset about Deborah leaving. I didn't want it to ruin the remainder of our wedding night, so I made sure to put on a brave face, so joking about it right now is not a good idea."

"I'm sorry, honey, I didn't mean to be so insensitive. I'm truly sorry that she left—I know how much she means to you."

"I'm really going to miss her." As I say the words out loud, it comes to me. I realize that Deborah is the one who switched the champagne to sparkling water. It had to be—no one else knows I'm pregnant, and I know our staff would never be so careless. She and Elvis must have been in the cottage for one last visit. I find myself standing in the middle of the room holding the note, with Kanoa asking why I'm smiling. I tell him yet again that it's nothing. I set the note on the edge of the bed and excuse myself to use the bathroom. I slip on one of the lightweight cotton robes we offer our guests and splash some water on my face.

I reenter the bedroom and see that Kanoa has read the note, as he is still holding it in his hand. He places it back on the bed. "Honey, I need to run to the kitchen. I'll just be a few minutes."

"Listen Kanoa, if you're going to the kitchen for champagne, don't bother. The staff didn't make a mistake."

"What are you saying?"

I reach for Kanoa's hand and pull him in close to me. "I'm saying they didn't make a mistake. Someone asked them to replace it with sparkling water."

"Who would do that? Are you trying to tell me that *Tūtū* did it?"

"Yes."

"Why? What's the purpose?"

And just like that, the light goes on in Kanoa's brain. His eyes light up like floodlights and he is smiling from ear to ear.

"Are you saying what I think you're saying?" he asks as he pushes me forward a bit and rubs my belly.

"Yes," I say. "We are going to have a baby."

Kanoa hugs me so tight I have to remind him that I need to breathe. I say, "In case you haven't noticed, I've not had a drink in almost two weeks."

"What? But I saw you drinking."

"It's been water or virgin drinks."

"Oh my God, Abby! I'm the luckiest man in the world. How did I get so lucky to deserve you, and now a baby?"

"I wanted to tell you two weeks ago, but then I thought about what a great wedding present it'd be. I had planned on telling you privately before the fireworks— that way we could share it with all our guests."

"Why didn't you? Why'd you change your mind? This is fantastic news."

"Because when I went to see Deborah and Elvis after the ceremony, she told me she knew I was pregnant. Let me tell you, *Tūtū* was over the moon about our pregnancy."

"Then why'd she leave?"

I don't want Kanoa to see the deep disappointment in my face. I turn away before explaining to him. "Because she promised you she would. We've fulfilled all her wishes."

"But Abby, it's not something I ever believed in."

"That's the problem, you didn't believe in her—but let's not go there. It's over. She wants us to be happy, so let's drive on."

"I'm sorry, Abby. If I could change things, I would. You mean the world to me. Now I feel like a shit and an even bigger shit for not getting you anything. You told me you didn't want a gift."

"You being alive is gift enough for me, and now we are going to have a baby! Let's just be grateful for everything we have. I don't need material things. In case you haven't noticed, I'm not the same Abby you first met. I just need you."

It doesn't seem to matter that I wasn't going to drink. Kanoa insists on going to get a bottle of champagne, and I'm not going to deny the man celebrating the conception of our child. As soon as he leaves, I plop myself on the bed. This has been one very long and exciting day.

I must have nodded off, but the pop of a champagne cork wakes me up. I hear Kanoa's footsteps coming towards the bedroom.

"Sorry, being pregnant has me nodding off a lot and it's really late. Have I been asleep long?"

"Not really. I'm kind of glad you've been sleeping—you need your rest. Plus, I've been gone a little longer than I had anticipated, so I'm sorry for that. I went to retrieve your wedding gift."

"I thought we'd decided I didn't need anything."

"I heard what you said. I didn't buy this, I begged and groveled for it. Tell her, *Tūtū.*"

"Yes, he did," Queen Deborah says as I watch her enter the bedroom, along with Elvis.

I'm in a state of shock as Deborah continues speaking. "Kanoa found me by the lagoon having one last ride," she says. "Of course, Kanoa has probably never told you that I've been watching him by the lagoon since he was a little boy." She looks over at Kanoa. "I'm sure your parents didn't know you were there, young man," she laughs. "My boy begged me not to leave. He said that he believes in me and that he would try to make things better between us if I stay."

I never thought this could happen to me, but I'm speechless. It takes the King to snap me back into this odd reality, in which we are all living. Elvis asks, "Maybe, when your honeymoon is over, if you wouldn't mind, I'd like to hang out in my old cottage, or bungalow as Cilla and I used to call it back in the day. I wouldn't want Deborah to be lonesome on any night, if you know what I mean?"

And just like that, we are *'ohana.*

ALOHA

Made in the USA
Las Vegas, NV
12 May 2021

22871008R10273